A LESSON IN LOVE

Derek pinned Meghan in his embrace, drawing her roughly against his brawny chest.

"It seems that you are sorely in need of some lessons in love . . . and I shall be most obliged to serve as your instructor," he whispered hoarsely as he lowered his lips to hers.

Meghan struggled uselessly to free herself from Derek's strong embrace, and it seemed like an eternity before he withdrew his burning mouth from hers.

"Aren't you going to scream?" he mocked.

"Get out of here!" Meghan hissed between clenched teeth.

"Not yet," he breathed against her silky throat.

To her complete horror, Derek began to place tiny featherlike kisses upon her neck and cheeks. Then, with fierce and fiery passion, he kissed her mouth, forcing it open as his tongue thrust deep inside.

Finally, to Meghan's profound relief, Derek withdrew his lips and whispered thickly, "Ah, little one, I'll wager that pompous ass you are to wed never kissed you like this. . . ."

YOU'LL ALSO WANT TO READ . . .

TIDES OF ECSTASY

Luanne Walden

ZEBRA BOOKS

KENSINGTON PUBLISHING CORP.

ZEBRA BOOKS

are published by

KENSINGTON PUBLISHING CORP.
475 Park Avenue South
New York, N.Y. 10016

FOURTH PRINTING MARCH   1984

Printed in the United States of America

To Pete

Part One

The Encounter

Chapter One

Meghan Elizabeth Bainbridge awoke later than usual to the bright rays of sunlight that spilled magnificently through the delicate lace curtains into her bedchamber. She threw the coverlets aside and bounded to the window, where she rested her elbows on the sill and silently watched a robin hop from limb to limb. Meghan scarcely noticed the chill of the mid-May morning as she waltzed back to her bed and, with the spirit of an untamed three-year-old, threw herself down on it in a most unladylike fashion. She raised her hands high above her head, yawned, and giggled shamelessly as she wiggled her toes.

Soon she heard the familiar sound of her maid stirring in the anteroom and realized that she was about to be ushered from her cozy bed. Millie peeked into the room, but upon finding her mistress already awake all pretenses of discreetness quickly vanished.

"'Tis about time ye was up 'n' about." The servant came full into the room with all the force of the King's army.

Meghan looked at the servant through beautiful, bright green eyes and smiled. "And just how do you expect me to sleep, may I ask? What with you clamoring about in the outer room like a wild bull," she teased.

"Humph!" Millie snorted. "Wild bull indeed! Out of that bed with ye now. Mercy, a body might think that ye was a fixin' to spend the day abed, and this bein' the most important day of your life."

"Second most important," Meghan corrected her.

"What?!" The maid stopped short and looked directly at her mistress for the first time that morning.

Meghan sat up in the huge bed and hugged the downy soft pillow to her knees. "Tonight the engagement will be announced," she explained. "But the *most* important day of my life will be the day I become Lady Meghan Beauchamp, beloved wife of Lord Charles Beauchamp, the most dashing man in all of London." As she spoke, Meghan stood upon the mattress and performed a somewhat clumsy pirouette, after which she immediately dropped into a very low curtsy.

"Excuse me!" Millie replied in an exaggerated voice.

"Oh, Millie," Meghan said, as she fell back upon the bed, "you mustn't tease me, not today." She pretended to pout. "Besides, I saw a robin this morning. Perhaps it will serve as an omen, a sign that good things are about to happen, especially at tonight's party."

"Robins!" Millie spat disgustedly. "Me with a thousand things to do on this day, and all ye can speak of is robins." She walked to the bed to stand before her mistress. "Now I heartily suggest that ye drag yourself from that bed and hurry on downstairs to breakfast with your father. He's in a nasty mood, he is, and I daresay that the last thing on *his* mind this morn is some silly bird a flittin' about in a tree." She held out a blue velvet robe for her mistress and Meghan slipped into it.

Meghan was prepared to make an angry retort to the older woman, but decided that she would let nothing spoil this special day for her. Instead she turned to Millie and offered her a brilliant smile. "Really, Millie, what a way to speak to me. Do you think that Papa would approve?"

"I've spoken to ye thusly since ye was a babe at your mother's breast, and I'm too old and contrary to change

8

me ways now."

"Just the same, I think you should exhibit a little more respect in my presence. Mind your ways and curb your chatty tongue, else I may be inclined to find a more congenial person to replace you." Meghan playfully reminded the servant as to who was in charge, realizing all the while that Millie knew she would never carry out such a threat.

Meghan stepped into silk slippers that complemented her robe, selected a gold-handled brush from the dressing table and began absently to pull it through her hair.

Meanwhile, Millie busied herself with tidying the room and laying out the dress her mistress would don following the morning repast. But when she turned from her labor she was quite distressed to discover that Meghan still lounged about the room.

"Stop dillydallying, Missy!" Millie automatically reverted to her pet name for Meghan. "Hurry down to breakfast, I said. His lordship is in no mood to be toyed with this day." She directed her mistress toward the door.

"Oh pooh, Millie." Meghan paused before the mirror to adjust the sash that held her robe securely in place. "I assure you that I am accustomed to Papa's erratic moods. What has upset him this time? Did Cook put too much sugar in his tea again?"

"If only 'twas that simple, Missy. But from the sound of things 'twould seem that a far greater disaster has befallen Bainbridge House this day," she said mournfully.

Meghan waited for the servant to continue, but when Millie showed no sign of doing so, Meghan asked, "And just what might this *disaster* be?"

It was true that Millie had taken care of her for as long as Meghan could recollect, and she loved the old servant dearly. But at times such as this, when Millie would prattle on endlessly without getting to the point, Meghan could almost envision herself strangling the old woman.

Millie opened her mouth to speak, but the response to Meghan's question was never uttered because at that precise moment there came a thunderous knock at the chamber door.

"Meghan!" boomed a voice from the hallway.

Meghan felt certain that the shout had been heard throughout the entire city. "Yes, Papa." She didn't wait for Millie, but scampered to the door and opened it herself.

"Do you intend to join me for breakfast, or shall I instruct Cook to dispose of the meal since you appear content to wile away the day upon your feather-soft bed?" His eyes bore down upon her.

Meghan stared into those black, glaring eyes, more than a little stunned by the ferocity of the man who stood angrily before her. She had witnessed a mood such as this only once previously, and the man who had been responsible for it was now safely tucked away in his eternal resting place. That had been the penalty for crossing Lord Thomas Bainbridge. Meghan quickly searched her memory to see if she might inadvertently have done something to ignite the flaming temper of the man in the doorway. Thankfully, she could think of nothing.

She swallowed slowly and lowered her gaze to the floor. There were few things in the world that she feared, but she was quick to admit that her father's wrath was one of them. Whoever had brought this black mood upon her father had cause to worry. But she, for one, did not intend to blacken it any further.

"I was just on my way down—" she began.

But Thomas had already retreated down the hallway.

He waved his hand impatiently as if to command her to silence. "I have no desire to hear your lame excuses, daughter. However, I demand that you present yourself before me in the library in exactly five minutes, no longer."

"Yes, Papa." But Meghan's words fell upon an empty corridor.

"See, Missy. I told ye so. Didn't even bother to send one of the servants. Came up hisself to call ye down to breakfast. *That* should tell ye somethin', Missy." Millie ceremoniously folded her arms firmly across her matronly bosom and nodded her head knowingly.

But Meghan only half heard those final remarks, for Millie had no sooner begun her speech than Meghan picked up her skirts and flew down the steps to the library, pausing briefly to catch her breath and regain her composure before pushing the door open and entering the room.

The library was Meghan's favorite room in Bainbridge House. It was one of the more adequately supplied libraries in all of London, and her father had permitted her unlimited access to the wide variety of exquisitely bound volumes. The bookcases stretched from floor to ceiling on all four sides of the room, the sturdy oak door was the only entrance, and a single window provided light from outside.

But on this particular morning the drapes had been drawn, so the room was dimly lit. This in itself served to create a disquieting aura as Meghan carefully stepped inside the room. The thickly padded carpet muffled her entrance, giving Meghan ample opportunity to observe her father as he sat at his desk directly opposite the door. Thomas Bainbridge shared his daughter's love for the room and it had become customary for them to share a few quiet moments together in the mornings by having their breakfast served to them in the library.

Somehow, though, Meghan sensed that this particular breakfast might not be at all pleasant.

Bainbridge looked up from his morning cup of tea, which today contained a liberal dose of brandy. This was indeed rare, for Thomas seldom indulged in anything stronger than an occasional glass of wine or, as the years slipped by, his customary nightcap. But he was of foul disposition this morn and felt that he might very well partake of several more drinks before the day reached its wretched conclusion. His eyes fastened upon Meghan's slender form as she stood by the door, and as he gazed at her he silently wished for at least the thousandth time since the day of her birth that she had been the son for which he had so fervently prayed. On today, of all days when he desperately needed a son to assist him in upholding the Bainbridge family name, who was he forced to turn to? This . . . this simpering female.

With this thought in mind Thomas brought his fist crashing down upon the desk with a resounding thud. "Damn it, girl! Do you intend to stand there and breakfast?" he bellowed.

Meghan stiffened noticeably as she pulled herself up to her full height. This was one time, she decided, that her father was not going to intimidate her.

"Is this an indication as to how the day is going to progress, Papa?" She marched across the room to stand before his desk. "For if it is, permit me to caution you now, sir. I will not abide such intolerable behavior."

"*You will not*—" he began furiously, scarcely believing his ears.

"No, Papa!" Meghan's eyes were as fierce as her father's. "Not on the day upon which the announcement of my engagement to Charles will be made. Or has the fact that a small fortune has been lavishly provided for a grand party suddenly eluded your memory?" She paused briefly to catch her breath. "No, sir, you *must* control your disgraceful temper this once," she said unwaveringly.

Thomas, eyes wild with rage, stood up from his chair so abruptly that he sent it rocking precariously behind him. And had it not been for the servant who stood by to tend to his master's needs, the chair would have likely crashed upon the floor. But, as it was, Thomas's chair was returned to its proper place a bit more gently than it had been sent from it.

Bainbridge turned to the bewildered servant. "Leave us!" he commanded. "My daughter's tongue has a severe bite about it this morning, and it is best that only one of us be subjected to its vindictive sting."

Father and daughter locked glares and neither one spoke until they heard the familiar click of the door which assured them that the servant had vacated the room. Thomas stepped around the desk and grabbed Meghan brusquely by the shoulders. "If you ever have the audacity to address me thusly before my servants again, I shall personally render ten lashes upon your fine, stubborn back within full view of the serving staff. The spirited Bainbridge blood may run through your veins, but you lack the tenacity and the experience to bully *me* about. Do you understand?"

Meghan did not reply.

Thomas's grip tightened and he shook her roughly. "I said, do you understand?"

Meghan nodded weakly.

"Very well. Now sit down and listen to what I have to say."

Meghan took a seat opposite her father and stared blankly at the food before her, the meal looking suddenly cold and unappealing.

"Are you not going to eat?" he asked gruffly, returning to his chair.

"I have suddenly suffered a loss of appetite," she

murmured quietly.

"As have I." He tossed a piece of hot buttered bread onto his plate and turned his attention instead to his tea which by this time had grown distastefully cold. "It's not enough that I have received alarming news this morning that might severely alter all of our lives, but I must additionally contend with a lovesick daughter whose single concern is of a niggling engagement party."

Meghan observed her father move to the bookcase into which a small liquor cabinet had been installed and was amazed to see him secure a bottle and fill a glass with brandy.

Thomas, glass in hand, again turned to address his daughter. "Would it interest you to know that there exists a strong possibility that no betrothal will be announced this evening?" He stood over her now, his mocking eyes biting into the softness of her vulnerable flesh.

Meghan's breath quickened. "What do you mean?" she demanded. "Of course the betrothal will be announced. Why do you say such a thing?" The words came out in a rush, and her thoughts raced wildly as she waited for her father to explain his statement. Then she drew upon the only conclusion which she thought might make her father voice such an absurdity.

"Oh my God! Charles has been hurt! That's why there will be no betrothal." She suddenly grew weak with uncontrollable fear.

Thomas threw back his head and laughed so loudly that Meghan thought the very foundation of the house must be shaking. "If only it were that simple, my dear daughter. But fear not, no injury has befallen your precious Charles."

Meghan exhaled a grateful sigh of relief and relaxed a little as she continued to observe her father. She was determined to hear him out, if only for the sake of gaining an opportunity to best him at his own game, but she was growing exceedingly weary with the proceedings.

The elder Bainbridge took a drink from his glass and savored the fiery liquid before he continued. "Of course, after he learns of what will transpire here this noon, Charles may very well decide that marriage to you will be out of the question."

Meghan could bear it no longer and started for the door. "You speak in riddles," she called bitterly over her shoulder. "I'm going to speak with Charles and ask him what he knows of this."

"No! As of yet the hapless groom-to-be knows nothing of what I am about to tell you. Come, sit down and I will reveal to you the news with which my manservant awakened me this morn."

Meghan reluctantly allowed herself to be led back to the chair. She did not want to remain in the room a second longer. Something told her to run, to flee this man and the tidings he was about to disclose. She watched her father refill his empty glass and steadied herself in the chair. Not only was he in one of the foulest moods she had ever had the misfortune to witness, but he was drinking heavily as well. And she did not know if she could cope with him should he succumb to the influence of the wicked spirits.

"Do you remember Derek Chandler?" he asked suddenly.

"Elizabeth spoke of him frequently." Meghan recalled the name. "He was her son."

"He was her bastard!" Thomas roared.

Meghan frowned slightly at the remark. "I was quite young when you took Elizabeth Chandler to wife, but I do remember that she had a son named Derek. Has he done something to upset you, Papa?"

"He has."

15

"What?"

"He is coming here." He dropped down into the chair he had vacated earlier and rested his head wearily on one hand while he spoke. "Why did I ever marry that accursed woman?" he said more to himself than to Meghan.

"Was it not for love?" Meghan asked softly.

"It was not!" he shouted gruffly. "I have loved no other woman in my life besides your mother."

Meghan was only too aware of this. She remembered little of her own mother, being only three years of age at the time of her death. But she did have a fond recollection of a golden-haired woman with a soft voice and ever-present smile who was always there to tend to her little hurts and soothe her with a comforting lullaby until she drifted off to sleep at night. The circumstances leading up to her mother's death were even more remote to Meghan, but the horrible night of the death itself was forever imprinted upon her mind. Meghan closed her eyes and it was almost as if she were three years old again, prancing about the nursery in her pink gingham gown.

"I hate pink!" she had spewed at Millie.

"Now, Missy. Ye are too little to be hatin' anythin'," Millie gently scolded.

"But I do. I wish I were a boy. Then I would not have to dress up in these silly dresses, and I could ride my pony and get dirty and no one could scold me because I would be a boy and boys are supposed to do such things. Papa wishes it, too. I have heard him say it many times, *how I wish Meghan had been a boy.*" She wrinkled her nose in exaggerated imitation of her father.

Millie put her sewing aside and looked down at the girl who sat contentedly at her feet playing with a rag doll. "Come, child. 'Tis time to make ready for bed."

Later that same stormy night Meghan had been

16

roughly awakened from a sound sleep to stare drowsily into two cold and savage eyes. "Papa?" She struggled to sit up in the huge bed.

"Come with me," he had ordered.

She had obediently followed her father from the room and down the dark corridor to her mother's bedchamber. Meghan had not been permitted to see her for several days, excuses being that her mother was too weak to receive her, and she was greatly surprised to discover that her father intended to admit her now. Upon entering the room, Meghan scampered past him and raced to the bed where her mother lay. The room's total darkness was intermittently relieved by flashes of lightning; a storm had been raging all night. It was during one brief flash momentarily illuminating the room that Meghan began to sense that something was awry. Catherine Bainbridge had been ill for some time, and Meghan had grown accustomed to the whitish pallor of her mother's skin, but it had never before been this pale.

"Mama." Meghan gently reached for the hand that had so often caressed her, only to release it immediately as she felt the icy coldness of its lifeless touch. "What is wrong with my mother?" she cried.

"*What is wrong with my mother?*" Thomas cruelly mimicked the child. His two strong hands enveloped Meghan and trapped her within their iron grip forcing her to look at the pitiful figure on the bed. "I will tell you what is wrong. She is dead!"

The final word reverberated within the small child's head like the raging thunder in the night as she struggled hysterically to free herself from the imprisonment of her father's brutal embrace. But as the reality of his statement registered in her mind, Meghan's slight frame gave way to violent spasms of sobbing.

"No!" she exclaimed as tears streamed down her

cheeks. "She cannot be!"

"Yes, she's dead right enough. My beautiful, beautiful Cathy." The child suddenly realized that her father, too, was in tears. "It's all your doing," he ruthlessly accused her. "She never regained her strength following your wretched birth. Had you been the son for which I prayed I might have been able to endure all this."

Meghan struck out at him with her tiny fists to no avail. "Look at her!" He jerked the child's head in the direction of the bed. "Look, so you may never forget what you have brought about!"

Meghan had lapsed into hysterical screaming at that point and, to this day not knowing how, managed to wrench herself from her father's cruel grasp. She blindly stumbled from the room, and two soothing arms gently enfolded her and carried her back to the safety of her own chamber.

Knowing the master, Millie could but guess as to what had occurred in Lady Catherine's bedchamber, but daylight had begun to creep through the nursery window before the child finally calmed down enough to go to sleep.

Meghan's eyes again focused on the man she knew to be her father. He had most assuredly achieved his purpose . . . she had never forgotten.

It had been less than a year later when Thomas met and wed the lovely Elizabeth Chandler. Meghan had found her to be a great comfort, and she had grown to love her stepmother quite dearly. But Elizabeth had succumbed to a deadly fever the previous fall once again leaving Meghan alone with her father. A father who did not attempt to hide the fact that he held no great concern for his only offspring.

Oh, Charles, she thought to herself. If you would but come this very minute and rescue me, it would be none too soon.

"Then why did you marry Elizabeth, Papa, if not for love?" She had noticed his curious eyes upon her, and she did not care to have him question her about her musings.

"Necessity," he stated flatly. "Your mother's illness cost me much financially as well as emotionally, what with the various doctor and medical bills. Then, after she died, I began to squander much away on poor investments and I visited far too many gambling houses." His tone was direct, and far from apologetic.

Meghan had heard tidbits of the story from Millie, but much of the information had been kept from her.

"It was through an acquaintance at one of these gambling establishments that I was introduced to Elizabeth Chandler. She was well-connected, but her parents pampered her overmuch and governed her with a light hand. Consequently, she met and had a brief affair with a Jonathon Marley with whom she conceived that bastard who will arrive shortly."

"I take it that Mr. Marley refused to do the honorable thing and marry Elizabeth." Meghan urged him on, not wanting him to lapse into another tirade about Derek Chandler.

"Why should he? He had broken the seal and tasted of the heady brew. No, the Chandlers could find no other suitor for their soiled daughter until I happened along, the hapless widower who was down on his luck. Even knowledge of my financial situation did not deter them. They were more than willing to pay the price to see their tarnished daughter safely installed within the hallowed halls of matrimony."

"But what of Derek?"

"She brought him with her, the bitch, as if to install him in my household. But I hastily put an end to that foolish notion by signing him on as a cabin boy on a ship destined for America. I had heard no word of him since that day almost fifteen years ago—until I received this." He handed her an unsealed letter.

Meghan took the message from her father and quickly scanned the bold script. "According to this, he will be arriving at noon. It must be nearly that now, Papa." She glanced at him thoughtfully. "I wonder what he wants."

"I think, madam," a deep and husky voice announced from the doorway, "that I can perhaps satisfy your curiosity on that score."

Meghan and Thomas whirled simultaneously to meet the intruder. The tall stranger was successfully blocking the doorway, while a servant tried to push past him and gain entry to the library. Finally realizing that his efforts were futile, the servant called from the hallway, "I'm sorry, m'lord, but the . . . ah . . . *gentleman* would not wait to be announced."

"It's all right, Jules." Thomas allowed his eyes to rest darkly on the unannounced visitor. "I am expecting Mr. Chandler."

Chapter Two

Derek Chandler leaned his long, agile frame against the door and smugly observed the nervous servant beat a hasty retreat. He then turned to the occupants of the room, and, with a slight movement, he pushed the door closed with the heel of his boot before entering the library.

Thomas and Meghan watched as he came full into the library with all the grace and confidence of a lion returning to the lair after a long and successful hunt. If he were aware of the close scrutiny he was receiving from the two Bainbridges, he gave no indication. In fact, he embarked upon a cursory inspection of his own.

His unfaltering gaze took in the older Bainbridge first. He looked a great deal older than his fifty-four years. There was a thinning and graying of the once rich, black mane, and dark lines of worry creased his brow.

So, he *is* worried, Derek smirked to himself. And well he should be, for after I finish with him and his precious family, he will rue the day he separated me from my mother.

Derek shifted his eyes till they came to rest upon Meghan. She had positioned herself beside the desk as if she thought the sturdy piece might provide sufficient protection from him. He allowed his eyes to roam freely and leisurely over the slight but amply proportioned figure. She had certainly grown into a beautiful young thing. Long, honey-brown hair hung loose in thick layers and cascaded freely down her perfectly rigid back. Her emerald-green eyes returned his curious perusal and were wide with anticipation as to the reason for his visit and, he thought, held a touch of bitterness. Her soft, sensuous mouth looked almost ready to spew forth all manner of insults upon his unsuspecting head, and he would have laughed out loud at the picture she presented had she not looked so serious.

He permitted himself the pleasure of a long, lingering look. She was nearly a foot shorter than he, but his initial impression was that she could turn into quite a little hellcat if set upon. One of these days, he decided, he would find out. Yes, by God in heaven, he would. He would sample this tasty morsel. He would take advantage of her womanly body then return her to her father, soiled and humiliated. Yes, that should aptly repay the years of suffering his mother had been forced

21

to endure at the hands of Thomas Bainbridge. Lost in thought as he was, Derek momentarily forgot himself and took a step toward Meghan.

Thomas had begun to grow weary with the lengthy silence and as he observed the man he hated regard his daughter with open lust, an intense anger began to steep within his belly. But when this bastard, son of a whore stepped toward Meghan he could control his temper no longer. He held no great fondness for the girl, but she *was* his daughter, and this foulest of all God's living creatures was not going to lay his filthy hands upon her.

"Chandler!" Thomas spoke harshly. "Now that you have all but raped my daughter before my very eyes, could we get down to business?"

"Forgive me, Thomas," Derek offered a mocking bow, "and you, Miss . . . it is Meghan, is it not?"

Meghan nodded slowly. She was still a little taken aback by the awesome aura that surrounded this ruggedly handsome stranger and could not readily find her tongue.

"As I said, forgive me, but I was taken with your daughter's beauty." Derek cast a scornful glance at his adversary.

"Enough of your shenanigans." Thomas stormed to his chair and sat down. "Get on with it before I tire of your presence and have you cast from my home."

"That would not be wise." Derek quietly rebuked the threat. "So you would suspect me of some devious ploy." He chuckled as he planted his large, rugged frame in the chair that Meghan had previously occupied and flashed a wicked grin at Thomas. "I assure you, I have not come to pillage and plunder."

"Then why did you come?" Meghan asked hesitantly.

"Ah, the fair damsel does possess a tongue." Derek laughingly teased her.

"Chandler!" Thomas shot him a warning glance.

Derek settled back in the chair and crossed his long legs as he drew an expensive gold case from his coat pocket. It was an elegant case, Meghan noted, attractively embellished with minuscule diamonds and rubies. From this elaborate case he withdrew a slender cigar and carefully prepared it for smoking.

Meghan surveyed him discreetly from her sanctuary behind the desk. His movements were nerve-rackingly slow and deliberate, as if he purposely intended to goad her father into further temper. She had never in her life seen a man so meticulously fondle a cigar. He ran his fingers gently up and down the slender rod with the delicacy of a lover. Meghan's face pinkened as she pondered the metaphor and grew a shade darker when she discovered Derek's chocolate-brown eyes fixed thoughtfully upon her.

He smiled confidently, as if reading her thoughts, and drew sensuously on the cigar. Eyes never wavering, he addressed her. "In answer to your question, dear lady, I have come to collect what is due me."

"And what might that be?" Thomas scowled.

"Oh come now, Thomas. You needn't play your little games with me. You know very well my reason for coming here. However, if you insist," he sighed tediously. "I have come for the Chandler family jewels."

"The jewels!" Meghan's startled reply was barely audible.

"It would seem that your father has failed to inform you of my dearly departed grandfather's last will and testament. I happen to have a copy on my person." He passed the document to Thomas.

Thomas quickly scanned the paper before him and then in one swift motion he ripped the document in half. "That is what I think of your grandfather's will." He ceremoniously deposited the remnants in the waste

23

basket beside his desk.

Derek regarded the man with such a cold, callous glare that even Meghan's blood ran cold. "As I stated, that was merely a copy. The original is with my lawyer. I must warn you, Thomas." All pretenses at goading the man had vanished and Derek leaned forward in his chair to accentuate his statement. "That is a perfectly legal document and while my grandfather made provisions that I could never claim the estate, he did name me heir to the Chandler family jewels following the passing of my mother. It is my understanding that she is dead."

"She is," Meghan whispered softly.

Derek glanced at Meghan strangely, totally surprised to detect the sorrowful note in her voice.

"How did you learn of her death?" Thomas asked coldly.

"Little thanks to you," Derek replied tersely. "Suffice it to say that I have friends who keep me well-informed." He leaned forward and flicked the cigar against the ashtray. "Will you honor the document, sir?"

Thomas grunted sourly. He would not give this bastard the satisfaction of knowing that his own lawyers had taken the will apart word by word, syllable by syllable, and to his complete dismay had found it to be legally inviolable.

He turned cold eyes to Derek. "I shall."

"A most sensible decision. May I see them?" Derek asked.

"*Now?!*" Thomas was genuinely astonished. "Good Lord, do you take me for a ninny? The collection involves an extensive number of jewels, sir. As you well know, your mother's family was indeed fond of costly gems and the collection is one of the most famous in the whole of England."

"I am well acquainted with their value. My interest

24

now lies in viewing the pieces to ensure that the collection is intact." Derek impatiently extinguished the cigar. "May we continue? I would like to see them."

"For obvious safety precautions I don't keep the jewels here," Thomas explained.

"Then I suggest you collect them. I shall return this evening with my lawyer. I warn you, Thomas, the jewels best be here." In response to Derek's threatening glance, Thomas rose from his chair and stalked out of the room in a furor.

Meghan had gone to the window during the last exchange and pulled the drapes open. She had heard very little of the conversation after her father announced that he would relinquish the jewels to Chandler. The jewels that were to serve as her dowry. What would she do now? Charles had been relying on them to use as collateral in some sort of business venture. She had understood that much from snatches of conversation she had overheard between Charles and her father. Would he want her now? That is what her father had meant when he suggested that the betrothal might not be announced this evening.

"I fervently pray that I am not the cause of such a distressing frown," a deep voice whispered closely behind her.

Meghan whirled and found herself in Derek's arms.

"You *are* a comely wench."

"Let me go!" Meghan screeched and wiggled from his grasp. "Where is my father?" she demanded.

"He has gone to gather up my inheritance," Derek calmly informed her.

During their short struggle the sash on Meghan's wrap came undone and the folds fell apart briefly. Meghan hastily retrieved the errant sash, but not before Derek's observant gaze caught a fleeting glimpse of one soft, white breast beneath the sheer material of her gown. His hand ached to caress the fleshy orb, but even as he lifted his hand to do so, Meghan quickly removed herself from his reach and secured the sash.

Derek coughed sharply to clear his throat. "I'm surprised you did not hear him leave. He made quite a to-do."

"My thoughts were elsewhere," Meghan replied absently.

"Ah, yes. The dowry, no doubt. Whatever will Charles do now?" Derek inquired coyly.

"How do you—" she began.

"How do I know about Charles Beauchamp?" He completed her question. "The same way I learned of the party to announce your betrothal. It *was* to be this night, was it not?"

"It is tonight," she corrected him. "Charles loves me and wishes to marry me. He will not let this paltry matter deter our marriage."

"We shall see. Your Charles is a very greedy fellow."

"Don't speak of Charles in that manner." Meghan raised her hand as if she intended to strike him, but she quickly found her arm caught in a viselike grip.

"I shall speak of the swine in any manner I choose, my sweet." His manner was ruthless, and Meghan was suddenly wary of this brooding stranger.

Meghan struggled in vain for her release. She was obviously no match for his superior strength.

"In answer to your question," his voice was coolly reserved despite the squirming girl trapped in his arms, "I learned of your betrothal through the same friends who informed me of my mother's death."

Meghan found herself relaxing in his arms and the muscles in Derek's hard body did likewise. Seeing her chance, Meghan sought to escape her captor. But his

26

reflexes were finely tuned and he quickly pinioned her in his embrace again, drawing her roughly against his brawny chest.

"Methinks that madam is sorely in need of being taught a valuable lesson in deportment, and I shall be more than obliged to serve as her instructor," he whispered hoarsely as he lowered his lips to hers.

Meghan could do little but submit. Her struggles were useless and it seemed an eternity before he withdrew his burning mouth from hers, and only after he had conducted a thorough exploration of the sweetness of her virtuous lips.

She mustered up all the courage available to her, and in a steady but weak voice she managed, "I shall scream if you do not release me at once."

In her intense desire to be free from this blackguard's embrace, Meghan had failed to notice that Derek's adept fingers had untied the sash that secured her robe. With one swift movement Meghan found herself standing before this offensive stranger in the flimsiest of garments.

Meghan was completely mortified. No man had ever seen her in such a state of near undress. She tried desperately to retrieve the fallen garment, but Derek kicked it from her reach.

"Are you not going to scream?" he mocked. "I'm certain the servants would love to have a juicy tidbit to bandy about should one of them happen upon us now." He laughed haughtily.

"Get out of here!" she seethed between tightly clenched teeth.

"Not yet," he breathed against her silky throat.

To Meghan's complete horror, Derek began to place tiny featherlike kisses upon her neck, her cheeks, and then he kissed her mouth forcing it open as his strong tongue, tasting faintly of tobacco, thrust deep inside her mouth. Meghan felt herself weakening, almost relenting to his ardent caresses, but a tiny voice somewhere in the recesses of her mind reminded her that this was not Charles, and even he had never dared to kiss her thusly.

Suddenly, and to Meghan's profound relief, Derek withdrew his mouth and whispered thickly "Ah, little one, I'll wager that pompous ass you are to wed never kissed you like this."

"He, sir, is a gentleman. A term I am certain no one has ever associated with you," she added bitterly.

"For that small blessing I sincerely thank the Lord above," Derek bellowed scornfully. "For were I gentle, I never would have tasted the sweet nectar of your lovely lips, and never, *never* would I have dared to do this."

He watched her eyes grow round with bewilderment as his sunbrowned hand effortlessly pushed aside the protective garment, permitting him to caress her breast. He heard her sharp intake of breath as his thumb gently massaged the tiny nipple into vibrant life. Her entire body quivered as he lowered his head and allowed his tongue to lightly flick the taut peak, finally drawing the rigid bud into his mouth.

Meghan's humiliation was profound as tears welled up in her eyes, and she lifted two trembling hands to his shoulders and tried to push him away. "Pl—please . . ." she stammered. "Someone may come in." The words crackled piteously in her throat and to her extreme relief he succumbed to her pleas.

Derek's eyes were dark with desire as he looked into hers and pulled her tightly against him. Through the material of his immaculately tailored pants she could feel the impatient bulge of his restless manhood, and she averted her eyes in acute embarrassment. But his fingers firmly caught the tip of her chin and lifted her head until their eyes again locked.

"Don't be ashamed, little one. It's only natural for a man's desire to rise when presented with the fetching sight of a lovely maiden. And had we been anywhere except this house I would have gladly taken you and suffered no compunctions whatsoever." He ran his fingers through the silky tresses of her hair.

"You speak of me as though I were a strumpet you had purchased on the street." Bitter tears burned in her eyes.

"All women are whores at heart," he stated flatly. Derek stepped to the discarded robe and bent to retrieve it. "Oh, you play the virgin well since no doubt you are still an innocent. But I'll wager that your precious Charles will find you most willing to relinquish *that* coveted possession when he receives you upon the marriage bed." He gently placed the robe around her shoulders and retied the sash. "Now that you have been properly chastised, and with your permission, I shall take my leave." He bowed mockingly before her.

"You may go and, I pray, never return," she cried bitterly.

"Oh, I shall return, you may rest assured, for you see I still have some unfinished business to conduct with your father." His hand reached for the doorknob, but he turned to address one last comment to Meghan. "A caution, madam. If you are ever foolhardy enough to raise a hand to strike me again, I shall do more than make you suffer a few embarrassing caresses. I shall break your lily white neck." He held his large hands up before her as if to illustrate his promise.

The last sound that Meghan heard before collapsing to the floor in a heap of tears was the click of the door as it closed behind the departing Derek Chandler.

29

* * *

Thomas pulled his horse to a halt, leaped from the steed, and tossed the reins to a somewhat stunned stableboy. He barked orders over his shoulder to the boy as to the care of the animal and roughly implied what the lad would encounter should these directions not be promptly followed. Needless to say, the young servant dropped all thoughts from his mind of other chores and scurried off to tend to the sweating stallion.

Meanwhile, Thomas swiftly made his way from the stables to the door of the spacious town house. Without even bothering to sound a knock, Thomas impatiently shoved the door inward and rushed past a bewildered butler. He quickly scanned the first floor rooms and, not finding the object of his search, he then made his way to the stairs. But it was here that he found his path substantially blocked.

Matilda, Charles Beauchamp's faithful housekeeper for ten years, was not about to let the crazed man past her. "The master's orders were explicit, Lord Bainbridge. He don't want to be bothered, not for *any* reason." The housekeeper locked angry stares with Thomas.

"We shall see about that." Thomas attempted to dart past her, but Matilda quickly stepped in front of him.

"Why you sniveling little mouse. You dare to accost *me*!" he snarled indignantly.

"I ain't accosted ya, *yet*," she reminded him.

"I shall insist that you be severely punished for this outrage. Now, announce me to Lord Beauchamp at once," he commanded.

"There's no need for that." A third voice joined the exchange, and Thomas's eyes shot upward to discover Charles slowly descending the staircase. "I fear that your presence was made known to me the moment you

30

crashed through the front door. The knocker was placed there for a reason, Thomas. Next time, see that you make use of it," he added curtly.

"But what of her insolence?" Thomas nodded toward Matilda.

"What of it?"

"I *demand* that she be punished for her impertinence." Thomas looked at him harshly, disbelieving that Charles would permit one of his servants to insult a guest in such an atrocious manner without fear of retribution.

"For what?" came the haughty reply. "I can hardly punish Matilda for obeying my orders. This is my home, Thomas, you make no demands here." Charles made his way down the remaining steps and paused before the affronted man. "Come inside the study. You obviously have something you wish to discuss, otherwise you would not have arrived in such a furor."

Charles opened the study door and waited as Thomas stormed past him to claim a chair. "Matilda," he sighed. "I fear that I am sorely in need of a drink. Fetch me a decanter and two glasses."

Charles sat complacently in a brown velvet, over-stuffed chair and meticulously nursed his brandy. He relaxed his medium sized frame and allowed his thoughts to wander freely for a moment as he studied the man in the chair opposite him. His bright blue eyes perused Thomas with an impatient scrutiny as he ran his fingers through his mussed blond hair. His eyes then fell on a darker hair, the color of shimmery onyx, that rested on the sleeve of his hastily donned robe. He thoughtfully plucked the strand from the expensive fabric and watched it float to the carpet. He then returned his gaze to Thomas. The man had damnable timing.

31

"A bit late in the day for napping," Thomas remarked snidely.

"I assure you, Thomas, I was not *napping*. I might add that your interruption came at a most . . . *awkward* . . . moment," he stated pointedly.

"Humph!" Thomas snorted.

"Don't sound so disapproving, Thomas. In fact, it might do your disposition a turn for the better were you to indulge in an occasional tumble yourself." His lips parted in a sinful grin. "Lord knows you are in need of *something* to improve your ghastly temperament."

"Is my daughter aware of your carryings on?" Thomas would not allow the conversation to be maneuvered in the direction of his private affairs.

"That naïve little creature?" Charles scoffed. "She suspects nothing. Why, I wager I'll be able to service her and still manage a discreet assignation or two on the sly."

"I have no desire to hear of your intended dalliances," Thomas grunted sourly.

"Of course, how crude of me. A gentleman doesn't candidly talk about his intentions of bedding a lady, and certainly not with said lady's father." He laughed aloud. "I wager you have come to discuss something a bit more distracting, say perhaps the arrival of one Derek Chandler to our fair city."

"How did you know?"

"When one has much to lose on a business venture such as ours, he generally makes it his responsibility to know what is about." Charles rose from his chair and walked to a table from which he picked up a bulky folder and casually dropped it into Thomas's lap. "That is a record of Chandler's activities since his untimely arrival from America some three weeks ago," he said.

"He has been in London three weeks and you didn't

32

bother to tell me?" Thomas's face grew scarlet with fury.

"Yes."

"Why?" he demanded.

"And have you raving like a madman? You probably would have done something irresponsible, such as attempting to dispose of the bastard." Charles retained his impassive attitude, despite the fact that he was growing increasingly weary of Thomas and the entire proceedings. "You have an unnatural dislike for the man, and I could not risk the chance that you would spoil our plans for the jewels."

Thomas realized that Charles was right and his temper momentarily subsided. "He wants them, you know."

"Of course he does." Charles returned to his chair.

"What are we going to do?"

Charles placed the tips of his fingers together, and rested his chin pensively upon them. "Give them to him. The will is quite legal from all standpoints as you well know," he reminded Thomas. "When does he want them?"

"Tonight."

"I suspected as much. His ship is due to return to America in three days; so that leaves us precious little time. We shall have to act quickly." He laid his head upon the back of the chair and concentrated on a tiny speck upon the ceiling.

"I thought you said the will was ironclad," Thomas reminded him.

"Yes, we cannot go about breaking the will, but that doesn't place us above breaking the law." He grinned slyly. "If he comes tonight that should place him at your home in time for the festivities . . ." His voice trailed off thoughtfully.

"You intend to go through with the betrothal?" Thomas was more than a bit surprised.

"Too many people are aware of the impending announcement. It would be an embarrassment for all concerned were I to back out now," he said, with a low chuckle, "especially when our dear Captain Chandler graciously *returns* the jewels to us."

Charles rose from his chair and went to stand by the door. "As I was saying, Chandler will no doubt put in an appearance at the party; so as host it is your duty to see that our *guest* receives a proper English welcome by making sure that he gets properly bloody drunk. You must be discreet, of course. But don't fret, Thomas, for my men will take care of the more difficult details."

"No more disruptions, please, Mattie," Charles said to his housekeeper once Thomas was gone.

"Aye, sir."

He swallowed the remaining contents of his glass and placed it on a table in the hallway. He began to whistle a breezy tune as he leisurely climbed the carpeted stairway. Coming to a halt before his chamber door, he paused briefly to undo the belt at his trim waist. As he stood there the door suddenly opened from within and a comely woman in her mid-twenties beckoned him to enter the room.

"All is well, my dear." He drew her to him and pressed his lips against her long, raven hair. "The plot has been sufficiently laid." He chuckled. "And now let me see if I can oblige you in a similar fashion." He closed the door with one hand while encircling the woman's waist with the other, and the room resounded with the combined laughter of its two occupants.

Millie discovered her mistress lying in a crumpled

34

heap upon the library floor. She had taken note of the master's departure, and shortly thereafter she had seen the visitor follow suit. She had waited several minutes before seeking out her mistress, but upon finding Meghan in such a distraught condition, Millie cursed herself for not having entered the room when she knew Meghan to be alone with the stranger.

"What did that scoundrel do to ye?" She knelt considerately beside the fallen girl.

Meghan raised her head from her folded arms and tried vainly to compose herself. She wiped at her eyes with shaky fingers as she slowly rose to a standing position. "He . . . did . . . nothing," she finally managed weakly.

"Ye lie, Missy. Look at ye. I've never in my eighteen years of lookin' after ye seen ye so. Tell me what the rake was about so he may be properly punished," she demanded.

Meghan whirled on her maid with an embittered scowl on her pretty face and fire in her voice. "I said he did nothing," she said. "I grow weary of your inquiries, Millie, and would retire to my chamber. Bring me a cold compress for my eyes, for I don't wish them to be red and swollen this evening." Without another word she swept past the astonished maid and flew up the stairs to the sanctuary of her room.

Once behind the sturdy oak door Meghan flung herself upon the bed and released a fresh flood of tears. But suddenly she sat up and determinedly brushed her tousled hair from her face. She stood up and clutched a pillow to her breast as she began to pace furiously about the room.

"*How dare he!*" she said aloud, though there were no ears to hear her utterances save her own. "How dare he treat me as though I were a common trollop with whom

35

he could take his pleasure and then cast nonchalantly aside." Meghan stalked to the dressing table and plopped down in a huff before the mirror. She selected a brush and began to pull savagely at her hair.

"I shall inform Charles of his lascivious behavior toward me." Her eyes brightened eagerly as this idea sprang to mind, but then she raised her eyes to the mirror and absently touched her fingers to her lips.

It was almost as if she could still feel the pressure of Derek's mouth as it had claimed hers in that most passionate of kisses. And she dared not look at her breast, for she feared that the imprint of his lips might be forever branded upon the soft, white flesh as it had been upon her memory. Meghan closed her eyes as she recalled the ferocity of his kisses and the burning touch of his caresses.

"No," she finally decided, "I cannot tell Charles. He would be compelled to defend my honor by calling the scoundrel out and might possibly be killed." There was no doubt in her mind as to the capabilities of the man who had so suddenly entered her world and had proceeded to turn it topsy-turvy.

Again she spoke aloud to the mirror, "I may have been forced to suffer the indignities of his lechery this once, but I vow before God in heaven that Derek Chandler will *never* touch me again."

Chapter Three

When Derek left Bainbridge House he instructed his carriage driver to return him to his lodging. Once inside the common room of the inn, Derek called for a tankard of ale and retired to a vacant corner where he could reflect upon the morning's happenings.

His thoughts inadvertently focused on the scene with Meghan. He had not meant to push her so far, at least not yet. Oh, he would have his way with her and claim his vengeance upon her family, but raping the girl within earshot of the servants was not the way to achieve his goal. But he would have to act quickly, for his ship, *The Lady Elizabeth*, sailed in just three days, a short length of time for him to successfully bring about the ruin of the Bainbridge family.

He had an uneasy feeling about the girl, for in reality his grievance rested with Thomas Bainbridge. There were few things that Derek despised, but he hated Thomas—hated him with a fierce passion that had simmered for fifteen long years. And now that he had the opportunity to vent his stored-up wrath, Derek knew that he would not desist until Thomas had been repaid in kind for the outrages that had been committed against his mother. And if that meant that the girl suffered as well, then so be it. After all, she was a Bainbridge too.

The one bright spot in Derek's life had been his mother. She had been a beautiful woman: full of love, life and giving. Thomas had snatched him from his loving mother at the sensitive age of fifteen and cast him into the world to fend for himself. Then he had taken Derek's mother, that delicate blossom, and suffocated her within his black house of hate. The blossom dried and withered under the constant strain and finally succumbed to the evil treatment of her tormentor.

Oh, Thomas had not literally murdered Derek's mother, but he had assuredly been to blame for her death. He locked her away from the things she loved best, never permitting her to leave his estate or receive guests. He shut her away and condemned her to die, his punishment for Elizabeth Chandler's one mistake . . . a mistake that she was never allowed to forget her entire life.

Derek could forgive Thomas for the hardships he had personally endured, and perhaps he should even extend the man his gratitude for forcing him to accept the responsibilities of manhood at such a young age. It had certainly taught him how to deal with the inhumanity of others.

Derek had begun his adventure by sailing as a cabin boy on a ship destined for America. He had encountered all manner of hardships in this position and had been the brunt of many an experienced sailor's practical jokes. He had begrudgingly tolerated his fate in the beginning, but when one of his shipmates emptied the dottle of a burning pipe down his breeches, Derek decided to stomach no more of their tomfoolery. In the ensuing fight, Derek managed to display a physical prowess that earned him the respect of the entire ship's crew while he battered his opponent so severely that he had to be confined to his bunk with injuries for the duration of the voyage.

The captain had surveyed the young lad with a raised eyebrow as he himself tended to Derek's bloody fists. "Since ye've seen fit to makin' one o' me best men unserviceable I'm to thinkin' that maybe ye can take on his duties 'til he's recovered."

Derek had been unable to believe his ringing ears.

"I know yer young, but anyone what can handle Big Jake the way ye jest did is deservin' the chance to prove hisself aboard me vessel. Well, lad, what do ye say?"

Derek had readily accepted the challenge, and he

38

adapted so smoothly to the life of a seaman that anyone observing him would have thought that he had been born to it. He continued to climb the ladder of success and at the age of twenty-five was captain of his own ship, quite an accomplishment for one so young.

One position led to another, until Derek turned from commanding his own ship to establishing a private shipping firm. As his profits mounted so did his assets. He invested in a plantation and purchased his own warehouse. He reasoned that in doing this he could cut costs by eliminating middlemen.

He grew cotton, rice, and other good sellers on his plantation, stored it in his warehouse, and shipped it on his own vessels. All of this coupled with the investments of other thriving entrepreneurs had contributed to a most profitable enterprise for the twenty-nine year old Chandler.

Yes, he could forgive Thomas for his own *misfortune*, but the man must pay dearly for the maltreatment of Derek's own beloved mother.

Meghan nervously adjusted the bodice of her gown for the third time. "Oh, Millie, this just won't do!" She impatiently stamped her foot.

"Come now, what is wrong?" The maid came to stand behind her mistress.

"Have you no eyes? The bodice is much too revealing. I dare not breathe for fear my breasts will tumble out." She tried unsuccessfully to pull the décolletage higher to obscure more of her alluring flesh.

Millie smothered a titter. "'Tis just your nerves, Missy. The dress is fine. Just look at ye." She led Meghan to the mirror.

Meghan had to admit that she had never worn a

lovelier gown. It was made of gold silk that shimmered glamorously in the candlelight. The sleeves fell in billowy puffs to her elbows then tightened to a firm band at her delicate wrists where the lace trim came to a point across her slender hands. The high waist gathered in tiny folds beneath her bosom and cascaded luxuriously to the floor. The bodice was square, and the décolletage was cut precariously low so that it forced her breasts to be mounded high above the bodice.

Meghan breathed a sigh and swore silently that she would die of shame if anything came unfastened. She then turned her attention to her coiffure. Millie had worked an absolute wonder by piling the hair high upon her head and arranging a pattern of feathery curls about her face. She then arranged a number of ringlets to cascade freely down the back to complete the style.

"If ye should happen to come tumblin' out o' that dress mayhap Lord Beauchamp might be persuaded to advance the weddin' date." Meghan's self perusal was interrupted by Millie's gay voice.

"Hush your foolishness, Millie, and bring me the necklace," she said more harshly than she had intended. It is the party, she thought. That combined with the disturbing events of the morning had put her nerves on edge.

Meghan had decided to ornament her ensemble with a single piece of jewelry: a diamond necklace in the shape of a heart, the minuscule diamonds having been exquisitely inlaid in a gold setting. It had been given to her upon her eighteenth birthday by her stepmother. Meghan cherished it, not only because she knew it to be costly, but because it was from Elizabeth.

Meghan struggled with the clasp for several minutes before relenting to Millie's gentle fingers. "The way you're carryin' on a body might suspect this to be your weddin' night." She secured the clasp and turned her mistress to face her. "Ye be a beauty, Missy," she said as tears of pride and joy welled up in her eyes. "The guests be arrivin' soon. Ye best scurry on downstairs to your father."

Meghan gave the old woman an affectionate hug then carefully lifted her skirts as she passed through the doorway. She slowly descended the staircase and came to a halt before the library door. Meghan could not be sure, but she thought she heard her father conversing with someone on the other side of the barrier. It was probably one of his cronies arriving early to discuss some dull matter of politics, she decided as she shrugged her shoulders and turned towards the main ballroom.

The clean smell of freshly polished furniture mingled with the fragrance of fresh-cut flowers greeted her when she crossed the threshold. The room was spotlessly clean, an indication that the diligent serving staff had labored vigorously to prepare the room for the party they knew would mean so much to their mistress.

Meghan observed the waiters as they received last minute instructions from the butler, and she listened to the array of confused musical notes as the musicians began to tune their instruments. She then made her way to the buffet that was laden with tiny hors d'oeuvres. After the guests had eaten their fill of these appetizers the table would be refurbished with plates of beef and ham, vegetable dishes of various kinds, tiny loaves of hot, fresh-baked bread, and finally a delicious assortment of pastries, sweets, and fruits. The huge crystal punch bowl in the center of the table was filled to the brim with an icy champagne punch and, on impulse, Meghan filled a crystal goblet and sipped thoughtfully from it while visions of the gala evening ahead floated through her imagination.

41

"What have we here?" A voice Meghan had come to recognize all too well mocked her from the doorway. "Can it be that mademoiselle enjoys a tot now and again, or is she merely trying to deaden her senses for the impending evening that is to be spent in the arms of her *beloved*?"

Meghan stared into those laughing eyes and longed to pluck them from their sockets.

"In either case, may I join you?"

Meghan observed with cold, steely eyes as Derek Chandler served himself a glass of champagne. "If you have come for your inheritance, Mr. Chandler, my father is in the library. Now, if you would be so kind as to join him I shall continue with more pleasant thoughts until my guests arrive," she suggested, but to no avail, for to her supreme consternation he fell into step beside her.

"My attorney is with your father at the present," he informed her. "They are in the midst of signing a few papers, nothing that needed my personal attention. Besides, your beloved was casting such lethal glares in my direction that I felt the need for more agreeable companionship, and who should I happen upon wandering about this great hall but a princess herself." He bowed over her hand and would have placed a kiss upon it had she not yanked it from his grasp.

Meghan ignored his incessant babbling except for the part that concerned Charles. "Charles is here?" she asked excitedly.

"I suspected that particular bit of information might interest you." He toyed with the stem of the delicate goblet. "Yes, your fair-haired friend thought it his business to interfere where he has no concern."

"But it *is* my affair, Chandler." Charles's husky voice penetrated the air behind them.

42

Meghan whirled to find Charles standing in the middle of the ballroom. The look in his eyes was murderous as he observed his adversary conversing casually with his fiancée. She interpreted the look and immediately disengaged herself from Derek.

"And how, sir, do you justify such a ridiculous statement?" Derek was unmoved by the intrusion and continued to sip his drink.

"The jewels were to be Meghan's dowry to me, promised by her father." Charles came forward to stand beside Meghan and placed his arm around her possessively.

"Unfortunate turn of events for you that I have returned, a likelihood that you and Thomas apparently had not counted on," Derek mocked him. "But in any case the jewels were never his to *promise* to anyone. They were not a part of my mother's dowry. As I recall there was a rather substantial sum of money that was to serve that purpose." Derek drained the goblet and casually sauntered over to the buffet where he proceeded to replenish the glass. "But why quibble over a fortune in gems when you can pleasure yourself with this fetching trinket till your dying day?" The look he directed at Charles was arrogant and smugly reserved.

Meghan felt the muscles tighten in the arm that surrounded her waist and for a moment she feared that the two men might grow weary with bandying curt phrases about and go after each other with fists flying. But just as suddenly as he tensed, Charles relaxed.

"How right you are, Chandler," he laughed and placed a less than passionate kiss upon Meghan's brow. The effect was the same. He had successfully demonstrated his ownership of the girl. "I must warn you, though. I may allow one promised treasure to slip through my fingers, but never two." He started to lead

43

Meghan from the room. "If you will excuse us, we must see to the arrival of our *invited* guests. You will, of course, be staying on to congratulate us." Charles smiled wryly.

Derek clicked his heels together and mocked a bow. "But, of course."

Charles' first inclination as they emerged from the room was to question Meghan about her association with Chandler. They seemed to be getting along quite fondly when he discovered them in the ballroom. He cast a quick glance at her. The foyer was already brimming with people, making it virtually impossible to broach the subject immediately. But later, later he would interrogate her, and her answers had better meet with his liking.

"Chandler, can this not wait till the morrow?" Thomas asked tiredly from his chair in the library.

"I'm afraid not. When I take my leave tonight it is my sincerest intention to never grace this hall with my presence again," Derek replied icily. "It has nothing to do with your hospitality you understand. I simply find the inhabitants a bit shallow for my liking."

David Sinclair, the lawyer who had accompanied Derek to see to the transition of the inheritance, found himself trying to maintain a calm atmosphere. He had already interceded between the pair twice, and he knew not how long the two men could insult each other before tempers flared again.

The lawyer drew a handkerchief from the lapel of his jacket and wiped at the beads of perspiration that speckled his forehead. "Derek, please, if you insist I will return tomorrow to claim the necklace. The other pieces are intact. Let us leave Lord Bainbridge to his daughter's engagement party."

Derek cast a warning glance at the attorney then casually selected a cigar from his pocket. He lit the cigar and inhaled heavily before turning his back to the two men. The evening had progressed well enough thus far. Thomas, though none too pleased with the proceedings, appeared resigned to the fact that he had to part with the coveted jewels. He had even attempted to be cordial, which only inspired Derek's suspicions.

Thomas was up to something. That much was obvious, and if Thomas had something up his sleeve that meant Charles likely had a hand in it as well. Derek made a mental note to be on his guard the duration of the evening.

He turned around and began to rummage thoughtfully through the velvet-lined case that contained his inheritance. It was full to the point of overflowing with gems of every size and description. The Chandler family had taken great pride in their collection, as well they should. Derek had taken upon himself the tedious task of checking each item against a detailed list which gave a complete description of every piece in the lavish collection. He had meticulously examined each item to ensure the authenticity of every stone, and it had been during this inspection that he discovered the missing necklace.

It was described as a cluster of diamonds inlaid in a heart-shaped gold setting. Derek had calmly asked as to the whereabouts of the necklace and had been none too pleased to learn that Bainbridge's daughter wore it about her pretty neck at that very moment. He did not care about the necklace, but the fact that this snooty upstart of a girl thought that she could ignore the will and his rightful claim to the inheritance brought his blood to an unbearable boil.

"There's no need to wait for the morrow." He closed

45

the lid abruptly and in one swift movement locked the case. Pocketing the key he turned to his host, "I have yet to felicitate the bride-to-be. I must seek her out and extend my *condolences* posthaste," he added sarcastically.

"And, of course, you will see fit to inquire about the necklace," Thomas offered dryly.

"That is a distinct possibility."

"And most likely create a scene," Thomas added.

Derek turned blazing eyes to Thomas, and David Sinclair braced himself for the coming onslaught.

"Perhaps the circumstances of my birth did brand me forever a bastard," Derek snapped viciously. "They did not, however, deny me the tutelage befitting a gentleman. I do know how to conduct myself among people who are above my station," he whispered hoarsely and stalked to the door.

Derek placed a hand that trembled with anger upon the doorknob and turned to spit out one last remark at Thomas. "Be warned, Thomas. *When* I decide to embarrass you there will be no advance warning. My strike will be quick, but I daresay your suffering will be long and slow."

As Derek opened the library door he cast a final glance at the case containing the jewels. "Watch those for me, David. I don't trust the bloody bastard."

Charles grasped Meghan tightly about the waist as he led her expertly across the dance floor. The orchestra played a waltz, one of Meghan's favorites, which Charles had requested in order to spirit Meghan away from a group of friends to accompany him on the dance floor. Meghan tried to concentrate on the waltz and its intricate steps as well as on the man who held her in his arms, but her thoughts irrevocably returned to the moments she had spent alone with Derek.

46

Derek. She did not even like the presumptuous dolt. He had the manners of a rutting boar and acted like one whenever he was near her. He was forever looking at her with his piercing brown eyes, which seemed to strip the very clothes from her back with every sensuous glance. She shivered involuntarily. This was madness. Why should he, of all men, affect her this way? The mere mention of his name, his commanding presence in a room, sent her senses reeling.

It's just the festivities, she decided firmly. Any girl would suffer from nerves at such a turning point in her life.

"Why do you frown so, my pet?" Charles whispered in her ear.

Meghan shivered slightly as the excitement of his nearness sent a wave of pleasurable gooseflesh tingling down her erect spine. "Forgive me, Charles," she spoke quietly. "I didn't mean to frown."

"Then by all means, dear heart, place a smile upon your lovely lips, else the loose tongues amongst us will assuredly start to wag. Lady Trepinger has already spotted us. No doubt she will scurry off to exclaim to her boorish friends that she witnessed the downcast bride-to-be suffering the attentions of her intended."

"Oh, Charles, do you think so? I was merely lost in thought. I didn't mean to appear inattentive." She cast a worried eye in the direction of the woman of whom Charles spoke.

"Don't look so forlorn." He squeezed her arm reassuringly. "I was merely jesting. It would seem that your nerves are on edge." He successfully camouflaged the thoughtful scowl that briefly darkened his brow. "Perhaps you would enjoy a glass of champagne."

"Oh yes, that would be lovely." Meghan readily agreed and allowed Charles to lead her away from the remaining couples.

Charles deposited Meghan discreetly in an alcove slightly away from the bustling activity of the party. The evening was overly warm despite the mid-spring season, and Meghan soon found herself stepping through the garden doors to seek respite from the stuffy ballroom. The moon shone brightly over the garden, and the freshly pruned hedges and topiary shrubs cast eerie shadows.

The softly murmured giggles and contented sighs that echoed through the dimly lit shadows soon made Meghan realize that she was not the first to abandon the party for a breath of fresh air. A slightly knowing grin appeared upon her lips as she heard the familiar sound of the slap of a well-placed hand upon unprotected flesh which was quickly followed by a feminine voice breathlessly exclaiming, "You musn't do that!" Suddenly overcome by an overpowering sense of love she hugged her arms to her body and silently prayed for Charles's quick return, so they too could join the carefree lovers among the shadows.

Meghan was aroused from her daydreams by the sound of footsteps directly behind her. She turned abruptly expecting to find Charles returning with the promised champagne, and was supremely agitated to discover that the footfalls did not belong to Charles, but to Derek.

The moonlight was reflected in his eyes and they sparkled like two shimmering black onyxes. He ambled slowly to her side, sensuously nursing a drink.

Meghan's first impulse was to dart away from this man and flee to the comparative safety of the hall. But Derek anticipated her escape and clamped a sturdy hand upon her forearm.

"I . . . I thought that you were Charles," Meghan

said with a nonchalance she did not entirely feel. She was furious with herself. Why did this rake unnerve her so?

"Obviously." His keen eyes twinkled devilishly as they scanned the shadows. "Tell me, have you chosen a secluded nook where you may lure your Charles for a few stolen kisses?" The grin that brightened his handsome face was wicked and Meghan longed to wipe it from his smirking lips.

The remark caused Meghan's face to turn a deep scarlet. It infuriated her that this rogue, who stood before her like a proud peacock unruffling its feathers, might have read her thoughts as easily as if she had uttered them aloud. "You are truly a fiend, Mr. Chandler. A gentleman would not make such a ribald statement to a lady."

Derek relaxed his hold on her arm, but did not release her entirely. And when he spoke again it was in that same confident manner that Meghan had grown to expect whenever he talked. Only this time he spoke more softly. "If you find it so terribly difficult to address me by my Christian name at least exhibit common courtesy by prefacing my surname with the title of Captain. It's one I have justly earned.

"As for my being a gentleman, I thought I made myself clear on that score earlier today. But since the incident seems to have eluded your memory perhaps I should freshen it for you." He started to pull her to him.

"*No!*" Meghan succeeded in jerking her arm from his grasp. "I distinctly recall the incident and the likelihood that I shall permit an atrocity such as that to recur is scant indeed," she replied defiantly.

So engrossed was she in escaping the clutches of the menacing scoundrel that Meghan failed to notice the rising crescendo of her voice. Many of the concealed couples became unsettled by the raised voices and sought to make their way back to the gay atmosphere within the ballroom.

"You really must learn to control your flamboyant behavior, my sweet, else you may very well find yourself alone with me in this romantic Eden," Derek murmured craftily. "Do you dare discover how a deserted moonlit garden stimulates my passions? Let me assure you that this morning's display was but an enjoyable prelude to the inestimable pleasures awaiting you." He chuckled at her obvious displeasure with his playful banter.

Meghan shivered uncontrollably as Derek fingered the silky curls that lay against her cheek. The effect of moonlight upon her skin was radiant and though it took a great deal of obvious self-control Derek finally managed to remove his hand and force his concentration to the task at hand.

"Come." He offered her his arm. "Walk with me. There is a matter I would like to discuss with you."

Meghan cast a wary eye at Derek and glanced over her shoulder to search for Charles, but he was nowhere to be seen. What could be keeping him? she thought desperately.

"Your father is looking after Charles." Derek read the question in her eyes. "He knows that I am with you. Come." He again proffered his arm. "I promise not to ravish you in the secluded darkness."

Reluctantly Meghan accepted his arm and strolled with him along the walkway until they were sufficiently distanced from the laughter and music of the house.

"Why did you seek me out?" Meghan paused before a bench and indicated that she would like to sit down.

"My reasons were twofold. I had a desire to tour the

50

garden." He motioned for her to sit. "I must admit that the scenery from my vantage point is particularly breathtaking," he added huskily.

Meghan raised her dazzling green eyes questioningly to his and was chagrined to discover that his gaze rested not on the surrounding landscape as she had expected. Instead his sultry eyes were focused upon the soft curves of her breasts as they protruded from her gown. Meghan immediately felt herself flush.

"Such innocence is most charming." Derek's lips came dangerously close to her own.

Afraid that he might renege on his promise of good behavior, Meghan hurried on, "And the second reason?"

"The necklace you are wearing. Are you not aware that the shiny bauble now belongs to me?"

Meghan's hand flew to her throat where the gem rose and fell with her every breath. "No! It's mine!" she exclaimed.

"How did you come by it?" Derek inquired quietly.

"Elizabeth . . . your mother gave it to me on my eighteenth birthday," she explained.

"Your father said as much," Derek agreed. "But since Mother never signed a document stating as much, the trinket is still officially a part of the Chandler jewels," he informed her. "Therefore, it's mine."

"Captain Chan . . . Derek," she spoke his name for the first time and was surprised at the pleasant feel of it upon her tongue. "I know that you despise my father for the suffering your mother endured. I won't pretend to be ignorant of my father's villainous ways, but I assure you that I did not emulate them. Your mother was as dear to me as was my own; therefore, I beseech you," she raised tearful eyes to him, "do not take this precious gift from me."

Derek studied the girl for a long moment. The tears

51

were genuine and the words she spoke were probably true. But if he wavered now he would not be able to successfully avenge his mother.

"I must warn you, madam," he stood up and pulled her to her feet, "I am unmoved by feminine tears. Regrettably I must demand the necklace."

Meghan thoroughly scanned the rigid face for some indication that he might relent. She saw none.

"As you must, *m'lord*." She dropped into a very low curtsy before him and then drew herself up to stand directly in front of him. With carriage erect she determinedly lifted her hands behind her neck and bitterly struggled to unclasp the necklace. At last she succeeded, and, with a look of excruciating vehemence, she dropped it into Derek's open palm.

"It's indeed merciful that your mother did not live to see what you have become. She often spoke of you and wondered how you had fared. She rather hoped that you had become quite the gentleman, caring for your fellowman and bestowing upon him the kindnesses that were denied you. Yes, it's fortunate she did not have to suffer the disappointment of a reunion with a black-guard such as you," she spat scornfully and whirled to take her leave of him.

But Meghan had taken no more than two steps when she found herself caught in his crushing embrace. "You really must learn to tether your spiteful tongue." He pulled her tightly against him.

Meghan opened her mouth to protest but quickly found it covered by his. Instead of the piercing scream she had been prepared to sound she vaguely became aware of a soft, whimpering noise that originated in the back of her throat as, to her horror, she discovered that she was responding to Derek's demanding kiss.

He ruthlessly parted her lips and thrust his tongue

inside her sweet-tasting mouth, driving all thoughts of resistance from her mind. It was Derek's turn to experience surprise as Meghan did not try to dissuade him, but accepted his tongue and caressed it with her own.

An eternity later Derek withdrew his mouth and deliberately placed a kiss on the curve of each voluptuous breast. "You little vixen." He breathed heavily. "You are no better than I for all your pretentions. I might even go so far as to suggest that you are a wanton."

Meghan could not deny his accusations. Who knew better than he that she had just responded most shamefully to his overtures? With her eyes downcast she turned from him. "Charles is waiting. I must go to him before he grows impatient and comes to search for me," she muttered forlornly, ashamed that she had reacted so exuberantly to Derek's kiss.

"Let him wait," Derek ordered candidly.

"But . . ."

Meghan became aware that Derek stood close behind her, and she jumped involuntarily when she felt the warmth of his fingers upon her neck. What was he about now? Did he mean to do her some physical harm?

But just as quickly he withdrew his hands and stood away from her. Meghan cautiously raised her right hand to her throat to discover that he had replaced the necklace, and she lifted her eyes in total confusion to survey his face.

"You may keep it for the evening," he said, in answer to the unspoken question. "Your guests may notice its absence and begin to question you. Then you would no doubt point me out as the unscrupulous villain," he sighed wearily and started to reach for a cigar. "Besides, it's not you I wish to humiliate, but your father."

"In doing so you shall force me to suffer humiliation as well," she reminded him.

"That's likely," he agreed.

Meghan sighed. "I shall have my maid return this to you on the morrow."

"No, you shall deliver it to me," he stated flatly.

"*I cannot!*" she protested.

"You are in no position to argue. Perhaps you would like your Charles to learn of the enchanting episode that occurred this morning," he casually suggested.

"He would not believe you!" she gasped.

"Really? I wager that there are few damsels who possess such a charming birthmark as you. If memory serves me correctly, and it usually does, it was the tiniest diamond-shaped mole at the side of your right . . . no . . . left breast." He arched one eyebrow to ensure that she fully captured his meaning.

She did. Eyes filled with tears of indignation, she stumbled blindly ahead. "Then he will call you out!" she exclaimed.

"In which case, I shall be obliged to kill him," Derek assured her.

Meghan's mind raced with the possible alternatives available to her. She could either relent to the wishes of this man and visit him in the privacy of his quarters, or allow him to enlighten Charles of her indiscretions of the morning. She wanted neither event to materialize, but even as she pondered the hopeless situation she knew what she would do.

Derek acknowledged his minor victory. "I am staying at the Hilltop Inn."

Meghan nodded.

"I shall expect you early. The proprietor will direct you to my quarters. Come alone."

"How can I?" she objected. "There will be

questions."

"You appear to be a resourceful creature. I'm quite confident that you will devise some believable tale." He bowed and pressed his lips to her dainty hand. "Till the morrow."

"Chandler!" Thomas's voice boomed from the darkness.

Meghan quickly pushed away from Derek and smoothed the skirt of her gown before turning to await the emergence of her father from the shadows.

Thomas came to stand beside Meghan. He immediately noticed the anxious look upon her face and surmised that Chandler had succeeded in upsetting her. It was just as well that he had insisted Charles wait inside, for the two hotheads more than likely would have engaged in some sort of skirmish. Ah well, Chandler would be taken care of in due course. And if he knew his daughter she had probably held her own with the rogue.

"Charles is anxious to make the announcement. The hour grows late and a few of the guests are expressing a desire to leave," he explained.

"I was about to rejoin you." She eagerly welcomed the opportunity to deliver herself from Derek's over-powering presence.

Derek stood aside as father and daughter made their way back to the garden doors that permitted entrance to the ballroom. He looked on in smug amusement as Meghan cast a worried frown over her shoulder at him. Their eyes locked for a fleeting moment before she turned her attention to her father and the proceedings before them.

"Where is she?" Charles demanded.

"She needed a moment to freshen up." Thomas

explained as he reached for a glass of champagne from a tray being passed among the crowd. "From the looks of things she and Chandler had been arguing before I happened along. I think she fared well enough."

"Good, but I pray he did not exhaust her. I, too, have a matter to discuss with your lovely daughter before I retire this evening. Did I tell you that I discovered her alone with Chandler earlier? They seemed to be having quite a familiar tête-à-tête when I interrupted the quaint scene."

"*You* can't be jealous!" Thomas roared. "Not after your indulgence this afternoon. How utterly hypocritical of you." He choked back a laugh. "Besides, you have no need to fear that Meghan will be taken in by him. She thinks as little of the bastard as do we."

"In any case, I intend to speak with her about him," Charles reiterated.

"Tell me, Charles. I'm puzzled." Thomas lowered his voice so that his remarks would not be overheard by a passer-by. "How do you intend to explain the reappearance of the jewels to Meghan?"

"She will never learn of it. Once I have recovered the gems I shall conclude the transaction with my contact who at this moment waits only to finalize the deal and return to America."

"Can this contact be trusted?"

"Implicitly." Charles' manner was reserved. "We have discussed this before," he added impatiently. "If you don't trust my judgment you should never have agreed to place the jewels at my disposal." His voice was cold, but he forced a smile. "Meghan is coming," he cautioned Thomas.

"Charles, forgive me for keeping you waiting, but I looked an absolute fright." She smoothed the folds of

56

her gown with anxious fingers.

"Forgiven." He planted a chaste kiss upon her cheek. "Besides, you are well worth the wait."

"Come, let's make the announcement while there is a pause in the dancing," Thomas suggested.

Even as he talked he moved toward the huge buffet table. Pausing before the punch bowl, he refilled his goblet and those of Meghan and Charles, and then turned to his audience.

"Ladies and gentlemen, I believe that many of you may have already guessed the purpose for this gathering." Thomas paused until the calculated whispers died down. "As you all know, Charles Beauchamp has been a close friend of our family for many years. Recently the man exhibited the profound good sense to approach me and request the hand of my lovely Meghan in marriage, and I am elated to inform you that I have happily consented to the match."

"But more important," Charles interrupted, "Meghan has agreed to be my wife." He pressed her fingers to his lips in a romantic gesture.

Derek stood partially hidden in the alcove that led outside and observed the proceedings with a mixture of amusement and disgust. The poor, misguided wench. Did she not realize that the two men were manipulating her to gain their own means?

Derek laughed to himself and stared thoughtfully into his drink—a drink that had been forced into his hands by an over-zealous servant. So, this was their ploy.

Ever since his arrival at Bainbridge House, Derek had seldom been without a drink in his hands. As he finished one, a fresh drink was magically waiting nearby. Evidently they intended to get him intoxicated and then spirit away the jewels, no doubt inflicting sufficient damage upon his person in the process. Derek grinned ruefully and returned his attention to the scene before him. Unexpectedly, he felt a pang of sympathy for Meghan.

I am no better than Thomas or Charles, he admitted to himself for it is also my intention to use her to humiliate her family. He sighed softly, finished off his drink, and began to pick his way toward the couple who were receiving congratulations from various well-wishers.

She certainly is a spirited young thing, Derek continued his silent ponderings. She, if none of the others, will survive my assault.

"Have you decided upon a date for the wedding?" one of the guests was inquiring as Derek approached the newly betrothed couple.

"No," Charles responded. "But fear not, I shall not tarry many more days before I make the lady officially mine," he added good-naturedly and watched as the well-wisher took her leave of them, silently thankful that she was the last of the lot. But when he turned to make an offhand comment to Meghan, Charles came face to face with Derek.

Chapter Four

The two men locked hate-filled glares and several tense moments passed before either one spoke. Derek towered a good three inches over Charles and was broader through the shoulders. But Derek sensed that for all of Charles's meek appearance, he would be an able adversary. Indeed, he mused, conquering Charles Beauchamp might prove to be a pleasurable challenge, whether it be in a physical contest, or a battle of wits.

Derek was the first to break the silence and when he spoke his voice was cool, with an aristocratic air of self-assurance. "It would appear that I am the last of your guests to extend my heartfelt congratulations." He smiled smugly.

"Thank you." Meghan's voice was barely audible above the continued noise of the crowd and resumed orchestrations. She had been unconsciously holding her breath while the two men assessed each other. "You're very kind."

Charles was not to be so amiable. "And now that you have made the gesture you may take your leave of us." He pointedly turned his back on Derek and started to usher Meghan toward the dance floor.

Derek, not one to be so easily dismissed, stepped in front of Charles, thereby impeding their departure. "Come now, Charles. It has always been my under-standing that a learned gentleman possesses better manners and certainly accepts defeat with a more gracious attitude." Derek noticed the nervous twitch near the corner of Charles's mouth and knew that he had succeeded in irritating him. "It was merely my intention to ask your permission to dance with your lovely fiancée. Is that unacceptable to you?"

Derek intentionally raised his voice so that this last statement could be overheard by several of the re-maining guests. And he lifted one eyebrow in a questioning pose as he calmly awaited a response.

Charles was acutely aware that many onlookers were interested in the outcome of the situation. "Of course," he replied dryly. "That is, if Meghan has no objection."

Both men turned inquisitive eyes toward Meghan. She, in turn, looked at Derek then at her betrothed and then once again focused her determined emerald-green eyes on Derek. This brazen scalawag might possess the damaging means with which to blackmail her, but she would be damned eternally to hell if he would make her cower before her guests. She performed a token curtsy before Derek and extended her hand to him.

"We shan't be long, darling," she called over her shoulder to Charles as she traveled the short distance to the dance floor. There she allowed Derek to take her into his arms as the orchestra began to play a popular waltz.

Derek did not attempt to make conversation, but rather devoted his concentration to leading her through the intricate steps of the dance. Meghan, in turn, let her thoughts stray to the man in whose arms she was held.

She had always considered Charles to be an excellent dancer, but Derek was even more proficient than he. What manner of man are you, Derek Chandler? she wondered silently. You were born a bastard, yet you carry yourself with the air and pomp of any well-groomed aristocrat. You were denied the love and comfort of your mother at an impressionable age, and yet you seem to have managed well for yourself.

She unconsciously smoothed the blue velvet dress coat where her hand rested upon his sturdy shoulder. The material was exquisite and costly. He was obviously quite wealthy by his own right and apparently had no pressing need of the jewels he so strongly desired. No need, that is, other than sustaining his damnable masculine pride. It was the same with all men.

Meghan could not help but feel a twinge of admiration for the man even though he posed a threat to her.

He had most assuredly overcome numerous barriers to have achieved his present station, for the lot of a bastard, even an industrious one, was seldom easy.

Ah, well, she sighed inwardly. He will be gone from my life in a few days and it will matter naught.

Meghan suddenly became aware that the music had ended, but she still remained firmly ensconced in Derek's embrace. She felt her face redden and quickly pushed away from him, then glanced furtively toward Charles to see if he had detected her faux pas. He had!

Derek chuckled aloud as he followed the direction of her frantic gaze. "It would appear that you have a bit of explaining in store for you, sweet." He recaptured her hands and pressed a quick kiss to each one. To anyone looking on it had all the appearances of a friendly parting. "My sincere thanks for the waltz. It was most enchanting." He winked at her.

Meghan stood with mouth slightly gaping as Derek presented his back to her, and, with that self-assured gait she so despised, he leisurely strolled to the door and quit the ballroom. Meghan again turned to search for Charles and was horrified to see him stalking toward her, the most deadly expression blackening his handsome face.

Charles was barely by her side before he grabbed her roughly by one arm. "I should like a word with you, *darling*," he spat the last word scornfully.

"A moment, please," Meghan replied weakly, trying desperately to regain her composure.

"*Now!*" he commanded.

The pressure on her arm increased so that Meghan feared the bone would snap. There was little that she could do except allow Charles to escort her from the ballroom and down the hall to the sitting room.

Charles wrenched open the door and flung a helpless

Meghan across the threshold. He then stepped inside the room and viciously slammed the door behind him. The room was dark except for a small fire burning in the fireplace, but Meghan found that she was thoroughly chilled despite the cozy blaze. The fire cast an eerie light upon the room and their shadows appeared ominous as they danced upon the wall.

Meghan turned cautious eyes to Charles. "Charles?" she began shakily. She had never seen him in such a violent rage, and she was more than a little frightened.

"Be silent!" he commanded. "Do you take me for a complete fool, Meghan?" He stepped toward her angrily. Meghan instinctively moved away from him, but soon found her arm again caught in a bone-crushing vise. "I demand to know your feelings for that bastard!"

"I . . . I have none." She fought for self-control. But as she struggled to extricate herself from his grasp, the flames from the fire caught the reflection of the diamond necklace and it sparkled like a tiny sunburst at the hollow of her throat.

"So," he seethed bitterly. "It appears that Chandler forgot to claim his prize after all—*or did he*?" he added accusingly.

Meghan read the inference in his statement and recoiled involuntarily. "No," she whispered hoarsely. "You are being unjust, Charles."

"Am I?" His claw-like fingers encircled the gold setting and in one swift movement he ripped the treasured necklace from her neck. Charles regarded the gems for a moment then discarded it disgustedly upon the floor.

Shocked and frightened, Meghan felt a slow, painful awareness awaken within her as she suddenly realized that she knew very little about the man she had consented to wed. "He simply allowed me to keep the necklace for the evening with the promise that it will be returned to him on the morrow. And now you have ruined it," she accused him.

"Chandler be damned!" he shouted angrily. "Do you think me gullible enough to believe that out of the kindness of his black heart Chandler deigned to grant you some small comfort? You forget that I was witness to the way he regarded you earlier in the ballroom and again as he held you in his arms and whirled you about the dance floor. Believe me it was apparent to everyone watching that Chandler desired more from you than a pleasant smile and a kind word!"

Meghan pulled viciously at his grasp and turned fiery eyes to her betrothed as she successfully gained her freedom. "I reiterate, Charles. Your accusations are falsely leveled. You may believe me or not, but in either case," she added vehemently, *"leave me alone!"* Meghan pushed abruptly past him and marched determinedly toward the door.

Enraged by her actions, Charles grabbed her and spun her around to face him, and slapped her harshly.

Meghan's hand flew instantly to the burning flesh and she fought bitterly to control her tears. For the first time in her life Meghan knew intense hatred as she glared at the man who was to be her husband. She might have laughed aloud at her near folly had the realization not been so shattering. She would never, *never* marry this wretched man.

"Ah, I read your thoughts, madam," Charles baited her. "Had you witnessed this side of me before you would never have consented to marry me."

Meghan withdrew a little as his evil laughter enveloped the room. "It's not too late to cancel the wedding," she said defiantly.

"That is where you are vastly mistaken, my sweet."

His face drew close to hers and she could feel his breath, hot and moist upon her cheek. "The decision to marry me was never really yours in any case," he went on. "Your father and I decided months ago that the Chandler jewels would be placed at my disposal."

"For what purpose?" Meghan asked hesitantly.

"I was going to sell them to an American buyer I met in France last summer then split the profits with your father. Oh, I know you think me to be quite wealthy, but I've recently suffered some rather *heavy* losses at the gaming tables, and my share would have kept us comfortably until I was on my feet again."

"But why offer me in marriage? Why did Papa not simply *give* you the jewels?" So much had happened to put her mind in a whirl of confusion that she could not think clearly.

"You may not have been aware of it, love, but Elizabeth Chandler was indeed fond of you. So much in fact that she persuaded her father to add a condition to the will—that if Derek Chandler could not be found and summoned to London to collect his inheritance, then the collection could serve as your dowry." His temper had mellowed somewhat during his explanation, but Charles still regarded her with a calculating stare. "Don't think for a moment that your unsavory behavior has altered matters. We shall marry!"

"But Derek has returned to claim the jewels," she said. "Surely you can gain nothing by marriage to me now."

"Oh, to be so innocent, so utterly uncalculating." He absently toyed with the pins in her hair, removing them one by one to permit the thick tresses to cascade freely over her shoulders and down her back. "They will be mine again to be sure. So you see, my darling, I still have need of you as a wife." His voice was tender as he

64

pressed his lips along her neck and shoulders.

Meghan was openly repulsed by his amorous attentions, and she tried unsuccessfully to push him from her.

"Surely you don't intend to deny your beloved a few loving caresses, not after the way you so blatantly lost yourself to a veritable stranger. You have embarrassed me before a number of old and influential friends. Therefore, I feel that I must demand retribution for your humiliating oversight." He had her arm again and was dragging her along behind him. Roughly and without warning he pushed her down on the sofa. "I have a desire to sample the treasures you evidently relinquished to Chandler, else he never would have left the premises without that accursed necklace!"

Meghan struggled to sit up, but her efforts proved futile, for Charles savagely pushed her back. And for the third time since rising from her bed that morning, on a day that was supposed to be a joy for her, Meghan Bainbridge found herself at the mercy of an obdurate, overbearing man. She was rapidly learning what it meant to be a member of the fair sex.

Charles's blue eyes were filled with angry lust, and Meghan was so terrified that she lashed out at his unprotected face with her right hand. Charles howled in painful fury, and she once again felt the sting of his hand against her tender cheek. Through her tears, Meghan saw a streak of blood where her nails had raked his left temple, and she would have squealed with delight at her small triumph had her own situation not been so perilous.

"You little bitch!" he mumbled beneath his breath. Even as he spoke his hands found the bodice of her gown, and in one violent motion he ripped away the exquisite material of her dress and exposed her heaving

65

breasts. "Tell me, did you play the coy virgin with your bastard lover?"

Charles's hands upon her breasts were brutal, pinching and squeezing with every ruthless touch. They did not seek to give her pleasure—as Derek's had—but to mete out punishment, a punishment that Meghan felt was unjustified. She could no longer endure Charles's attack and began to struggle furiously.

But her resistance merely aroused Charles all the more. He covered her trembling breasts with fiery, demanding kisses and bit at the taut nipples, while frantically seeking to raise the skirts of her disheveled gown. Angered by her struggles, Charles cruelly bit into the sensitive flesh.

Meghan cried aloud. She had never before experienced such excruciating pain and it was with renewed vigor that she fought him all the more. But when she became suddenly aware of his stiffened manhood roughly prodding the softness of her inner thigh, Meghan summoned all her faculties. With one final burst of energy, Meghan thrust her knees forward and caught Charles squarely in his unprotected groin. The act brought about immediate results as Charles rolled from her and onto the floor where he twisted back and forth in obvious agony, clutching his hands to the injured appendage. Meghan did not wait for him to recover. She sprang from the sofa, gathered her tattered dress about her and ran from the room. And she kept running until she reached the safety of her own chamber.

Millie folded the ruined gown and turned inquisitive eyes to her mistress who sat staring blankly out the window. Meghan had supplied no specific details, but even a blithering idiot could determine that the young

66

couple had quarreled. "'Tis just as well," she mumbled to herself. "I never was fond of the bloke in any case." She sadly shook her head as she again regarded her mistress. It pained her sorely to see Meghan so out of sorts.

"Must you dawdle?" Meghan snapped irritably.

The churlish remark stung Millie, but she masked her hurt feelings. "I was waitin' to tuck ye in, Missy," the maid whispered softly.

Meghan was too overcome by shame and rage to be easily consoled. It had not been her intention to vent her anger on Millie, but there was no one else upon whom she could relieve her frustrations. "I'm too old for that."

Dawn was approaching, and it would soon be time for her to keep her appointment with Derek. She no longer fretted over his threat of blackmail, but Charles had foolishly informed her of his intentions to steal the jewels from Derek. It would please her immensely to warn Derek of Charles's plot, thereby thwarting his plans to recover the jewels. For if he didn't possess the jewels, he would have no need of her as a wife.

"Humph! Ye were not too old last night," Millie reminded her.

Meghan turned an unsmiling face to her maid. "I'm sorry, Millie. I didn't mean to be cross with you, but it has been a rather full day and although I am weary, I feel far from sleepy. You may retire, but I prefer to sit here a little longer."

Millie cast one last concerned glance at her mistress, then shrugged and left the sullen girl to seek out the comforts of her own bed.

It had taken Derek but a moment to collect his lawyer and inheritance after abandoning Meghan to fend for herself against an irate Charles. That was one confrontation he truly would have loved to have witnessed.

Derek gave the address of David Sinclair's house to the driver and climbed in beside the mellow attorney. Derek genuinely liked the man even though he found him to be a bit passive and wan for his taste. Derek sincerely doubted that the attorney had had a hearty drink, meal, or woman in the last fortnight. But to each his own, for as long as David performed his duties properly and skillfully, Derek cared not about his personal habits.

Derek picked up a canvas bag that lay neatly folded upon the seat beside him. Without a word he pulled the key from his pocket, unlocked the leather case, and began transferring the jewels to the canvas bag while David looked on in silence.

When they drew up in front of their destination, David looked pointedly at Derek. "Are you certain you want to place these in my care?"

"I have no alternative," Derek replied. "But if you're skittish about the idea, I can take them with me."

"No," the attorney said as he reached for the latch. "It's the least I can do, considering what lies ahead for you. I only hope you live to retrieve them."

"I guarantee you, David, if anyone attempts to relieve me of my inheritance this eve they will find several surprises in store for them," he reassured his friend.

The two men shook hands, and Derek thanked the lawyer for his valuable assistance. As the door closed behind David, Derek leaned through the window to address him. "One of my men will call for the package on the morrow." He then leaned back against the seat and rapped the top of the carriage with his knuckles to signal the driver to resume the journey.

Atop the stately carriage the driver clicked the team into a lively gait in the direction of the waterfront. He had heard nary a sound from the interior of the carriage; therefore he was dumbfounded to suddenly hear the high-pitched sound of his fare's voice, quite noticeably slurred with drink, raised in boisterous song as they neared the inn.

The melody he sang was quite popular about the taverns of London. It told of the misfortunes of a certain young lass who was forced to fend for herself while her husband went off to war. It went on to describe, in vulgar detail, her antics as she turned to the only position available to her, the town whore, in order to care for herself while her errant husband played at being a soldier. There were several stanzas to the song, and the man within the carriage seemed determined to sing them all.

The driver was more than a little mystified by this sudden outburst, and he pulled up abruptly before the inn. But still the singing continued and every so often a distinct hiccup could be heard interspersed with the lyrics. The driver jumped from his perch and reached for the door, only to have it kicked open from within to reveal a very disheveled passenger inside.

Derek's hair was mussed, his stock untied, his frilly white dress shirt was open to the waist displaying a multitude of curly black hairs upon an expansive chest, and he positively reeked of whiskey. The driver stumbled backwards after inspecting the man and rubbed his eyes in disbelief. This drunken sod bore only a vague resemblance to the distinguished gentleman who had earlier entered his carriage.

Unexpectedly Derek careened forward and came to an uncertain vertical position, his foot on the top step, as he clutched drunkenly at the carriage door for support.

As he stood there, precariously tottering back and forth, he brought his song to a climactic conclusion, holding the final note long and loud. Amid angry shouts that were hurled at him by the inn's disgruntled lodgers, Derek disembarked from the carriage. His movements were far from the lithe, self-assured ones that one usually associated with him. Instead his boot misjudged the last step sending him sprawling clumsily to the dirty street.

The driver, happy to be free of this strange passenger, did not wait to see to Derek's condition, but jumped to his seat and sped away. His departure was followed by a string of coarse obscenities that were shouted by an indignant Derek.

Once again on solid ground, Derek leveled the bottle of whiskey to his lips and drank earnestly from its contents. But finding the bottle empty he hurled it disgustedly in the direction of the now vanished carriage. Lovingly he patted the leather case tucked beneath his left arm and began to drunkenly zigzag his way to the door of the inn. As he moved in an apparent stupor, his dark eyes danced alertly about, suspiciously scanning the surrounding blackened streets and alleyways—any likely spot where someone might lay in wait to ambush him.

Derek burst through the inn door and staggered across the common room to the stairway. As he stumbled up the first few steps he cautiously surveyed the room for anything out of the ordinary. The night clerk sat slumped at his station, snoring loudly, undisturbed by Derek's noisy shufflings. Finding nothing amiss, Derek made his way up the stairs without further delay.

* * *

"Watch it, Toby! Let's not rouse the bloke," the man cautioned as the one called Toby labored to pick the lock to Derek's door.

"That's not likely, Dewey. What with the stupor 'ees in 'eed like as not sleep through the practiced ministrations of a dozen doxies with ease," Toby snickered.

Dewey glanced up and down the hall nervously. "'Urry up with that lock jest the same," he whispered. "I'm feelin' jittery, I am, and besides which, I don't 'ave a 'ankerin' to tangle with that bloke be 'ee drunk or sober."

Toby successfully accomplished his task and stood up proudly. He was a good head shorter than his accomplice, but both men had the well-worn appearance of toughened hooligans.

Toby's balding head caught the glare of the hall lantern as he turned to his partner. "Blimey, Toby," Dewey said as he retrieved the man's cap from the floor. "Cover that shine afore ye blind me."

"'Ush yer trap!" The shorter man's hand fell to the latch and he deftly opened the door. "On yer guard now."

The two men stealthily entered the room. Dewey closed the door, and they paused momentarily to allow their eyes to adjust to the darkened room.

"I'll see to 'im," Toby offered as he made out a form on the bed. "You try'n' find that fancy case 'ee was carryin'."

Suddenly from behind the two men the door crashed open and the ominous figure of their would-be victim framed the doorway. In each hand he held a sinister looking pistol. He meticulously cocked each weapon and carefully aimed it at the two would-be thieves. "Well, well, well. What have we here?" he grinned evilly. "If you two *gentlemen* are in need of quarters, I suggest you

71

speak with the man downstairs, for this room is presently occupied."

Dewey glared at Toby. "Ye said 'ee was so drunk 'ee could 'ardly stand," he accused.

Toby brandished his partner with a look that was meant to silence him. It did. "If ye'd put those guns aside, gov'ner, maybe we could talk this over."

"As I see it there's nothing to discuss. I apprehended the two of you in the process of burglarizing my quarters. What do you have to say for yourselves?" Derek's voice remained calm as he silently calculated the capabilities of the two crooks.

"We meant ye no 'arm," Dewey broke in nervously. "'Twas the jewels we came for."

"Really?" Derek's eyes fell to the knife that Toby held purposefully in his hand. "And what were you going to do with that, manicure my nails while I slept? No, the only thing we need discuss is how I am going to dispose of you two hoodlums."

Dewey had rapidly lost his taste for the entire situation and without warning he darted for the door and pushed Derek off balance. Derek struggled to regain his footing and in a flash was chasing the scoundrel, finally catching up with him at the head of the stairs. He slapped the hood across the face with the butt of one of the pistols, and then, grabbing the man by the scruff of the neck and the seat of his breeches, he hurled him down the stairway. If the night clerk was awakened by the clamor he showed no sign of awareness.

Dewey struggled to his feet and limped noticeably toward the door. But he turned to shake a menacing fist at Derek who stood at the top of the staircase. "Bastard! Ye busted me leg," he whined piteously.

"Come sniveling about my property again and I'll break your bloody neck," Derek promised him and whirled to cautiously retrace his steps to his room.

The chamber was empty when he returned, or so he thought, for just as he stepped across the threshold something swished through the air from the direction of the window. Derek reacted swiftly and narrowly avoided receiving Toby's well-aimed knife through his heart. As it was, the knife grazed his arm, then glanced off the door behind him and fell harmlessly to the floor.

Derek bolted to the window, but his assailant was nowhere to be seen. Viciously he slammed his fist against the windowsill as he shouted into the darkness, "Should you be foolish enough to return, you filthy bastard, you'll discover that I shan't hesitate to use these." He angrily waved the pistols out the open window, but the only response to his threat was the sound of hurried feet as they scurried along the cobblestones.

Chapter Five

Meghan quickly rose from the window seat where Millie had left her earlier and walked to the wardrobe. There she selected a riding habit of green velvet, choosing the warmer material because the morning air was still quite chilly. She dressed rapidly and pulled on black riding boots, then crossed to the dressing table to arrange her hair. She brushed at it furiously until it shone, then tied it at the nape of her neck with green and gold ribbons. Satisfied with her appearance she stepped to the pitcher and bowl that stood on the commode beside her bed. The water that she splashed on her face was ice-cold, but she was determined to wash the sleep and tiredness from her bleary eyes. Besides, she did not want Derek to think that she had spent a sleepless night pondering his intentions.

Meghan collected her cloak and paused to scribble a vague note to Millie. She had caused the woman enough grief for one night and did not want to further worry her by disappearing without notice.

She slipped quietly out the door and tiptoed past the maid, who snored loudly as Meghan crept noiselessly by her bed. Once in the hallway she wasted little time and quickly made her way to the sitting room.

Meghan rushed straight to the fireplace, choosing to ignore the sofa where Charles had tried to rape her, as if by shunning the scene of the horrible incident she might erase it from her memory. The flames from the fire had long since died down and the ashes were cold, leaving the room in a blanket of darkness. She decided against using a lamp, fearing that she might draw the attention of an early rising servant. Instead she knelt on her knees before the fireplace and began searching with her hands along the plush carpet for the diamond necklace, for in her haste to flee Charles she had inadvertently left it in the room.

"It should be right . . . about . . . here," she whispered softly, but her exploring fingers could not locate the errant gem. "Unless, of course, Charles took it with him," she added despairingly. The thought was not only dismaying, it angered her greatly. But then she squealed aloud as her anxious fingers locked around the tiny gem. Meghan immediately clamped her hands to her mouth to prevent any further utterances and waited carefully to see if anyone would respond to her outcry.

No one did.

Hastily she scrambled to her feet and made her way to the stables directly behind the stately mansion. She stepped into the dimly lit stable and cautiously secured the door behind her. Meghan glanced around for the stable boy and groom and was profoundly relieved to discover that they were evidently still abed.

"Good morning, my love," she whispered soothingly to one of the horses as she paused before a stall which bore the nameplate "Champion." "Could I perhaps interest you in a little outing on this fine morning?" She gently stroked the horse's magnificent head.

The horse whinnied what Meghan interpreted an affirmative reply, and she accordingly disappeared into the tack room to collect the necessary gear. But upon her return Champion began to move about restlessly in his stall.

"Shhh, Champion," she quietly scolded. "Do you want to wake Rafferty? He would be none too pleased to discover my plans for the day." She opened the stall and led him to the middle of the stable to accomplish the task of saddling the huge stallion. By the time she had readied the horse he was more than a little anxious to commence his morning exercise.

"Anxious," she crooned into the horse's ear.

Meghan led him to the door that opened at the rear of the stable. She paused just outside to close the door then led Champion to a large rock which she stood upon in order to climb upon his noble back without assistance. The rock had been placed there years before to serve this particular purpose.

Meghan directed the high-spirited stallion away from the house. The route she intended to follow would take longer, but she wanted to avoid the house for fear that someone might observe her unchaperoned departure. It would be discovered soon enough as matters now stood.

She held tight upon the reins, curbing the horse to a slow pace. She had been forced to neglect Champion for the past few days what with her preoccupation with the engagement party. A frown darkened her pretty face as she reflected on what a fiasco that had turned out to be.

She sighed and leaned forward to stroke the horse's sturdy neck. "Rest easy, Champion, we have but one unpleasant errand to tend to. Then we shall be free to race through the hills and meadows beyond the city."

Meghan left Champion at a stable near the inn. The stable boy had just risen and was washing the sleep from his eyes when Meghan appeared in the stable yard perched atop Champion. The boy could scarcely believe his eyes. The establishment seldom stabled a horse of that caliber, and it was *never* visited by a lady the likes of which sat upon the majestic steed. Meghan left Champion with the still blubbering boy and hastened the three blocks to the Hilltop Inn.

The waterfront district was hardly the place for well-bred young ladies to be found wandering about, especially without a proper escort. Murders occurred almost nightly in this section of the city, and Meghan's single thought was to deposit the necklace with Derek, warn him about Charles and take her leave of him.

Meghan was indeed thankful that the Hilltop Inn was considered to be one of the better establishments on the block. The waterfront was famous for its drunks, muggers, pick-pockets and prostitutes as well as the squalid buildings that housed these undesirables. At least Derek had displayed the good sense to choose a respectable place to reside during his stay in London.

"The Hilltop Inn" read the large, black letters on the

76

sign that swung squeakily back and forth in the gentle morning breeze. Meghan paused thoughtfully beneath the sign before entering the building. "What an odd name for an establishment that sits not more than a few blocks from the docks. Why, I can see the topmasts of several ships from where I stand," she said, half-aloud.

"So ye be wonderin' 'bout the name, miss," said a voice from the entrance to the inn.

"Yes, I am." Meghan glanced at the cheery face that grinned at her and could not help but return the smile.

"Me name is Bromley, miss. I came down from Durham 'bout two years ago. Had meself a dandy inn up there, I did. She was called the Hilltop Inn as well. She sat right at the top o' the lovliest knoll ye ever laid eyes on. A green meadow ran t' the side o' her and a brook just bustin' with trout ran behind her. Aye, 'twas a fine inn." His eyes glistened as he envisioned the establishment he had once owned.

Meghan realized that he was rebuilding the image in his mind, and she allowed the man a few moments before she continued. "It sounds like the perfect paradise, Mr. Bromley."

"Aye, she was that, a paradise." He shook his head as if to erase the vision and turned to her. "When I came down to London no other name 'twould come to mind; so that's how she came to be called the Hilltop Inn and sittin' 'ere on the waterfront. Must admit," he continued "many people stop out o' curiosity 'bout the name and end up stayin' the night. And you, miss, what is a fine lady such as yerself doin' in this part o' town, and you with no one to see to ye?"

"I have an appointment to speak with one of your lodgers," she explained and stepped past the man to enter the common room.

"Aye, and who might that be?"

"Captain Chandler," Meghan whispered lowly.

"And why would a proper lady such as yerself be wantin' t' visit a gentleman alone in his chambers?" He regarded her disapprovingly.

Meghan pulled herself erect before the man and looked him square in the eye. "The matter is one of business. It's personal *and* private." She raised her voice, irritated that the man should dare to question her motives. Certainly he did not suspect that she had an assignation with Derek.

"Beggin' yer pardon, miss. 'Tis only that—"

"Yes, I accept your apology," she interrupted tartly. "I have not the time to stand here and chat the morning away. Your story about the inn was enchanting, but if you would kindly direct me to Captain Chandler's room, I shall waste no more of your time."

"Aye, miss. Turn right at the top of the stairs. 'Tis the third door on the left."

"Thank you." She turned and walked briskly to the stairway, took a deep breath and ascended the steps. Fearing that she would turn coward and flee should she take even a moment to deliberate, she rapped sharply upon the door as soon as she arrived in front of it.

"Come in." Derek's voice summoned her lazily from within.

Damn his insufferable hide anyway. He was always so cocksure of himself. "Oh, how I wish I could be around the day he is delivered his comeuppance," she breathed lowly. Her cheeks were red with anger as she threw open the door and stalked inside. She came up short, though, at the sight with which she was greeted.

"Close the door, sweet." Derek smiled wryly from the bed.

At her were leveled two pistols. He was naked to the waist, the sheet drawn over his flat, muscular belly, and

78

as far as Meghan could ascertain he was naked beneath the sheet as well.

"I should like to leave it ajar." How she managed to sound so calm was an enigma to her.

Derek's eyes twinkled merrily as he leaned forward as if to rise from the bed. "Very well, if you won't, I suppose I shall be forced to see to it myself." He casually lifted one corner of the sheet.

"No!" Meghan shrieked and ran to the door and swung it closed.

"Come, sit here beside me." He motioned to a spot on the edge of the bed.

Ignoring him completely Meghan selected a straight back chair, carried it a safe distance from the bed and firmly implanted herself upon the hard seat. It was uncomfortable, but she reasoned that it was a good deal safer than placing herself upon the rogue's bed.

"I mean you no harm," she informed him tartly. "And I assure you that I carry no concealed weapons on my person."

Derek dropped the guns to the pillows that had served to camouflage his bed when the intruders had attempted to burglarize his room and to Meghan's complete horror, he started to rise from the bed. She immediately clamped her eyes shut, and her pulse quickened when he spoke.

"The guns were not meant for you. But you are vastly mistaken when you claim to carry no concealed weapons."

Meghan's eyebrows lifted in question at this statement, but still her eyes remained tightly closed.

Derek chuckled as he moved to stand in front of her. "You are a female," he went on to explain. "If that were not enough in itself, you also possess a cunning mind, a willful disposition, and an extremely potent tongue. The combination would make most ordinary men turn tail and run. It is indeed fortunate that I am no ordinary man," he added snidely.

"Come now, open your eyes," he coaxed her. "I am no beastly ogre who would lure you to his den then toss you upon the sheets and have his way with you. Had *that* been my intention I daresay I would not be wasting my time *talking* with you. Besides, while I shall admit that you are quite a tempting morsel, I tend to fancy a more gentle, agreeable wench to warm my bed. And from my observances of you thus far neither of those adjectives apply to you."

Meghan flew into a rage. "Why you . . . you . . . spineless son of a guttersnipe," she spat at him. Her eyes snapped open to glare into his laughing ones. "Who are *you* to insult *me*?" Her tone was harsh, but her eyes never wavered from his.

"I see the talons are sharp and at the ready." He laughed good-naturedly. "Don't be angry, my sweet," he said in a soothing voice, "but we could hardly conduct business with you sitting like a statue, eyes glued shut as if you fully expected to be accosted at any moment, now could we?"

Meghan lowered her eyes then and saw that he *was* clothed, but only in his trousers. They were skin tight and left little to the imagination, but at least he was not stark naked as she had supposed. She folded her hands primly in her lap and again met his intense gaze. "I thought you to be . . ." She glanced hastily toward the bed, her sense of propriety not allowing her to complete the awkward statement.

Derek threw his head back in exaggerated laughter. "You thought me to be naked!" he bellowed. "What? And find myself castrated by one glare from your devilish, green eyes." He caught her chin and forced her to look at him. "I assure you, Meghan, while you might not fancy my *charms* there are those who do, and above all else I hold my masculinity quite dear to me." He stopped suddenly as his eyes fell upon the dark bruise that shadowed her right cheek and he softly fingered the blemished area. "How did this happen?"

Meghan was taken aback by the serious, almost gentle tone in his voice. "It's nothing." She brushed his hand aside and went to stand by the window.

"Did your father strike you?" he persisted.

Meghan shook her head. "No, it was Charles." Her voice was so low that Derek had difficulty hearing her. "I came to warn you." She turned to look at him. "He intends to steal the jewels from you."

"Why should you trouble yourself to warn me?" Derek asked suspiciously. "Surely you have been slapped before?" he taunted her.

But Meghan refused to let him goad her. "I have decided that I cannot marry Charles," she continued. Her staunch Bainbridge pride would not allow her to confess that Charles did not truly love her, but merely coveted the profitable concessions their marriage would bring. "Charles is a deceitful cad. I discovered many things about him last evening that I could not live with. His intention to rob you of your inheritance is merely a minute part of it." She again faced the window. "I may be many things, as you have generously brought to my attention, but I could never knowingly allow harm to befall another human being, even one who so enormously detests me."

Derek stared at that proud straight back. So she was not a part of their scheme to seize the jewels. He didn't know why, but he was genuinely pleased with this discovery.

Derek put his hands on her shoulders and gently

turned her to face him. "I don't detest you," he stated simply, and Meghan knew that his words were sincere. "In fact I should like to thank you for your warning, even though it has been delivered a trifle late." He indicated the wound on his arm. The blood had long since dried which made the cut look worse than it actually was. "Your estranged fiancé sent his hired ruffians to do their dirty work earlier this morning. And while one of them did manage to leave his mark on me," he lifted the injured arm gingerly, "they did not succeed in their task. The jewels are still safe."

"Oh, Derek, I was never interested in your inheritance. You must believe me." She looked at his face and was relieved to find that for once it did not mock her. "You need tend to the wound at once," she cautioned him.

"It's merely a scratch." He was quite surprised to note the concern in her voice. "There is no need to fuss over such a paltry injury."

"Nonsense," she scolded. "With any open wound there is always the danger of infection. You sit on the bed and I shall collect the things I require." She left the room before Derek could protest. She returned shortly carrying a pan of hot water, a roll of bandages and a bottle of whiskey. She placed these articles on the table by the bed and went to retrieve the soap and towel from the washstand.

"There," she said and sat down on the bed beside him. She lathered the cloth with the clean-smelling soap and carefully lifted his arm. She looked at him questioningly, thinking that he might not trust her to tend to the nasty cut and offered the cloth to him, but Derek shook his head.

"I'm at your mercy," he said.

Meghan quickly cleansed the wounded area and

carefully examined it. "The cut is not deep," she informed him, "but if it is to heal properly it will require a few stitches. Do you have a needle and thread?" she asked.

"Madam," he replied patiently, "do you mistake me for a seamstress?"

Meghan smothered a giggle and shook her head. "No," she murmured quietly. "This will have to suffice, I fear." She reached for the whiskey bottle. "It will sting a little," she cautioned.

"Yes, go ahead."

Meghan poured a generous amount of the brown liquid on the wound to cleanse it and was about to replace the bottle on the table when Derek took it from her hands and turned it to his lips. She then took the roll of bandages from the table, wound a strip tightly about his arm several times, tore a section in two and securely anchored the bandage.

"There." Meghan surveyed her handiwork. "Is it too tight?"

"It's fine." Derek flexed his arm to test the dressing. "You are an efficient little nurse," he said lightly and glanced at her admiringly.

Meghan stood up and reached into the pocket of her riding habit. "Here." She thrust out her hand in which she held the diamond necklace.

"I fear that the clasp has been damaged," she explained and her face reddened slightly as she recalled the humiliating confrontation with Charles. "I shall gladly make retribution for the damages," she offered shyly.

"That won't be necessary."

"Then I must go."

"Just a moment." Derek halted her movement toward the door. "I'm curious. What sort of tale did you contrive to satisfy your father?"

"I told him nothing," she stated truthfully, deciding not to mention the note she had scribbled to Millie. "It's Saturday and I often ride out to the family's country estate on Saturday to check on matters for Papa and place flowers on my mother's grave."

"And do you usually make this journey unescorted?" Derek raised an unapproving eyebrow.

"No, our groom accompanies me."

"But not this day?" Derek inquired.

Meghan shook her head.

"Then you must permit me to see you there and back." He selected a fresh shirt from the bureau drawer and slipped it on.

"No!" Meghan exclaimed. "I'm capable of finding my way."

"I'm sure you are." Derek struggled into his boots as they continued their argument. "But you need not protest further, for I'm going to escort you." He located waistcoat and coat and went to stand beside her. "Besides, I would like to see my mother's final resting place. It's the least you can do," he added.

Meghan could formulate no reply to this, so she abruptly stepped past him and led the way to the stable where she had left Champion. She was furious with him for being so presumptuous as to think that she would welcome his company. And she was angry with herself for not steadfastly refusing his offer, for she could have easily returned home and made her trip another day. These thoughts were still whirling through her mind when she entered the stable yard. The stable boy recognized her immediately and ran to fetch Champion.

Derek took one look at the spirited animal and dubious of Meghan's ability to handle him, he suggested that she might like to hire a carriage.

"Nonsense," she responded airily. "Champion needs the exercise and I am looking forward to the ride. It's much too beautiful a day to spend cooped up inside a stuffy, old carriage. But, of course, if the idea of a ride makes *you* skittish . . . ." she challenged him.

"I shall choose a mount," he said tersely and vanished within the stable.

He was gone for some time and Meghan seriously entertained leaving without him. "He would only follow me," she surmised. "Then I would be forced to endure his wrath as well as his company."

Meghan swore she could hear Derek angrily haggling with the young stable boy as she sat impatiently upon her mount. Both she and Champion were eager to be on their way, but Derek appeared momentarily leading a grey mare of obvious good stock.

"Champ, old boy," he sauntered over to the stallion and patted the horse's flanks, "meet Clarabelle." He winced openly at the name.

Meghan's sour mood seemed to vanish instantly. "Oh, Derek, that can't possibly be true. What an atrocious name for such a splendid animal."

The stable boy had stood by the door silently watching the exchange, but he suddenly hurried forward. "Mum," he snatched his hat from his head as he addressed Meghan, "that's me master's 'orse . . . 'is pride 'n joy. If'n anythin' should 'appen to Clarabelle . . ." He dared not to imagine his fate should some misfortune befall the animal that had been placed within his care. "Yer friend would settle fer no other."

"There were no others worth choosing," Derek patiently explained.

"Me master returns by nightfall on the morrow," the boy again spoke directly to Meghan. "If'n Clarabelle ain't 'ere, 'e'll throttle me good."

"The animal shall be returned long before that," Meghan assured him. Then she added with a sarcastic glance in Derek's direction, "Besides, Captain Chandler may be many things, but I sincerely doubt that even he would stoop to thievery." She gently tapped Champion's flanks with her riding crop and directed him down the street.

Derek jumped to his mount and caught up with her as she rounded the corner two blocks away. Neither one of them spoke as they rode through the city streets and Meghan forcibly restrained Champion till they were reasonably clear of the crowded city. But once they had traveled a safe distance from the noise and smell of London, Champion's sensitive nostrils sensed the fresh aroma of the country and he was no longer content to progress at such a sluggish pace.

Meghan eased him from the road, turned to Derek, and said, "Race you to that clump of trees." She pointed to a small group of trees across a wide meadow.

Derek nodded, and the race began.

Meghan allowed Champion free rein and had to do little else save cling to her saddle. The wind whipped her hair about wildly, and her face was flushed with the exhilaration of the ride. As they drew near the trees she pulled in the reins and slowed Champion to a walk. She then turned to search for Derek and discovered him rapidly approaching her.

"That is a magnificent animal!" he exclaimed.

"Humph! And I suppose the horsewomanship I displayed had little to do with my *superior* ride?" she pouted.

"Had I been astride Trojan instead of this milkweed I guarantee the results would have been significantly altered," he stated flatly.

"Is that your horse?" she asked.

"Yes."

"Well, words mean precious little when actions speak differently. The fact remains that I did indeed win."

"Yes, that's true," he conceded. "And to the victor go the spoils. Tell me, my sweet, what of my meager spoils would you desire?" He drew his mount up close and stared into her dazzling eyes.

Their eyes met for a brief instant, and Meghan felt her pulse quicken and her knees grow weak. Had she been standing she felt certain that they would have buckled beneath her and sent her sprawling to the ground. Oh, what wicked demon has possessed me that he should arouse these sinful feelings within me? she thought to herself.

Meghan drew back in the saddle and tossed her curls at him. "Lunch!" she proclaimed. "There is a little inn just beyond the woods there. Perhaps you could procure some food for us."

"Lunch!" he cried. "It's barely past the breakfast hour."

"Yes, and I had none, nor did I eat last night or yesterday. Your sudden appearance has certainly altered my dining habits," she teased him. "I *am* starving, Derek. "Please," she whispered softly and fluttered her long, black lashes at him.

"How can I possibly refuse?" He tweaked her nose. "I am your slave, m'lady. Lead me to your inn."

Meghan laughed happily and maneuvered Derek through the thickly wooded area. Not more than fifteen minutes lapsed before they emerged into a bright clearing. "There." Meghan pointed to a grey building.

They pulled up before the building and Derek slid to the ground and tossed the reins to Meghan, then disappeared inside the small inn.

Meghan watched him, silently praying that no one

87

had seen them ride up together, for she traveled the route often and could easily be recognized by several of the locals, especially the owners of this particular inn. She and Rafferty usually stopped here to sup on their return trips from the estate. They would think it odd to find her with someone other than Rafferty, especially someone like Derek. No one could ever mistake *him* for a groom.

It was at that moment that Derek reappeared beside his mount to interrupt her musings. "Where shall we dine?"

"I know just the spot."

"Lead on." He jumped back into the saddle and followed her out of the yard and onto the main road.

They rode on for quite some time before Meghan suddenly veered off the road and into a grove of trees. She directed Champion through the trees to an isolated clearing through which ran a glistening brook. Meghan halted her mount and twisted in the saddle until she could see Derek who rode a few paces behind her. "Is this satisfactory?"

Derek responded to her question by sliding to the ground and going to assist her from Champion's back. "It's fine, m'lady." He lifted her gently from the saddle and eased her to the ground.

Meghan spread her cloak upon the grass for them to sit upon while they ate and waited there while Derek collected the basket of food and came to share the cloak with her.

"What did you get? I must warn you that I am simply famished."

"You're in luck, m'lady. The Latimers were more than generous, especially when they discovered that it was Mistress Meghan Bainbridge they were serving. Why, they simply could not do enough for you it seemed."

Meghan sat up on her knees and her hand flew out to catch the sleeve of his shirt. "Oh, Derek, you did not tell them—"

"Rest easy." He pulled his arm away and continued unpacking the basket. "I explained that I was your cousin. Your groom was abed with the chills, and I had graciously taken a day off from prayer study to escort you to the Bainbridge estates."

Meghan sighed heavily then suddenly burst out giggling. "Prayer study! *You!*" She pointed at him incredulously and fell back upon the cloak as she tried to stifle her laughter.

"I fail to see the basis for your annoying display, madam." Derek observed her calmly, a slight grin twitching at the corner of his sensuous mouth.

"If the Latimers only *knew*," she tittered uncontrollably.

"Shall we return and enlighten them?" Derek meant only to tease her, but Meghan took the question seriously.

"N-n-*no!*" She brought her laughter to an abrupt conclusion, and a disheartening frown shadowed her pretty face.

"Still worried about your precious reputation, I gather," he said sourly. "Even when you have decided that Beauchamp is not the love of your life."

"But that doesn't mean I do not wish to wed someone, Derek. And a girl with a sullied reputation would be hard-pressed to find a respectable gentleman who was willing to marry her." She greedily accepted the drumstick he offered her.

Tearing off a hunk of bread, Derek tossed it unceremoniously upon her plate. "Are you referring to my mother?" he asked dryly.

Meghan considered his question as she wiped at the corner of her mouth with her napkin and she searched his face for some indication that he might be angry with her. "No, Derek," she replied softly. "Elizabeth never entered my thoughts. I simply don't wish to take any chances with my own reputation, that's all."

Derek accepted her explanation and turned his attention to his meal. Presently he said, "How much farther must we ride?"

Meghan finished the last of her chicken and accepted the wine bottle from him. "About half an hour, if we ride hard." She glanced at Derek's plate then at the bottle in her hand. "But then I suppose we are in no great rush."

"Mrs. Latimer forgot to include drinking cups," he said, then added sarcastically, "Have you aversions to drinking from the same bottle as has a bastard?"

"Derek! That was not the reason for my hesitation. Faith, I scarcely ever think of the circumstances concerning your birth. Were it not for you I daresay I would never think of them," she stated curtly. "I was merely wondering . . . are you not going to eat the remainder of your chicken?"

"You little glutton." He laughed as he watched her rummaging through the basket.

"Are there no more of those little cakes? They were positively scrumptious. Ah!" she squealed with delight as her fingers encircled the last one.

Derek observed her with fond amusement. "If you aren't careful you will grow to be as round as Aunt Sophie," he cautioned her.

"Who is she?" Meghan paused curiously just as she was about to bite into the tantalizing morsel.

"My housekeeper."

"Oh, and how *round* is she?" Meghan asked.

"Well, whenever I return home from a voyage, or an extended business trip, Sophie is always there to greet me with a great big hug." He thoughtfully rolled a blade of grass between his perfectly white teeth.

"And," she prompted.

"I have yet to make my arms reach all the way around her."

Meghan dropped the cake instantly to the ground. She quickly drank from the wine bottle to wash down her meal and passed it back to Derek who was still chuckling at her reaction to his story.

"Are you ready to continue with our journey now that your appetite has been satisfied?" he asked, taking his napkin to wipe away the dribble of wine that clung to the corner of her mouth.

Meghan stood up and smoothed the material of her riding habit. "I would like to pick a bouquet of spring flowers in the meadow if you have no objections."

"Go ahead. I shall clean up here," he offered. "Careful crossing the brook."

Derek watched as she gingerly picked her way across the stepping stones to the other side of the stream and began to gather the brightly colored flowers. She was a beautiful girl, easy to be with, definitely not the whimpering, clinging-vine variety he so carefully avoided. There was no longer any need to carry out his plan to violate her. She had canceled the wedding to Beauchamp on her own and had come of her own volition to his room at the inn then permitted him to ride with her to the Bainbridge estate. This in itself, when bandied about the snooty London parlors, would render her unmarriageable to anyone of quality. His task was complete. He had brought about the humiliation of the Bainbridge name. It was no longer a *task* to bed the girl, no, it had now become an intense desire.

"Derek!" Meghan called for the third time. "Can you not hear me?"

Derek shook the stimulating thoughts from his head and turned his attention to Meghan who stood calling to him from the far side of the bank.

"Yes, what have you done now?" He stood with his arms crossed, grinning at her.

"I cannot cross back over," she explained.

"And why not?"

"I can't seem to locate the stepping stones I used and there exists the further problem of balancing myself and holding up my skirt from the water without dropping the flowers," she went on patiently.

"My, my," he clucked his tongue. "It would seem that you are presented with quite a dilemma. Perhaps I shall find you here on my return from the estate," he teased her.

"Derek!" she screeched. "You would not dare leave me!"

Suddenly he stepped into the water regardless of his footwear and marched determinedly to where she stood. He swooped her into his arms, retraced his steps through the clear stream and settled her gently upon Champion.

"No, m'lady, I would not leave you. I fear for the safety of any unsuspecting travelers who might happen upon such a troublesome wench." He swung himself into the saddle and they continued their journey.

Derek was indeed shocked. He had expected a more dignified structure than that which stood before him. The house was comfortable to be sure, but it noticeably lacked the grandeur that he had anticipated of a Bainbridge estate house.

Meghan read his thoughts. "It's not what you expected."

"To be frank, no. I *had* envisioned something a bit more . . . spacious," he admitted.

"After my mother died, Papa never enjoyed staying here. Consequently he devoted his time to his affairs in London, and his money went to the upkeep and maintenance of Bainbridge House," she explained as she ascended the steps to the front door.

"Who manages the properties?" Derek inquired as he followed her to the house.

"Fergus, but he usually goes into the village to visit his mother on Saturday." She threw open the door and wiggled her nose in distaste as a musty odor enveloped her sensitive nostrils.

"It would appear that he tends to neglect the house," Derek muttered dryly.

Meghan left the door standing ajar and went to open the windows throughout the house in an attempt to air it out.

"So this is it." Derek frowned slightly as he stepped into the sitting room behind Meghan.

She had just thrown open the window and paused momentarily to let the fresh, cool breeze wash over her before turning away. She caught a glimpse of the sky as she turned and the dark grey clouds that were rolling rapidly in from the west, coupled with the increasing wind gave her cause to anticipate an afternoon storm. Well, the showers were usually brief this time of year. They would undoubtedly have plenty of time to travel back to London before dark. "I'm sorry, what did you say?" She brushed her hands together to shake the dust from them. The house *was* in quite a state of disarray. She would need to reprimand Fergus.

"I was merely admiring the enchanting surroundings in which my mother found herself imprisoned for her last fifteen years." His voice was composed, but bitterness glittered brightly in his eyes.

"This was not her *prison*," Meghan protested. "It was her home and believe it or not, she dearly loved it here." She tried to keep her voice calm.

She could well remember the two occasions on which she had spoken rashly to Derek, and her lips still burned from his angry reaction to her outbursts. She was totally alone with him now. There were no servants just beyond the door who would answer her cries and no crowded ballroom into which she could escape. There were but the two of them.

"My mother would never have *loved* being cooped up here," Derek said shaking his head firmly.

"She was not *cooped up*," Meghan insisted. "I preferred to spend my holidays here instead of London. Papa was always so busy that I rather think he preferred I come here, also." There was a far away, saddened tone to her voice. She walked the few steps to the sofa and sat down before the marble fireplace. "Anyway, Elizabeth was not confined to the house, just the grounds."

"And I suppose I am to *thank* your father for this great kindness he bestowed upon his *wife*!" Derek spat bitterly.

"No, Derek, I don't expect you to understand my father's ways, for I don't always understand them myself," she admitted. "I only ask that you let me explain how things truly were."

Derek studied her for a long moment and decided that it would do him no harm to listen to her. "Very well. Fxplain away the years of pain and anguish that my mother endured in this bleak shell of a house."

Meghan ignored his belligerent remark and proceeded with her account. "Your mother and I used to go riding every day and we had the most divine talks. She would talk about her family and . . . and you. And of course she had a garden that she adored." Meghan paused again as she witnessed the look on Derek's face. It was positively murderous.

"You make it sound as if her life here was one gala event after another," he said angrily.

"No, but you are vastly unfair to imagine that she was chained to her bed from sunup to sunset," she retorted in a voice every bit as hard as his had been.

Derek took a step toward her, but halted abruptly as he glared into her upturned face. He would not believe her! He *knew* that Thomas had treated his mother cruelly and heartlessly. Refusing her access to society was just one example, but then to hide her away in this hole . . . it was unforgivable. He could not . . . *would not* believe this girl who thought him gullible enough to accept her picture of rides through overgrown meadows and digging in an insect-ridden garden as being sufficient activities to ensure his mother's happiness.

Derek cleared his throat and when he again spoke it was with forced composure. "I believe we came to view the gravesite."

"Yes," Meghan stood up quickly, "it's a short distance behind the house. Follow me." She exited through the main door and went to collect the flowers she had left in the basket on Champion. But when she turned from her task she found Derek staring at the sky behind her.

He stood at the top of the steps, hands on hips, feet planted rigidly apart while the wind gently whipped the strands of hair that curled down his neck to the collar of his shirt. She could almost picture him in that rugged pose as he stood aboard the deck of his ship bellowing orders to his crew. He certainly did strike an impressive figure and, were it not for this conflict that existed between them, she could almost imagine them becoming fast friends. Yes, she would like to have Derek Chandler for a friend, for he would make a most formidable enemy.

Meghan shook her head to bring her thoughts back to the matter at hand and started around the house by way of a well-worn path. She had not spoken a word to Derek, yet she knew he followed, for she heard his footsteps on the path behind her. Presently Meghan came to a stop before a small, white picket fence. Her hands rested on the gate as she scanned the headstone. It read:

CATHERINE SHEFFIELD BAINBRIDGE
1781-1805
MY LIFE, MY LOVE, MY EVERYTHING

Thomas Bainbridge
Adoring Husband

Meghan pushed aside the gate and went to kneel by the headstone. Silently she pulled the weeds that had grown around it since her last visit. She then removed the dried flowers that were a reminder of the last time she had been to the grave and replaced them with the sweet smelling flowers from the meadow. Meghan stood then and finding her work to be satisfactory, she whispered a quiet prayer and opened the gate and stepped onto the path. She did not dare look at Derek for fear that his face might have assumed a smug look of self-satisfaction, and she could not bear to have him mock her at her mother's grave.

Derek's notable figure blocked the path so she could not pass him. But had she looked at him, Meghan would have seen that the expression that shadowed his handsome face was neither smug, nor self-satisfied.

Instead it was deeply saddened with the compassion one feels for one who has suffered the loss of a dear one. Derek shifted his feet uncomfortably. It bothered him not a little that he could feel compassion for a girl whose family had caused him so much misery. He gently touched Meghan's shoulder. "My mother," he whispered.

But Meghan did not hear him, for her thoughts were turned toward the sky. The wind was growing increasingly stronger and thunder sounded in the distance as the darkening sky grew threateningly ominous.

Derek noticed the direction of her gaze and his attention was immediately drawn to the treacherous looking sky. He surmised that it was only a matter of minutes before the heavens opened up and thoroughly drenched them. Again he touched her shoulder.

This time Meghan nodded and led him further down the path, across a narrow bridge, and up a grassy knoll to the shelter of a monstrous oak tree. Beneath this tree rested Derek's beloved mother. There was no elaborate picket fence to border her grave and, of course, no costly marble headstone. The headstone was of granite and said simply: Elizabeth Chandler Bainbridge, 1771-1819.

The anger and hurt burned brightly in his eyes and he felt an incredible urge to lash out at someone. Had Thomas been present, Derek would have taken his spite out on the man.

Meghan discerned the look on Derek's unhappy face and she hastened to explain, "This is where she asked to be buried, Derek. Elizabeth would come here and sit for hours at a time to view the countryside and to think. She is not placed so far away from my mother because Papa wished it this way. This was her favorite place, and she requested that this be her final resting place."

Meghan did not wait for Derek to respond, but

stepped forward to place a tiny bundle of flowers by the headstone and whispered so softly that Derek could not distinguish her words, "He has come home at last, Elizabeth. I have brought your Derek to you."

Meghan stepped a few paces away so that he might have a private moment with his deceased mother, and she felt a stab of sorrow rip at her heart when she saw him wipe a tear from his cheek. She could not bear to see a man cry, and she would have called anyone else a liar were they to say that they had witnessed Derek Chandler give in to such a tender emotion. Yet, she had seen it with her own eyes, and her heart went out to him in this painful reconciliation between son and deceased mother. But, of course, she would never allow Derek to know that.

The peaceful moment was abruptly interrupted as a flash of lightning and an uproarious clap of thunder tore across the sky. Derek shot a glance heavenward toward the rapidly approaching storm clouds.

"Get to the house quickly!" he shouted above the rising wind. "I'll see to the horses." He called over his shoulder as he ran down the slope.

But Meghan did not immediately heed Derek's warning. As the rain began to drizzle she knelt down beside the gravesite and whispered against the gusting wind, "You can be proud of him, Elizabeth. Oh, he is stubborn and argumentative and *completely* exasperating, but from all appearances he seems to have done quite well for himself. Yes, you can rest easy now and be proud of your son."

Derek ran the entire distance from the oak tree to the front of the house where the horses were tethered. Quickly he led the animals to the shelter of the barn, removed the saddles, rubbed each one down and found a generous helping of oats for their overdue supper. He then bedded them down for the night, for there was no doubt in his mind that there would be no return trip to London till the next morning.

He secured the barn door and sprinted toward the house, but just as he rounded the corner of the house the heavens released their torrential downpour. Derek burst through the door and quickly slammed it against the wind and rain.

"Meghan!" he bellowed above the crackling thunder.

Derek shook his head furiously and hundreds of tiny droplets of water flew from his glorious black hair. He relieved himself of his dampened coat and walked straightway to the sitting room where he fully expected to find Meghan, but instead he discovered a mild hurricane raging as the wind whipped the curtains about in a frenzy and rain gushed in through the open windows.

Once he'd pulled them closed, his thoughts again focused on Meghan, and he realized that she had not responded to his summons. Surely she was not still outside in this ghastly weather. Perhaps she had gone upstairs. Derek quickly made his way to the foot of the stairs. "Meghan!" he shouted again.

Derek had placed his booted foot on the first step to ascend the staircase when the front door was suddenly flung open. Derek took one look at Meghan's disheveled condition and determined that she was thoroughly terrified.

"God above!" he exclaimed as he rushed forward. "What are you doing out in that?"

Meghan's reply was obliterated by a flash of lightning and a clap of thunder so loud that it shook the very foundation of the house. Meghan was so frightened that she sprang forward and vaulted into Derek's sinewy arms.

Somehow Derek managed to close the door against the turbulent wind and still keep Meghan secure in his embrace. Actually there was little he could do, for she clung to him with a ferocity that fully astonished him. Yet, even as he smoothed the wet curls from her devastated face he realized that she clung to him out of fear.

"I distinctly recall instructing you to return to the house," he scolded her sternly. "Had you heeded my advice you would now be warm and dry. Instead look at you. You closely resemble a drowned muskrat." He attempted to ease her tension by drawing her attention away from the storm. "What kept you?"

"I . . . I had to talk to . . . Elizabeth." Her teeth chattered as her rain sodden clothes clung tightly to her body, enveloping her in an aqueous blanket that chilled her to the very bone.

Derek stared at her in total disbelief at her absurd statement before releasing her. "Come, I shall build a fire to warm you." He led her by the hand into the sitting room.

Derek had no idea how long it had been since the grate had held a fire, but at least there was an ample supply of firewood in the basket. And for that he was immensely thankful, for he knew that there would be nary a dry twig outside. Derek had a promising blaze underway before he again turned his attention to Meghan and only then because a not so distant clap of thunder elicited a jump and a squeal from her.

His gaze slowly wandered down her trim figure, over the firm, young breasts, the slender waist, and the softly rounded hips. "It's no wonder her skirts sway so temptingly," Derek sighed beneath his breath. Finally his eyes came to rest at her feet where a substantial pool of water had gathered about her boots.

"Well, young lady," he brought her chin up so he could gaze into her eyes, "it's time you got out of those wet garments." He laughed openly as she withdrew from him as though he were afire.

"I think only of your welfare," he continued cunningly as she backed still further away from him, stopping only because her leg caught the edge of a chair and she stumbled backwards into it. "It would not do for you to catch a chill." He chuckled at her obvious discomfort. "Perhaps there is something upstairs you could change into," he offered casually.

"No, there . . . there is nothing." Meghan was utterly shocked by his suggestion. "What I did not take with me to London I gave to Fergus to distribute among the tenants."

"Your generosity somehow amazes me," he said wryly before exiting the room. He returned shortly carrying an armful of blankets that he had discovered in an upstairs wardrobe. "These will have to suffice." He dropped them at her feet then resumed his vigil at the fireplace. "Remove your wet clothing so you won't catch a chill," he ordered.

"No," Meghan whispered defiantly.

"Shall I assist you?" Derek stepped menacingly near her chair.

"You would not dare!" Meghan breathed hoarsely.

"Wouldn't I?"he countered.

Meghan studied the hard lines of his face, and what she read there completely unnerved her. He would assuredly do what he threatened without any qualms whatsoever. She shuddered more from this disturbing thought than from the wet clothes that were draped about her. She realized they needed to be changed and, given another situation, she would likely do so without giving it a second thought, but she had never disrobed before a man before and she certainly was not about to begin the practice with this rogue. It was a simply horrid experience just being stranded in the same house with the scoundrel, but to be clothed only in a mere blanket? The idea alone made her cringe. A blanket was insufficient protection from his flaming eyes and roaming hands. Why, who was to prevent him from . . . her eyes closed tightly. . . . No, she must not think about *that*!

"Well, what shall it be?" Derek's eyes danced in gay apprehension to her answer.

"Humph!" was her reply as she stooped to retrieve a blanket. Meghan flounced past him and left the room, closing the door roughly in her heated departure. As she ascended the steps to one of the bedrooms, she covered her ears to muffle the sound of Derek's laughter as it followed her up the staircase and echoed down the hallway.

Meghan was gone but a few moments and had it not been for the raging storm outside she would not have hastened her return to Derek's irksome presence. She might despise the man, but at least she felt protected with him nearby.

Meghan reentered the sitting room to find that Derek still stood in a thoughtful stance beside the fireplace. She quietly positioned a chair before the blaze and spread her riding habit upon it posthaste. But she paused uncertainly with her undergarments and glanced bashfully at Derek.

"I *am* familiar with what lies beneath a lady's skirt," he assured her.

Meghan threw her chemise on the chair in a huff and hurried to remove herself as far away from him as possible, and yet remain close enough to the fire to enjoy its comforting glow. In her flight she tripped over a loose corner of the blanket and as her hand flew out to steady her balance, the blanket fell away from her shoulders to expose one tempting breast for a fleeting moment.

Derek's ever observant eyes caught a glimpse of that breast, the nipple rosy and taut from the chill of the room, and almost immediately he was burdened with a throbbing sensation in his loins. He turned his back to her so she would not witness his awkward condition. But in doing so, Derek failed to see Meghan gather the blanket tightly about her and regally stride to the sofa where she gracefully sat down. Nor did he witness her indulge in a childish prank as she thrust out her tongue at his back in a most unladylike gesture. No, had he observed *that* he might very well have turned her over his knee.

Derek, his passions having temporarily abated, turned once again to Meghan.

She noticed the movement and looked at him sourly. She also took note of his clothes and though they were not as soaked as hers had been, they were damp enough to invite a chill. She swallowed hard. The next words she spoke were going to be the most difficult in her entire life. "Are you not going to do the same?" She indicated his wet clothing and the blanket that now enveloped her and quickly came to regret her words.

"Why, madam," he looked pleasingly shocked, "do I dare hope that you proposition me?"

Meghan's face instantly grew red with resentment as she hissed at him, "You flatter yourself, sir. I simply don't wish to be faced with the tiresome task of seeing to your recuperation should you become ill. But upon second thought I wager I'd be a good deal safer were you confined to a sick bed!" Her eyes burned brightly

103

with animosity.

Derek shortened the distance between them in two quick strides, and, grabbing her by the shoulders, he jerked her roughly to her feet. "Were I stricken with the very plague and but a moment from death's awesome grip, you would not be safe from me. That is *if* I decided I wanted you." His breath was hot against her flesh.

Meghan stiffened in his grasp and tried desperately to keep the blanket wrapped securely about her. She wanted to avoid another confrontation, for she realized that if Derek should decide to take her there would be little she could do to stop him. But her fears were for naught, for Derek suddenly released her from his vise-like grip. Off balance, Meghan stumbled backwards onto the sofa.

"Your concern for my welfare is most surprising," Derek said sarcastically as he returned to the fireplace to allow the heat to dry his rain sodden clothes.

Meghan was determined to avoid another argument, and she strived to bring the conversation around to a harmless topic. After all, they had spent the day together riding and picnicking, laughing and talking, and never once had he gazed at her, his eyes glittering with passion. She studied his tall, muscular frame as he leaned forward to bank the fire. He could be quite friendly with her when he permitted himself. Her thoughts wistfully turned to the luncheon they had shared earlier. "It's because I am a Bainbridge," she sighed softly.

Cautiously, clutching the blanket close to her, she slipped to the window to view the rain. "Please, let it have slackened enough to permit us to return to London," she whispered prayerfully.

But even as her hand reached to spread the lace curtains she knew her prayers to be in vain. The steady rhythm of the water against the windowpane, the flashing lightning, and pounding thunder made her realize that while they had already suffered the worst of the storm it was far from over. They would not be able to return to London before daybreak.

Her shoulders dropped like a dead weight. "When Papa learns of this, he will . . ." Meghan released the curtain and shivered nervously, unable to complete her musings. She could not sufficiently envision the ferocity of *that* encounter, nor did she wish to.

Meghan was so engrossed in her dilemma that she failed to notice Derek abandon the warmth of the fireplace and come to stand behind her, nor did she become aware of him until he encircled her waist with his arms and drew her against his muscular chest.

Meghan was too fatigued to resist his advances. "Do what you wish," she sighed heavily. "It matters precious little now."

"How gallant." Derek pressed his body closer to her soft, pliable curves. "The cringing virgin prepares to sacrifice herself to the brown-eyed monster." He nuzzled her ear.

"Please, Derek," she moaned at his mockery. "I have had no sleep since early yesterday morning. I'm more than a little weary of bickering with my father, fighting off your advances, and being slapped around by my fiancé. In short, I am weary of domineering men. After tonight I will be blackballed by every decent family in London, and Papa will likely exile me to a convent in Europe." The mere thought made goose bumps run up and down her spine. "So do what you want. Do it, then leave me be."

For an indeterminable length of time the only sounds in the room were the splashing of the rain against the window and the crackling of the fire in the grate. In fact she might well have imagined herself to be alone in the musty room were it not for those ever-present arms that held her in a tight embrace.

"I suppose it is too much to hope that there might be something to eat or drink in the house." Derek's husky voice finally broke the suspenseful silence.

She was puzzled by the sudden change in conversation, and she cocked her head so that she could better see his eyes, as if they might hold the answer to her questioning thoughts. But Meghan was unable to ascertain anything from the cool gaze that met hers.

"I'm sure there is nothing to eat," she hesitantly answered. "But there is brandy."

"Where?"

Meghan directed him to the liquor cabinet and tried to relax while he was gone. But her reprieve was short-lived, for he soon returned and thrust a glass of cognac into her hands. Then he led her back to the sofa and seated himself beside her.

"Drink it," he commanded. "It will help you sleep."

Reluctantly Meghan raised the glass to her lips and sipped the fiery brew. Ordinarily she abhorred the taste, but she was uncommonly cold and tired, and the brandy quickly spread a warm, cozy feeling within her that had been alien to her of late. She hurriedly downed the remainder of the drink and shyly extended the glass to Derek for him to refill it. After he complied, she followed suit with the second glass.

No more than five minutes had lapsed before Derek heard the soft plunk of the glass upon the rug as it slipped from Meghan's hand. He retrieved the glass and placed it on the table beside the sofa. He turned his gaze to Meghan where she peacefully slept in the corner of the sofa.

Derek gently lifted her into his arms and mounted the

staircase that led to the upper chambers of the house. He felt along the hallway and opened the first door he encountered and deposited Meghan upon the bed therein. He left her a brief moment while he returned to collect the remainder of the blankets and firewood from the sitting room. And when he rejoined her in the chamber he quickly set about building a fire to remove the chill from the dampened room. When that task was completed, Derek turned to face the bed, but the sight that greeted him caused the breath to catch in his throat.

Meghan had obviously changed positions in her sleep, for the blanket had fallen away to reveal her voluptuous, naked body to him. Derek moved cautiously toward the bed, fearing that any sudden movement might awaken her and cause the lovely vision to disappear.

But he need not have bothered, for she slept soundly. The disturbing events of the past two days had taken their toll on her nerves, and once she had finally yielded to the comforting sleep, Derek would soon discover that it would take more than the squeak of a loose floor board to rouse her.

Derek strode over to the bed. He untied the ribbons at the nape of her neck and spread the heavy tresses upon the pillow. He stood back to gaze at her and as the flickering firelight played upon her flesh, he felt a sudden warmth spread to his loins as he surveyed every inch of her tantalizing form.

"Oh, my innocent lamb," he whispered huskily. He leisurely discarded his clothing and climbed into the bed beside Meghan. Raising himself on one elbow above her, he peered down into her sleeping face and shook his head slowly. "Poor little lamb. It certainly was your misfortune to meet up with such a wolf as I."

It was then that his wandering eyes fell upon the ugly

bruise that marred her otherwise perfect breast. He frowned angrily as he realized the identity of the culprit who would dare to treat her in such a barbaric manner.

"The swine," he mumbled harshly. "I shall see Beauchamp properly punished for his brutality." He gently brushed his warm lips against the bruised flesh, but as he did so the nipple stiffened immediately in response to his practiced touch and he groaned involuntarily.

"Ah, you are so vulnerable, my sweet, lying here in my arms this way. You make it quite difficult for me to remember that you are of gentle birth and not some doxie who has agreed to warm my bed for the night."

He paused for a moment as he realized that he was speaking aloud to her. "So lovely," he sighed. "And so terribly, terribly irresistible." He slowly lowered his head until his lips came to rest against hers.

Chapter Six

Meghan stirred restlessly as she reluctantly awakened from a marvelous sleep. She had been dreaming that someone held her snugly in his arms throughout the night, but now the illusion had deserted her and warmness had vanished as well.

"Millie," she moaned sleepily, still too drowsy to open her eyes. "I'm cold."

Almost immediately an additional blanket was placed over her. Meghan sighed contentedly and snuggled further down in the soft bed. "Thank you," she managed softly.

"You're quite welcome," a masculine voice cooed beside her.

Meghan's eyes flew open instantly as the sound of that voice painfully reminded her that she was not safely tucked in her bed at Bainbridge House, but here in the country with Derek. What in the name of heaven was he doing in her bed? Did he not even have the common decency to seek separate sleeping quarters? Meghan raised her eyes, now completely void of sleep, to stare into Derek's grinning face.

"Actually, love, it's I who should be thanking you." He smoothed her hair as it gently flowed across his pillow.

He was propped up on one elbow, staring down into her bewildered face. His wicked eyes were gleaming and it was a full minute before Meghan's muddled brain completely comprehended the implied meaning of his statement and her mouth flew open to protest, "No!" she squeaked. "You did not."

"I did not what?" His sensuous eyes had taken on a sparkle of feigned innocence.

"Oh you—you!" Meghan could think of nothing severe enough to call him; so she decided to remove herself from his offensive presence. She threw back the coverlets and jumped to her feet, but only too late did she realize that she was completely naked before Derek.

"A most charming nightdress." Derek's passionate eyes slowly appraised her young, shapely body.

Wildly Meghan lunged for one of the blankets to cover her nakedness, but Derek anticipated the maneuver and craftily removed them from her reach.

"Ooohh!" she shrieked. "You are the most disgusting . . . despicable . . . the poorest excuse for a man that

109

I have ever had the misfortune to set eyes upon," she spewed at him.

"Oh really?" He looked affronted by her verbal attack. "That's odd, for you didn't seem to think so last night." He grinned slyly.

Meghan's mouth again dropped open at his repeated implication that they had been intimate during the night. The mere notion that he could use her body and she not recall the experience stunned her for only a moment; this startling revelation was quickly replaced by a rising anger that burned within her and threatened to erupt violently.

Derek stared at her as he tried to interpret the expression on her face. But he was none too surprised when Meghan rushed forward and snatched a pillow from the bed and began to pummel his body with vicious blows. Derek alertly raised one arm to ward off the blows and with the other, he grabbed Meghan firmly about the waist and lifted her onto the bed. But the battle was not yet to be concluded, for Meghan continued to scratch at him with her long fingernails and when he imprisoned her hands in his, she kicked at him.

"Stop it, you little minx!" he commanded. But when Meghan failed to comply with his order Derek sat up on the edge of the bed and with considerable difficulty, he managed to drag her across his lap. "Someone should have done this long ago," Derek said, not half as perturbed as he sounded. He then proceeded to turn her over his knee and brandished her unprotected backside with precisely placed blows from his large hand.

Meghan's lovely hair tumbled about her in wild disarray and her thoughts were in a similar state of confusion. She was bitter and humiliated that Derek would dare to treat her this way, and she was

110

embarrassed at the tears that swelled up in her eyes.

Meghan suddenly grew weary of the struggle and lay limp across his lap. She realized that if she were ever going to escape him that day, it would be wise to pretend that she had succumbed to his will for the time being.

"That's much better." Derek relaxed his hold when she ceased grappling. He gently turned her over in his lap and eased back against the headboard. It took him a moment to find a comfortable position, but not once did he release Meghan from his grasp. Once settled he looked down into her eyes. They were still bright with unshed tears and her cheeks were wet with those that had escaped their prison.

"Derek?" she whispered softly, her mouth turned down in a pout like a young child's after it has been reprimanded.

"Yes?"

"You . . . you . . . did not . . ." she stuttered.

"Hmmmm?" The sudden desire to kiss those pouting lips was great, and he did not try to suppress it as he brushed his lips against her quivering mouth.

"That is to say, *we* did not . . ." She could not bring herself to put the question that plagued her into actual words.

"Yes?" He grinned at her amusingly.

"But I don't feel as though . . ." She blushed under his watchful gaze and hurried on, "That is, I . . . I don't remember . . ." Her voice faltered and she looked desperately into his mocking eyes hoping to detect something that might indicate that she was the brunt of one of his cruel jokes.

"What!" His eyebrows shot upward as if in bewilderment. "You don't remember?" he gasped. "That says precious little for my performance. Perhaps an encore is in order." He playfully traced a pattern around the nipple of one quivering breast.

"*No!*" She squirmed away from him, but Derek was quicker than she anticipated, and he once again drew her into the circle of his arms.

Meghan's mind raced with thoughts that were as jumbled as the emotions that coursed through her body. She was both embarrassed and mortified to have awakened in the same bed with this man, and she felt a bitter animosity begin to build inside her to think that Derek would have the unmitigated gall to defile her body while she slept. Why, the whole situation was utterly preposterous!

Surely, I could not have slept while he . . . She somberly considered the dilemma before her. Unless . . . unless, oh, why did I drink that accursed brandy?

Meghan peered up into Derek's face—that ruggedly handsome face that patiently awaited her reaction to his insinuations. She could not seriously think him capable of doing such a thing, but then a twinge of doubt gnawed at her as she recalled the one factor that might spur him to such drastic action. Her name. He hated her because she was a Bainbridge, the offspring of Thomas Bainbridge, and the tool through which he could gain revenge upon her father. He had not been sufficiently satisfied to learn that she had canceled her marriage to Charles. No, he had not halted his assault until he had rendered her unmarriageable to any man, for she could not now offer herself as an innocent bride to an unsuspecting groom.

Meghan averted her stony gaze to the window, and when she spoke her voice was as cold as was the expression on her face. "You are to be commended, Captain Chandler. It would appear that you have won."

"Won?" He questioningly placed his hand on her chin to force her eyes back to his, but she savagely

112

pushed it aside.

"Don't play coy with me," she said irately. "It has been your intention to destroy my family ever since you arrived in London. Well, it appears that you have accomplished your chicanery through me. But pray, don't puff up like a proud toad and boast of your victory," she cautioned him in a shaky voice, "for surely you must realize that you had a most gullible, yes, stupid victim." Her eyes filled suddenly with fresh tears.

"No," he whispered. "You are neither gullible nor stupid, but rather very beautiful and desirable, and no match for me." His lips burned against her throat and shoulders, and his hand caressed the silky flesh of her stomach then slowly edged its way upward to gently cup first one breast, then the other.

Meghan felt her body tingle with his sensuous touch, and she visibly strained to quell the rising surge of her own passion. Why was he doing this to her? Why would he not leave her be now that he had accomplished what he had set out to do? She must force her concentration on something, *anything* other than the strange, thrilling sensations that were coursing through her body like the swift wind in a rampaging storm. But even as her reason cried out for him to stop her body willed him to continue, for it had barely been introduced to these new sensations, and the desire to experience them to their ultimate conclusion was strong within her.

Derek sensed her acute tenseness, and interpreting it to be extreme revulsion to his lovemaking, he rolled away from her to sit on the edge of the bed. His serious gaze drifted over the dormant figure on the bed. What would become of her now?

Actually her alternatives were few and Derek could not see her stationed in any one of them. She was too well-bred to seek out a position as a governess, and he was quite certain that life in a secluded convent would not suit her. That left but one option for her, but try as he might Derek could not convincingly imagine Meghan as a prostitute selling herself to the riffraff of London. Then what would happen to her?

Irately Derek stood up and struggled into his trousers. What do I care? he reasoned to himself and concluded buttoning his trousers. He was just about to reach for his shirt when the door to the chamber swung open and Thomas and Charles burst into the room.

Meghan clutched the blanket to her heaving breasts and sprang upward in the bed. Her eyes were bright with surprise and apprehension as they quickly scanned her father's face. But her expression changed noticeably to fear when she read the outraged fury that transformed his features.

"Papa! What are you doing here?" she managed from trembling lips.

"Silence!" he bellowed. "You slut!" He distanced the space between them in three quick strides and yanked the blankets from her grasp. In one swift motion he sent the covers billowing over the foot of the bed and left Meghan's lovely body hopelessly exposed to the three pairs of masculine eyes in the room.

"Why so modest? You evidently paraded yourself before this bastard. Why not let the world view you for what you are, a shameless whore," he spat venomously. "It's already common knowledge about the streets of London how you visited this whoreson in the privacy of his chamber, and had Millie not shown us the note you left divulging your ultimate destination, we would still be searching for you. What's wrong, daughter?" His eyes raked her disgustedly. "Did you find the London

114

waterfront to be too disreputable a place to carry on your whoring ways?" he shouted hysterically, and losing all reason, he grabbed Meghan viciously by the shoulders and shook her with all his strength. "You are no better than *his* mother, sluts the lot of you!" He raised his hand to strike her, but the blow was never to reach its target.

Derek had been mildly surprised to see Thomas and Charles, but perhaps it was for the best. If a showdown was in order then let them get on with it. He had been greatly agitated when Thomas so crudely exposed Meghan's innocent body and ruthlessly slandered her. What rational man would treat his own daughter, flesh and blood, in such a degrading fashion? But when the coward grabbed that lovely body and began to shake it so villainously, Derek had been unable to control his rising anger.

As he observed Thomas lift his hand to strike Meghan, Derek sprang across the bed with the agility of a cat and knocked Thomas to the floor. "Swine!" Derek spewed at the fallen man. "You lowlife bastard! Your argument is with me, not the girl. If it's a fight you seek then perhaps you would like to take me on!" Derek suggested bitterly.

Derek glared at Thomas as the older man clumsily returned to his feet and awkwardly made his way to where Charles stood calmly surveying the situation. Satisfied that the man would molest Meghan no further, Derek collected his shirt from the chair and carefully draped it about her sagging shoulders.

"You need not gawk at us," Derek sneered at the two men. "I have successfully accomplished my goal, Thomas. Your name will no longer hold the importance it once did, and this lovely maiden won't be able to provide you with the wealthy son-in-law that you

115

fervently seek." He paused when he noticed the astonished look of surprise that suddenly dressed Thomas' face.

"*Maiden?*" he growled scornfully. "That particular term no longer signifies." He turned with a scathing look toward his daughter. "Get dressed. We shall ride for London before word of *this* scandal arrives there ahead of us."

"No," Derek said firmly. "I shall return Meghan to you in due course."

"*What!*" Thomas's face grew red with anger.

"You need time to cool your temper. No telling what you might do to her in your present state," Derek calmly informed him.

"He's right, Thomas," Charles spoke for the first time. "The damage has been done. Let Chandler return her to London."

Thomas looked first at Derek, then at Charles, and a dark scowl appeared on his face. Gone were his hopes and dreams of at last achieving financial security. He glared at Derek with open hatred and secretly vowed to himself that Chandler would pay for his actions. If it took him the rest of his life he would hunt Derek Chandler down like the dog that he was and destroy him.

Thomas abruptly turned toward the door. "I shall deal with you in London." The words were meant for Meghan and though they were stated calmly, she shuddered at the implication of his words. Thomas was at the door when he noticed that Charles had not offered to join him. "Are you coming?" he asked, the anger slipping back into his voice.

"Not just yet. I would like a word with the clandestine couple," he said smoothly. "Go ahead, and I shall join you in a moment."

116

The room fell silent, but it reverberated with the sound of Thomas's angry footsteps as they echoed down the stairway. It was a full three minutes before Charles spoke, and when he did his eyes were fixed squarely on Meghan.

"You stupid, stupid chit," he said slowly, savoring each word as he voiced it. "We could have had so much together—money, travel, anything you desired would have been yours for the asking. I could have even tolerated a lover or two had you exhibited the proper discretion, of course. But really, Meghan, to fling everything aside just to warm this fellow's bed for one night. . . . He shook his head distastefully and added dryly, "I trust it was worth it."

"You could have given me nothing but anguish," Meghan replied, as she stood stiffly by the bed, clutching Derek's over-large shirt to her bosom. "I would never have rested a single night knowing that the luxuries that surrounded me were purchased with your blood money. At least you and Papa shall never profit from the illicit use of Elizabeth's jewels," she said as if she had won a great victory.

"Yes, Chandler has seen to that," Charles agreed. "But then he has also seen to you, my sweet. Tell me, what will you do now that no worthwhile gentleman in London will touch you?" he asked smugly.

"I shall manage." She held up her head proudly, refusing to be intimidated by his egotistical attitude. "A girl does not always have to marry in order to survive."

"True. And I'd wager that the good Captain here could introduce you to his acquaintances on the waterfront who could further instruct you in the ways of your newly acquired talent, just in case," he sneered.

"Enough!" Derek shouted. "I have listened to enough of your senseless prattle, Beauchamp. Vacate the premises at once, else I shall be sorely tempted to call you out. And while I'd be the first to admit that I'd derive immense pleasure in putting an end to your miserable life, I fear the additional strain would be a bit much for Meghan." Derek clenched his fists tightly behind his back to check his temper.

Charles seemed outwardly unmoved by Derek's threat, but inwardly he wanted to avoid an altercation with him if possible. Charles was not usually cowardly, for there were few men who outskilled him with a sword or pistol. But one glance at the expression on Derek's face made him realize that this was an adversary to be kept at arm's length, for he would not be easily vanquished.

"No need to become rattled, old boy," said Charles as he turned to the door. "Tell me, Chandler. What are you going to do now that you have ruined Meghan's chances for a suitable match? Even the foulest of blackguards would at least offer to make the lady respectable after what you have done."

"The *lady* came to me," Derek reminded him. "And were I inclined to enter the world of wedded bliss, I would not be inclined to take a Bainbridge to wife." Derek did not observe the stricken look that darkened Meghan's face at his blunt statement. "I shall see to the girl and account for my actions, but don't expect more of me. Now, if you would be so kind as to leave us." He marched past Charles and held the door for him, indicating that the conversation had reached its conclusion.

Charles cast one final look at Meghan, shook his head slowly, and walked past Derek and out of the room. Derek swung the door closed behind him and turned to find Meghan glaring at him savagely, her eyes blazing as they shot daggers at him from their fiery depths.

"For your esteemed information," she seethed bitterly, "I'd as soon spend the remainder of my days in a convent as be saddled with the likes of you for a husband."

"*Really?*" Derek's eyebrows raised in amusement. "Perhaps that can be arranged." He strolled over to her and nonchalantly pulled her into his arms. "But it would be a vast injustice to allow such a sensuous body to wither away in a convent," he whispered against her ear. "No, the notion I am presently entertaining is much more pleasant, to be sure."

Meghan was not certain that she wanted to know what his plan was, but she found herself asking him just the same.

"Oh, one might say that I have grown used to your vexatious presence, and I'd like to set you up as my mistress before I sail for America. I make several trips to England yearly, and it would be to my liking to know that I have a soft, warm wench waiting to welcome me after a long, tedious voyage." He deftly parted the folds of the shirt that hung loosely about her and placed a trail of sensuous kisses from the pulse that pounded in her throat to the luxurious valley between her breasts.

Meghan could scarcely believe that she had heard him correctly. To be honest, she had not quite known what to expect, but this blatant suggestion that she become his whore momentarily stunned her. But she soon recovered her equanimity, and pushing away from him, she raised confident eyes to his amused ones.

"I whore for no man," she informed him, and the fire in her voice matched that in her eyes. "Pray, Captain Chandler, don't concern yourself with my welfare, for I shall certainly manage." She turned away from his perturbing gaze. "My clothes?" she questioned. "I should like to leave for London promptly."

119

"As you wish. I'll get the horses," he offered, pulling on his boots. He paused for a moment, scanning the room for his shirt when he remembered that Meghan still wore it about her unclad torso. "My shirt, madam." He haughtily extended his arm toward the garment.

Meghan selected a blanket from the bed with which to cover herself. Then she removed the fine linen shirt and hurled it at his head. .

Derek hastily donned the shirt and clicked his heels together as he performed a mocking bow before her and said, "Your clothing is where you left it last evening." He placed his hand upon the doorknob and turned to flash her a devilish grin. "Were I in your position, I'd not be so hasty to spurn my offer. Why, I can handily name a score of women in New Orleans alone who would slit your pretty throat to obtain the station I just offered you."

"Ooohhh! You . . . you . . ." Meghan looked about her wildly for something to sling at his insolent head. But finding the room void of anything that would inflict a severe injury, she had to be content to lash out at him with her only available weapon, her tongue. "You arrogant clod! You conceited, pompous boor!" she screamed. "You possess the audacity to take advantage of me while I sleep, then you generously offer to engage me as your personal concubine!" She stamped her foot for emphasis as she continued her tirade, "Did you actually expect me to fall to my knees in thanks for your offer? Forgive me my noticeable lack of gratitude." She went on, as her eyes glittered angrily in the morning light, "Get out of here! Get out of my sight! I hate you! *I hate you!*" Meghan clamped her hands over her mouth and sank down onto the bed.

The tears that had been threatening to overflow their boundaries came in a rush as the full weight of her disgraced position became clear to her. Was this now the only alternative available to her? Was she destined to become the pleasure puppet of some uncaring man? Meghan wiped savagely at her tear-ravaged face and lifted her gaze to meet Derek's, only to discover that she was completely alone in the room.

The return trip to London was made in awkward silence since Meghan spent much of the ride pondering the shambles in which her reputation now lay. She had almost successfully carried out her wish to avoid speaking to Derek, but when she turned down the street that led to Bainbridge House, she noticed, to her supreme agitation, that Derek followed her.

She abruptly jerked Champion to a stop and turned to face him. "I no longer need your escort. I assure you that I quite know the way to my own home," she informed him dryly.

"On the contrary." His tone was equally as dry. "I said that I would see you safely home. I am a man who stands on his word, madam. I shall see you to your door, and then you'll never need cast your lovely eyes on my lecherous hide again." He started to move on, but Meghan was not to be budged.

"No," she said unwaveringly.

Derek brought his mount beside hers, and leaning forward in the saddle, he caught her by the chin and forced her to look at him. "I see that the spanking you received earlier today did little to cure your obstinate tendencies. Perhaps a more public thrashing might do more toward dispelling the outlandish behavior you so often exhibit."

Meghan pulled away from him. "You would not dare!" she warned him brusquely.

"Meghan, you above all should know by now that I

would dare to do whatever pleases me." He chuckled wickedly as he dismounted and went to stand by Champion, taking care to hold the reins to prevent her from bolting away from him. "I wager that the sight of Lady Bainbridge, skirts over her head, tumbled over a gentleman's knee and receiving a sound spanking might give the neighborhood something to gossip about." His hands were placed firmly about her waist, and he was prepared to pull her from the saddle. "And it just might serve to quell that damnable tongue of yours."

"That won't be necessary," Meghan said hurriedly as she realized that he was completely serious. "I *had* hoped to be rid of you, but a few moments more of your abominable company could do me no more harm than it already has. You may escort me home." She sat tall and proud in her saddle.

"I'm surprised that you've not yet learned that a man prefers a woman of a more passive nature when it comes to openly expressing an opinion," he scolded as he strode back to his horse.

"I suppose most of your *lady* friends are content to lie submissively while you coo loving phrases in their ears," she stated hotly.

"Something on that order." Derek smiled smugly as he climbed back into the saddle.

"And I'd safely wager that not one of them is capable of voicing a single intelligent thought," she spouted indignantly.

"It's not their *thoughts* that interest me," Derek informed her tartly, and Meghan again lapsed into silence.

Once again astride Clarabelle, Derek trotted along beside Meghan until they arrived at their destination. He watched as she handed over her mount to a servant and scurried up the steps to the august mansion. Once at the door, though, he noticed that Meghan paused as if she were hesitant about entering the house, and she turned to glance at him.

Derek immediately kicked his horse into a trot and left the girl to her troubles. "Surely, Bainbridge won't harm the girl," he mumbled to the animal. "Oh, he will likely be in a tizzy for a while and probably threaten to do all manner of things, but to inflict actual punishment upon the lass for my devilment . . ." He paused for a moment and shook his head determinedly. "No, if I thought the man capable of that I'd never have returned her to him." Derek cast one final glance at the house, nodded his head slightly at Meghan, then continued on his way.

Meghan watched until the horse and rider disappeared around the corner and sighed heavily as if a cloud of sadness had suddenly settled upon her shoulders. "You ninny!" She checked herself. "He has caused you nothing but sorrow since the unhappy moment you laid eyes upon him," she reminded herself.

But even as she pushed the huge door open she could not shake the feeling that she would miss his devilish grin and ribald laughter. Yes, she might even miss his roguish manners. But all thoughts of Derek faded as she slipped quietly into the house and hastily made her way to her chamber. Once safely ensconced within the security of her room, Meghan released a profound sigh of relief and collapsed upon her bed.

"Well, 'tis 'bout time ye meandered on home."

The voice surprised Meghan so that she jumped immediately to her feet. She whirled around to find Millie standing in the doorway. "Oh Millie!" She again sank down upon the bed. "You startled me."

"Aye, that don't surprise me none. Not after the way ye sneaked in here as if ye expected a scoldin' from me.

123

'Tis not me ye should be fearin', Missy, but your father." She gently pulled Meghan from the bed and led her into the adjoining chamber.

"Where is Papa? I might as well face him now and get it over with," she managed bravely.

"Ain't here." Millie began undoing the fasteners on Meghan's clothes. "Not to fret now, Missy. Your father rode off earlier. Said he had business to tend to and he'd be late returnin'."

"Is that all? He said nothing about me?" Meghan asked and the nerves along her spine tensed anxiously as she awaited her maid's reply.

"Nay," Millie lied. She didn't want to upset her mistress by confiding that his lordship left explicit orders stating that Meghan was not to leave the house once she returned to it. "Now, what ye be needin' is a nice relaxin' bath." She pointed to the steaming tub. "I've had it warmin' for ye all mornin' and when I seen ye turn up the street with that nice Mr. Chandler, I sent word for the maids to carry it up."

"Thank you, Millie. You are a dear and you take such good care of me." She slipped gratefully into the tub and slowly eased her weary body into the pleasantly hot water. Then suddenly all of Millie's words sank in, and she sat bolt upright in the tub. "*Nice!* How could you possibly associate such a word with Derek Chandler? He is far from nice!" She scooped up the rose-scented soap and lavishly lathered her arms with it.

Millie chuckled at her mistress's words as she went about the task of laying out a dress for Meghan to don following her toilette. After selecting a pale blue muslin gown from the overflowing wardrobe, Millie reentered the room. She carried the dress to the bed and meticulously spread it on the lace coverlet. "If ye'll permit me to say as much, he seemed like a well enough

124

behaved gentleman when he was here the night of your engagement party. And he's a right smart lookin' fella, too." She picked up a can of water and poured it over Meghan's head to rinse the rose-scented soap from her honey-brown tresses. She then placed a fluffy towel about Meghan's head and vigorously rubbed the curls.

"Well, you have assessed him incorrectly," Meghan assured her as she submitted to the older woman's ministrations. "He is a simply horrid man, and I pray that I never have the misfortune of seeing him again." She stood up, and wrapping a towel about her, she stepped regally from the brass tub.

In the distance the sound of thunder echoed in her ears and Millie walked to the window and pushed the curtain aside. "'Pears 'nother storm be brewin'. 'Twas worried I was 'bout ye last night, knowin' how much ye dislike storms." She turned to look at her mistress and was perplexed by the faraway expression that shrouded Meghan's delicate features. "I'll be here t'night, Missy. No need to fret." She dropped the curtain and went to assist her mistress with her dress.

Meghan rolled over in the roomy bed and drowsily pushed at the rough hands that were trying to wrestle her from her comfortable sleep. A blinding flash of lightning momentarily lit up the room, and Meghan sat bolt upright as the memory of a similar night flashed through her mind. Again the rough hands were angrily dragging her from the warmth of her bed.

"Papa?" Meghan managed above the roaring thunder. "What . . . what do you want?"

"Shut up, bitch!" He slapped her ruthlessly across the face and jerked her violently to her feet. "You have made me the laughingstock of the entire city."

He raised his arm as if he intended to strike her again,

125

and Meghan lifted her hand to shield herself from the blow. He reeked of liquor and Meghan realized that he had been drinking quite heavily. But instead of weakening his movements the liquor seemed to endow him with a Herculean strength that rendered her helpless before him. She looked about her anxiously for some means of escape, but no attempt was to be made, for she suddenly found her wrists bound securely to the bedposts. A flash of lightning permitted her to see the riding whip that lay at her father's feet, and as Meghan was shoved roughly to her knees, she suddenly realized what was about to take place.

"No, Papa, please!" she shrieked pitifully.

"*No, Papa, please,*" he mimicked her and grabbed her nightdress at the back of the neck, pulling it tightly about her throat to momentarily choke off any further protests. "You're no better than a whore. You've disgraced your family and your mother's sacred memory, and for that you will be appropriately punished. I have decided upon twenty lashes, a scant punishment indeed considering your outrageous behavior." He leaned down and grabbed her face between his massive hands and jerked her head around to look at him. In the intermittent flashes of lightning, Meghan could see the murderous expression that darkened her father's face. "After which I relinquish all claim on you as my daughter. You are to remove yourself from this house and *never* set foot in it again. Should we meet hereafter in passing along the street, do not bother to address me, for I shall not acknowledge you. Do you understand?" He released her, and Meghan's head fell limply forward like a rag doll's as the ferocity of her father's decree left her feeling empty inside.

But Meghan was readily brought back to the reality of the situation as the material that covered her back was savagely torn away. Involuntarily she tensed as she awaited the first blow to sting the snowy soft flesh of her unprotected back. Prepare herself though she might, she did not expect the severity with which her father delivered the blows to her back. With each one an ugly welt arose, and by the time the tenth stroke had stung her flesh there were trickles of blood oozing from the open cuts.

Meghan did not cry out, though the tears fell freely down her cheeks. She bore her agony in tearful silence and still the blows continued until—could she be imagining the sound of running footsteps along the corridor, the pounding on the door, and the shouts from the hallway? Vaguely she became aware that the beating had stopped, but only to begin again with renewed vigor and increased intensity. This time she was unable to stifle the agonizing scream that escaped her trembling lips just before she lapsed into blessed unconsciousness.

Derek sat near the window in his darkened room and stared pensively toward the wharf where his ship rested at anchor. It was late. He was uncertain as to the exact hour, but it appeared that he was destined to go without sleep this night. Even the young lady who had graciously accompanied him to his room following supper had failed to provide him with the needed outlet for his mounting tensions.

But Derek was alone now, with only his cigar and the diversions of his own tempestuous thoughts to entertain him. He leaned forward in his chair and flicked the ashes out the open window. Elbows propped on the window ledge, Derek continued his silent surveillance of the night-darkened city, and kept a watchful eye turned toward the heavens which threatened another storm. As he did so his thoughts immediately turned to the one subject he had tried adamantly to expel from his memory: Meghan.

"God above!" he swore aloud. "Why are my thoughts preoccupied with a mere chit of a girl who has expressed her profound hatred of me?" he grumbled. "Why, if the truth be known, I care as little for her."

Then why did he keep recalling the sweet pressure of her lips beneath his and the thrill of her satiny skin against his own? He could almost hear the soft, lazy tone of her voice when she spoke his name as if it were a piece of fine, bone china that might shatter if treated too harshly.

Derek shook his head, as if to empty his mind of these disturbing thoughts and stood up to light the lamp. His tall frame cast eerie shadows in the flickering candlelight as he paced back and forth, puffing contemplatively on his cigar.

"Damn it!" he muttered and whirled at the door to retrace his steps to the window. "In my dealings with her thus far she has proven to be little more than a raging hellcat, always hurling some spiteful insult at my head." He could not help but grin as he remembered the defiant way she cocked her head whenever they argued. And more often than not, he admitted to himself, he had been to blame for getting her riled.

"What am I going to do about her?" he sighed forlornly as he realized that she had inadvertently wormed her way under his skin. "She refuses to be my mistress, and marriage is out of the question." He shook his head sternly.

Derek halted his soul-searching long enough to pour himself a drink from the nearly empty bottle on the dressing table. He then continued to pace, drinking as he walked. An hour later, when he was interrupted by a sharp knock at the door, he was no nearer a solution to the problem that vexed him than when he had started.

Derek strode cautiously to the door and opened it but a crack to peer out into the dimly lit corridor. He didn't actually believe that Beauchamp was brazen enough to set his hired thugs on him again, but one could not be overly careful when dealing with the likes of that scalawag.

"It's Nathan, Captain. I overheard something that might be of interest to you."

Derek swung the door wide and stepped aside to admit his first officer to the chamber. "Has it to do with *The Lady Elizabeth*?"

"No, Captain," Nathan quickly assured him. "The ship's safe."

"Then what brings you here at this ungodly hour? It must be bloody well important for you to give up your last night in port over it." Derek made his way to the dressing table and refilled his empty glass. "Care to join me?" He motioned to his guest.

"No, thank you. Begging your pardon, Captain, I believe the news I have shouldn't be postponed any longer. I was having a few drinks in a pub near the inn when Thomas Bainbridge stopped in. His lordship was pretty much into his cups when he came into the tavern, and it wasn't long before he started waving a riding whip about, telling anyone who would listen how he was going to teach his upstart daughter a well-deserved lesson when he returned home." Nathan noticed that Derek's expression had changed drastically from agitation to fury.

"*What*? Are you sure, Nat?" Derek caught him by the shoulders.

"I've been watching Bainbridge for you for years, Captain. I know the bastard when I see him."

"Not that. About the girl. You think he intends to

129

harm her?" Derek was already pulling on his coat.

"That's what it sounded like to me." Nathan watched Derek's flurry of activity with mild perplexity. "I know how you feel about the family, sir, but I've observed the young miss during my surveillance for you, and I seriously doubt her ability to stop Bainbridge if he did attempt to carry out his threat."

Derek shot an anxious glance at the window and discovered that the storm had erupted and the rain plummeted to the ground in a fury. "Damn it!" he exclaimed. "We'll need to summon a carriage, and Lord only knows where we'll find one at this hour and in this weather." Derek scooted out the door with Nathan close on his heels.

"There's one downstairs, Captain," Nathan informed him.

Derek halted in midstride on the staircase and cast his friend a suspicious frown. "And just what made you so bloody certain I'd dash off to rescue the fair damsel?" The fact that he was indeed on his way to assist Meghan seemed inconsequential to him at the moment.

"Just a hunch." Nathan shrugged his shoulders. "It's just that ever since you took up with the girl you've changed somehow. I can't explain it, but you have," he stated awkwardly.

"I haven't *taken up* with the girl," Derek said, his voice tainted with righteous indignation.

"As you wish, Captain. But if you ask me, I think that perhaps you've finally met your match." He gave Derek a slight push to start his momentum downward.

"Hah! That will be the day!" was all he could manage before he was shoved through the inn door and ushered into the waiting carriage.

Their journey was hampered somewhat by the pouring rain, but the driver was well-skilled and diligently prodded his team through the rain-slickened streets until they arrived at Bainbridge House. Derek was the first to emerge from the carriage. He hastened up the slippery steps to the house, and he was already removing his rain-drenched coat when Nathan joined him in the foyer.

"The door was slightly ajar," Derek whispered hoarsely. "I imagine the servants are abed by now."

"Perhaps I was mistaken, Captain." Nathan looked about him cautiously. "Nothing seems amiss."

"Perhaps, but I hardly think that Bainbridge makes a habit of leaving his front door ajar at this hour of the night." Derek tossed his coat on a nearby chair and turned his gaze to the staircase.

"He *was* well into his cups. . . ." Nathan began.

"Nevertheless, it won't hurt to inspect the house now that we're here." Derek put up his hand to silence his friend and walked soundlessly to the stairway.

He had traveled no further than the first step when he heard a woman's high-pitched scream which was quickly followed by hurried footsteps. Derek wasted little time in bolting up the stairs, taking the steps three at a time. At the top of the stairs he came face to face with the source of the scream.

An older woman stood before one of the chamber doors, pounding her fists against the wooden plank and demanding entrance to the room. She voiced no alarm at seeing Derek in the house; instead she rushed forward to beg his assistance. "Oh, please, sir," Millie cried, as she grabbed him by the shirt sleeve and pulled him toward the door. "Help me! He's beatin' her, he is. Me poor baby. Please, ye've got to help me!" she pleaded piteously.

Derek gently pushed the woman's hand aside and darted quickly to the door. He, too, pounded on the door and called for it to be opened, but his shouts also went unheeded. Derek placed his broad shoulder against the sturdy oak door, and leaning his full weight into the structure, he heaved with all his might, but to no avail. As Derek glanced around for something he might use to break open the obstacle he suddenly found himself chilled to the very bone by the painful scream that emerged from the blockaded room and with a burst of rage, he kicked the door open in one vengeful blow. The scene which he came upon was to become branded into his memory for the remainder of his life.

Meghan lay in a crumpled heap upon the floor, arms lashed cruelly to the bedpost. Her gown lay in torn strips about her waist and her back was a series of ugly, crisscrossed welts. Several of the slashes had caused open wounds, and blood oozed from them to worsen the already foul situation.

Thomas Bainbridge straddled his bound daughter and continued to lash out at her unprotected flesh. He was quite oblivious to Derek's emergence upon the scene, else one glance at the younger man's seething face would have caused Thomas to cease the inhumane punishment at once.

In a savage rage, Derek leaped forward and jerked the bloodstained whip from the deranged man's hands, and in one violent motion, he shoved him away from Meghan. Derek then turned his immediate attention to the stricken girl, noting first that Nathan blocked the doorway to prevent Thomas from escaping.

Millie was struggling futilely with the leather strap that bound Meghan to the bed when Derek quietly pushed her hands aside as his more capable ones assumed the task. "Bring me something to tend to her wounds," he whispered kindly. "I'll see to this."

"Leave her be!" came the commanding roar from

132

Thomas. "She has received only that which she richly deserved. She's going to suffer the way she caused me to suffer these many years." He took an angry step toward Meghan and would have grabbed her roughly had Derek not interceded.

"Don't touch her again," Derek cautioned in a hoarse voice that Nathan knew to be dangerously threatening.

Thomas pulled back sharply and appraised Derek with glassy eyes. "Touch her?" he questioned vaguely. "I intend never to set eyes on the chit again, let alone dirty my hands by her touch. Just prior to your unwarranted trespass, I disowned her completely and banished her from my home. She is to be out of this house by morning and she is *never* to return." He turned on his heel to leave, but paused at the door to issue a final statement. "Since you will soon be departing, perhaps you'd consider taking my estranged daughter along with you and depositing her somewhere en route, I care not where." Pushing Nathan aside, he stepped out of the chamber and strode off to his own room.

Derek had but a moment to contemplate Bainbridge's declaration, for Millie hurried into the room with an assortment of medications. "I heard what he said," she wailed, and pushing the tray of ointments into Derek's hands, she rushed to Meghan's side where she knelt to cradle the unconscious girl's limp head to her breast. "Oh, me baby, me poor, poor Missy. What is to become of ye?" She cried huge tears as she rocked Meghan back and forth.

A pitiful moan escaped Meghan's parched lips as her pain-racked body stirred slightly. As Millie continued the rocking movement Meghan groaned and her eyelids fluttered open momentarily.

Derek leaned forward and touched Millie softly on the shoulder. "Come," he whispered, "you need to

133

gather your wits about you, so you can help me see to her back."

Millie nodded hastily and stood up. "Aye, what would ye have me do?"

"Bring me soap and fresh water to cleanse the cuts," he instructed and waited till the maid had left on her errand before he attempted to move Meghan.

He was more than a little thankful that she was already unconscious, for he could well imagine the intensity of the pain. Tenderly Derek picked Meghan up in his arms and gently eased her onto the bed. He carefully removed the remnants of torn gown from her upper torso, and a renewed rage was born within him as he saw clearly the mass of crisscrossed lines that marred the otherwise flawless skin. It was at that moment that Derek decided upon his course of action, and he crossed the room to issue orders to Nathan, who immediately exited to follow his instructions. He then hurried back to the bed where Millie had begun to cleanse the nasty cuts.

Millie raised tear-filled eyes to Derek. "What'll ye do with her?" she asked as a tear rolled down her wrinkled cheek.

Derek glanced at the maid then turned to the window, where he planted his feet firmly and clasped his hands behind his back as he stared out into the darkness.

"I shall take her with me," he said shortly.

"*To America*?" Millie's eyes grew round with surprise.

"Yes, to America." He moved from the window and stared down at the battered girl on the bed. "Don't sound so disheartened. America is not so far away that you could not see one another again."

Millie completed her ministrations and stood up stiffly. "There's nothing left for me mistress here, Captain Chandler, and if she remained his lordship

134

would likely make life miserable for her. Nay, me concern lies not in where ye be takin' her, but what your intentions be after ye arrive there. She be a good girl, Captain. Well-bred and gently raised and I'll not have her ill-used by any man," Millie informed him flatly.

"I shall provide for her until she meets someone she chooses to wed, or until she attains a suitable position. In either case, I assure you, madam, she will be well cared for. If you so desire I can send you word of her welfare by the captains of my ships when they are in port. Aside from this, you must not expect more of me." He locked stares with the maid, and seeing the relenting nod of her head, his gaze softened. "Prepare a small trunk of her belongings. I wish to leave this house without delay."

Meghan stirred and shifted her position slightly. She had been vaguely aware of the events that followed the brutal beating her father had inflicted upon her. Could it possibly be true? Was Derek actually taking her with him to America? How could anyone assume that she would want to cross the street with him, let alone an entire ocean? No, she must not allow this obscene situation to develop any further. A moan escaped her lips as she struggled to voice her opposition to the proposed plan, but her protests soon subsided as she felt her body being lifted into surprisingly strong, yet gentle arms. Suddenly she felt very safe and secure in these arms as they carried her through the damp, chilly night to the awaiting carriage.

The gentle rocking motion of the carriage helped her relax and quite naturally she leaned back against the leather seat. But the pressure against her raw flesh was electric, causing Meghan to cry out in agony. Almost

135

immediately she again found herself enveloped by that same pair of strong, compassionate arms that drew her near and nestled her tenderly. Meghan sighed contentedly in wonder. Could this possibly be Derek? The same Derek who hated her and had inadvertently brought her world crashing down about her? Suddenly she no longer cared and discovered that she was content to luxuriate in the warm caresses and softly spoken words that gently assured her she was safe and would be taken care of. With these thoughts lazily floating through her mind Meghan drifted off to a much-deserved sleep.

Chapter Seven

Meghan could recall little about her first days at sea, but the few incidents she did recollect gave her virtually nothing to be mirthful about. Her head throbbed constantly with the unfamiliar rocking motion of the ship. Ship! She again vaguely recalled the night of the beating and the circumstances that had temporarily placed her under Derek's guardianship. She shuddered at the mere thought, then put it from her mind. Her back ached too severely for her to consider anything save relief from the persistent, nagging pain. And then, as if someone had read her thoughts, a hand appeared with the cup of soothing liquid that brought almost instant sleep and respite from the dreaded pain. Meghan weakly attempted to raise her hand to the one that held the cup, but the effort proved to be too strenuous and the words of gratitude she longed to express died upon her lips.

But just prior to dozing off into a painless sleep, Meghan again wondered about the identity of the person who was taking such diligent care of her. Were the hands that provided the medicine also the ones that gently administered the soothing balm to her tortured back?

Meghan sighed. Whoever it was, was certainly being kind to her, and above all she could appreciate kindness after the atrocities that she had lived through recently. It was with these thoughts that she drifted off into a deep sleep.

Meghan was to do this for the better part of her first week aboard *The Lady Elizabeth*. She would drift out of her sedated sleep long enough to murmur incoherently and then lapse into unconsciousness for hours on end.

It was exactly one week from the day they departed from London that Derek entered his spacious cabin to discover Meghan feebly attempting to rise from her bed. He was at her side immediately and gently pushed her back within the confines of the covers. "I see that the sleeping princess has finally awakened from her nap." He eased himself down onto the bed and offered her a breezy smile. "How do you feel?"

"Tired," she admitted in a small voice, "and very weak. Have I been asleep long?"

"You have shuttled in and out of unconsciousness for a week now, but this is the first day you have spoken a completely coherent sentence and displayed the vivacity to attempt to rise from your bed." As he spoke he leaned toward a bedside chest and retrieved the jar that sat upon it. "Turn over," he instructed, but his voice had a gentle ring to it. "Let me have a look at your back."

Meghan complied with his request and lay quietly as he gently spread the soothing salve on her rapidly healing flesh. It was only after he had completed his task and returned the jar to the chest that she dared to verbalize the question that so haunted her. "Does it look so very awful? Will there be any ugly scars?"

"None as I can see." Derek wiped his hands on a towel as he glanced down into her hopeful face. "Oh, there may be a slight blemish or two, but nothing for you to worry your pretty head over."

Meghan rolled carefully to her back and clutched the sheet to her naked bosom. She looked squarely into Derek's intense eyes as she posed her next question, "But how? Papa was quite thorough."

"True, but the salve I used was of a special mixture, the prescription for which was given me by my mother. The primary base is honey, then, of course, there are the particular herbs which must be blended with exquisite precision. The honey is the main ingredient, though. It softens the skin and encourages proper healing." He halted abruptly as he realized that he sounded more like a physician than a ship's captain.

"Then it *was* you who took care of me?" Meghan gasped. She had not meant it to sound like an accusation, but she was so surprised at the thought that she could not control her tone.

Derek stood up hastily, and for the first time since she had met him, Meghan actually saw him redden with embarrassment at the revelation of his tender and intimate ministrations.

"It's not my common practice to allow subordinates to loiter needlessly about my cabin, madam. Since you were here, it was most convenient and efficient for me to assume the responsibility of caring for you."

"*Your cabin!*" Meghan cried out.

Derek laughed aloud. "I am truly distraught to have inconvenienced you, m'lady, but unfortunately this vessel was designed for cargo rather than passengers.

138

Had I not seen fit to quarter you here, I would have had no alternative save to house you with the men." He casually sauntered over to the sturdy, ornately designed desk and absently fingered the papers that lay thereon. "Granted," he chuckled as an amusing anecdote sprang to mind, "I *am* acquainted with a number of *ladies* who might aspire for such a pleasurable voyage, but indeed, Meghan, I had not thought to include *you* amongst them."

Meghan cast him a scornful look. "I grow increasingly weary with your insipid prattle," she said. "If I'm doomed to be sequestered in this drab cabin with you, perhaps you could exhibit the common decency to drape a blanket to partition the room."

Derek guffawed loudly. "*Common decency*, madam? Just who do you think saw to your personal needs while you were ill and abed?" He raised a pointed eyebrow and derived obvious delight in her sharp intake of breath and sudden flushed skin.

"Rest easy, my sweet. I'm not so love-starved that I have taken to the ravishment of innocent, young ladies while they sleep."

"It did not deter you before," she coldly reminded him.

"Ah, but you make reference to a dark and stormy night when lusty temptation far surpassed the bounds of sensible reasoning. I was inebriated with your sultry beauty and mesmerized by the silky softness of your skin. I am a man, no more, no less. What was I to do save sample the heavenly feast that was so provocatively displayed before me?" Somehow he was again sitting on the edge of the bed. "Tell me, were you me, what would you have done?"

Before Meghan could respond, they were interrupted by a knock at the cabin door.

"Enter," Derek bellowed.

Meghan observed in silence as a man she judged to be a year or two younger than Derek cautiously entered the cabin; when he noticed that Meghan was fully awake and attentive, he doffed his hat to her. "Good afternoon, m'lady. It's good to see you looking so fit and lively." He offered her a friendly smile. "I trust this means you are feeling better today."

Meghan's angry eyes shot daggers at Derek, but she managed a curt nod at the seaman before she turned from them both in a huff and presented them her back.

"Lady Meghan is indeed much improved. Can you not derive as much for yourself from her sunny disposition? Well, Nathan, you obviously have something to dispatch to me. Out with it."

"Yes, sir. The men have completed repairs on the topmast and are ready for your inspection."

Meghan listened to the sound of receding footsteps and held her breath tensely until she heard the reassuring click of the door closing behind the two men. Then she turned over on her side and pummeled the pillows repeatedly with her tiny fists, pretending all the while that it was Derek's pompous head she pounded rather than the downy, soft cushions.

When Derek returned shortly before dinner, he discovered that Meghan had donned a dressing gown and robe and was sitting in the window seat, aimlessly staring out at the vast expanse of blue ocean. He removed his sea-dampened coat and began to warm his hands by the small stove in the center of the room.

"The ocean breezes are still capable of chilling one to the bone even if it is spring," he said.

"But summer rapidly approaches, and I daresay we will welcome a cool breeze when the hot sun bears down upon us," Meghan said in reply.

"Yes," Derek grunted, totally puzzled by her ever-changing moods. "Are you no longer angry with me?" he asked uncertainly.

Meghan shook her head, and the knot of curls she had tied loosely at the nape of her neck fell free, sending her long tresses cascading in disarray about her shoulders. "No," she admitted hesitantly. "I should indeed like to thank you for taking such diligent care of me. I'm quite certain that I was a tiresome bother for you." She continued to stare out at the rolling waves on the sea.

"Not at all—" he began, but was prevented from further discourse as the door to the cabin lurched open, and an extremely young man entered carrying a large tray that was laden with a vast array of delicacies.

"'Ello, miss. The Cap'n said ya was feelin' better, so Cook up'n fixed ya a regular feast, he did. Said the young lass'll likely be needin' to get her strength back, 'specially since yer travelin' with the Cap'n. He says—"

Derek coughed loudly and relieved the young man of his burden. "That will be all, Tim," he said harshly. "We'll serve ourselves and ring for you should we require anything more."

The young cabin boy departed, but Derek turned in time to receive Meghan's cold glare. Derek placed the tray on the table and raised his hands above his head in mock surrender. "Meghan, I assure you that I have not been wagging my tongue. A ship this size—well, the men are naturally going to assume that I . . . that we . . ." He collapsed helplessly into a chair and looked at her hopefully. "Do you not think we can call a truce for the duration of the voyage? I'm not certain that I can withstand the pressures of captaining a ship safely across the ocean and engage in a nightly battle of wits with you." He rose from the chair and went to stand before her. "I am at your mercy, madam." He claimed one of her hands and bowed grandly before her as he pressed it to his lips.

Meghan burst into a fit of laughter at the pitiful character he projected and at last cast a brilliant smile at him. "A truce it is then. Now, sir, shall we seal this agreement with that elegant meal your presumptuous cook prepared for us? I *am* in need of rebuilding my strength, albeit for reasons other than those suggested."

She attempted to stand, but fell back helplessly onto the window seat and glanced apologetically at Derek. "I fear that I'm not as strong as I believed myself to be."

He gallantly proffered his arm so she might steady herself as he led her to the table. The meal was every bit as delicious as it looked. They both ate heartily, though Meghan declined the rich dessert, fearing that she might overdo and upset a still queasy stomach. When they finished their meal, Tim cleared away the dishes, and Derek deposited Meghan in a chair by the stove to ward off the chill of the spring evening.

Meghan insisted that he enjoy his afterdinner cigar in the comfort of his cabin rather than prowling about the lonely decks. Derek drew up a chair and spent the remainder of the evening amusing her with anecdotes of his early years as a seaman. And he paused only when he noticed Meghan valiantly endeavoring to suppress a weary yawn.

"Forgive me," Derek said, rising immediately. "You must certainly be tired, and here I sit, boring you with these endless tales of the sea."

"They are not boring," she insisted. "Indeed, they are most delightful. The fault lies with me, I fear, for I do not seem to be an attentive listener this evening."

"Nonsense." He was already pulling her to her feet. "You will undoubtedly grow stronger with each passing day, but in order to do so you must have sufficient rest." He directed her toward the bunk.

Meghan sat down tiredly on the huge bed. She knew it was unusual for a ship's cabin to harbor such an outsized berth, but she had refrained from commenting on it, fearing Derek's no doubt scandalous explanation. Suddenly a thought did occur to her, and she ventured, "Where have you been sleeping?"

"A chair or the floor. Wherever I happened to be when overwhelmed by exhaustion," he replied absently.

Meghan shrugged off her robe and folded it neatly over the end of the bed. "That could not possibly offer sufficient comfort for the captain of a ship." She stood up uncertainly, taking care to steady her wobbly legs. "I insist that you sleep in the bed tonight, and I shall make a pallet on the floor."

"That won't be necessary," Derek said in a tone that indicated that the matter was not open for discussion. "I have an errand to attend to," he added. "I shall return presently. Pray, do not concern yourself with my sleeping arrangements as I shall assuredly make do. Goodnight, Meghan." He reached for the latch on the door, but turned abruptly as he heard Meghan softly utter his name. He saw that Meghan had wriggled to the far side of the bed.

"There's no need for either of us to sleep upon the floor, for there is plenty of room for both of us here," she said solemnly, and Derek knew that she was offering him the use of the bed for sleeping only. "Besides," she continued as an air of lightness entered her voice, "I'll not have you rendering us to the bottom of the sea simply because you lack adequate rest to make responsible decisions. That won't do. Moreover, we have a truce, do we not?" Her mouth parted in a shy smile.

Derek nodded stiffly and opened the door. "Go to sleep. I shan't be long." The door closed behind him.

143

*　　*　　*

They went on in this fashion for some time. Derek was always careful to join her abed after determining that she was asleep. And he likewise made certain to rise first in order to spare her an awkward confrontation. However, one particular morning, Derek awakened to discover Meghan nestled comfortably across his chest and was presented with the task of getting up without awakening her. As he lay there, silently pondering the various possibilities available to him. Meghan's eyelids fluttered open sleepily.

She sighed and rolled over to her back, stretching her arms luxuriously high above her head, which pulled the fabric of her nightdress tight across her voluptuous bosom. "Good morning, Derek," she murmured lazily.

"Good morning." He returned the greeting a trifle harshly. Tearing his eyes away from her breasts, he rose from the bed to instigate a fumbling search for his clothes in the semidarkness of the cabin.

If Meghan noticed his gruff tone, she gave no indication. "I was having the most delicious dream before I awakened," she said sleepily.

"Madam," Derek said, "I'm unaccustomed to frivolous chatter at this ungodly hour." He struggled into his boots to complete his outfit and straightway made his way to the washstand. "Indeed, it would suit me if you were to return to your dreams."

"Humph! Had I known you were this surly in the morning, sir, I most certainly would have preferred my dreams to your company."

Derek dried his face and hands on the towel by the basin and turned to confront her. "I diligently tried to avoid awakening you."

"I can appreciate your consideration, but the fact

144

remains that I'm very much awake. This being the case, do you suppose I might join you at breakfast? It's dreadfully boring dining alone every morning," she confessed.

"I'm truly sorry you find the voyage so tedious. Had I been astute enough to foresee your boredom, I surely would have engaged a troup of jesters to entertain you," he replied tersely.

Meghan ignored the jibe completely and continued along her own train of thought. "Why do you leave the cabin so promptly each morning? Is the thought of spending this extra time with me so very unpleasant?" She could not fathom why the idea distressed her.

Derek was quick to reassure her. "No. I've a ship to manage and I can't do that properly if I dawdle about in bed all day, now can I?" He crossed the room and lifted her chin so that he could gaze into her eyes. Even in the dim light of the cabin they sparkled brilliantly.

Dare I tell her the truth? he sighed inwardly. How could he delicately explain to Meghan that the reason he avoided her companionship was due to his rapidly increasing desire to sample her more womanly charms? This morning, finding her so unashamedly sprawled across his chest had nearly caused him to seek fulfillment of his gnawing passions. Even at this very moment his body yearned to experience the softness of her young flesh pressed against his.

Derek blinked his eyes and the torturing image vanished from his thoughts. "You may join me for breakfast, but only if you promise to tether your chatty tongue," he cautioned her.

Meghan sat pensively in the window seat, obediently mending a shirt that Derek had requested she see to. She chuckled to herself as the events of the morning repast flashed through her mind. Not only had Derek kept a running conversation going throughout the meal, but he had lingered needlessly over his coffee and had to be summoned on deck by his first officer.

Meghan placed the shirt in her lap as she fondly reflected on the occurrences of the day. She had spent much of the morning tidying up the cabin, and following lunch, she had ventured out on deck to enjoy her daily constitutional. How surprised and flattered she had been when Derek asked if he could join her. She could still feel the gentle pressure of his hand on her arm as he escorted her about the deck, painstakingly explaining to her the more easily grasped mechanics of a ship. Meghan had found his conversation utterly fascinating.

But whether this was to be attributed to the fact that sailing was a new experience, or that Derek had taken the valuable time to devote to her still puzzled her. She only knew that she was happier this day than she had been in weeks, so happy, in fact, that she had been singing while she mended Derek's shirt.

"Derek's shirt," she said aloud. As her delicate fingers reached for the fine linen fabric, her eyes drifted seaward. But she was ill-prepared for the black horizon that greeted her gaze.

"Surely I have not daydreamed the afternoon away." Meghan glanced hastily toward the door, half-hoping to find Derek returning to share supper with her.

He was not there.

There was only one other plausible explanation for the blackened sky and the uncommonly rough sea: a storm. Meghan shivered despite the warmth of the room. She had been positively terrified of storms ever since the night of her mother's tragic death. She stood up suddenly, heedless of the falling shirt. An inland

146

storm was bad enough, but a storm at sea against an unprotected ship—

Meghan screamed aloud as an abrupt lurch of the ship sent her tumbling to the hard, wooden floor. Minutes later, Derek entered the room amidst a peal of thunder and a galing wind to find Meghan slumped on the floor. As quickly as he could—for even his great strength was severely tested by the ferocity of the wind—he bolted the door against the storm and started to go to Meghan's aid. The ship careened again, throwing him against the desk, but Derek finally managed to secure his balance and carefully made his way to Meghan's side.

"Are you all right?" he asked anxiously as he assisted her to her feet.

She slowly nodded. "I'm a little frightened," she admitted.

"That's understandable. It does look as if we're in for a bit of nasty weather." He glanced over her shoulder and out the window, his expression growing increasingly grave.

"What are we to do?" Meghan asked as she nervously followed his gaze.

"There's nothing we can do except ride the storm out." Derek looked down at her panic-stricken face and felt a pang of remorse that she should be subjected to the mercy of the raging storm. Had he left her in London she would have doubtless found sanctuary with a considerate, family friend; now, instead of being safely housed in a posh London parlor, she must face the fury of the advancing tempest that might handily send *The Lady Elizabeth* and her passengers to a watery grave.

"Don't worry, pet. *The Lady Elizabeth* is a sound vessel. We'll come through this in fine fashion." He sounded so convinced that Mother Nature would not dare cross him too severely that Meghan's fear began to subside a little.

"Should you not be at the helm?"

"Nathan is manning that position." He coaxed her away from the window so that she would not be able to view the approaching storm clouds that would likely disturb her even more. "Nathan is the best helmsman around and far more qualified than I to guide us through this."

Meghan seriously doubted this statement, but she said nothing; she was thankful that Derek was near her.

As they began to make their way toward the center of the room an enormous clap of thunder caused Meghan to jump and clamp her hands tightly over her ears. And at that exact moment the ship rolled precariously to one side, sending the couple sprawling onto the bed. Meghan immediately started to extricate herself from the bunk, but Derek placed a restraining hand upon her arm.

"It's safer here." He circled her waist with his powerful arms and gently pulled her into his embrace.

Later, when each had time for reflection, neither could recall exactly how it happened. But suddenly, Derek became aware of her upturned face in the dim light and his lips sought and captured hers. The sweet taste of her mouth spurred on his long-suppressed passions, and he gently forced her lips apart, running his tongue over the succulent crevices of her unexpectedly yielding mouth.

Even as he kissed her, Derek's hands effortlessly untied the laces of her bodice. Eagerly, he lowered his burning mouth to savor her firm, young breasts and gently nibbled at each one until the nipples grew firm and erect. Derek took great delight in the excited tremors that shook Meghan's flushed body, and he hungrily sought to pleasure her more. He gently pushed her back onto the bed and expertly began to remove her dress. His eyes drank in her glorious beauty, committing to memory

148

every inch of her sultry flesh.

The storm completely forgotten, Derek stood up and quickly discarded the constricting garments that held his already swollen manhood at bay. When he turned to her, Meghan gasped openly as her innocent eyes beheld for the first time the sight of a man sexually aroused. But curiosity overruled her timidity and she marveled at the exquisite specimen of a man Derek presented.

And then he was beside her, his inquisitive fingers exploring her everywhere—touching her breasts, her stomach, creeping lower still to probe the very essence of her womanhood. Meghan squirmed, and in her desperate attempt to evade his persistent hand, she unwittingly gave him better access to the coveted prize. She cried out with unexpected pleasure as her struggles moved her firmly against his gently prodding hand.

Meghan vaguely heard the chuckle that resounded in Derek's chest, and she directed her questioning eyes to his, thereby, giving his hungry lips access to her mouth, her eyes, her neck . . . Only once did Meghan open her mouth to protest and she quickly discovered her objecting lips claimed in a breathtaking kiss that rendered her senseless to all else.

Derek could not deny himself a second longer and he rolled until her body was draped with his. In the dim light he observed her eyes grow wide in wonderment as his knee spread her thighs and his throbbing shaft frantically sought entry to her body.

Meghan lay in breathless anticipation. And in that first spectacular moment when man and woman become as one, she was so caught up with the turbulent storm that raged outside and the one that held her in a state of emotional frenzy that she did not notice the brief burning sensation between her thighs as Derek thrust forward and successfully entered her. Indeed Meghan was

149

conscious of little, save Derek as he moved against her and inside her, arousing sensations that she had never before experienced. She circled his neck with her arms and clung to him desperately, pressing her breasts against his hard, muscular chest as she strained against him, matching him thrust for thrust. It was almost as if her inner being knew something of which she was ignorant and raced ahead of her, urgently struggling to experience some final, exquisite release.

Then suddenly as the thunder cannoned about her head, Derek found release, bringing the curious struggle to an abrupt conclusion and leaving her with a peaceful, yet distinctly unsatisfied feeling. As Derek rolled away from her, Meghan timidly reached over to caress his handsome face and as he drew her to him and whispered tender offerings in her ear, she fell into an exhausted sleep in his strong embrace.

Meghan slept soundly into the night and upon awakening, discovered the cabin completely shrouded in darkness save for the single lantern that swung above Derek's desk. He sat behind the desk, busily writing in one of his many ledgers, and Meghan propped herself silently on one elbow to better observe him. What a strikingly handsome man he was, so tall and muscular. Why had she been so blind to his rugged, good looks before? Perhaps tonight would be the start of a new and different relationship for the two of them.

"It's several hours before dawn," Derek said, when he realized she was awake. He had recognized the glow of contentment in her expression, and he decided to interrupt her concentration lest she begin to place excessive importance on their lovemaking. She had been everything that he had imagined, and he could foresee that she would likely serve him well for the duration of the voyage. But he was sorely disturbed by her serene expression as she gazed at him with what Derek considered to closely resemble an affectionate smile. It suddenly became quite plain to him that he would indeed have to reinforce his position on matrimony. For though it may be true that he took great delight in her companionship in bed and fully intended to continue to do so while they remained on ship, he did not intend to allow their relationship to blossom into a *permanent* arrangement. No, should he detect her attempting to steer him in that direction, he would assuredly set her straight.

"Is there coffee?" She noticed the pot on the stove.

"Yes, and a plate of food should you be hungry. Tim brought it shortly after the storm abated. You were sleeping so soundly that I decided against disturbing you." He pointed to the covered dish on the table. "It's cold by now, but it should prove to be filling."

"That will do nicely. I *am* famished." Her voice faltered as she glanced about, vainly searching for something with which to cover her nakedness.

The dress she had worn earlier had been haphazardly tossed aside, and now it lay neatly folded across the back of a chair, far from her reach. But as Meghan silently deliberated as to the method of seizing the dress without attracting Derek's attention, he crept to stand beside the bed. In one swift motion, he plucked her from the berth and stood her on her feet before him.

"You cannot possibly mean to exhibit modesty after what we shared today." He removed his shirt and routinely placed it about her, securing each button with a maddening slowness.

Derek fastened the final button and held her at arm's length in front of him. "Even clad in my oversized shirt you are the most captivating wench I have laid eyes on in many a day."

"Derek." She grew increasingly nervous under his sensuous perusal and timidly lowered her lashes to avoid his disturbing eyes. "What happened between us—"

"Was a most beautiful and gratifying experience and should thusly be regarded." He cupped her chin in his hand and planted a feathery light kiss upon her lips. "Now you must see to satisfying your hunger. But I fear the fare may be sadly lacking in that respect. That is, if you are as ravenous as was I following our little *episode* this afternoon.

"And one more thing," he went on as Meghan moved toward the table. "I can't hand over my shirt to you at every turn, nor am I willing to quit the room whenever the whim strikes you to robe or disrobe. I beseech you to overcome this annoyingly timid nature. I don't consider the opportunity to gaze upon you in your natural state an unpleasant chore. Faith, I await it with great zeal, but that doesn't mean I'll throw you to the bed and ravish you with every glance." He sighed heavily and returned to his chair behind the desk. "In short, Meghan, I only ask that you try to relax and make yourself as comfortable as circumstance allows. Don't feel intimidated by my presence."

"I will try to be more at ease," she promised meekly.

She seated herself at the table and proceeded to devour the food. Even though the fare was cold, it did replenish her hollow stomach. After completing her meal, Meghan glanced around casually in search of something with which she could occupy her time. She had just awakened and was not yet ready to return to bed regardless of the hour.

Meghan rose and went to a bookshelf behind the desk to retrieve a book of sonnets. She then positioned herself by the dim light of the lantern and once settled, she began to absently thumb through the pages.

Derek's sharp cough interrupted her reading, and she glanced up to find him watching her.

"Yes," she said innocently. "Am I disturbing you in some way?"

Derek's gaze lowered to her breasts, whose distinct outline could be detected through the worn material of his shirt, and he felt the familiar warming glow spread throughout his loins. Yes, she disturbed him all right. Of this, he was certain, she was well aware. How quickly the feminine mind apprehends the artistry of coy seduction, he mused to himself. Derek cleared his throat before he spoke. "You block the light and it hinders my vision as I endeavor to write," he patiently explained before redirecting his attention to the ledgers.

"What are you writing?" She discarded the book and rested both elbows on the table, propping her chin in her hands and cocking her head at a slight angle as she carefully studied him.

"An account of the storm. Any damages that the ship might have incurred. Things of this nature must be recorded in the ship's log." His patience was beginning to wear thin.

"Have you ever lost any men at sea?"

"Every voyage has its casualties of which you may be presently included if you don't cease this tiresome badgering of me with trite questions." His anger was not as great as he pretended it to be, yet he wondered at the lightness of her attitude.

"Now what are you recording?" she persisted, a wicked grin parting her luscious lips.

In utter exasperation Derek tossed the quill onto the desk and stared at her hopelessly. "If you must know, I'm commenting on Nathan's heroic performance during the storm. It's due to his skillful manipulation of the ship that you are now sitting here, provocatively tempting me and pestering me. I might further add that were this a naval vessel rather than a merchant ship, I would recommend that Nathan be awarded a citation for his brave conduct during the tempest."

Meghan contemplated this for a moment then her face lit up suddenly in a scintillating smile as a positively shameless notion occurred to her. "And what of me?" A flirty smile widened her lips. "Should *I* not receive a citation for *my* performance?"

Derek reacted to her coquettish suggestion by throwing back his head in genuine laughter. "A meritorious citation is usually bestowed upon one who performs a valiant deed which in due course secures the safety of the ship, or saves the life of a crew member or subsequently the entire crew," he explained as he circled the desk and pulled her against his broad chest. "While I'll readily admit to the valor of your deed, I must likewise point out that I, alone, was the benefactor." He kissed her nose and abruptly released her as he turned toward the door. "As to your *reward*, I shall prescribe something presently," he tossed casually over his shoulder.

"Where are you going?" Meghan's soft voice followed him across the room.

"On deck for a breath of fresh air and, hopefully, respite from your persistent questions." He again laughed.

"Are you not coming to bed?"

"I'm not tired. Visions of a most beguiling wench keep springing to mind . . . taunting me . . . repudiating sleep. I was most anxious to have her bucking beneath me a second time tonight, but, alas, the fair damsel fell victim of a sound sleep. Most frustrating, I can assure you." He sadly shook his head.

154

"I'm not asleep now," she whispered lowly and looked meaningfully into his sparkling eyes.

Derek considered her statement for a brief moment before he hurriedly retraced his steps and swooped her up into his arms. He swung her full circle at least three times before returning her to the floor. Anxiously, his hands reached to undo the buttons of the shirt, but Meghan stepped backwards and shook her head.

"No, let me."

She meticulously undid each button one at a time, drew the shirt open, and with a seductive shake of her shoulders, sent it fluttering to the floor. The shadow from the lantern cast an eerie glow about her, and giving in to the illusion, Derek imagined that this was what a goddess such as Aphrodite would have looked like. He exhaled slowly and stepped closer to enfold Meghan in his arms, thereby assuring himself that the lovely apparition would not disappear.

Meghan willingly accepted his arms about her, and she fervently returned his kisses as their tongues locked in a passionate frenzy and each one thoroughly explored the sweetness of the other's hidden treasures. Then she was in his arms and he was carrying her toward the bed. As he carefully placed her on the spacious berth, she lay back on the pillows, lazily content to wait for him to join her on their tempestuous throne.

Once again Derek discarded the constricting trousers and sat down on the bed. "Listen," he said, reaching out to smooth her hair as it fanned out on the pillow.

"What?" she replied huskily.

"How quiet it is. There is no storm with which we can match the tempest of our lovemaking." His hands were rhythmically stroking her body as he spoke, warming her blood and preparing her flesh for the imminent happening.

"It's just as well, for I don't like storms." She stopped one of his hands as it passed over her breast and pressed it tightly against the passion-swollen sphere, thrilling at the sensation it ignited. "They frighten me."

"I've noticed," he remarked. "Earlier today and at your father's estates as well. It stormed that day if you recall." He rested a hand on either side of her and stared down into her beautiful face. "Tell me why they frighten you, pet." He gazed intently into her eyes and was entranced by the shimmering, liquid pools.

"There was a terrible storm on the night my mother died. I was quite young at the time."

"I know," he murmured.

"Mama was seriously ill and I wasn't permitted to see her for several days until one night Papa dragged me from my bed and ushered me roughly into her chamber. It was frightfully dark and the lightning kept flashing, illuminating my mother's form on the bed." Her face was alive with anguish as the story unfolded. "I ran to her, but she was . . . she was dead. Then Papa started screaming that it was my fault, that I was responsible for her death. And he forced me to look at her . . . to . . . to . . . touch . . ." She turned her face from him in despair as the memory of that horrid evening overcame her.

"I understand," he said soothingly. "It was a dreadful experience for one so young and impressionable to be made to endure. But Meghan," he gently turned her face to him again, "you must remember that I'm here to protect you from future storms."

Meghan blinked back her tears and offered him a faint smile. She timidly reached out and let her hand wander down his chest to his firm stomach and shyly rested it upon his thigh. In fascination she looked at his now limp member and, uncertainly, she lowered her hand to fondle it.

Meghan was unprepared for the fierce reaction she caused as the inert flesh began to harden and grew until it became a throbbing scepter, ready to rule her and take her to yet unknown heights of ecstasy.

Derek groaned as Meghan's still timid and inexperienced overtures thrilled him beyond expectation. Breathlessly he rolled atop her, frantically seeking to pleasure her as she had pleasured him.

"Derek," she hoarsely panted his name.

"Hmmm?" His lips were near hers, ready to claim them in a fiery kiss.

"What is to become of me? I mean, after we arrive in America." She was totally perplexed as to why the answer to this particular question suddenly meant so much to her that she had to voice it at such an inopportune moment.

"Shhh! Always the incessant chatter," Derek playfully chided her as his able fingers masterfully explored her breasts, neck and shoulders, once again stirring the flame of newly experienced rapture. "You speak of matters that need wait for a more convenient time." He hovered over her, his manhood hard and pulsating as it urgently sought the intimate crevices of her body. "And now, permit me to present you with my own particular medal of valor." He chuckled sinfully as he plunged deep into her and reveled in her startled gasp as she involuntarily clasped him to her.

For the second time that night life's forming fluid spewed into her as Derek found turbulent release in the recesses of her body. And while Derek collapsed into a peaceful sleep beside her, his arm possessively curled about her shoulders, Meghan lay awake as she pondered the outcome of their second coupling.

Again she had felt no more than a curious, peaceful

feeling of contentment when the act had been culminated. Her body had not responded as had Derek's when he attained fulfillment. Certainly he was doing his utmost to delight her.

No, she decided firmly, *I* must be doing something wrong.

She glanced at Derek and traced the line of his jaw with her finger, causing him to stir restlessly and draw her tighter against him. How quickly one's attitudes and impressions can alter, she mused, silently recalling how only a few short weeks had passed since the emotion-packed morning when she had violently expressed her hatred at him.

And now . . . now what? Was it possible for a fierce hatred to mellow and be converted to a blossoming love? Did she dare permit herself to believe that she was falling in love with Derek? And more importantly, could she dare hope that one day he might return her love?

Meghan continued to stare at him, but soon her fitful thoughts were transferred to troubled dreams as she drifted off to a restless sleep.

Chapter Eight

Meghan awoke before Derek, and in the dawn's early light, she repositioned herself to better scrutinize the features of the man who slept serenely beside her. She ran her fingers along the thick, curly hairs of his chest, playfully spelling his name then her own and finally enclosing the invisible names with a heart. Meghan was giggling to herself at her own lightheartedness, when suddenly she heard rapping at the cabin door.

Stealthily so as not to disturb Derek, she moved to the end of the bed and stepped out. Stooping to the floor, she recovered Derek's abandoned shirt and wrapped it around her as she hurried to the door.

The caller proved to be Tim who entered the room carrying a breakfast tray, but upon finding Meghan scantily clad in his captain's shirt, the young cabin boy's lips immediately twisted into a sly, knowing grin. "Mornin', ma'am. Trust ya had an *agreeable* night." He placed the tray of food on the table and gathered the dirty dishes from the previous evening.

"Quite, thank you," she replied curtly, a trifle dismayed that Derek's men should view their sleeping arrangements with such open mockery.

"Shall I wake the cap'n?" The boy seemed determined to continue with his little game.

"That won't be neccessary, Tim." She pointedly directed him to the door and secured the latch before returning to the bed to awaken Derek.

Humming softly to herself, Meghan lovingly reached for Derek's shoulder to gently shake him from his dreams. But suddenly her hand froze in mid-air as her eyes fastened upon a blotchy stain that darkened the sheet, and upon closer examination, Meghan determined the stain to be dried blood.

But how could that be? It was not yet her time. . . .

Her eyes grew steadily wider as she recalled a brief conversation that she had one time with Millie. It was one of the rare occasions that the personal servant had endeavored to explain to the young, inquisitive girl any of the gnawing mysteries of the intimacies

159

shared between a man and a woman.

"'Tis but one way a husband knows for certain that he be receivin' unspoiled goods . . . 'tis if the maid spills blood on the weddin' night," she had spoken bluntly.

Meghan recalled how at the time she had cringed at the mere thought and had fervently prayed she never be made to suffer such a horrendous ordeal. Now, as she stood gaping at the dark patch, the shock of the revelation just made known to her began to subside and was replaced by a slow, burning anger that brewed deep within her and threatened to explode at any moment.

She moved away from the bed to contemplate her next maneuver, but her eyes never wavered from the occupant of the bed. And she silently cursed herself for ever considering that she might be capable of loving such a damnable cur. Deciding upon a forthright course of action, Meghan stepped to the washstand to retrieve the pitcher and with the vessel in hand, she returned to empty the cold contents upon Derek's regal head.

Meghan retreated somewhat as he responded to the abrupt awakening by snapping to a sitting position, sputtering, and cursing all in the same breath. Hands frantically pushing the water from his eyes, Derek furiously scanned the cabin. The shock at discovering Meghan, pitcher still in hand and looking daggers at him, was apparent on his startled face. He slowly measured her up and down, and it was with controlled effort that he attempted to conceal his rage.

Derek swung his feet to the floor and addressed her hoarsely, "Explain yourself, madam! And I should caution you to make it a good one, else I shall be sorely

160

tempted to satisfy an overwhelming yearning to soundly thrash you."

"But, sir," she performed a mocking curtsy, "would you harm an ignorant maid whose wont was but to serve her master by assisting him with his morning bath?" She spat the words at him viciously.

"Be warned, Meghan." He stepped threateningly close to her, completely oblivious of his naked appearance. "I'm in no mood to be trifled with."

"You didn't take me the night we spent together at the cottage!" she blurted out hysterically.

Derek followed the direction of her gaze to the bed where his eyes beheld the basis for her display of animosity.

He turned to her calmly. "*I* never said I did."

Derek's blasé attitude momentarily rendered Meghan speechless, but she quickly recovered her voice and lashed out at him again. "But you led me to believe . . ." She faltered confusedly. "You did not deny it!"

Derek shrugged his rugged shoulders and strode to a sea chest where he drew out his clothing for the day, and he unceremoniously dressed as he spoke. "It's true that I did not deny it. But then who am I to shatter the dreams of a pretty, young maid?" He turned a devilish grin to her in time to avoid the pitcher that she hurled at his head.

In less time than it took the piece to splinter against the bulkhead behind him, Derek narrowed the distance between them and stood grasping her cruelly by the shoulders.

"You played me false." Hurtful tears of pride and anguish sprang to her eyes. "Had you but *explained* to Papa, perhaps I could still have made a suitable marriage in London."

"Explained what, my sweet? You forget that he

161

happened upon the quaint scene that revealed you so provocatively sprawled upon my bed. Do you really think he would have believed me had I attempted to explain that I had not bedded you?" He released her from his hurtful grip and absently played with a heavy curl that hung loosely about her breast. "Why, every capable man in London would have laughed me out of town for a fool as well they should, for indeed I must be a fool for waiting until yesterday to make love to you." He tried to place a kiss against her troubled lips, but Meghan savagely pushed him away.

"So, it is to protect your precious male pride that I have been brutalized and disowned by my father. It is to satisfy your deranged craving for revenge that I have been cast from my home and country to the shores of some uncivilized land." Her voice grew taut with bitterness as she spoke.

"I had no inkling your father would react in such—"

But Meghan refused to listen to him and she ranted on. "Were this itself not enough to endure, I have been placed under the guardianship of a rake whose single aspiration is to satisfy his lascivious desires upon me."

Infuriated by her harsh attack, Derek wound his hand in her hair and jerked her head back so that their fiery eyes met. "If memory serves me," he said, his breath hot against her throat, "I did not have to resort to rape in order to sample the sweetness of your virginal charms. Indeed, I have known practiced whores who were not as anxious to spread themselves beneath me as were you!"

He released her so suddenly that she lost her balance and stumbled to the floor upon her knees. She was furious at his insult, but, nevertheless, she rose to her feet with as much grace and dignity as she could muster. The look she bestowed upon him was positively scathing. She marched to the small sea chest and savagely jerked open the lid.

"I *demand* separate quarters for the duration of this disgusting voyage. I absolutely refuse to remain closeted with a bastard who so thoughtlessly—" She came up short as Derek's powerful fingers dug sharply into the soft flesh of her shoulders and twirled her around to face him.

"You forget yourself, madam!" His lips all but met hers as he carefully presented his warning. "Tread gently, my sweet. The last man who was foolhardy enough to call me that lies at the bottom of the sea."

Meghan threw her head back defiantly and her eyes narrowed determinedly as they indicated her resentment for him. "*Bastard!*" she whispered deliberately.

Derek's masculine pride was stung no less by the blatant insult than was Meghan's delicate cheek as his hand shot out with lightning quickness to deliver a blow that sent her falling back upon the bed. Derek immediately regretted his reaction to her remark, and he would have cradled her in his arms to comfort her had she not hurled him a deadly look and crawled to the far corner of the berth to avoid his touch.

Derek strode angrily to the door when suddenly a method of taming the spiteful vixen occurred to him.

Hand resting lightly upon the latch, he leaned a shoulder to the wall and casually said to her, "You asked me what your fate would be once we reach America. In truth, at the time I had not yet decided your destiny. But your audacious display has encouraged me to decide upon a disciplinary course of action." He noticed her quick intake of breath as she awaited his next statement. "I've an *acquaintance* in New Orleans who is in need of some fresh material with which to entertain her customers." He paused to see if she had

163

grasped the direction of his conjecture.

She had.

"Of course," he continued, "you *are* in dire need of instruction as to the particulars that please a man, but with careful tutelage you will no doubt be suitable." He jerked open the door. "I, of course, am the likely candidate to serve as your tutor." He observed her eyes grow round with horror and decided to leave her with one final statement for contemplation. "Yes, I daresay you will arrive in New Orleans with quite an extensive repertoire."

"*No!*" she gasped, thoroughly horrified by his suggestion.

"Ah, but yes, my sweet. I might likewise add that it would serve you well to endeavor to please me. For if I find displeasure with your behavior henceforth, I may very well be tempted to turn you over to my men. They are not as select as I in the type of women they choose." He slammed the door behind him as he left her alone to ponder his declaration.

Meghan clasped her arms about her knees and rocked back and forth, silently condemning herself for her impetuous behavior. Only a few hours had lapsed since she had been locked in a stormy, passionate embrace with Derek, imagining herself to be in love with him and wistfully praying that he would one day love her too. But now she realized her folly and could only speculate at Derek's next move.

He had said she must learn the ways of a whore. Could he actually do that to her? Was he capable of holding her tenderly one moment then casting her ruthlessly aside to be used by countless other men the next?

Men, she thought contemptuously. The only thing the whole lot of them can do efficiently is hurt.

She gingerly caressed her bruised cheek. First it had been her father, then Charles, and now Derek. No. She must be honest. Of the three, Derek had proven to be more solicitous of her welfare. Had he not cared for her when her back lay open and bloodied by her father's hand? And how had she repaid him? With loathsome words that had hurt him deeply.

Derek did not return for the noon meal, nor did he appear to share supper with her. Meghan sullenly ate alone, wondering what sort of devilment he might be contriving.

Clad in nightdress and robe, Meghan sat before the mirror, somberly brushing her hair when he finally returned. He said nothing, but crossed immediately to a screen in a corner of the room. He moved the screen to reveal a bathtub which he proceeded to carry to the middle of the spacious cabin.

Meghan had been permitted the luxury of a tub bath only once since boarding the ship. Derek had explained that fresh water was as precious as gold on an ocean voyage and tub bathing had to be limited accordingly. But evidently Derek had received water from somewhere, for he most assuredly was preparing to bathe.

Meghan regarded the tub longingly, mentally recalling the relaxing feeling of a warm, leisurely bath.

Derek had departed again, but returned shortly carrying two buckets of steaming hot water which he emptied into the tub. He continued with this procedure until the tub was nearly full. Then, tossing the last bucket aside, Derek tested the steamy liquid and finding it to his satisfaction, he removed his clothes and eased himself into the tub.

"Meghan!" he bellowed, causing her to jump at the sound of his rough voice. "Fetch the soap and towels and bring them to me." He rested his head against the back of the tub and pretended to close his eyes while in fact he watched her as she scurried to carry out his command.

"I was unaware that there was water aplenty for bathing," she said softly, proffering the bar of soap to him.

"Yesterday's storm replenished the rain barrels, permitting me the opportunity of such a luxury." He lightly grasped her hand as she started to move away from him. "Have you no welcoming kiss for a man who has labored hard all day?" His eyes danced with merriment as he awaited her response.

She had no alternative. Had he not specifically warned her of her fate should she fail to accommodate him? Meghan leaned forward awkwardly and gently brushed her lips against his. She then pulled away shyly.

"Very sweet. And while I might find your innocence refreshing, a good deal of the men you will be entertaining won't." He wrapped a wet arm around her and drew her halfway into the tub with him. He crushed his lips to hers in an almost painful embrace as he roughly parted her lips and ravished her mouth with his tongue. Abruptly, he released her and laughed aloud, for she clung breathlessly to the side of the tub for support. "*That* is how I expect to be kissed in the future."

"I shall endeavor to remember." She could barely hear her own voice above the intense pounding of her heart. And she desperately fought to control the tears of pain and humiliation that threatened to spill down her cheeks as she again started to retreat from the tub.

"I did not bid you leave," he reminded her. "It would seem that I've suddenly grown lazy and shall require your assistance in washing me." He offered her the soap, but another appealing thought occurred to him, and when she nervously extended her hand to accept the clean smelling soap, Derek purposely hesitated. "But first I have a request." His eyes raked her up and down. "Disrobe for me, please."

Meghan gasped openly at his absurd suggestion and shook her head vigorously.

But Derek was not one to be denied and he tapped his fingers impatiently against the side of the tub. "I am waiting."

Meghan read the determination in his eyes, and her fingers begrudgingly undid the sash at her waist. She reluctantly slipped the robe from her shoulders, but she turned her back to him when she lifted the gown over her head and promptly wrapped a towel around herself. If anything, the towel only served to enhance her seductiveness. She stepped toward the tub to perform her bidden task, a victorious smile on her lips, but the smile quickly faded when Derek dropped the soap into the depths of the murky liquid.

"How clumsy of me." He flashed a grin at her. "Retrieve it, won't you, love? I'd like to collect my wayward thoughts so that I might devote my entire concentration to the remainder of the evening. You will be thorough, won't you, sweet?" he added suggestively and he chuckled heartily as he leaned back against the tub and crossed his arms behind his head.

Meghan eyed him warily and courageously plunged her hand beneath the water, desperately groping for the elusive bar of soap. Without suffering excessive embarrassment, she located the bar and removed it from its watery depths with a relieved sigh. Vigorously, she lathered a sponge and applied it to his arms, chest, stomach and legs, cautiously avoiding his eyes as she did so. Finally completing the task, she rose to a standing position and peered down at him scornfully.

"Are you not forgetting something?" His voice had a lazy, almost drugged tone about it.

"Derek, please . . ." She pleaded in total exasperation.

"My *back*." He leaned forward.

With a heavy sigh, she again dropped to her knees and energetically scrubbed his back, taking care to massage away the tension in his shoulders. Then, staunchly determined that Derek could satisfactorily cleanse any remaining parts that she had overlooked, Meghan hurriedly retreated to a remote corner of the room to observe him rise from the tub and briskly dry himself with a towel. After completing this ritual, he secured the towel about his trim waist and stepped to the door to summon Tim to empty the contents of the tub.

Meghan watched the activities in subdued silence and was amazed to discover Tim carrying in fresh buckets of water to refill the tub. She raised questioning eyes to Derek as he closed the door behind the young cabin boy.

"There was enough water to accommodate another bath," he stated simply and gestured toward the object of discussion, but still her feet remained glued to the floor beneath her. "If you have no desire to bathe I shall call Tim and have him remove the tub." Derek took a half-hearted step toward the door.

"No!" She scurried to the bath, tying her hair in a loose knot high atop her head so as not to wet it. She cast a wary eye at Derek then with a shrug of her shoulders she permitted the towel to flutter to the floor. She gracefully stepped into the tub and gradually lowered herself into the steaming water.

"Thank you," she murmured gratefully.

"Believe me, pet, it's my pleasure." He held a fragrant bar of soap and a sponge in his hand and even as he spoke he gently rubbed the two together to create a generous lather.

"I'm not lazy, nor have I toiled all day." She tried to force a lightness to her voice, but it shook noticeably regardless of her futile efforts. "Why don't you relax with a glass of brandy and a cigar? I'll just be a few moments."

"No, my sweet. Turn about is fair play. You were kind enough to accommodate me. I must surely return the favor." He eased her forward and gently stroked the sponge along her rigid spine.

He routinely did the same with her arms and legs. At last his eyes rose to meet hers and she became acutely aware of his warm perusal as his eyes, almost black with desire, burned a path slowly downward till they finally rested on her breasts. The beautiful orbs were pink from the heat of the water and the taut nipples created a most tempting distraction for Derek. The sponge inevitably captured these quivering mounds and as Meghan struggled for equanimity, Derek made certain that each perfect sphere received a thorough cleansing before continuing his ministrations. On down the sponge traveled, maneuvered expertly by Derek's educated hand, over her stomach, taunting her, teasing her, until at last he withdrew his hand from the water.

Meghan breathed a sigh of relief and started to remove herself from the bath when the bar of soap *slipped* from Derek's nimble fingers and splashed noisily into the water. Meghan sat back suddenly startled, but she was ill-prepared for the impending shock as Derek's submerged hand, under the auspices of retrieving the errant soap, clamped between her thighs and skillfully began to massage the sensitive region that served as the

169

repository for her passions.

Meghan gripped the sides of the tub with both hands so fiercely that her knuckles turned white. She struggled frantically to drive the maddening sensations that he was creating from her mind, but to no avail. How could she ignore the monumental feelings that were coursing through her, bringing her blood to a boil? She opened her mouth to beseech him to halt the torture, but was horrified to hear a series of whimpering moans emitted from her lips instead.

Derek chuckled aloud at her futile attempts to disregard her own responses, and placing one arm under her knees and one around her waist, he lifted her glistening body from the water and stood her momentarily on the floor while he toweled off the excess moisture that clung to her. Deftly, his masterful fingers loosened her hair till it tumbled carelessly about her shoulders. Then he carried her still damp body to the bed and placed her upon the fresh smelling sheets. Removing the towel that clung to his waist, Derek quickly resumed his preliminary ministrations before seeking to culminate the passionate interlude.

His hands traveled leisurely over her body and his lips left a scorching trail from her mouth to her stomach. Meghan had never dreamed that over-whelming sensations such as these existed and her feeble attempt to discourage him was rapidly supplanted by an all-consuming need to fulfill the tumultuous, driving emotions that Derek had aroused within her.

She gasped suddenly as Derek's tongue briefly entered her and as his tongue skillfully flicked at the highly volatile flesh, Meghan's eyes sprang open with the thrill this new experience evoked. "Derek," she whimpered his name as her arms instinctively reached out to encircle his neck.

"Yes, love." He brought his mouth near hers and she felt his erect manhood gently probing against her inner thigh, impatiently seeking the passageway which would quell its burning desire.

But Meghan could only whimper his name over and over until he covered her trembling lips with his burning mouth. Then he was inside her, driving hard to seek the divine release that lay at the end of the exhilarating journey. He positioned one arm beneath her hips and as their bodies closed with each commanding thrust, he pulled her against him, causing her to cling to him desperately and cry out with pleasurable surprise.

Vaguely, she did not know exactly when, Meghan became keenly aware of a new sensation running along the base of her spine and branching out through her body. It began as a scant pressure somewhere in the depths of her being and began to build with an increasing rhythmical crescendo, mounting and mounting . . . until . . . suddenly Meghan cried out and arched against Derek violently as wave after wave of ecstatic convulsions flooded her body.

But still Derek continued to move inside her . . . deeper and deeper . . . filling her completely. And with each demanding thrust there came a new wave of sensual delight that left her breathless, beseeching him to stop lest she be driven insane from sheer rapture.

After what seemed to be an eternity to Meghan, Derek, too, found release and lay exhaustedly spent atop her, his hands still gently fondling and caressing her.

As the climactic tremors slowly subsided, Meghan's eyes filled with tears of emotional relief and she did not try to dissuade them as they rolled uncontrollably down her ravaged cheeks.

Derek, realizing that she had experienced sexual

171

fulfillment for the first time, gently wrapped her in his arms and tenderly rocked her back and forth till her tears gradually subsided. He gazed down at her tear-stained face and marveled at the innocent beauty it still possessed. Derek pushed a few errant strands of hair away from her delicate features and lightly rested his hand on her breast as he said, "Did you think that the man was the only one who derived pleasure from this?" He softly pressed his lips to the hollow of her throat as he gently massaged her breast with one hand and held her to him with the other.

"I . . . I . . . didn't know," she sobbed against his sturdy shoulder.

"Now you do, love. Now you do," he murmured quietly against her ear and continued to cradle her in a warm embrace until she drifted off to sleep, contented to have his reassuring arms securely wrapped about her.

Three weeks had lapsed when Derek paused on the deck of his ship to allow his eagle-like eyes to scan the passing shoreline. He estimated that it would be at least two hours before they reached the port of New Orleans, and there still remained a multitude of things to be accomplished before he could allow the crew to disembark.

He searched out his first officer and barked out a list of commands. Satisfied that Nathan would do a commendable job of tending to these affairs, Derek headed toward his cabin. He gently pushed the door open and moved soundlessly to the bed, easing himself carefully onto it so as not to awaken Meghan.

He grew warm with desire as he looked at Meghan's trim but womanly figure, her breasts heaving up and down with each breath she took.

He sighed quietly as his eyes fell upon her hands that

172

were still clenched in tight, little fists even though she slept soundly. What a fine pugilist she had become since their first encounter when she had willingly given herself to him and he chuckled as he wistfully recalled the night just spent. Gingerly, he lifted a hand to finger the painful shoulder, and he realized he would bear the mark of her brutal attack for quite some time to come. But the struggle had been well worth it.

He grinned as he recalled how valiantly she had fought him. In the end, however, the victory had been his. For even though she had steadfastly resisted his advances as her mind had commanded her, her body had responded to him in such wild abandon that even he had been overwhelmed by her uninhibited display.

"Ah, yes," he whispered. "I think that I shall miss you more than even I thought was possible." He leaned over and brushed his lips against her brow.

His hushed words had been truthful. He *would* miss her and not just for the pleasurable distractions she provided him in bed, but as a companion in general. In the weeks they had shared together while on ship Derek had spent a great deal of time with Meghan, finding her to be intelligent and witty and a competent conversationalist.

"If only I weren't such a confirmed bachelor," he mused aloud, but straightened abruptly on the bed as a brooding frown darkened his handsome brow. There was another obstacle that substantially blocked the trail of matrimony to Meghan. She was the daughter of Thomas Bainbridge. It was indeed odd how that significant factor had almost slipped his memory entirely during the lengthy ocean voyage. But the scowl vanished instantly as all thoughts of marriage evaporated and another, more appealing suggestion sprang to his mind. His plantation was not so far removed from

173

New Orleans that he could not venture into town if the urge to visit Meghan should ever strike him. And with this agreeable thought piercing his mind, Derek was once again reminded of the task that lay before him. "Ah, well," he sighed aloud. "It's best to get it over and done with."

He glanced fondly at Meghan as she lay curled on her left side, facing him. And Derek purposefully raised one, large hand and brought it down with a resounding *whack* upon Meghan's meagerly protected backside.

Derek roared mightily with laughter at the sight of Meghan's astonished face as her eyes jerked open and she came to a ramrod-straight position on the bed. Her eyes spit venom at him and had she carried a heavy object in her hands, Derek felt certain that she would have hurled it at him.

"Good morning, pet." He grinned deviously.

Bright, unshed tears laced her eyes in response to the painful slap, and though her mind reeled with insults, she could as yet not find her tongue. Clutching the sheet tightly to her bosom, Meghan shot Derek a murderous glare then rolled over to her side and presented him her back.

"The sun is high in the sky and yet mademoiselle appears content to lie in her bed." He pressed his hand against the small of her back. "Do I dare permit myself to hope that this gesture means that you wish me to join you so that we may engage in one final romp before we go ashore?" He chuckled throatily as Meghan recoiled from his touch. "We have time aplenty before we arrive in New Orleans," he assured her.

"You impudent dolt!" she seethed hotly between drawn lips and turned on her back to better deliver her missive. "I'd as soon make my bed with a pit of deadly vipers than welcome you to my cot with open arms,"

174

she cried indignantly.

Derek's sharp eyes never wavered from her breasts which heaved violently as her anger increased. He slowly stood up and with meticulous precision began to remove his clothing.

Meghan watched him with growing dismay. At first she had played his game, quietly submitting to his lusty demands, fervently praying that he would withdraw his threat of abandoning her in a New Orleans brothel. But the taunting had continued until, in complete desperation, she began to resist his amorous advances. But her struggles had proven futile against Derek's superior strength. And many had been the nights when Meghan found her wrists dragged above her head and pinioned there by one of his powerful hands while he fondled her with the other and molded his body to hers as he repeatedly lifted her to new plateaus of sensual delight.

Now Meghan's gaze rested on Derek as he stood before her, unashamedly taunting her with his impressive naked body. She sighed wearily and knew that while she could do little to prevent the imminent scene, neither would she make an effort to aid him in his lascivious plunderings. She was determined that she would lay motionless beneath him while he had his way with her, thereby diminishing his pleasure.

Derek guffawed aloud as if he had managed to read her very thoughts. He sat down upon the bed and his eyes burned a path from her head to her toes then retraced their blazing trail to meet her glaring eyes. She stiffened as he settled one hand between the valley of her breasts and expertly began to fondle the now familiar flesh. He placed his other hand behind her head and as his menacing eyes openly laughed at her, he ruthlessly yanked the sheet away to expose her naked splendor while simultaneously jerking her forward to wrap her in his steely embrace and claim her mouth in a passionate kiss.

Meghan forced her body to lay limp in his arms as she meekly allowed him to brush her lips aside and ravage her mouth with his experienced tongue, fighting all the while the response that threatened to yield to him despite her frantic efforts to quell it.

Derek suddenly pulled away from her and cast Meghan a mocking glance, immediately recognizing the coy game she played. He released her from his embrace and silently surveyed her passive form, head turned to one side as if her thoughts centered around a multitude of insignificant trivialities, and the man who hovered above her with erect manhood existed in some faraway and remote place.

With an oath and a scowl, Derek flopped down onto his back. But the victorious smile that instantly dressed Meghan's lips was short-lived, for Derek thrust his arm beneath her and plopped her upon his expansive chest. "It would appear, love, that your heart is not fully devoted to our lovemaking." He lazily caressed the softness of her cheek with the knuckles of his work-hardened hand.

"There is no *love* involved in your play," she responded coldly.

Derek calmly ran his hands up and down her silky back, creating luxurious tingles along her spine that Meghan could not ignore, regardless of her efforts. She squirmed and tried to evade his grasp only to have Derek pull her even tighter against him, crushing her breasts flat against his hard chest and sending her hair cascading in wild disarray about her shoulders and across his chest. Derek wove his hand in those honey-brown tresses and pressed them to his sen-

176

suous lips.

"My sweet, innocent Meghan," he sighed wistfully. "Have you not yet learned that *love* has little to do with the pleasure I derive from your splendid body?" He coaxed her head downward till their lips touched in a gentle embrace.

Meghan was the first to withdraw from the kiss, a pained expression shadowing her pretty face. "But . . . but there should be." Her voice quivered noticeably and she carefully avoided the inquisitive look that Derek cast in her direction. "For it is wrong to regard such an intimate act so casually."

"Really?" He studied her proud features for a moment then with an amused nod of his head, he added, "Yes, you would think that, what with your upbringing."

"There is nothing wrong in the way in which I was raised." Meghan bristled. "Was it wrong for me to have learned to respect and revere love as being a precious thing shared between a man and woman?"

"No, pet." Derek had preoccupied himself by nibbling on her ear lobe while she spoke. But with the unpleasant turn in the conversation he realized he would be hard-pressed to persuade Meghan into a romantic mood. With a sigh he crossed his arms behind his head and focused a pensive look upon her. "But you mustn't expect everyone to share your sentiments. I, for one, am quite satisfied with the life I lead. I have no family ties, no responsibilities save those I choose, and better still, I have no clinging wife to question my every move. No, no, *this* is much more to my liking," he continued as he caressed the supple flesh along her shoulders. "A brief, yet gratifying interlude in which we revel in the pleasures of one another's embrace which subsequently culminates with no binding commitments.

"You may have your *love*, Meghan, but you may rest assured that I shall never be enslaved by that emotion." His eyes grew suddenly dark with thought and narrowed slightly as he considered her closely.

"Why do you stare at me so?" She grew uneasy under his watchful perusal.

Derek drew a long breath and proceeded carefully. "The day of the storm . . . I did not take you with force, nor later that night. Indeed, you were a most willing and satisfying wench," he reminded her.

Meghan shrugged her shoulders and drawing away from him, she rolled to her back and heaved a noncommittal sigh.

Derek followed her movement and turned on his side to rest his weight upon one elbow. "Your actions, madam, do not serve your philosophy." He leaned even closer till his lips rested a breath's pace from hers. "Meghan, it was not in love you gave yourself to me, was it?" His eyes grew black with serious intent.

Meghan swallowed hard and tore her eyes from his. "No, Derek, it was not in love," she whispered softly.

He moved to the edge of the bed and quickly retrieved his clothes. "Good, for while I'll readily admit that I've grown quite fond of you, I don't make it a habit to fall in love with beautiful, young girls." He finished dressing and went to pull her from the bed. "You would do well to find someone nearer your own age who can satisfy your lusty cravings." He playfully squeezed her buttocks as he drew her close to him. "For whether you admit it or not, you happen to be one passionate lass." He planted a brief kiss upon her lips and crossed to the door. "We shall arrive in New Orleans shortly, but it will be some time before we disembark. You are welcome to come on deck whenever you have properly

178

attired yourself so that you may view the city which will serve as your new home."

And with that, he left a befuddled Meghan to contemplate his parting words, looking toward a future that grew bleaker with each passing moment.

Part Two

The Conflict

Chapter Nine

When Meghan emerged from the cabin a short time later to view the city of New Orleans for the first time, she was not overly impressed. It looked to her like any other city, with rows of brick buildings at the water-front, their tiled roofs reaching skyward. Meghan shrugged indifferently and turned from the railing. Perhaps if her circumstances had been altered she might find the prospect of visiting a new country more to her liking, but as the matter presently stood her mood was far from festive.

Her wandering gaze settled upon Derek who was avidly engaged in an argument with a man Meghan had never before seen. The stranger, apparently having had his say, abruptly stalked to the side of the ship and descended the ladder to his awaiting dinghy.

Whatever the man's business, it had served to place Derek in a black mood. Meghan had turned again to view the landscape when she suddenly discovered Derek at her side. She looked up into his face, half expecting him to relieve his raging temper on her, but instead she found a thoughtful frown darkening his handsome features. Meghan studied his rugged face for a moment before hastily averting her gaze to the shoreline. She smoothed the folds of her pale blue traveling gown and lifted a hand to her coiffure to ensure that the curls remained in place. The continued silence on Derek's part unnerved her and she wanted to draw him into conversation. "Who was the man with whom you were arguing?"

"That impudent dolt!" He gestured hotly toward the dinghy as it slowly moved through the water toward shore. "His name is Simmons and unfortunately he is the dock foreman. He rowed out to inform me that we will have to wait till the morrow to unload our cargo. There are other ships ahead of *The Lady Elizabeth* and the wharves are crowded. No amount of persuasion would convince him otherwise."

"It's well that not everyone bends to your will. It would like as not make you more narcissistic and unyielding than you already are." She aired her opinion sincerely though not unkindly. And she thought to herself how she would love to just once gain the advantage against this towering man as the departing dock foreman had apparently done.

"An astute observation," Derek concurred. "And one I am certain you derive great pleasure in voicing. But come," he took her arm, "the hour grows late and I'm not wont to wile away the minutes discussing my disposition be it agreeable or not."

"But where are we going?" Meghan cast a skeptical glance toward Derek's cabin, but to her profound relief she discovered him edging her in the opposite direction.

Derek heaved himself over the ship's railing and stood on the ladder before he bothered to answer her question. "To New Orleans. I have decided to situate you with my acquaintance, so I can tend to the business of my ship on the morrow." He lifted her slender frame over the side of the ship and steadied her in front of him. "Hold tightly to the ladder and follow me."

Meghan glanced reluctantly at the water below her, seriously doubting herself capable of doing what he

184

asked, and she pulled away from him with obvious misgivings.

Derek recognized her fear and offered her some reassuring words of encouragement, "You'll do fine, Meghan. I'll be here if you need me."

Meghan did as he instructed, clinging to the rope as though it were life itself as she heeded Derek's directions. She slowly scaled the rope ladder until at last she swung away from the ship into Derek's waiting arms and was delivered safely into the launch that was secured to the larger vessel.

"Good girl!" Derek said proudly as he placed her near the stern, and seating himself facing her, he maneuvered the bow toward shore and began to row in that direction.

"Are we the only ones going ashore?" Meghan's eyes rested on Derek as he effortlessly powered the launch through the calm water.

"My men signed a contract to deliver the cargo to port. An extra night aboard ship will only serve to whet their appetites for the more pleasurable activities awaiting them in the city once they are free. I shall no doubt find the cargo unloaded in record time tomorrow." He chuckled slightly, then fell into silence as he focused his concentration on piloting the launch to the wharf.

Meghan followed suit and tried not to think about what awaited her in New Orleans.

Once securely anchored to the dock, Derek leapt from the boat and assisted Meghan. Without a word he took her arm and directed her through the throng of people that crowded the wharf. But as they slowly progressed through the milling crowd, Derek became increasingly aware of the numerous glances and outright stares the stevedores cast in Meghan's direction.

The astute observer would have noticed the smile upon Derek's lips twist suddenly into a frown as he contemplated the excessive attention she drew.

Meghan, however, was aware only of the iron grip that Derek had on her arm. She was perplexed when he jerked her forward without warning and literally dragged her through the remaining assembly. Derek did not cease the maddening pace till they covered a number of blocks and just when Meghan feared she would collapse from sheer exhaustion, he halted before a house.

Meghan peered speculatively at the red brick rather elegant looking structure and turned pensive eyes toward Derek.

"Behold, your new home," he said and escorted her to the door.

But before Derek could knock the door was flung open and a young beauty, strongly perfumed, richly clad, and profusely made up, stepped out and immediately wrapped her arms around Derek's neck. She then proceeded to bestow upon him a kiss that Meghan thought surpassed all that was decent. She watched in silent agitation and a small spark ignited in the pit of her stomach as a gnawing urge to snatch the harlot's arms from Derek's neck and scratch her make-up coated face was forcedly suppressed.

But to Meghan's intense surprise, Derek pulled the girl's arms from around his neck and put her from him. "Hello, Regina," he said dryly.

"Is that all you have to say after all these months, Derek Chandler?" She placed a hand against his chest and gently rubbed it up and down. Then for the first time she noticed Meghan, and the two girls regarded each other shrewdly with thoughtful stares that suggested their instant dislike for one another.

If Derek noticed the girls' inspection of one another, he paid no heed. "Regina, be a dear and tell Dulcie that I have returned from London and would like to speak with her."

"Anything you say, sweetkins." She moved so that her breast brushed against Derek's arm, and throwing a haughty look at Meghan she disappeared inside the building.

Derek held the door for Meghan to pass before him, but she stood immobile, refusing to move. "You aren't going to make a spectacle of yourself, are you?" He raised a questioning eyebrow.

"No, I simply prefer to wait for your here, *sweetkins*," she said, perfectly imitating Regina's lazy accent. "Besides, I fear I might place a damper on your evening when I am forced to snatch that insipid little tart baldheaded." She fumed openly, unaware of the jealous connotations of her speech.

Derek laughed softly to himself, and placing his arm around Meghan's waist, he gently nudged her forward and inside the house. "I see right away that I shall have to warn Dulcie that you and Regina have conflicting personalities so she can arrange your chambers accordingly."

The impact of his statement served to sober her immediately as the purpose of this visit was again made apparent to her.

The hallway was fairly dark despite the bright sunshine outside and Meghan squinted to accustom her eyes to the extreme change of lighting. When she was at last able to differentiate her surroundings, Meghan was quite astonished at the plush interior of the establishment. Surely this was no ordinary brothel.

The floor was padded with a thick carpet of a rich red hue and the walls were mirrored completely from floor to ceiling. Meghan continued her inspection as she was escorted into a much larger and more brightly lit room. Here, too, the decor was lush and expensive. Again the thick carpet and ornate mirrored walls were present, and crystal chandeliers adorned the high ceiling. Meghan's observant emerald eyes skimmed over the bar that took up one side of the room, then came to rest upon the rows of green felt-topped tables. It must also serve as a gambling establishment, she decided. She opened her mouth to speak with Derek, but discovered that his interest lay with the woman who stepped from behind the bar and hastily moved toward them.

The woman was older than Regina and carried herself with a mature grace. Meghan decided that this must be the Dulcie with whom Derek requested to speak.

"Derek!" she squealed with delight. "Regina said you were here." She squeezed his hands between hers. Then she noticed Meghan and flashed her a friendly smile. "And who is this, Derek? You can't mean to tell me that you've finally—"

"No, Dulcie," he laughed. "I have not lost complete hold of my senses. This is Meghan Bainbridge. A friend. Meghan, this is Dulcie. She is the owner of this establishment."

As the two women exchanged friendly greetings, Derek spied a figure leaning serenely against the bar which caused him to immediately inquire, "Is that Garth McTavish?" His voice carried a distinct rankled tone.

"Now, Derek. I know that you and Garth have had your differences in the past, but he works for me and does a good job. I can't tell you the countless times he's saved the place from being torn to shreds," she informed him quietly. "Just stay away from him, so you don't give him an excuse to stir up trouble," she cautioned.

"He is scum, Dulcie, and no self-respecting woman, or man for that matter, would have him in their employ," Derek said curtly.

Dulcie laughed at his easy temper. "That's my affair, isn't it?" she said good-naturedly. "Why don't you take Meghan upstairs, so she can freshen up? Then join me in my private dining room for a quiet supper." She noticed that Derek's sullen eyes still glared hatefully at McTavish and she gave him a little push toward the door. "Go on. If anyone knows the way, *you* certainly do."

With a snort, Derek grabbed Meghan roughly by the arm, causing her to stumble against him. As the two righted themselves, Meghan caught a glimpse of the man Derek had been discussing and the sight made her blood run cold. She unconsciously tightened her grip on Derek's arm and turned abruptly, closing her eyes in an attempt to block from her mind the deadly, leering grin she had witnessed on the man's face. She was indeed grateful when Derek ushered her from the room and up the wide, majestic staircase.

Once alone with him in the privacy of their chamber, Meghan descended upon Derek with a flurry of questions. "Who was that awful man?"

"The term *awful* hardly describes the lowlife bastard," he spat bitterly.

She stared at Derek and tried to interpret the strange mood that had enveloped him. In her dealings with this explosive man thus far, Meghan had witnessed his various humors, but even her father had not received the look of intense hatred that Derek had bestowed upon the man downstairs. The look on Derek's handsome face was chilling, and Meghan felt certain that death could be read in those dark, piercing eyes. She shuddered and

189

glanced to where he stood by the window. Could he do that? Was he capable of taking a human life?

Derek stared out at the Mississippi River as it rolled lazily by, and Meghan wondered about his thoughts. She crossed to the window and slowly lifted a hand to rest lightly on his arm. "What is it, Derek? What has this Garth McTavish done to make you despise him so?"

Derek averted his gaze from the window and his expression softened noticeably as he appraised her earnest concern. He absently lifted a sunbrowned hand to caress the velvety fineness of her cheek. "The tale is unpleasant and not intended for the ears of delicate, young ladies such as yourself." There was a forced lightness in his voice, but a frown still tugged at the corner of his mouth.

But Meghan was determined that he should confide in her and she swallowed hard before voicing her objection. "Since I am to remain here, do you not think I should know about the unsavory man so that I may avoid him?" she persisted.

Derek started to scold her for her stubborn ways, but checked himself as he realized the logic of her statement. "Very well." He dropped his hand from her cheek and walked to the bedside commode where there rested a decanter of brandy. Derek poured himself a glass of the fiery liquid before he turned to address her.

"I have a plantation about a day's journey north of the city which I purchased a few years ago from a man named Sam Iverson." Derek finished his drink and sat down on the plush sofa, patting the space beside him as an invitation for Meghan to join him.

Meghan moved quietly from the window to place herself beside him and as she smoothed the skirt of her gown, Derek continued his narrative. "McTavish had served as Iverson's overseer. I retained him because he was familiar with the plantation operations. At that time I was in the process of establishing my shipping and warehouse franchises, and I needed McTavish to run the place during my frequent absences. That was to be my greatest blunder," he said morosely.

"What did he do?" Meghan asked softly.

Derek pulled her closer to him and draped his arm about her shoulder. "McTavish was cruel to the plantation slaves. He worked them long and hard and brutalized them for the most trivial of deeds. I was unaware of this, of course, until a neighbor apprised me of the situation."

"But, Derek," Meghan interrupted, "if he was so mean, why did the slaves themselves not come to you?"

"There's much you need learn about this country and the sometimes peculiar ways of its inhabitants. You shall soon learn that a black man is often reluctant to speak out against a white man for the simple reason that his word will hold no credence. Had the slaves come to me they feared I would do nothing, choosing to believe McTavish over them. Consequently, McTavish would have made them suffer more severely whenever I was away from Chandalara, my plantation."

Meghan raised her eyes to study the set lines of his handsome face. "I don't believe you would have been so cruel and unjust," she murmured quietly.

"No. I would have investigated their allegations, but it's useless to reflect upon what might have been." He rose suddenly and again took up his stance at the window. "McTavish murdered one of the plantation slaves who was the father of a young girl that McTavish had taken a fancy to. To shorten a lengthy story— McTavish raped the girl. When her father learned of this, he set out to kill Garth, but the old man never had a chance." Derek lowered his head sadly.

191

"But was nothing done? Did he not stand trial for murder?" Meghan found it unthinkable that a man could commit such a crime and not be suitably punished.

"It was determined that Garth acted in self-defense," he stated bluntly.

"But you said he raped—"

"I know what I said!" He whirled on her. "I also said it was a tale not for your ears, but you insisted. Meghan, rape is not easily proven in any case, but when you happen to be a young, attractive slave subject to your master's will . . . well, it's virtually impossible." His tone calmed and he again stared out at the landscape. "It's little consolation, but I released him from my employ immediately following the unfortunate incident."

"What happened to the girl?"

"She discovered that she was pregnant and unable to bear the shame and cope with the death of her father, she took her own life." Derek paused, then added softly, "She was only sixteen."

Meghan gasped, completely horrified by this revelation and immediately crossed to stand behind him. On impulse she ran her arms around his muscular torso and clasped her hands together across his chest. "And you blame yourself?" She pressed her cheek against the hardened contour of his back.

"I was responsible for the safety and welfare of everyone at Chandalara." Derek slammed his fist against the windowsill.

"But you cannot be responsible for the irrational behavior of an obviously deranged man. I saw the look on his face, Derek, and he truly looks demented." She dropped her hands and he turned to retrieve them before they fell to her side.

"You continually amaze me, Meghan." He pressed each hand to his lips. "After the way I have treated you, you can still seek to comfort me. You are a rare gem indeed." He brushed his lips against her hair, only to have her pull away abruptly.

"Oh, not so rare apparently," she laughed brokenly. "Else I could not be so easily cast aside."

"Meghan," he murmured softly and started to move toward her, but he was momentarily checked as the door crashed open and a young girl burst into the room and flung herself into Derek's surprised arms.

"Derek!" she cried joyfully. "Aunt Dulcie told me you were here. You simply must tell me all about your trip. Where did you go? What did you do? Who did you meet? What did you see?" she asked all in one lengthy breath.

Derek laughed good-naturedly and held the girl from him. "Slow down, Gretchen! I'll tell you all about my trip in good time." He crossed to the decanter and refilled his glass.

"Aunt Dulcie thought that your young lady might need a fresh change of clothing." She turned to Meghan. "Oh, you are every bit as beautiful as Aunt Dulcie said. Are you going to marry her, Derek?" she asked gaily.

Derek had just taken a healthy drink from his glass and with the impact of her question, the liquid spewed forth from his mouth as if someone had slapped him heartily on the back. "Get out of here, you little squirrel, before I turn you over my knee." His anger was forced, but Gretchen tossed the dress on the bed and scurried from the room in any case.

Derek was still mumbling something about troublesome women when Meghan said, "It appears that you have a rather *avid* group of admirers."

193

"And each one vying for my favors." He grinned shamelessly. "I told you as much in London."

"Ooohhh . . . you conceited rogue!" she seethed hotly. "It *would* suit your colossal ego to have a covey of skirts competing for your attentions."

Derek crossed to her in two short strides and pulled her roughly against him. "And what of you, Meghan?" He looked deeply into her eyes. "Would you compete for my favors?"

Meghan pushed away from him haughtily and stepped to the bed. "With every eligible chit in New Orleans throwing herself at your feet, why should you concern yourself with my insignificant feelings?" She picked up the borrowed dress from the bed and began to non-chalantly press the wrinkles from its folds.

"Ha, I assure you, madam," he chuckled at his own humorous thought, "it's not my *feet* at which they throw themselves!" He successfully ducked the pillow she hurled at him and raced to the door. "I'll return later to claim you for dinner. See that you are ready." He hurriedly closed the door amidst a flurry of bitter oaths.

Meghan stomped her foot and fumed silently for allowing Derek to so easily manipulate her, but despite her agitation, she was ready when he called for her.

"You look absolutely ravishing," he said thickly as she turned from the dressing table to face him.

Meghan followed the line of his gaze as it caressed her from head to foot and silently wished she had not changed from her original dress. The one in which she was currently clad was indeed lovely, but Meghan seriously felt that it was far too immodest to wear to a simple supper.

The skirt was full and made of a soft pale green material that billowed gracefully about her dainty feet.

It narrowed tightly about her waist and the material for this, as well as the bodice, what there was of it, consisted of a dark green velvet. The sleeves were billowy puffs of material that capped her upper arms, and just below the bodice the material parted in the shape of a diamond and extended all the way to her navel, revealing a good deal more of her silky flesh than Meghan considered necessary. To worsen matters, the bodice was extremely tight, forcing her breasts into two round protrusions that rested high above the décolletage of the dress.

She had viewed her reflection in the mirror for a long time and would have changed back into her original dress had Gretchen not retrieved it for laundering.

"A most charming display." Derek looked pointedly at her voluptuous bosom. "You simply must have a gross of these made, exactly like this one," his eyes glazed over with desire, "and send me the bill."

Meghan tried desperately to force more of her breasts inside the scanty compartment, but with little success. "Gretchen is obviously smaller through the bosom than I." She wanted fiercely to wipe the leering grin from his face.

"The gown belongs to Regina, for Dulcie would never permit her niece to wear such a garment. But you are correct about one thing. Regina *is* considerably less well-endowed." He glanced purposely at her breasts and knowingly chuckled as he took her arm and escorted her from the room. "But you need not fear, pet," he leaned over to whisper intimately, "I rather prefer buxom women."

Meghan winced at his candid appraisal of her personal anatomy and angrily jerked away from him. "I can manage by myself, thank you." She swept past him and flounced down the hall.

Derek wistfully viewed the sensual sway of her skirts before he proceeded down the corridor, finally catching up with her when she paused uncertainly before a door. "Stubbornness does have its disadvantages," he quipped. "I heartily suggest that you check your behavior if you intend to dine with me this evening. If not, I may very well be forced to turn you over my knee and send you off to bed like the spoiled brat that you are." He ceremoniously escorted her back up the hall to the door of the private dining room.

"*Alone,* I pray," Meghan flashed heatedly.

"Perhaps. We shall see." He brought her hands up to his lips. "However, since this may very well be our last night together, I wouldn't want to deprive either of us of the pleasures of a fond farewell." He flung open the door and gently pushed Meghan across the threshold. "Behave yourself, little one," he cautioned and delivered a playful slap to her backside, "else Dulcie may decide not to keep you. Then you just might discover yourself in more dire straits."

Meghan sat quietly throughout the meal, speaking only when spoken to and smiling occasionally at some amusing anecdote. She absently picked at the succulent dishes that adorned the table and explained away her waning appetite as fatigue resulting from the tedious voyage.

"But, my sweet, you simply *must* try the shrimp. It has been prepared in the tastiest sauce." Derek plucked one from his plate and extended it before her lips. "Be a good girl and open your mouth," he coaxed her.

Meghan looked at him imploringly, but when she recognized the determined look in his eyes, she obediently opened her mouth and allowed him to plop the shrimp therein.

"Delicious," she mumbled sullenly and Derek returned his attention to Dulcie and their conversation.

Meghan grimaced as the strong, spicy flavor of the meat exploded in her mouth. She reluctantly swallowed the tangy morsel and was immediately overcome by a wave of nausea. She sat very still to allow the queasy feeling to pass before she addressed her hostess. "Dulcie. Forgive me, but I am suddenly quite exhausted. With your leave, I shall return to my room and rest for a while." She did not dare glance at Derek, fearful of the disapproving scowl she was sure to find on his handsome face.

The older woman was genuinely concerned at Meghan's sudden pallor and at once urged her to retire to her chamber. "Of course, dear. Derek was a beast to have forced you to join us this evening considering your weakened condition. I'll send Gretchen to prepare a warm bath for you," she offered.

"Thank you. I should like that very much." She nervously avoided Derek's questioning appraisal and quickly scampered from the table.

Derek stood as if to escort her to their chamber, but Meghan motioned him back to his chair. "There's no need for you to interrupt your supper. I can find my way."

Derek and Dulcie watched until the door closed behind her youthful, swaying skirts then Dulcie questioned, "How long have you known her, Derek?"

"We met fifteen years ago when my mother married her wretched father. She was just a child," he said airily and reached for the flagon of wine to refill his glass.

"Humph! She is little more than that now," Dulcie reminded him. "But that's not what I meant and well you know it." She looked at him pointedly. "Have you

197

bedded her?''

Derek choked down a piece of bread and turned a quizzical gaze upon his hostess. "I hardly consider this polite table conversation. What are you getting at?''

Dulcie logged one last thoughtful glance at the closed door and shrugged her shoulders. "Oh, just call it womanly intuition.'' She smiled at him. "Now tell me. When will you cease this tiresome game and tell the child that you'll not be leaving her here?''

Derek gulped down the remaining contents of his glass before answering. "When I feel she is suitably chastised and will behave like a proper young lady. And just what makes you so certain I'll not leave her?'' he asked curiously.

"I'm wise to your ways,'' she laughed. "But this time, my friend, I think perhaps you have acquired more than you bargained for. Meghan is a beautiful, well-bred lady, and you cannot use her at your whim then cast her aside like some gutter strumpet. It would destroy her, and though you'll not likely admit it, the girl *has* found a place in your stubborn heart.'' She raised her hand to silence him as he scoffed openly at her words. "No, hear me out. It's a tiny spark now, to be sure, but I'm certain it could easily blossom into an all-consuming flame if you'd allow it. Don't deny her, Derek. Don't deny yourself.''

"And what, pray tell, do you suggest I do with her?'' he asked brusquely.

"Why marry her, of course,'' she decreed without hesitation. " 'Twould do you a world of good.''

Derek swore mightily and rose from the table, nearly knocking his chair over as he retreated to the door that opened onto the courtyard. "I ask for advice and you condemn me for life! Marry her! Bah! Thank you, but I shall endeavor to solve my own problems.'' He bowed to

198

her curtly and exited to the courtyard in hopes that some fresh air might clear his troubled thoughts.

Meghan closed the door to the private chamber and sprinted up the staircase and scurried down the dimly lit corridor to her room. But just as her hand circled the doorknob, she was grabbed roughly and whirled around by two strong hands. Before Meghan could utter a protest her lips were covered brutally by her unknown assailant's. She recovered quickly from the shock of her attack and struck back with all the strength she could muster by raking her nails down the side of her attacker's face.

The man let out a howl and an oath and shoved Meghan gruffly against the wall. "Damnit, Regina! What the hell is wrong with you?"

Meghan's eyes grew wide with horror as the identity of her violator became known to her. She stared into the angry eyes of Garth McTavish as his hand checked the damage inflicted by her razor sharp nails, and Meghan reached frantically for the door, only to have Garth open it and roughly push her inside the room.

"Get out of here!" she screamed as she cautiously backed away from his reach, her eyes fervently scanning the room for anything she might use as a weapon. "Leave me alone! I'm not Regina!"

"No, that's a fact, but you got what I'm after just the same. Fact is, you spit fire like a ragin' hellcat and I like that in a woman. And yer softer, more ladylike than Regina is. I ain't had me a *real* lady 'afore, and I've a hankerin' to sample me one now." He lunged forward and grabbed her by the arm just as she tried to sprint around the bed to escape him. "Now, you just relax, honey, and ole' Garth'll be real good to ya." He lowered his mouth and covered her face and throat with wet, repulsive kisses that sickened Meghan.

Wildly, she searched her mind for a route of escape and luckily recalled how she had eluded Charles's unwanted advances. With some effort she pretended to respond to his kisses to draw him off guard and prayed silently that her scheme would be successful a second time. As Garth fumbled with the laces that held her bosom in check, Meghan thrust her right knee into her would-be assailant's already throbbing groin.

With a cry, Garth released her and stumbled backwards. "You little bitch!" he swore. "You'll pay for that, my fine lady!" he snarled viciously. Garth lashed out with one hand and caught her dress in the diamond-shaped opening.

Meghan was horrified at the sound of rending material as her flawless breasts were helplessly exposed to his lecherous eyes.

"Meghan." The door flew open and Gretchen entered the room, lugging two buckets of hot water. But she stopped short at the sight her startled eyes beheld.

McTavish whirled on the bewildered girl angrily. "Get out of here, girl," he shouted. "The *lady* and I have some unfinished business to tend to."

"Gretchen, *please!*" Meghan pleaded as she clutched the torn gown to her breasts. "Don't leave me alone with him!"

Gretchen stared at them for a long time before she formulated her reply, and Meghan feared for a moment that she might actually leave her alone with the madman. "Get out, Mr. McTavish, or I'll summon Captain Chandler. I assure you, he won't take this lightly and if he doesn't kill you, Aunt Dulcie will certainly terminate your employment. And between the two of them, you'll most likely never work in this town again," she spoke each word deliberately.

McTavish deliberated over this ultimatum for several tense moments. It was true that Chandler and Dulcie could make life difficult for him, but it just might be worth it to bed this vixen just once. He continued to eye Meghan hungrily, but then reason overcame lust, and he realized the folly of attempting such a thing with Chandler still on the premises. There would be ample time to satiate himself with the girl once Chandler had left. "All right, I'll be going," he drawled slowly and stepped away from Meghan, but he paused before Gretchen to issue one last threat. "You'll find yourself sorry that you crossed me," he hissed at the young girl. "And as for you," he swore vehemently to Meghan, "you ain't seen the last of me!" and vacated the room.

Meghan heaved a huge sigh of relief, but she abruptly clutched wildly at her stomach as she experienced another attack of nausea. She quickly made her way to the basin where she became violently ill.

"Are you all right?" Gretchen was immediately at her side.

"Yes." Meghan reached for a towel to blot at her reddened face. "I fear that my stomach is yet unaccustomed to your rich and spicy cuisine. And then that unfortunate man further unsettled my nerves." She sank wearily down upon the bed. Meghan gripped the bedpost for support and fought to regain her composure as she watched Gretchen prepare her bath.

"You'll feel better after a soothing bath." Gretchen helped her out of the torn dress and into the tub.

"Thank you for coming to my aid." Meghan scrubbed at her delicate skin as if she thought to wash away the memory of the disgusting man's hands upon her body. "But I fear you have only succeeded in acquiring the scoundrel as an enemy as well."

"Don't worry about me." Gretchen poured another

201

bucket of steaming hot water into the bath. "I came to live with my aunt when I was twelve years old. That was five years ago and no man has so much as looked at me wantonly. Partly because they respect my aunt as the proprietress of this establishment, but *mostly* because they fear her wrath if they dared to anger her," she stated matter of factly. "No, don't fear for me," she repeated. "Aunt Dulcie will care for me just as Captain Chandler will most certainly care for you." She placed a fluffy towel within Meghan's reach. "Will you be needing any further assistance?"

"No, thank you," Meghan assured her. "You've been a dear, but I'm quite all right now."

"Don't hesitate to ring for me if you need anything." She paused at the door. "Oh, I brought you a nightdress. It's on the bed," she added before she slipped quietly out the door.

Meghan donned the filmy white nightdress and transparent robe, vaguely wondering why she even bothered, for the ensemble revealed nearly as much as it concealed. Then she climbed wearily into the window seat to sort out her jumbled thoughts. She drew her legs up to her chest and locked her arms around them as she rested her head on her knees. Suddenly she began to weep. She cried for the outrage that had been attempted on her body. She cried for Derek. For now that he had fulfilled his threat by bringing her to Dulcie's, she would undoubtedly never see him again. And finally, Meghan cried for herself—a stranger in a new land with no friends and no one to whom she could turn for help.

She remained in that position long after the sobs that wracked her body had subsided. She was absorbed with her troubles and consequently did not hear the click of the door, nor the muffled footsteps that cautiously crossed the carpeted floor and paused uncertainly

202

before her. Meghan became aware of another presence in the room only when she heard her name spoken softly.

"Meghan?" Derek whispered. "Are you all right?"

Meghan lifted red, swollen eyes and a tear-stained face in utter disbelief. "Derek . . . you're . . . you're still here?"

"Of course. Where did you expect me to go?" he asked quietly.

Meghan could not formulate an answer. Instead she threw her arms around his neck and hugged him tightly.

Completely taken aback by this emotional display, Derek placed his arms around her and held her close to comfort her. "I was enjoying an afterdinner cigar in the courtyard when Dulcie informed me that she was receiving several inquiries as to the identity of the enticing angel provocatively reposed in the upstairs window. It would seem that you have gathered quite a following downstairs, my lovely. But, alas, their journey has been for naught since you already have a captivated admirer." He braced himself for one of her crisply phrased retorts and was genuinely surprised to receive none.

"You do stand out like a beacon in this white gown." He maneuvered her away from the window and tilted her face upward so he could better study her. "What is it, Meghan?"

"What have I done to make you hate me so?" she blurted, as a fresh stream of tears swept down her lovely face. "I'm truly sorry for the harsh words I hurled at you aboard ship. They were cruel and unkind and you were right to be angry with me, but I have done nothing to deserve *this*," she sobbed.

"Shhh . . . shhh." He clasped her to him until her sobs dwindled. "I don't hate you, Meghan," he whispered softly. "The words you spoke have long been forgiven . . . and forgotten. If anyone had a right to voice bitter thoughts that day it was you, for of those involved in the sordid affair concerning my inheritance, you were the most innocent and yet you have suffered the most." He smoothed her hair as it fell around her silky shoulders. "And for that, my dear, I am truly sorry." He stepped away from her.

But Meghan clutched at his arm to prevent his total withdrawal. "Then . . . then I beseech you, don't leave me here. I shall do any reasonable task you request of me. I am quite willing to accept a position as a governess, or even a scullery maid if that is all that is available." She searched his serious face for a moment and then her voice rang with utter desperation as she voiced her final plea, "But *please* don't leave me here at the mercy of that dreadful man!" She raised tear swollen eyes to appeal to him.

Derek's face went white and he unwittingly grabbed Meghan's arm brusquely. "What man?" He gripped her shoulders and brought her frightened face up to meet his enraged one. "Was it McTavish?" His voice shook with uncontrollable fury at the thought of the vile man abusing Meghan's delicate body and when she hesitated with her response, he shook her roughly. *"Was it McTavish?"* he roared savagely.

Meghan had never seen him so furious, and she withdrew from him in fear. She could not find the strength to sound a verbal reply, but with deliberate effort she mustered enough courage to bob her head up and down as an affirmative response.

"Did he hurt you?" he demanded.

Suddenly Meghan's head shot back and she stared into his face with eyes flashing wrathfully. "Of course, he *hurt* me! Did you expect him to be gentle?" She jerked away from him in disgust and returned to the window where she rested her aching head against the glass as she stared up at the starlit sky. "But he did not rape me, if *that* is your concern. Oh, he tried right enough, but luckily Gretchen came in before he could . . ." Her voice trailed off aimlessly, and she closed her eyes as she recalled his rough hands and lips harshly caressing her. She sighed tiredly. "Now I fear he may harm her."

"No, he won't," Derek said flatly. "The intolerable bastard shall be dead before the sun rises."

He stalked toward the door, but halted abruptly in midstride as Meghan suddenly burst into laughter. Derek turned slowly to stare at her in total bewilderment.

"Forgive me." Meghan fought to control the fitful spasms. "But why should *you* wish to murder a man who simply desired the same thing of me that you take night after night? I see no difference."

In less time than it took her to utter the words, Derek crossed the room to stand before her. "There is one devastating difference and you would do well to commit it to memory." He took her face between his large hands and forced her to look at him. "You belong to me and *no one* takes that which is mine unless I give them leave to do so." He voiced each word precisely.

Meghan cringed at the ferocity of his words, but somehow found the courage to continue. "But how can a few scant hours possibly matter to you? For tomorrow you will be gone and he shall but try to take me again." She removed his hands harshly and lowered her gaze. "Shall your conscience be eased once you've denounced your claim on me? Can you truly cast me aside to be used by countless other men in such a casual fashion?" The pain-filled expression she cast at Derek was too much for him to bear.

"Meghan," he whispered gently and stepped forward to draw her tenderly into the circle of his protective embrace.

"No!" She misinterpreted his intent and struggled frantically to escape his grasp.

"I mean you no harm." He easily lifted her into his arms and carried her to the bed. After laying her upon the turned down sheets, Derek extinguished the candles and bolted the door. Then he returned to her and sat down on the edge of the bed. The moonlight danced eerie shadows across the floor as Derek reached out to smooth the hair away from her tear-ravaged face.

"Meghan," he repeated soothingly. "I'm not going to leave you here. I issued that threat in anger, and although I may have been sincere in my intent at the time, I have since determined that I cannot in good conscience leave you in a place like this. For even though Dulcie's Image is perhaps the most reputable establishment of its kind in the city, it is still no place for you." He lowered his hand to caress the satiny skin of her shoulder.

Meghan hastily scrambled to her knees and with trembling fingers, she brushed the tears from her eyes. "Do you truly mean that?" She fervently scanned his face.

Derek nodded. "You are free to do what you wish."

Meghan regarded him pensively. "But . . . but I'm not sure. I mean . . . I don't know what to do. I know nothing about America. Whatever shall I do?" she asked in a quivering voice. Meghan looked at Derek helplessly. She had longed for the opportunity to be free of him, and now that the possibility was near, she was not entirely certain that she savored the idea.

Derek eased her carefully back against the sheets and cupped her chin in his hand. "Rest easy tonight, my

206

sweet, and we shall discuss your future in the morning." He tucked the sheet under her chin and tenderly stroked her cheek for a lingering moment before retiring to a nearby chair to engage in thoughtful deliberation.

He remained in the chair till the early morning hours, alternately smoking cigars and drinking whiskey. And though his eyes wandered about the room, his thoughts never strayed from the occupant of the bed. Derek likely would have spent the entire night in the chair had he not become aware of Meghan's troubled murmurings that threatened to disturb her slumber. As he watched, she scooted closer to the middle of the bed and threw out one arm as if to seize some evasive object. Derek curiously rose from the chair and inched closer to the bed to better decipher her muffled utterings and he was completely astounded to discover that the name she cried in her sleep was his.

A wide smile parted his sensuous mouth, and he slowly pulled off his clothes and climbed into the huge bed beside her. He wrapped his arms around her sleeping body and pulled her against him, observing that her tense body relaxed instantly and she returned to her peaceful dreams. Derek placed a lingering kiss on her forehead and stared at her luxuriously sleeping face as he whispered into her ear, "I think you shall be quite pleased with the offer I propose to you on the morrow." He chuckled softly before he, too, drifted off to sleep.

Meghan awoke the following morning with a light-hearted feeling and a song on her lips. She continued the airy tune in a mellow, sweet voice as she went about her morning ablutions and carried the melody with her when she responded to a light tapping at the door. The intruder proved to be Gretchen who thought the couple might enjoy a quiet breakfast in the privacy of their chamber.

Meghan thanked the girl for her thoughtfulness and the return of her freshly laundered frock and went to awaken Derek, so they might partake of their meal while it was still hot.

She sat down beside him on the huge fourposter and gazed at him for a moment before rousing him from his sound sleep. He lay on his back with one arm thrown carelessly above his head while the other rested lazily on his chest. His hair was noticeably ruffled and the slight grin that adorned his lips put Meghan in mind of a mischievous, little boy.

Too late she noticed the peaceful grin blossom into a devious smile as his two arms swiftly surrounded her and propelled her forward to sprawl across his broad chest. She looked down into the deep brown eyes that glistened in the early morning sunlight and his sensuously full lips murmured a husky good morning as they brushed against hers.

Meghan pulled away in feigned anger and playfully slapped at him. "You brute! Must you be about pawing me at every turn?"

"I can think of no better way to wile away the early morning hours." He grinned wickedly as his thumbs rhythmically massaged her nipples till the rigid buds strained against the sheer material of her gown.

Meghan swallowed slowly as the blood coursed through her veins like liquid fire. "Come," she managed weakly. "Gretchen has brought our breakfast and we should eat while the fare is still hot." She moved away from the bed, but he caught her slim hand in his to halt her departure and she turned a questioning gaze to him.

"The fare on the table is not all that is hot," he informed her shamelessly. "Besides, it's not food I *hunger* for and you well know it." His eyes twinkled sensuously as they boldly raked her up and down.

208

Meghan was well aware that the scanty gown only served to arouse Derek's passions and she attempted to draw him into conversation. "But the fare of which you speak could hardly satisfy *your* ravenous appetite for long. It would surely serve you better to feast on the meal that lay on the table."

"But a repast should provide pleasure as well as sustenance." His hand moved leisurely up and down her arm as he pressed his argument. "And at the moment I have an *urgent* need as well as desire to experience the former." He grinned menacingly and tugged her toward the bed.

But Meghan was not so easily maneuvered. She wriggled from his grasp and scampered to the table where she plopped herself down upon a chair behind a plate of delicious smelling food.

Derek muttered some unintelligible remark and rose grudgingly from the bed. He slipped into his white shirt, fawn trousers and black boots then sauntered slowly to the table and sat down opposite her.

It took all the self-control Meghan could muster to suppress a giggle as she observed the disappointed scowl on his rugged face as if he were a small lad deprived of some special treat. She poured each of them a cup of the strong coffee then lifted the covers from the plates to reveal the succulent comestibles thereon. She oohed and ahhed as each tasty morsel of the mellow omelet and the thick, juicy ham sent her taste buds reeling with mouth-watering delight.

"Am I to be subjected to this nonsensical jibberish throughout the entire meal?" asked an embittered Derek. "Or are you not capable of intelligent discourse this morning?"

"Derek," she chided. "Does the sight of me enjoying my breakfast disturb you so?" She lavishly spread a biscuit with creamy butter and topped it with a tremendous spoonful of savory, sweet honey.

"It's not the sight that proves bothersome, but the accompanying *prattle*," he muttered sourly beneath his breath.

Meghan shrugged off his mutterings and lifted her coffee cup daintily to her lips. "What are your plans for the day?"

"I shall see to the docking and unloading of my ship." He sliced a piece of the tender ham and plopped it unceremoniously into his mouth. "And you, Meghan. Have you given any more thought as to what you would like to do with your future?" He observed her closely.

Meghan shook her head vigorously and her unbound hair flew about her shoulders like fluffy wisps of clouds. "No, I thought that . . . perhaps you . . ." She fumbled about shyly. "*Would* you aid me in finding a respectable position?" she asked hopefully and was greatly relieved to see him nod his head affirmatively.

"I shall inquire about for you." He gulped down the remaining contents of his cup and Meghan refilled it for him. "As a matter of fact," he paused as if contemplating a serious notion, "one of my neighbors was seeking a governess for his daughter just prior to my departure for England. Of course, the position may have already been filled, but if you are willing to journey with me—" He broke off as her face burst into an eager smile and he correctly surmised the answer to his unfinished question.

"Do you really think he might employ *me*?" she asked brightly.

Derek returned to his breakfast with renewed vigor and nodded in reply to her question. "Jason Tyler and I are good friends and he trusts my judgment. Besides,

210

you would be a companion to his wife, Miranda, as well as governess to his daughter." He had concluded his meal, but lingered over his coffee as he watched her don her gown and arrange her hair in a becoming style.

"Is the Tyler plantation near yours?" she inquired gaily.

"I am a frequent visitor at Willow Wood."

"Then might it be possible for me to visit you at Chandalara sometime?" She looked at him hopefully.

"I would take great pride in showing it to you." He finished his coffee and went to retrieve his coat.

Meghan threw him a warm smile then averted her attention to the mirror where she viewed her attire with a critical eye.

"What troubles you, pet?" Derek stook behind her, one hand resting lightly on her trim waist.

Meghan met his eyes in the mirror and shivered involuntarily at the intensity of his gaze. "I fear I shall not make a suitable impression upon your Mr. Tyler. Millie must have packed my trunk in an incredible hurry, for this is the best of the lot and it is none too serviceable." She carefully fingered a tear in the hem.

"We *were* pressed for time that night and the old woman was distraught with concern for you." Derek turned her around to face him. "If a new frock will replace the unpleasant frown that currently darkens your pretty face with one of your bright smiles, I'll gladly purchase you a shipload of the frilly things." He cupped her chin in his hand and tilted her head back till their eyes met.

"One or two will be sufficient," she smiled sweetly. "And I shall repay you with my earnings as governess for the Tylers."

"Come then." He extended his arm. "We shall remedy the plight of your meager wardrobe posthaste."

211

Meghan accepted his arm as they left Dulcie's Image and made their way through the city streets to a dress shop that Derek proclaimed to be the finest in all of New Orleans. Silently, Meghan wondered why he would require the services of a dressmaker, but she refrained from asking such a personal question. She obediently followed him into the shop and all her uncertainties vanished as she admired the vast array of garments and materials on display.

Meghan was so captivated by the beautiful gowns and accessories that she did not notice the curtain at the rear of the shop part, nor did she see the attractive woman who emerged from behind the curtain and hurried forward to engage in familiar conversation with Derek.

Meghan's attention was directed toward an elegant gown, the color of which matched that of her emerald-green eyes. The gown was exquisitely designed and tailored to perfection and Meghan was drawn to it like a magnet. She was gingerly fingering the soft texture of the dainty fabric when a cough from behind her interrupted her concentration. She turned abruptly to discover that she was the object of close scrutiny from a woman Meghan estimated to be at least five years Derek's senior and whom, she decided, was most likely the proprietress of the shop.

"Where is Derek?" Meghan's quick eyes scanned the room for him, but he was nowhere to be seen.

"Captain Chandler thought you to be more enamored with the gown than with him," she laughed.

Meghan thought she detected a note of sarcasm in the shrill laugh, and she wondered if this woman, too, had at one time been Derek's lover.

"Come," the woman spoke with a heavy, French accent, "my name is Yvette and the Captain instructed that you remain here till he returns for you. We must hurry, *chérie*," she shooed Meghan toward the curtain at the rear of the shop. "There is a multitude of things to be done before he returns for you. Bah, men. What do they know of dressmaking? They are forever preoccupied with what lies beneath the garment to notice that each gown is painstakingly designed to entice their masculine appetites," she sighed. "Ah well, scoot!" She hurried Meghan into the spacious fitting room. "We have much to do and little time."

Meghan stood on a raised platform before Yvette, clad only in her chemise while the woman took a series of measurements and chattered away constantly while she worked. Yvette finally moved away and thoughtfully surveyed Meghan's svelte figure. "Mademoiselle does not bind her figure with cumbersome corsets," she observed.

Meghan mentally recalled distastefully the one time Millie had succeeded in coaxing her to wear a corset. "I find that they severely lessen the pleasure I derive from wearing beautiful gowns by constricting my freedom of movement," she said.

Yvette laughed loudly and heartily agreed with Meghan. "I would imagine that Captain Chandler rather agrees with your conclusion." She was unprepared for the resentful glance shot in her direction, and she hurried on hastily, "You are indeed fortunate, mademoiselle. I likewise do not relish the confines that a corset renders, but unfortunately my plump figure needs the restrictions that one provides." She smiled good-naturedly at her own fate and slipped through the curtain, returning shortly with a bundle of dresses clasped between her arms. "Perhaps mademoiselle would like to try some of these," she suggested.

One look at the attractive garments thrown across

Yvette's arms restored Meghan's jovial mood. "I would love that immensely, but you should never have brought so many, Yvette," she scolded. "Now I shall never be able to decide upon the *two* gowns I would like to purchase."

"Surely mademoiselle jests!" Yvette stared at Meghan in complete astonishment. "Captain Chandler left specific orders that you are to be outfitted with a complete wardrobe and there is to be a handsome bonus for me if the order can be filled by Friday." She slipped a gown over Meghan's head.

"But—" she started to protest, but Yvette silenced her with a look and devoted her attention to fitting the gown.

"Mademoiselle is slender through the waist, but quite full here." She indicated Meghan's ample bosom. "A most pleasing diversion for your dashing captain." She ignored Meghan's indignant sigh and stood back to better view the gown. "A handsome fit and it can be easily altered if it meets your approval."

"Oh, yes." Meghan eyed her reflection in the creamy yellow, moiré gown, but a frown shadowed her pretty face as she considered the revealing bodice. "But I hardly think this is the current fashion for a governess. Perhaps that blue cotton dress would be more serviceable."

"*Mon Dieu!*" Yvette had been pinning the hem and suddenly fell back on her haunches. "Forgive me, but I have been sewing gowns for Captain Chandler to present to his lady friends for several years. I think, perhaps, I am a more accurate judge of the wearing apparel he prefers on his ladies. I fear that if I permitted you to leave my shop in that . . . that nun's habit, he would never commission my shop again."

"Well, perhaps I shall take the yellow gown," she

214

said, relenting. "But I must insist on a few gowns that are more discreet." She indicated the revealing décolletage.

"*Oui*, mademoiselle." Yvette breathed a sigh of relief. "It's not proper for mademoiselle to display so much of her delicate flesh in every dress. Don't worry, *chérie*. Yvette will take care of everything."

"*Oui!*" Meghan eagerly nodded in agreement.

While Yvette waited on other customers, Meghan browsed through the shop, selecting slippers, laces, and other trimmings that would complement the gowns she had chosen. Meghan had long ago lost count of the gowns that Yvette insisted she take. There were morning dresses, traveling gowns, dinner dresses, and riding habits of every color and fabric imaginable, not to mention the necessary undergarments and nightdresses. Many of the gowns were already made up and needed but minor alterations. Still others were chosen from designs that Meghan selected from Yvette's collection, making suggestions and modifications where she deemed it necessary.

"However will you manage to complete all this by Friday?" asked a flabbergasted Meghan. "I see no one about to assist you."

"I have two girls who help me in the shop, but Tuesday is usually a very slow day, and I don't require their assistance." She looked up momentarily from the dress upon which she had already begun alterations. "But for a job of this size, I shall hire one extra girl to sew strictly on your wardrobe."

Meghan left the seamstress to her work and shuffled aimlessly about the shop until she became acutely aware of a presence behind her. She whirled quickly and found Derek standing before her, a satisfied grin on his attractive face.

215

"If memory serves me correctly, you were gawking at this very gown when I departed hours ago." Derek nodded toward the green dress.

Meghan's hand reached out to fondle the rich fabric. "I have never before seen a more exquisite gown," she murmured.

"Would you like to have it?"

"Oh, Derek, you have done so much already. I couldn't possibly ask you for this as well, for I'm sure it is quite costly," she said considerately.

"Nonsense. If you want the gown, you shall have it," he said flatly.

"But I'm sorry, monsieur." Yvette reentered the shop and overhearing their conversation, she hastened to explain, "The gown is a special order for a regular customer, and I regret to inform you that it is not for sale."

"Perhaps you could make another," Derek suggested.

"I fear that was the last of this particular bolt of cloth, but if mademoiselle would be interested in another color or material, I would be happy to make another," she agreed.

"No." Meghan's voice was laced lightly with disappointment. "I have no need of such an elegant gown." She dropped her hand from the dress dejectedly and turned a brilliant smile to Derek. "And how was your morning?"

"Hectic," he said tiredly. "Come outside with me. I have something to show you." He took her arm and maneuvered her toward the door.

"What are you being so secretive about?" She squinted her eyes against the bright sunshine. She quizzically followed the direction of Derek's gaze until her eyes came to rest upon the object of his intent. "*Champion!*" she squealed and ran forward to clasp her arms around the horse's magnificent neck. The horse affectionately nudged her shoulder with his nose and snorted a loud greeting to his mistress.

Derek watched the happy reunion from the sidewalk and congratulated himself for instructing Nathan to collect the steed from the Bainbridge stables before they sailed from London.

Meghan turned to Derek gratefully. "However did you manage—" she began, but Derek held up his hand to silence her.

"Did you think I would leave such a magnificent animal in the irresponsible clutches of a man like your father? Besides, you were being uprooted from your home and taken to a strange land. I merely thought the transition would be easier if you had something with which you were familiar." He stepped forward and gave the horse a friendly pat along its flanks.

Suddenly Meghan stepped around the horse and completely unconcerned with the gawks and stares of the passersby, she pulled Derek's head down to hers and kissed him ardently on the lips. "Thank you," she whispered softly.

Derek's immediate reaction was to wrap his arms around her and sweep her to him, but he restrained himself as he became increasingly aware of the shocked stares they were receiving from several people who had stopped to gawk. He reluctantly set her from him and shot her an inquisitive glance. "Do you no longer worry about your reputation?"

Meghan cast the pesky onlookers a haughty look. "Oh, pooh! Have they never before witnessed a simple kiss of gratitude?"

Derek coughed loudly and led her back inside the dress shop. "I assure you, madam." He leaned closer to her, so that she alone was the recipient of his next words. "Had I known you would be this *grateful*, I would have stabled the beast in my cabin aboard ship." He chuckled as Meghan flushed a deep scarlet. "Collect your purchases and we'll be on our way."

With a nod she scurried past him and disappeared through the curtain and returned moments later weighted down with a cumbersome parcel.

Derek immediately relieved her of the burden and turned a questioning eye to Yvette. "Is this everything?"

"Oh, no, monsieur. Those are merely the articles mademoiselle selected that require no alterations," she hurried to explain. "The remainder will be ready on Friday as agreed," she promised.

"Very well. We shall settle financial matters then." He held the door for Meghan.

"I'll need to see mademoiselle on Thursday for her final fitting," Yvette reminded them.

"She will be here," Derek assured her. And with that the couple departed from the shop to leave Yvette in a flurry of activity as she scurried about gathering the necessary materials to fill the extensive order.

Once on the sidewalk, Derek directed her toward Champion who tugged ferociously at his tethered reins in an attempt to be free. Meghan instantly reached upward to soothe his forehead and cooed lovingly in his ear to calm his nervous struggles.

Derek stepped to Nathan who had accompanied him and instructed him to see Meghan safely back to Dulcie's Image while he stabled the horse.

"Can I not accompany you?" Meghan asked hopefully.

"Why, Meghan," Derek offered in mock surprise. "I would be flattered were I not aware that your eagerness stems from a desire to be with this superb animal rather

218

than my own unimpressive self." His voice was rich with feigned sarcasm.

"I merely wished to ride him." Meghan hung her head dejectedly.

"I know that, pet." Derek sympathized with her. "But you could hardly hope to ride Champion wearing that." He pointed to her dress. "You have already scandalized my good name on the streets of New Orleans once this day. You could not mean to further tarnish *my* reputation." He lifted her hand to his lips and placed a kiss upon it. "There will be other days for riding," he assured her.

Meghan nodded slowly and turning away from Derek, she fell into step beside Nathan.

Derek watched until they disappeared around the corner then he cautiously reentered Yvette's dress shop.

Meghan excitedly tore open the package that held her new gowns and lovingly unfolded each one and hung them in the armoire as if they were priceless treasures. She glanced at the clock on the mantel and wondered at Derek's tardiness.

"Perhaps he is visiting one of his *lady friends* that Yvette so conveniently mentioned this afternoon," she spoke aloud. Her spine bristled angrily at the thought of Derek in the arms of some trollop, but then she remembered her own circumstances. "Well, at least I am no common slut he found on the street," she reminded herself with the haughtiness expected of one well-bred. "Perhaps he will realize *that* when I am not so readily available to warm his bed." She smiled to herself.

But all thoughts of Derek soon vanished when she plucked the remaining gown from the package. It was

219

made of a silky, melon-colored fabric. The gown was full-skirted and high-waisted and while the décolletage was not overly revealing, enough flesh would be exposed to entice the masculine eye. The bodice was square in cut and intricately inlaid with rows and rows of a chocolate-brown lace that Meghan knew matched perfectly the color of Derek's eyes. This same layered lace trimmed the hem of her gown and bound the sleeves of the dress tightly just above the elbow; then the material flared out and fell to her delicate wrists.

Meghan held the gown up to her and examined her reflection in the mirror. She then closed her eyes and visualized how she would look clothed in the dress, wrapped in Derek's sturdy embrace as he spun her around a dance floor. A breezy melody floated dreamily through her mind, and she soon discovered herself waltzing about the room.

Suddenly the room reverberated with the sound of boisterous applause and Meghan halted in midstep and whirled to find Derek casually leaning against the doorjamb, a dangerously wicked gleam in his eyes. Kicking the door closed with one booted foot, he quickly shortened the distance between them.

"It's indeed good to see you engaged in such frivolity. Tell me, does your gay spirit stem from your purchases at Yvette's?" His eyes danced lightly as they perused her shining face.

"Oh, yes!" She nodded happily. "But you commissioned far too much, for surely a governess would not require such an elegant wardrobe." She hastily hung the melon gown with the others. "And I don't know how I shall possibly repay you." A worried frown darkened her brow.

"You shall have need of the gowns," he assured her. "And unless I request payment don't insult me by

220

insisting to make retribution for a gift that I have readily given to you." He sat down on the arm of the sofa and gratefully accepted the glass of wine she extended to him. "Have you eaten?" He wisely changed the subject to prevent any chance of a rebuttal.

"No."

"Hungry?" He raised the goblet to his lips and drank thirstily.

"Starving!" she exclaimed. "I have had nothing to eat since breakfast."

"Good. I've instructed Gretchen to serve us here." He stretched lazily and stood to remove his coat.

Derek turned in time to detect her beaming face darken noticeably with disappointment. "What is it?" His tone was kind as he questioned the sudden change in her mood.

"It's nothing," she murmured and went to hang his coat in the armoire beside her things. "I had only hoped that we might dine out this evening."

"I'm sorry to disappoint you, little one." He tenderly locked his arms beneath her bosom and pulled her back against his chest as he planted a lingering kiss against the nape of her neck. "But I have invited Nathan to share our evening repast with us as we have some matters of business to discuss. There will be other evenings," he promised her.

"Yes," she sighed desolately, "just as there will be other days for riding."

Derek released her instantly. "You have never nagged at me before, Meghan. Pray, don't start the practice now," he warned. "It's a nasty habit and one I heartily detest."

Meghan nodded slowly and resigned herself to being closeted in the stuffy room instead of out viewing the sights of the city.

"We shan't leave for Chandalara until Friday." He returned to his chair. "I shall arrange for you to see the sights before we depart."

After dinner the two men retired to the desk that occupied the far corner of the room and soon their muffled voices could be heard as they engaged in avid conversation concerning Derek's business affairs.

Meghan nestled in a corner of the sofa with a book, but the words seemed to dance about the page and she soon abandoned the impossible task of reading the evasive text. Silently, so as not to disturb Derek and Nathan, Meghan moved to her perch on the window seat. She sat there for hours, staring at the starlit sky and the moon that hung like a halo in the heavens and tried to sort out her thoughts.

It was after midnight when she became aware that the room was in total darkness, and Derek stood behind her, his hands gently massaging away the tenseness in her shoulders.

"What are you thinking about?" He leaned forward and pressed a kiss to the nape of her neck and gently nibbled a path along her shoulders.

"Nothing special." She tried to suppress the warm, pleasing sensation that his caresses aroused in her stomach and that spread rapidly throughout the rest of her quaking body. "My thoughts have been confused as of late," she sighed nervously.

"Then come." He pulled her to her feet. "Let's collect our thoughts and force our energies on one common goal." His fingers skillfully unlaced her bodice and with one masterful sweep of his hands, she stood gloriously naked before him while her dress and chemise lay in a crumpled heap at her feet.

With the moonlight as her candle, Meghan viewed

Derek as he slowly stripped away his clothes to allow her to gaze freely at his powerful body. Without uttering a sound, Derek took her by the hand and guided her toward the bed, but she suddenly jerked away from his grasp and huddled near the window.

"No, please," she whimpered. *"Please."*

"Ah, my sweet, I cannot help myself," he whispered hoarsely and lifted her effortlessly into his arms and carried her to the bed, "for you see, I hunger for you in a way I have desired no other. Only you can quench the raging flames that burn in my soul this night."

He pressed her to the sheets and immediately covered her body with his own, his superior weight pinning her to the mattress. His lips claimed hers hungrily then burned a trail from the hollow of her throat to one heaving breast that was already swollen with passion. He took the pulsating nipple between knowing lips and tugged gently till Meghan writhed frantically beneath him.

"Give yourself to me, Meghan," he said thickly against her ear.

"I cannot," she sobbed.

Derek sighed deeply and moved upward slightly and with a sudden thrust, he entered the sweet passageway which would temporarily assuage his burning passions.

Meghan's mind commanded her to resist this domineering man's assault, but her own body's urgent need swiftly squelched any such notion. And once again her wicked body betrayed her as she rose with Derek and then gloriously fell to languish in the afterglow of love's violent passion.

The remainder of the week passed rapidly for Meghan. As promised, Derek escorted her about the city on Wednesday and she returned to Yvette's on

Thursday to be fitted for the remaining gowns. She returned to Dulcie's Image as soon as her duties as pincushion for Yvette had concluded, looking forward to a warm bath and a quiet evening alone with Derek. But she was dismayed to find a message waiting for her, stating that he would be detained indefinitely and that she should not wait up for him.

A trifle downhearted that Derek should choose to spend the evening elsewhere, Meghan picked at her meal morosely and stumbled into bed earlier than usual. She realized that the journey to Chandalara would be a taxing venture for her already exhausted spirit and she wanted to present an impressive picture to her future employer.

Meghan was certain she had been dozing only a few moments when she discovered someone kissing the dreams from her drowsy head. She slowly opened one eye to carefully scrutinize the culprit and instantly snapped it shut. Derek stood over her, a scandalous grin on his face.

"It's time to rise and shine, sweet." He ran a versatile hand along the well-rounded contour of her hips.

"It can't be." She glanced at him in sleepy disbelief. "I'm so tired. Can I not lie here just a bit longer?" She yawned and snuggled down under the sheet, pulling it tight about her chin and contentedly closed her eyes.

"You lazy dolt." She heard his throaty chuckle murmured near her ear. "Had I the time to spare, I'd crawl beneath those sheets and give you a ride that would indeed startle the sleep from your muddled head." As an afterthought he added, "But from the way you snored throughout the night, one would certainly assume that you had a most restful sleep." He turned from her, but his crafty eyes settled upon her reflection

224

in the dressing table mirror to observe her reaction.

Meghan considered his statement but a moment before she sat bolt upright in the bed. "Sir, *I* do not *snore*," she said with regal indignation. "Besides, how would you know if I did snore all night since you obviously had more important *business* to conduct elsewhere?"

Derek's eyebrows shot upward in mock surprise. "Can I be imagining things, or did I just detect a tinge of jealousy in your *accusation*? Surely, you can't be resentful of the prospect that I had an assignation last evening. Unless, of course, you are rankled because I was not here to see to your *needs* as well." He spoke the jibe airily, but his piercing eyes never wavered from her face as he awaited her response.

"Humph. You flatter yourself overmuch. Indeed, I was thankful for the reprieve," Meghan snapped at him. "I was merely curious as to your whereabouts and concerned for your welfare. The notion of you entertaining yourself with another woman never entered my head," she lied convincingly. Meghan then slipped nonchalantly from the bed, poured a generous amount of water into the basin and began to wash.

"If it would pacify your curiosity to hear from my own virtuous lips that I was not *unfaithful*, then so be it." He slipped up behind her and placed a kiss on her naked shoulder.

"You owe me no explanation," Meghan responded humbly, strangely relieved that Derek had not spent the night with another woman.

"No," he concurred, "but I have no aversion to telling you how I passed my evening. I assure you," he retired to the chaise longue to watch her don a dove-gray riding habit, "I would have much preferred to wile away the evening in your sweet arms. But instead, I *truly* was conducting business. You see, I sent Nathan to Chandalara to bring three of my men here with the necessary equipment to transport supplies home. They were later than I anticipated and I waited for them in my office at the warehouse to give them their instructions for today."

Meghan's lips formed a silent oh, but Derek continued without allowing her a chance to speak, "They are presently loading the wagons and the only thing that delays our departure is the fact that I stand here recounting the events of an extremely tedious evening to a scatterbrained young lady. Faith, I sincerely doubt that a *wife* would prove to be this troublesome."

"Wife, indeed!" Meghan clucked her tongue against her teeth. "The woman who makes the unfortunate decision to take you as husband will suffer a life of torment and strife." She anchored a gaily plumed hat atop her precisely arranged coiffure and collected her gloves and reticule from the dressing table. "Are you going to stand there and wile the day away? Faith, I shall never arrive at my new home at this intolerable pace." She swept past Derek, but paused at the door to wait for him.

Forever at a loss with her constantly changing moods, Derek plucked her portmanteau from the floor and walked crisply to her side.

"Meghan, you are perhaps the most exasperating, headstrong, mulish female with whom I have ever had the misfortune to become acquainted," he tartly informed her.

"I know." She smiled wickedly and reaching on tiptoe, she settled a provocative kiss upon his surprised lips. "Shall we go?" She tucked her arm in his as he led her from the room.

Chapter Ten

The sun was barely peeking above the horizon when the couple emerged onto the deserted street. The brisk, morning air proved to be quite chilly and Meghan huddled against Derek to share his warmth as they walked to Yvette's shop. Meghan alertly spied the wagon that was stationed in front of the dress shop and silently wondered if it belonged to Derek. But she had little time for further speculation, for Derek threw open the shop door and ushered her inside.

"Yvette!" he bellowed. "I have come to collect my goods and settle my account."

There was a flutter of muffled noises in the back room as the curtain parted to reveal a work-worn Yvette, eyes red and bloated from lack of sleep. She stepped toward them, still sewing the hem of a royal-blue, muslin cloak.

"There!" she sighed with satisfaction. "'Tis the last of the lot." She snapped the excess thread with her teeth and stepped to a table to wrap the cloak in paper.

"That won't be necessary, Yvette." He plucked the garment from her hands and placed it about Meghan, permitting his hands to linger along her shoulders. "I fear the crisp morning air might give mademoiselle a chill," he explained.

"Yvette, you have simply done wonders." Meghan marveled at the rich texture of the elegantly tailored cloak. "If my gowns are made this exquisitely, I shall undoubtedly be the most richly clad woman in all of Louisiana. New Orleans is indeed fortunate to have such a talented couturière. I have worn gowns sewn by London's finest, but I must admit that your workmanship far surpasses their meager efforts," she praised the seamstress.

"Mademoiselle is kind." Yvette's eyes brightened with the elaborate praise.

"Merely truthful," Meghan insisted as she raised her hands to fasten the frogs on her new cloak, only to discover that Derek's adroit fingers had already undertaken the task.

Once completed, he reached into his pocket and handed the dressmaker a leather bag that hung heavy with gold coins. "I trust that this shall be sufficient," he spoke in a dignified, businesslike manner.

Yvette's eager eyes mentally tabulated the coins and she turned to her benefactor with a wide smile. "As usual, monsieur has been most generous. You will find that one of your men has placed mademoiselle's belongings in your wagon."

Derek and Meghan retreated from the shop and made their way to the waiting vehicle. Derek placed Meghan's portmanteau alongside her other possessions then he assisted her to her seat atop the wagon between himself and the driver, he simply introduced as Elias.

"We shall join the remainder of our troup at my warehouse," he explained.

Derek's warehouse was located near the waterfront and as the wagon drew near the structure, Meghan spotted some wagons that she correctly assumed completed their entourage. But more to her immediate interest, her drowsy eyes fastened upon Champion who stood tethered beside a black stallion that was every bit as impressive as he. The fleeting chance that Derek might consent to allow her to ride Champion instead of the creaky, old wagon brightened Meghan's mood considerably, and she nearly knocked him over in her zeal to scramble from the wagon.

"Whoa!" Derek caught her around the waist and placed her on the ground beside him.

"Oh, Derek!" Her voice rang with excitement. "Might I ride Champion today?"

"Meghan, the animal *is* yours," he reminded her. "You need not ask my permission to ride him," Derek informed her testily and walked over to Nathan to discuss the arrangements for the journey.

Meghan's gaze followed his departure and she shrugged off his terse retort as she hurried over to the horses. Turning her back to the strange animal, she casually addressed Champion, "At least you don't snap at me," she sighed.

Champion leaned his handsome head down and nudged his mistress's arm with his nose and snorted. Meghan reached up to fondly rub the horse behind the ears and was duly startled when something warm was pressed against her backside. But her surprise changed abruptly to irritation when she suddenly felt herself propelled forward to land with a thud on the cold, hard ground.

Derek arrived on the scene moments later to discover Meghan trying to rise from her humiliating position on the ground. And amidst a flurry of tangled cloak, dress and petticoat, he was permitted a sultry view of her attractive legs.

"Meghan, we have little time to waste. It shall be dark when we reach Chandalara as it is and now I find you playing some childish prank." He clucked his tongue and forcefully suppressed a laugh. "Here, let me help

229

you." He offered her his hand, but she slapped it aside ferociously.

"You impudent clod!" She scrambled to her feet in a most unladylike fashion. "That . . . that scraggly mule," she thrust an enraged finger at the accused horse, who rolled his eyes and snorted an indignant denial, "pushed me down!"

Derek burst into uncontrollable laughter and carefully evaded Meghan's hostile glare. "I see that you have made quite a first impression on the lady." Derek heartily patted the guilty horse's flanks. "This is my horse, Trojan," he explained to Meghan. "Nathan brought him from Chandalara."

"Indeed. I should have known," she added sarcastically. "You more than likely taught the beast the charming maneuver."

Derek managed to stifle his laughter and suddenly stepped closer to Meghan, so close that even though their bodies did not touch, she was intensely aware of his masculine nearness.

"No, I did not teach him to fling young ladies to the ground, but he does resemble his master in one respect." His eyes twinkled merrily. "He cannot abide being ignored by a beautiful wench." He brushed a fleck of dust from her cloak and lifted her to her saddle. "Now, if you can avoid any additional disturbances, we shall depart for my plantation without further delay." He climbed to his mount and directed her to the head of the wagons.

Derek rode beside Nathan and Meghan settled in behind the two men to ride afront of the head wagon. But they had traveled only a short distance when Nathan turned his mount and rode to the rear of the train and Derek motioned Meghan to his side. Meghan spurred her mount forward and casting a wary glance

230

askance at Trojan, she settled Champion beside him. As they rode along the picturesque trail, they engaged in casual conversation, Derek taking the time to point out the more interesting plants and flowers that painted the breathtaking view.

They paused at noon to have lunch and rest and water the animals. The noon sun was high in the sky and the nippish air of the late June morning had been replaced by a sweltering heat that quickly encouraged Meghan to shed the warm cloak. As she walked to the blanket that Derek had spread beneath a magnolia tree, her fingers nimbly removed the pins that anchored her hat and she doffed this accessory as well.

"I suppose fashion is not so important in the wilderness." She smiled wanly at Derek.

"No," he agreed. "Come, join me in the shade." He offered her a hand to assist her to the blanket.

"Not just yet, thank you." She declined his invitation and tenderly rubbed her backside as if to explain her hesitancy. "I'm a little stiff. Perhaps I shall stroll a ways before lunch," she suggested.

"There is a brook just beyond those trees, should you desire to freshen up, but don't stray from the trail," he cautioned. "I did not bring you this far to lose you so close to home."

Meghan threw him a puzzled look at this last announcement as she turned and made her way through the clump of trees. She stepped into the small clearing and knelt beside the gently rustling brook. Reaching into her pocket, Meghan withdrew a lace handkerchief, dipped it into the cool water, and daintily dabbed at her sunburned face. Her fingers traced lazy patterns in the clear water, and she was submerged in her thoughts when a sudden noise behind her shattered the peaceful tranquility of the moment, startling her so that she

231

lurched forward. Meghan would have sprawled face first into the brook had two strong arms not encircled her waist and dragged her backwards to safety.

"I'm sorry," a masculine voice hurriedly apologized. "I didn't mean to frighten you."

Meghan looked up into Nathan's concerned eyes and breathed a sigh of relief. "Nathan. It's you. I could scarcely imagine who might have followed me." She smoothed her skirts and steadied her trembling fingers.

"I came to get water for the horses," he explained. Nathan considerately dipped a ladle from one of the buckets into the water and offered it to her. "Perhaps this will help." Meghan readily accepted it and drank thirstily of the cool, refreshing liquid.

Nathan then seated her upon a soft bed of moss under a nearby tree and went to fill the buckets. After completing this task, he sat down beside Meghan and looked at her intently. "Are you feeling better?"

"Much, thank you."

"Then I should take you back to the wagons. The captain will likely grow concerned if you stay away much longer. One can never tell what kind of varmints might be lurking about in these woods." He stood up and offered her his hand.

"Oh, pooh!" she pouted. "I'm not fearful of any *varmints*, as you call them. And I sincerely doubt that Derek will miss me overmuch." She could not help but notice the sympathetic expression that briefly passed over Nathan's handsome face.

"Miss Meghan," he began uncertainly, "perhaps you'll think me forward, but this needs to be said. The captain is not one to openly display his emotions and, at times, he is a difficult man to understand. Don't be fooled by his indifferent attitude," he advised.

"What do you mean?" she asked, totally perplexed by

232

his statement.

"My tongue wags too freely and had the captain overheard me, he most likely would have wrenched it from my head." He lifted the pails and retreated a few steps. "But since I have ventured this far, I will proceed a little further. The captain is an honorable man. You may find that hard to believe now, but I'm certain that in time you will learn the validity of my words."

"I seriously doubt that," Meghan said coldly.

"Perhaps," he agreed. "But you see, the captain is my friend as well as employer, and a man who has justly earned my respect. I know that he can be as stubborn as a mule when the notion strikes him, but if you'll pardon me, miss, so can you." He started to enter the thicket that led to the wagons, but paused to address her one last time. "Heed my words. Don't be too harsh in your judgment of him. His life hasn't exactly been a bed of roses and he sometimes makes rash decisions concerning his private affairs without fully considering the consequences. Be patient with him," he whispered softly.

And when Meghan looked up to question the rationale behind his peculiar oration, Nathan had disappeared through the thicket.

Within the hour, Meghan was once again atop Champion and the small company resumed its snail-paced journey. Meghan remained deep in thought, remembering the words that Nathan had spoken to her beside the brook. What rash decisions had he been talking about and how could any of them have anything to do with her? After all, she would soon be employed as governess for a respectable family, far removed from Derek. Then why did his speech so perturb her?

Meghan was engrossed in her own thoughts and did not observe the questioning glances that Derek cast her way as they slowly progressed along the winding trail.

But when he verbally expressed his concern for her solemn attitude, she merely grunted a noncommittal sigh, shrugged her delicate shoulders, and continued the journey in silence. A few more minutes passed by in this fashion and Meghan fidgeted in her saddle and sighed morosely, her eyes never wavering from the well-worn path that preceded her.

Derek could abide her abnormal behavior no longer and veering his mount closer to Meghan's, he swore, "Damn it, woman! Do you behave this way to purposely torment me, or does something pain you?"

"I am fine," she replied shortly, her eyes remaining glued on course. "Pray, do not concern yourself with me."

Derek pulled in close beside her and reached over to catch her just under the chin, forcing her to look at him. "But I *do* worry, my sweet. I have grown accustomed to your constant chatter and this sullen mood you have adopted both concerns and annoys me. Come now, say something to me, even though I know that I shall likely regret it."

"I have nothing to say," she replied simply. Meghan edged Champion away from him and quickened their pace, so that Derek lagged far behind. But only momentarily, for Derek easily overtook her and grabbing the reins from her hands, he jerked Champion to a sudden halt.

"Meghan!" His tone grew cold and threatening. "I shall overlook your blatant display of bad manners this once, but heed this warning: never, *never* again turn your back to me when I am addressing you. Do you understand?" The question was voiced with deliberate slowness.

She managed a stiff nod. "As you dictate, *m'lord*. I shall endeavor to commit your every wish to memory

234

and act accordingly," she said contritely.

"Faith, I have never understood your capricious moods," Derek sighed in helpless exasperation. "But at least I knew what provoked them. Presently, I fear that you have me at the disadvantage, madam. Could we not amicably discuss the issue that plagues you, so that we might restore a jovial smile to your pretty mouth?"

"I shall discuss nothing in front of your people, or your friend. I still have a shred of pride and dignity left and I shall not allow you to strip it from me by defacing me before your servants," she said proudly.

"As you wish." He jerked Trojan around abruptly and galloped back to the wagons to speak with Nathan.

Meghan observed the exchange with perplexed apprehension and wondered vividly as to what sort of devious plan Derek might have conjured this time.

He rejoined her moments later and instructed her to follow him. They rode a distance up the road then Derek veered off the main trail to a narrow, less traveled path which forced them into a single-file formation.

"The wagons shall never be able to maneuver on this trail." She broke the silence, glancing nervously over her shoulder to see if they did attempt to follow the hazardous road.

"An astute observation from one who appears to be totally swathed in self-pity. It amazes me that you noticed we tarried from the main road," he said snidely.

"Why are we going this way?" She disregarded his sarcastic intonation.

"Why, madam, have you so quickly forgotten our earlier conversation? Was it not you who demanded a more secluded place for our little chat?" he reminded her, then went on to explain, "I left Nathan in charge of the wagons. Their excessive weight severely impedes a speedy trip and at their present rate, they will not reach

Chandalara before noon tomorrow. As for us, we can travel faster alone. This trail runs parallel to my property, enabling us to omit several miles from our journey."

"Will we reach your plantation tonight?"

"Yes, but it will likely be late. We *could* stop for the night if the ride makes you weary," he offered.

"That won't be necessary. I shall manage," she said quietly.

"Good, for I have an intense longing to arrive home this evening," he stated simply.

Meghan lapsed into a hushed silence and vigilantly followed him as he piloted them along the narrow trail. They continued in this fashion for several miles, neither one speaking, the only sound disturbing the tranquility of the forest being the singsong warble of native birds and the frantic scurry of small wildlife as they hurriedly removed themselves from view of the human intruders.

While they traveled, Meghan silently recounted the events of the day . . . the curious exchange with Nathan, the puzzling remarks Derek had made, and his obvious eagerness to reach Chandalara. All of these factors contributed to setting her mind into a whirlwind of confused motion and she struggled to solve the problem that mentally tormented her.

"How long have you known Nathan?" she asked thoughtfully.

"Several years. We fought together in the war with England. After it ended, Nathan came to work for me and we have been friends ever since. When we are not at sea, he assists me at Chandalara." The road suddenly widened and he slowed his pace until she was beside him.

"Has he no family?"

"He's never mentioned any to me, but then I am not

236

as prolific in prying into personal matters as you seem to be," he scolded her. "But why this sudden interest in my first officer? Can it be that Nathan has stirred the yearnings of your cold heart?"

"That bizarre question does not warrant a reply; therefore, I shall not favor you with one," she replied disdainfully. "As for my interest in Nathan, we had an opportunity to chat earlier by the stream and from the things he said about you, I derived that he knew you intimately," she said simply.

"Oh, and just what did my *intimate* friend reveal to you about my personal character?"

"Nothing that I didn't already know." She avoided his intense stare. "Derek?" Her eyes remained glued to the path before her and her mood grew somber.

"Yes?" He eyed her curiously.

"There is no position waiting for me with your friend, Tyler, is there?" she asked candidly.

"I cannot possibly know that until we—"

"No, Derek, you needn't continue with your little game," she interrupted and looked at him. "I know that you concocted this whole story just to get me to come with you." She surprised herself with the cool reserve she maintained. "You must feel quite proud of yourself to be able to manipulate me thusly."

"Meghan."

"Don't bother," she snapped. "I am correct in assuming that your friend has no pressing need of a governess, am I not?" she persisted.

Derek was reluctant to respond to her inquiry.

"Well, am I not correct?" she demanded.

"Yes," he answered softly, but unlike one who might falter when discovered in the midst of an underhanded scheme, Derek did not. He remained unflappable. "When did you find me out?" he asked calmly.

"The possibility has been gnawing at me since I spoke with Nathan at lunch. That, coupled with some offhand comments you made led me to suspect that you had an ulterior motive in bringing me with you." She stared into the dark shadows of his sensuous eyes and discovered herself spellbound by the serious, brooding orbs.

A small deer wandered into the road ahead of them, but it bolted across the path to disappear in the thicket when it became alerted to their presence. The disturbance presented Meghan with the necessary distraction and enabled her to forcibly tear her eyes from his without permitting him the knowledge that his nearness could rattle her.

"I am curious, Derek." She forced her voice to maintain its reserved pitch. "When were you going to tell me the truth?"

"When the appropriate moment presented itself," he replied.

"I see."

"I must admit that you have accepted the circumstances much better than I anticipated." He eyed her suspiciously.

"I have accepted nothing, save the fact that you are perhaps the most unscrupulous man I have ever had the unhappy experience of meeting." Her eyes burned brightly. "Not to mention deceitful, loathsome and unreasonable."

Derek's husky laugh echoed throughout the forest and sent a covey of game birds sailing for the heavens. "It's good to see that my little deception has not inhibited your sugar-sweet tongue."

"When are we going back?" she asked abruptly and even though she sustained a blasé attitude, her voice trembled furiously.

"Where?"

"To New Orleans, of course, where I can find decent employment. I cannot possibly remain with you at Chandalara," she cried indignantly.

"But you shall. At least, until *I* decide that it is time for you to go elsewhere," he informed her.

"And just how will you present me at your home? It usually is not considered proper for an unmarried woman to travel about the countryside with a gentleman when she hasn't a proper chaperone. It tends to invite offensive gossip," she added scornfully. "Or is such protocol not adhered to in this uncivilized land?" Her voice grew steadily higher as she spoke.

Meghan had been foolish enough to believe that once she confronted Derek, he would return her to New Orleans. And now that he gave no indication of utilizing such an alternative, her despair was rapidly increasing.

"Tell me, Derek. Will you introduce me to your friends as your personal whore?" she asked bitterly and jerked Champion to a stop.

Derek flung her a chilling look and reached over to grasp her roughly by the arm. "You would do well to cease demeaning yourself in this manner. I do not consider you to be my *whore*. You do not sell yourself to me and Lord knows that you *give* nothing of yourself willfully," he added sourly. "Let me reassure you, Meghan, it's not my policy to bed the same woman with undue frequency. For if I honor a singular wench with my favors, it sets her to thinking ghastly thoughts that include marriage and children and tying me down, and if there is one thing I cannot abide, it is a female who squawks about these offensive matters."

His hand slipped up her arm and stripped a pin from her hair, permitting a single curl to tumble down her back. Derek lifted the curl and fingered it lovingly.

"You are different from other women that I have known, Meghan. You do not cling to me and make a bothersome nuisance of yourself, nor do you pester me about making you an honest woman." He pressed the honey-brown curl to his lips. "Perhaps it is this redeeming quality that so intrigues me," he sighed and dropped the curl over her shoulder. "Whatever it is, you have banked a fire in my loins that forever yearns for you, and I have discovered that I cannot release you . . . not yet." He dug his heels into Trojan's flanks and gently urged the horse forward. "But one thing you can well believe. Had I considered you to be a common whore, I would have left you in New Orleans to survive as one," he casually threw over his shoulder.

Meghan quickly caught up with him. "But . . . but *how will* you present me to your friends?" Tears welled up in her eyes as she realized the hopelessness of her situation.

"Regrettably, I have not yet contrived a suitable solution to that particular dilemma, but I shall undoubtedly think of some masterful ploy." He flashed her a fiendish grin.

"No!" she shouted adamantly. "I shall not be used this way. You cannot make me. You have no right!"

"Ah, sweet, but I do," he ruthlessly informed her. "Your father placed you under my protection and suggested that I leave you somewhere en route to my ultimate destination. My destination is Chandalara and that is where I have chosen to take you. Reconcile yourself to that fact, pet, no matter how displeasing it is to you," he said sternly. Then more gently, he added, "Come along, now. The hour grows late and I long to sleep in my own bed tonight."

"No!" she shrieked. "If you won't return me to New Orleans, I shall go by myself." She struggled to turn

Champion around on the narrow path, but with lightning speed, Derek grabbed the reins from her hands and brought his mount beside hers.

With some difficulty, he managed to lift her from Champion's back and placed her in front of him. But Meghan was not to be a docile passenger, for she ferociously slapped at his arms and face and when this proved futile, she bit him viciously on the hand.

"Ouch!" he howled. "You little vixen!" He grabbed her roughly about the waist and forced her back against his hard chest.

"I am suitably chastised, m'lord," she muttered sourly. "I should like to return to my own mount now."

"I think not. You might take it in your ridiculous head to run off again. Then I would be faced with the bothersome chore of chasing you down. No, this is a more satisfactory arrangement." He nudged Trojan forward and whistled for Champion to follow them.

They paused just before sunset to dine on the meager portions of bread, cheese, and meat from Derek's saddlebags. Derek fed and watered the horses and then assisted Meghan back onto Trojan and they continued their tedious journey.

As the sun crept behind the hills to the west and the full moon rose high in the sky, Meghan shivered and huddled against Derek for warmth. "How much farther?" she murmured sleepily, her head lolling against his broad chest, and she was asleep before she heard his reply.

An hour or so later, they emerged from the thicket into a clearing and in the distance, framed by the light of the moon, stood a majestic white-pillared mansion. Derek halted the horses and stared with pride at the impressive scene. It had been a long time since he had last stood in this spot and gazed at his home. He spurred

Trojan forward and tightened his grip around Meghan's slender waist. He had returned to Chandalara countless times before this, but this time he was filled with a strange feeling as he trotted toward the sanctuary of his home. He was suddenly overcome with a serenely contented sense of well-being, as if his estate now held some special, yet unexplored purpose for him.

"Meghan, my sweet," he whispered into her ear that had grown deaf with weary slumber, "we are home." He placed a light kiss on the top of her head and urged Trojan forward without further delay.

Meghan jerked awake as the drapes were snapped open to reveal a brilliant burst of sunshine. So startled was she by the abrupt awakening that Meghan did not immediately notice the robust figure of the black housekeeper who bustled about the room, neatly folding the clothes which had been carelessly discarded the previous evening. Meghan had just scrambled to a sitting position on the immense bed and was blinking the sleep from her dazed eyes when the chamber door was flung open.

"Sophie!" she heard Derek exclaim as he entered the room.

Meghan's sleep-clouded eyes had not as yet permitted her to clearly focus on him, but she did note the rankled tone in his speech and caught her breath in anticipation.

"Lawdy sakes, Massah Derek!" The housekeeper clutched at her heart. "You knows better'n t' sneak up on me."

"Sophie, I left explicit orders that no one was to disturb this room."

"I knows that, Massah Derek, but you wuz gone a mighty long time, so—"

"So you took it upon yourself to blatantly disobey my

orders," he finished for her.

"Well, now, I wouldn't use them words, 'xactly,'" Sophie said.

"Derek," Meghan interrupted, "why the fuss? Sophie has done nothing that warrants this display." She nodded at the housekeeper and was rewarded with a brilliant smile of gratitude.

"See, Massah Derek, the new Mrs. Chandler didn't think I wuz intrudin' none." Sophie shuffled towards the door and cast her master an offended look.

Meghan's eyes widened in bewilderment as the chamber door closed behind the servant. "What . . . *what did she say*?" Her voice trembled with fury.

"I believe she said the new Mrs. Chandler didn't think I wuz intrudin' none," he mimicked perfectly. He sat in a chair facing the bed and went on, "Actually the term new *was* redundant. Since there has never been an old Mrs. Chandler, you could hardly be the new one, now could you?" Derek's eyes twinkled as he taunted her.

"Indeed," she spat irritably, "the entire phrase was incorrect since I am not Mrs. Chandler at all! Am I?" she demanded. "Whatever led Sophie to make such a hideous assumption?"

"Well, the fact that you are presently resting your pretty, little rump upon the master's bed did little to discourage the theory." He grinned devilishly.

"*Your*—" She did not bother to finish her statement, but quickly got out of bed as if this gesture would disprove his allegation.

She carefully wrapped the sheet around herself to shield her nakedness from Derek's gaze, but her voluptuous curves were scarcely concealed by the sheet. Several nights had passed since he had last known the feel of that magnificent body against his skin. How he longed to run his fingers through her hair and caress

243

her soft flesh, forcing her rebellious body to respond to his lovemaking. Derek's eyes warmed with desire as he recalled the delight her body always supplied him, and he felt the familiar stirrings in his loins.

Meghan, too, noticed the gleam in his eye and the restless bulge that his tight trousers could not hide. She sighed dismally and quickly averted her gaze. She knew only too well what would likely happen before she was permitted to leave the room this day. And while she likewise knew that she could do little to prevent him from having his way, she could prolong the moment before he forced her into submission.

"You brought me here last night?" she questioned.

"Yes."

"Why?"

"Madam? Is it not proper for the mistress of the manor to share her *husband's* bedchamber?" He chuckled.

"You are *not* my hus—" The word formed a constricting vise about her throat and stuck there. Meghan shook her head in wild negation as if her denial of his outrageous statement would make it untrue. "Why must you persistently taunt me with your riddles? Are you not man enough to face me truthfully this once?" she asked crossly.

Derek was on his feet instantly. "If memory serves me, I have demonstrated the capabilities of my manliness on innumerable occasions," he thundered. "Perhaps we should dwell instead upon your ineptness at being a *woman*."

"The fact that you force me at will proves only that you possess superior strength, *not* your manliness." She ignored his reference to her. "Now, you shall answer my question. Why are you masquerading me as your wife?" Her bare foot patted impatiently upon the floor.

"In truth, I knew not what other action to take." He

244

shrugged his wide shoulders and sat down on the arm of the chair. "I have not kept the circumstances regarding my birth a guarded secret. Therefore, I could not very well introduce you as even a distant relative because my neighbors know that I have no family that would claim me." He absently fingered the material along the back of the chair. "So," he sighed, "my only alternative was to present you as my wife." He stood and walked to her.

One hand reached out and deftly traced the line along her collarbone and continued up her throat to gently cup her chin. He tilted her head back and stared intently into the emerald-green pools that were clouded with confusion.

Meghan's skin tingled where his fingers had touched her, and she shivered slightly. "But . . . but only last night you were emphatically averse to the prospect of matrimony," she reminded him.

"Oh, I will admit that the idea set sorely with me at first," he agreed. "But as I told you last night, I cannot release you just yet. So, if a simulated marriage is what it takes to keep you here, I shall gladly make the sacrifice and endeavor to play the devoted husband." He bowed before her grandly.

"And should I not agree to corroborate your story?"

"I don't recall consulting you in the matter," he said dryly. "You shall reconcile yourself to acting the part of the loving wife and concentrate your efforts at being mistress of this hall. Unless . . ." He raised his hand noncommittally.

"Unless what?" she asked reluctantly.

"Unless you want to be returned to Dulcie's Image and your friend, Garth McTavish," he slyly offered.

Meghan's lovely face turned white with bitter fury, and she turned her back to him with a huff in complete exasperation. "And what shall become of me when my

245

body no longer serves as a pleasant distraction for you? Will you then deposit me in the nearest brothel? How will you explain *that* to your friends?"

"I do not intend that this be a permanent arrangement, but if you agree to stay with me, I shall make the appropriate excuses when the time arrives for you to go your own way."

"Such as?"

"Many marriages of convenience survive with the spouses living apart. I shall inform those who inquire that you had a desire to return to your beloved England," he said simply.

Meghan silently considered all that he had said to her, then she slowly turned to face him and inquired, "And what do you intend to do about Nathan? *He* knows that, in truth, we are not man and wife."

"So he does." Derek strode to the dressing table and plucked an expensive-looking leather case from it. He sat down on the bed and opened the case that contained his inheritance. "But you need not fear. Nathan is my employee. He shall do as he is told," Derek replied stonily. "Now, come here," he suddenly commanded.

Meghan was disinclined to heed his command, and she squealed fearfully when he grabbed her roughly by the arm and dragged her to stand between his knees.

"Give me your hand," he instructed.

Cautiously, Meghan lifted her hand from her side and closed her eyes as she anxiously awaited the punishment she felt certain to be forthcoming. Instead, Meghan was greatly surprised to feel a slender band of cold metal gently placed upon the third finger of her hand. Her eyes fluttered open in genuine disbelief as they fell to examine the exquisite gem that adorned her ring finger.

"Derek?" she questioned softly.

"Is it not proper for a wife to wear such a bauble?"

246

"It's beautiful," she murmured and ran her fingers along the sleek, gold band with its bedazzling inlay of diamonds and emeralds. "I do not recall seeing this among the collection before."

"It wasn't," he explained. "A few of the pieces that my mother treasured were guarded for her by the family lawyer. When I returned to claim my inheritance, they were restored to me. This particular piece was secretly given to her by Jonathon Marley."

"Your father?"

"Yes. The trinket you now wear would have been Mother's wedding ring had she been permitted to wed Mr. Marley. I'm certain that Grandfather would have flung it in the Thames had he known that Mother accepted it." Derek's eyes grew dark with sorrow as he remembered his mother's illicit affair that had brought about his conception. "Ah, well." He snapped the lid closed and tossed the case onto the commode beside the bed. "It's yours now. Mother always insisted that my bride should have it."

Meghan lowered saddened eyes. "I am not your bride," she whispered faintly.

"You are, as far as I'm concerned—at least for the time being."

Meghan nodded weakly and turned the wedding band around her finger. "I shall treasure it as I am sure Elizabeth did."

"Well," he placed his hands on her shoulders, "do you not have a good morning kiss for your *husband*?"

Meghan sighed and leaning forward, she placed a rather perfunctory kiss upon his brow.

Derek pulled away from her in obvious disgust and studied her with a calculating stare. "Something troubles you, pet?" He lightly toyed with a wisp of hair that billowed about her shoulders. "Have I not yet made it clear that I require a more *eager* attitude from you?"

Meghan met his gaze with a calmly detached look, and when she spoke, her voice rang clear and firm. "I consented to masquerade as your wife merely because I fear the consequences of being returned to Dulcie's Image and that awful man. During my stay, I shall play the part of the doting wife to the hilt for the benefit of your friends, and I daresay that your home shall sparkle under my reign as mistress. But it is there I shall draw the line. You have left me little recourse save to corroborate your revolting lies. But do not think for a moment that this alters our situation." She removed his hands from her shoulders and stepped to the armoire to retrieve the riding habit that Sophie had hung there. "I shall not come willingly to your bed just because you have placed a ring on my finger and call me your wife." Meghan allowed the sheet to flutter to the floor as she attempted to wiggle into her chemise.

"This is a tiresome bother," Derek sighed wearily and jerked the undergarment from her hands. In one swift motion, he rent the delicate fabric in two and turned on her threateningly. "I shall not hesitate to do the same with your gown. Then you shall be forced to remain closeted with me until Nathan arrives with your belongings."

Meghan cringed as his arms enveloped her and lifted her in their sinewy embrace, and a surprised squeal escaped her lips when he abruptly dumped her upon the pillows. When she again dared to look at him, she discovered, to her acute dismay, that he had stripped away his clothing and stood before her in all his naked splendor.

"So, you would deprive me of my *husbandly* rights," he droned icily. Derek sat down beside her and gently ran a finger up and down her slender arm. "Meghan?" A

248

thought suddenly occurred to him. "Were we bound by the vows administered by a clergyman, would you then thwart my advances?"

"Were we legally bound by the church?" She soberly considered his query. "No . . . but in order for that to come about you would have to exhibit some sort of affection for me." She faltered momentarily, then continued, "And of one thing I am quite certain: you harbor no great love for me, Derek Chandler, only *lust*."

"Well, as long as you feel this way, I suppose I shall have to persevere in my endeavors to wear down your resistance. I admit that I grow increasingly weary of forcing my attentions on you, but I shall continue to do so, for there exists a flame within me that burns for you and have you I shall—willing or not." He brought his lips crushing down upon hers and pinned her struggling body against the mattress.

Outside the expansive mansion, the field hands lazily emerged from their quarters and slowly ambled toward the fields to begin the day's work. As they passed by the rear of the plantation house, their voices could be heard to blend together in song. The notes of the tune were picked up by the wind and floated up to the master's window. But the refrain went unheeded by the couple who strained upon the chamber bed to a melody of their own composition.

It was quite some time before they appeared in the downstairs dining room to partake of a late breakfast. And an amusing grin fashioned upon Derek's sunbronzed face as he casually contemplated Meghan, whose cheeks were still flushed from the fervency of his lovemaking.

Yes, he mused silently, I just might take a fancy to this arrangement.

Chapter Eleven

Meghan slowly donned the lavender-blue dress and matching bonnet and swirled around to scrutinize her reflection in the mirror. She dawdled about the room aimlessly, silently praying that Derek might forget about her existence and depart without her. But the sudden slamming of a door somewhere below, coupled with the sound of hurried footsteps up the staircase, soon led her to dispel any such hope. Half-expecting the door to be angrily flung open, Meghan braced herself for the sound of splintering wood. Instead, the door was gently pushed aside, and Derek stepped quietly into the room.

"Are you ready, sweet?"

"I . . . I do not feel at all well, Derek," she stammered. "Really, I don't."

"Nonsense." He stepped forward and took her by the hand. "You are merely skittish at the prospect of meeting my friends. Believe me, pet. The men will be utterly mesmerized by your charm and beauty, and the women, I daresay, shall positively turn pea green with envy. Yes, yours will no doubt be the name on everyone's tongue." He grasped her by the elbow and guided her toward the door.

"If you are trying to strengthen my confidence with your rhetoric, I must hasten to inform you that you are failing miserably," she muttered morosely.

"You will do fine," he assured her. "Just remember that you are my wife and conduct yourself in a manner befitting your station. But come along." He ushered her down the lavish staircase. "The reverend does not fancy latecomers to his services."

Meghan permitted Derek to lift her into the landau that waited to carry them to the church. She settled back against the leather seat as he climbed in beside her. As the landau rounded the bend that left Chandalara behind, Derek slipped his rugged hand around Meghan's and squeezed it comfortingly. She instinctively pressed closer against him and marveled at the secure feeling that enveloped her by just sitting next to this magnificent man.

Meghan sighed glumly as she raised her eyes to study Derek's sturdy profile and the square cut of his jaw. How ruggedly handsome he was. She allowed her thoughts to wander, and she reflected wistfully upon what their relationship might be like were their circumstances different. She looked away from him and gazed out the window at the passing landscape, fighting valiantly to control the nervous anxiety that gripped her queasy stomach and threatened to make her physically ill.

How long did he expect her to go along with this ridiculous charade? It had been but one day and she was already a bundle of nerves, careful to avoid long conversations with the servants lest she inadvertently divulge her true relationship with Derek. And she avoided Nathan altogether.

Meghan restlessly twisted her wedding ring round and round her slim finger, and when she again turned to Derek, she was jolted to discover his gaze thoughtfully perusing her.

"Something troubling you, little one?" He considered

251

the somewhat pale color of her face and silently rebuked himself for forcing her to accompany him.

"No, I'm fine." She managed a small grin.

"Now, pet, it's unlike you to try to deceive me, especially with me, since I have the uncanny ability to perceive your every thought," he teased. "Shall I instruct Robert to return us to Chandalara?" he added more seriously.

"No. I shall have to face your friends sooner or later, and I do not wish to arouse undue suspicion by avoiding them."

Derek acknowledged this statement by gently squeezing her hand then drew her close, and covering her mouth with his, he leisurely caressed her trembling lips. He pulled away and lightly chuckled at the pinkish color that blotted her cheeks. "Now, madam, a lustrous color has appeared on your cheeks. It's well, for I would not have my friends think I had chosen a wife who was frail and sickly."

When they arrived at the church the service had already begun, and Meghan was faced with the further humiliation of being escorted to Derek's pew while the eyes of the entire congregation turned to observe them. The service was long, almost unbearably so, and the topic of the sermon did little to lift her spirits; the reverend had chosen this particular morning to expostulate upon the evils of lust and infidelity and warned of the punishments awaiting those who blatantly disregarded these commandments of God.

It was with a sigh of relief that she stood alongside Derek to sing the closing hymn, and as his rich baritone blended with her own sweet voice, she wondered fleetingly if the words of the minister's sermon had affected him at all. When the service concluded, she accepted Derek's arm and smiled pleasantly at him as he led her from the church.

Immediately outside the door they were converged upon by a large group of curious well-wishers. Many of them had already learned of the confirmed bachelor's marriage and later, when Meghan questioned Derek as to how so many people were aware of their *marriage* when they themselves had announced it to no one, he explained, "The slaves have an uncanny system of communication. It's not unusual for the slaves of one plantation to make their masters aware of events that occur on neighboring estates."

The crowd continued to swell around the couple, each additional seeker hoping to have a better look at the young beauty who had managed to bring Derek Chandler to the altar. Meghan greeted each stranger gracefully, and as the new faces welcomed her into the community and readily accepted her as Derek's wife, she grew more and more at ease.

With each introduction her confidence grew, and a small spark of hope began to glimmer in her heart. If she could successfully win over Derek's friends and prove that she was indeed worthy of being a gentleman's wife, then perhaps she could persuade him to release her to make a life for herself. Or, her eyes flickered hopefully, perhaps Derek would discover the merit of having a wife and offer to truthfully install her in that honored position. Meghan sighed as she contemplated this last thought. There had been a time, not so very long ago, when she would have cursed herself for even harboring such a ridiculous notion.

"Darling?" Derek gently nudged her away from her silent reflections. "I would like you to meet my business associate, Wade Hampton."

Meghan looked up into startling blue eyes and graciously extended her hand. "It is indeed a pleasure to meet you, Mr. Hampton," she said sweetly and set about a cursory inspection of the man.

He was tall, but not as tall as Derek, and Wade was more slender. Wade was handsome, she decided, but then only in a boyish way, and he did not possess the rugged strength of character that Derek did. And when his hand closed around hers, she could not help but notice its delicate softness. Then Meghan laughed to herself as she realized her folly in comparing the man with Derek. Few men were as impressive as he.

"You must consent to call me Wade," the young man was saying to her.

"And I am Meghan," she replied and smiled happily into his bright blue eyes, the one striking feature he did possess.

"Derek, had I known this beauty was residing in London, I would have accompanied you on your journey and given you a run for your money, to be sure." Wade bowed over her hand and gently lifted it to his lips. "Derek, however did you get this beautiful creature to marry you?"

"It was not so difficult, Wade. I *do* possess a few hidden charms." He winked at Meghan. "And once I unleashed them on the unsuspecting maiden, she was hopelessly taken with me, and our marriage was inevitable." He nonchalantly removed Meghan's hand from Wade's clasp and placed a protective arm about her slender waist.

"Oh, pooh." Meghan giggled lightly, relishing in Derek's almost jealous response to Wade's attentiveness.

"Well, whatever your methods, Derek, you have certainly had good fortune in winning such a lovely as this." Wade recaptured Meghan's arm and guided her to the waiting landau. As they walked, he leaned forward to whisper in her ear, "You cannot have known Derek

254

for very long, my dear. Perhaps you will allow me to enlighten you on his rather nefarious past. Surely, once you have been duly informed of the rogue's notorious ways you will flee the rascal and take sanctuary elsewhere. My own home is not far removed from Chandalara," he added suggestively.

"Sir! Do you dare attempt to spirit me away from my husband beneath his very nose?" Meghan's response was gay, but her eyes darted around quickly to find Derek.

He was not far away. He had observed the exchange with obvious displeasure and had been within earshot of Meghan's coquettish question.

"Wade." He stepped between the couple and assisted Meghan inside the landau. "I honestly think that you jest, but in any case you would do well to remember that our partnership lies strictly within the business realm, and you sorely test our friendship with your banter. Meghan is my wife." He reached inside the landau to grasp her hand to accentuate his statement. "I do not take that fact lightly, nor should you." His tone was soft, but his message was explicit.

"Why, Derek, old boy," Wade slapped him heartily on the back. "I truly believe you've been smitten full score. Fear not, my friend, I would never seriously attempt to come between you and your lovely bride." He cast an appreciative glance at Meghan and started to move away from the landau. "By the way, am I still invited to Sunday dinner?"

Derek nodded as he swung into the landau beside Meghan. "Sophie would be unbearable the remainder of the week were you not present to charm her ornery soul every Sunday. We shall expect you at the usual time," he called out the window as the landau pulled away. Turning to Meghan, he explained, "Wade is a habitual

255

dinner guest at Chandalara on Sundays."

"I surmised as much." She scooted a little to her left to allow him more room, but Derek placed a firm hand upon her knee to prevent her retreat. "What does he do?" she asked curiously.

"You mean when he isn't behaving like a rutting stag around beautiful young ladies?" Derek said sardonically.

Meghan suppressed a giggle along with the urge to inform him that he usually displayed the same behavior when he was near her. The only difference being that he waited until they were completely alone when she could do little to forestall his lascivious attacks.

"Yes, you said he is your partner. What does he do?"

"Well, Wade has a fulltime job managing his plantation, but on the side he serves as my accountant. He handles the financial details of all my business affairs."

"I see. And you take care of the technical details." Derek nodded.

"It appears that you have assumed the greater of the responsibilities."

"I prefer it this way. Wade is more suited for the type of work I require of him," he stated simply.

"While you favor a more rugged challenge," she offered admiringly.

"Yes." He squeezed her knee suggestively. "Besides, I never was very good with *numerical* figures." He considered her sweet young face and could not resist the temptation to place his arm around her and draw her closer to him. And to his surprise, Meghan did not oppose the gesture.

"What did you think of Wade?" he asked casually.

"He was pleasant enough." She shrugged her shoulders as she plucked an imaginary piece of lint from her frock and carefully weighed her next statement. "But

256

just as you prefer a challenge in your working endeavors, so do I in the manner of men with whom I . . . uh . . . associate."

"Why, Meghan, do you imply that you consider *me* to be a challenge?" He raised an eyebrow in mock astonishment.

"No more than you think of me as one." She chuckled lightly at his befuddled expression and rested her head against his shoulder as the landau swayed gently towards Chandalara.

Meghan was soon to discover what the responsibilities of mistress of Chandalara would entail. The plantation was in a flurry of activity that entire day. Many of Derek's friends interrupted their Sunday afternoon by stopping off to congratulate the newlyweds and better examine the young miss who had finally coaxed Derek down the aisle.

She played the hostess with aplomb, serving cool drinks and delicious pastries and cookies that the cook, Lettie, had thoughtfully prepared. Meghan chatted with her guests in an easy, self-assured manner and was careful to cast affectionate glances at Derek now and again as was expected of any lovesick bride.

Darkness had fallen when Meghan finally bade the last visitor a fond farewell and wearily made her way to the drawing room where Derek conversed with Wade and Nathan. It was her intention to bid the gentlemen a good night and retire to her chamber.

The door to the drawing room was standing slightly ajar, and she pushed it open so quietly that no one in the room noticed her intrusion, thus allowing Meghan the opportunity to casually survey the scene before she made them aware of her presence.

Wade sat in a comfortable chair thoughtfully considering the flavor of a goblet of particularly satisfying, imported wine. Meanwhile, Derek and Nathan were silently bent over a game of chess, and from Derek's look of agitation, Meghan surmised that Nathan was soundly whipping his employer. She softly cleared her throat, and the sound brought Derek instantly to his feet; he crossed to her, taking her by the hand and leading her into the room.

"I did not mean to interrupt your game," she apologized.

"That is perfectly all right." He placed her on the sofa and waved his hand in the air as if to indicate that the game was insignificant. He then went to pour each of them a glass of wine. "Nathan held me in check in any case, and your pleasant diversion has exonerated me from seeing the game to its annoying conclusion." His smile was warm and reassuring. "Have the remainder of our guests departed?"

"Yes." She gratefully accepted the goblet of wine and leaned back against the luxurious sofa.

"Allow me to speculate." Wade leaned forward in his chair and smiled at her. "I'll wager that Olivia Davis was the last to depart."

"Why yes. How did you know?"

"Because, dear heart," Derek said as he sat down beside her, "Olivia is the local gossip. She takes it upon herself to personally inspect all newcomers. If she found you to her liking you have nothing to fear." He flashed her a wicked grin.

"And should she not?" A worried frown marred her pretty face.

"You needn't worry about that," Nathan offered. "You were a charming hostess." He rose from his chair and flung a pointed look at Derek. "In fact, if I may be permitted to say so, you have supplied Chandalara with

258

the sparkle it has long needed."

"Why, thank you, Nathan." Meghan smiled at him appreciatively.

Nathan nodded politely and directed his lanky frame toward the door. Bidding everyone good night, he withdrew from the room.

Wade, too, rose from his chair and made as if to leave.

"You musn't hasten your departure on my account," Meghan insisted.

"I really must be going. Besides, I shouldn't like to keep the newlyweds from their nuptial bed," he quipped.

"You must arrange to come again soon," Meghan invited, hiding her acute embarrassment at his ribald humor and finding it extremely difficult to act the gracious hostess.

"Yes, but only if you promise to sheath your bawdy tongue," Derek remarked dryly.

"Now, Derek," Wade chided, "were positions reversed, I could not in the next fortnight recount the cheeky comments you would expound. Just be thankful that I did not arrange for you to be greeted with an old-fashioned shivaree."

"What is a shivaree?" Meghan asked hesitantly, almost afraid to learn what the strange-sounding word meant.

"Believe me, darling," Derek said, "you don't want to know." He stood up to escort his friend to the door.

"Really, Derek. I *can* let myself out. Good night, Meghan. I pray that your night won't be tedious, seeing that you will be lying abed with this rogue." His eyes sparkled devilishly, but their luster dimmed noticeably when they beheld her angry face.

Meghan had endured quite enough of Wade's flippant

tongue, and she rose to stand by Derek, entwining her arm possessively through his. "I'll have you know that my husband is a perfect gentleman and I derive great pleasure from his nearness. Faith, Mr. Hampton, from what I have observed of your manners, you would do well to follow in his likeness," she said in a calm but lofty voice.

Wade guffawed loudly. "Bravo, Meghan! It's easy to see why Derek gathered you up for himself. Such devotion would be gratifying for any man." He smiled at her warmly and made a formal bow. "I apologize for my behavior, madam, and henceforth promise to conduct myself with the deportment befitting a gentleman in the presence of a lady."

"I accept your apology, and you may rest assured that I shall hold you to your promise," Meghan replied curtly.

Wade found his coat and turning to Derek, he said, "You won't forget what I said about Sam Iverson. Perhaps it's merely a rumor, but it would not hurt to check it out." He paused by the door.

"I shall look into the matter," Derek assured him.

"Good. Let me know what you uncover. One more thing. Deirdre will be returning shortly from her holiday in Europe and I'm positive she'll want to meet Meghan and plan some sort of reception for the two of you."

"Fine. We shall discuss it when she arrives home." Derek bade him a good evening, and the couple relaxed as they heard the click of the door that assured them they were completely alone in the handsomely styled drawing room.

Derek thoughtfully twisted the wine glass he held in his hand and carefully examined the slip of a girl who had just dealt so forcefully with a veritable stranger . . .

and in *his* defense.

"Derek?" Meghan said, misinterpreting his pensive look. "Have I done something to displease you?"

"What?" He stared at her dazedly. "No, no." He smiled warmly to reassure her and sank down into the chair that Wade had just vacated.

"Did you not insist that I *play* the role convincingly?"

"Yes, and that you did, my sweet. Although your parting speech did surprise me a bit." He chuckled and the sound reverberated deep in his chest.

"I found his constant badgering to be both boorish and offensive. He deserved a comeuppance and since you seemed content to stand idly by and suffer his churlish remarks, I was the only one remaining who could set him in his proper place."

"And you accomplished that feat in the most divine way. I could never hope to compete against your masterful tongue," he said, not unkindly.

They both lapsed into silence, the only sound being the ticking of the clock on the mantel. Meghan stood facing him, her eyes downcast, but it was as if some strange force that she could not resist commanded her to look at him. And when she did, she discovered Derek's gaze focused intently upon her.

"Come here," he whispered huskily.

Meghan stepped silently across the carpet to stand before him, gazing uncertainly into his warm, sensitive eyes. She did not offer him a struggle when he pulled her onto his lap. Indeed, she rested her head on his shoulder while he absently laced the fingers of one hand through hers. They sat like that for a long time, neither one speaking, contentedly basking in the undisturbed simplicity of the moment.

"Derek?" Meghan hesitantly interrupted the peaceful interlude.

261

"Yes, pet."

He released her hand for a moment and reached for his drink. But when he returned the glass to the commode and sought to recapture her hand, he discovered that she had moved it along the lapel of his silk coat, where she coyly traced abstract patterns.

"Who is Deirdre?" she asked softly.

"Wade's sister."

"Oh," she murmured.

Derek cocked his head at an angle, so he could better analyze the expression on her face.

"Why so pensive, sweet? Do you imagine that I've had past relations with Miss Hampton?"

"Have you?" she posed shyly, not certain that she wanted to know the answer, yet determined to hear it anyway.

"God above!" he exclaimed and slapped his knee. "You *are* direct, and such straightforwardness should be rewarded." He noticed that Meghan's hand stopped its playful wandering over his chest, and he sensed that she held her breath in nervous anticipation despite her cool façade.

"It would be folly for me to deny that at one time Deirdre and I were considered by the local grapevine to be the ideally suited couple. I shall spare you the incidentals, for the gossipmongers will no doubt fill you in eventually."

He paused and Meghan, thinking he intended to cease his narrative, pressed him further. "The two of you are no longer considered an ideal match?" she asked lightly.

"No."

"Why?"

"Pet, my friends would hardly expect me to carry on a relationship with Deirdre when I am *blissfully* wed to you." He laughed airily.

262

"Forgive me," she murmured sheepishly. "I still find it difficult to think of us in that context."

"Besides, our affair ended long ago, Meghan. If you must know, while I do enjoy the companionship of a female who is capable of intelligent discourse, I do not, however, relish an aggressive female business adviser," he said sourly.

"Deirdre interfered in your business dealings?" She could not believe that Derek would tolerate such a thing.

He nodded. "She tried, but it was when she attempted the same overbearing tactics in the bedchamber that I quickly decided she was not for me." He lazily ran a finger up and down her spine and pondered her subdued silence. "What? No more questions? Are you not interested in her rather peculiar, if not perverted, antics?" He looked deeply into her shimmering eyes and reveled in their innocence.

Hastily, Meghan shook her head in reply to his question and tried unsuccessfully to extricate herself from his lap.

"Sit still," he commanded. "I was merely teasing you. I would never subject you to that sort of evil. It would likely destroy the charming naïveté that I find so alluring about you." He kissed her pouting lips.

"I am no longer naïve," she reminded him in a soft voice that bore no accusing tone.

"In many ways you still are, little one," he reaffirmed. "Were you fearful that I might renew my association with Deirdre and cast you adrift?"

Meghan did not answer his question, but Derek's scrutiny of her face told him that he had guessed correctly.

"You little mouse," he scolded. "You are twice the woman that Deirdre Hampton is, and you are little more than a child. You need not fear that I'll return to her arms."

He positioned her on his lap more to his advantage, and while his sensuous lips descended upon hers in a tender kiss, his fingers expertly unfastened the laces of her bodice, freeing her breasts for his skillful manipulation.

Meghan's immediate impulse was to resist him, but the fervency of his kiss soon drove all thoughts of resistance from her head. Besides, she reasoned, she would never convince him that she could serve him well as a wife if she continued to spurn his lovemaking. Therefore, she might as well surrender, for he usually had his way with her anyway.

An eternity later, Meghan succeeded in pulling her throbbing lips from his mouth and playfully slapped at the hand that stroked the sensitive flesh of her breasts, arousing the nipples to proud, fearless peaks.

"What if Sophie should happen upon us?" She quickly tried to refasten the bodice of her gown, all the while repeatedly shoving Derek's persistent hands away.

"She retired to her cabin hours ago." He nibbled at her ear lobe. "Alas, there is no one to rescue the fair maiden from the evil clutches of the treacherous dragon. Capitulate, my love. You have no other recourse." He roared mightily and thrust his face into the still open bodice, shaking his head violently and growling gruffly as he playfully nipped at the vibrant flesh.

Meghan erupted with merry laughter at his light-hearted cavorting and with great difficulty, she managed to capture his head between her hands and force it from her.

"Derek!" She tried to sound stern.

"Yes, love."

He nonchalantly pulled her hands from his face and forced them behind her back. Then with a wicked chuckle, his teeth and lips returned to their plunderings and recaptured the lusty treasure.

"And . . . and what of Nicholas?" she pleaded. "He was still up and about when I came into the room. What if he should come to extinguish the candles? It would likely send him to his bed for days to find us thus entwined."

Derek released her and breathlessly contemplated her statement as his eyes boldly raked over her disheveled appearance. God, but she was magnificent! He considered the tangled hair that had come undone during their play and now hung wildly about her shoulders. His eyes fell to her lips, still swollen from his passionate kisses, and descended to her heaving breasts, the nipples firm and piquant from his attentive caresses. Her dress had crept upward to reveal one shapely leg and a helpless groan escaped his lips as he forcefully put aside the notion of mounting her on the drawing room sofa. Finally, his eyes returned to scan hers, which had grown wide with expectancy as to his next move.

"You are absolutely right," he sighed heavily. "It *would* shock the old boy." He stood up suddenly, scooping Meghan into his muscular arms, and in three long strides, he crossed to the door. "Lamentably, we shall have to adjourn to the upstairs chamber to resume our sport."

Somehow he managed to throw open the door, and they had just started across the hall to the staircase when Nicholas emerged from the shadows. Upon seeing his master and mistress, he mumbled a hurried apology for his intrusion and scurried into the drawing room, closing the door firmly behind him.

With a shriek, Meghan spread her hands over her bosom in an effort to cover her breasts from the servant's view and buried her head against Derek's shoulder. "I shall die of mortification," she cried piteously as he clamored up the wide steps three at a time.

Once inside their bedchamber, he placed her in the wing chair before the fireplace and crossed to the chiffonier to neatly fold away his clothes as he removed them. Having accomplished this, he slipped into a green satin robe and returned to Meghan. He knelt before her chair, thoughtfully considering the serious expression on her face and he swore silently as he damned the struggle he thought to be forthcoming.

"Do you still fret over the incident with Nicholas?"

"No," she whispered lowly.

With relief, Derek drew her from the chair and began undoing the hooks on the back of her gown. "Had this frock not cost so dearly, I would dispense with this formality and rip it from you without a moment's hesitation." He pulled it down to her ankles and Meghan mechanically stepped out of it.

"Derek? Wade said something about a Sam Iverson."

"Yes, he did. And you must thoroughly detest me if you choose to discuss that bastard at this particular moment." He lamely shook his head, hanging the dress over the back of a chair.

"No," she chided. "It's just that you mentioned him in New Orleans. Was he not the previous owner of Chandalara?"

"Yes."

He attempted to guide her toward the huge bed, but Meghan resisted.

"Meghan," his voice held a threatening aura, "you should know well enough by now that I am determined to have my pleasure. Now, come to bed," he commanded. "I should like to go for a *ride* this night." He smiled nefariously.

"It is not my intention to *deprive* you," she reassured him. "Faith, if anyone knows the folly of that, it's I. I am merely curious. Wade sounded ominous when he spoke of the man and he mentioned some sort of rumor. What did he mean?"

With a muttered oath, Derek collapsed upon the bed, and draping a weary arm around the intricately carved bed post, he said, "Wade has learned through a mutual acquaintance that Iverson has returned to the area, expounding the desire to take up residence again at Chandalara."

"But Chandalara is yours now. What can he possibly mean?" she persisted.

"Apparently he is claiming that I swindled him in some way. If truth be known, the drunken sot has doubtlessly squandered away the money he received for the purchase of Chandalara and he plans to bleed me for more. Well, he needn't attempt such a stunt with me, for the transaction was perfectly legal and my lawyer holds the deed for me."

"You are not telling me everything," she accused.

"Damn it, woman!" he swore at her, but when he read the genuine concern for him in her eyes his mood softened. "It would seem that he has threatened me with physical harm if I do not surrender my home to him."

"Oh, Derek!" She rushed to the bed and dropped to her knees before him. "You will be careful, won't you?" She took his hand in hers.

"Do not fret, little one," he comforted her. "Better men than he have tried to execute my demise, and all have yet to succeed. There now." He pulled her to her feet. "Set aside your fears, sweet. Come to bed, and let me hold you." He threw back the coverlets and discarded his robe almost in the same motion.

"And where is your carriage, sir?" she offered shyly.

"*What!*" The expression on Derek's handsome face was one of total bewilderment.

"For your *ride*," she reminded him demurely, a flush

that she could not control softly creeping over her young flesh.

Derek's deep chuckle filled the room as he watched her wiggle seductively out of her undergarments. He stepped to her, swooped her into his arms and carried her to the bed. After extinguishing the candles, he joined her in the wide berth and instantly wrapped her in his embrace and began to place a blazing trail of hot, demanding kisses from her mouth to her breasts.

Meghan placed a tiny hand against his broad chest to interrupt his fondling and grinned at him with devilish mirth. "And just where, sir, do you intend to take me at this hour of the night?" she demanded with feigned indignation.

"Oh, to sights unseen . . . to paths untrod . . . to heights heretofore unattainable . . ." His voice trailed off as his lips covered hers and the remainder of his narrative was lost in the ensuing storm.

Much later, after the passionate flames had found surcease and reason had been restored, Derek lay on his back with his arms folded behind his head and contemplated the shadows that haphazardly danced along the ceiling. The placid look on his face belied the turmoil that raged within him. In complete exasperation he ran his fingers through his thick, ebony hair and flopped to his side to better study Meghan, as if he might be able to find the answers to his gnawing questions by gazing into her sleeping face.

Would he ever be able to figure out this tiny slip of a girl? Only the day before, she had sworn vehemently that she would never surrender herself to him willingly, and yet, had she not just done so? Derek heaved his muscular torso up on one elbow and thoughtfully toyed with the honey-brown tresses that spilled across her bosom. He sighed at the loveliness of her face in the bright moonlight and suddenly felt a great weariness creep over him as he pensively shook his head.

No, she had not *completely* given of herself to him. Oh, she had tried, perhaps even *wanted* to, but there still remained that nagging thread of pride that held her in check and would never permit her to dishonor her noble birth by abandoning herself to a man to whom she was not properly wed. But there still existed the question as to the cause for this abrupt change . . . this . . . this *pretense* of submission, and Derek had to forcibly put aside the notion of shaking her awake and demanding a prompt explanation.

The moon slowly crept behind a covering cloud, and to compensate for the sudden darkness, Derek leaned closer to study the fine lines of her face. "Just what sort of schemes are you plotting in that shrewd mind of yours?" he whispered softly. "Can it be that you think you are capable of tempting me into a legitimate marriage?"

Meghan stirred in her sleep and suddenly became aware of an intensely uneasy feeling that warned of some lurking danger. She jerked awake from the depths of a deep sleep and her sleep-clouded eyes beheld the shadow that leered above her. In her confused state, she associated the figure with another who had twice awakened her from a deep sleep and the brutalities he had inflicted on her—*her father*.

"Papa? Papa, don't hurt me," she whimpered desperately.

All thoughts of badgering her with inquiries vanished as Derek realized the frightening nightmares he had inadvertently reawakened. In an instant he gathered her trembling body in his sturdy embrace and began rocking her gently back and forth to comfort her.

"It's Derek, Meghan. You are safe. Your father is in

England and cannot harm you," he reassured her.

"But . . . but what did you want?" she stammered.

Derek brushed the errant strands of hair from her face and stared into her eyes. Suddenly his musings of minutes before seemed trite and unimportant, and his questions, he decided, could wait for another less emotional time.

"It was nothing," he cooed softly and held her close to calm her trembling body.

"But—?"

"Shhh," he commanded and covered her lips with his to smother her queries and discourage any further protestations.

When Meghan awakened early the next morning, Derek was already gone. She scampered from the bed, quickly washed her face and hands and donned a modest gown. But when she arrived in the dining room, she was a trifle dismayed to discover that the table held only one place setting.

The scuffing of a chair against the hardwood floor startled Meghan from her musings, and she looked up to find Nicholas patiently waiting to seat her. Hastily, Meghan pushed aside the nagging memory of her disheveled appearance when they had last met and regally strode to the table.

"Has Master Derek departed already?"

She posed the question in a nonchalant manner, hoping that the fact that Derek had left without telling her his plans for the day might not appear unusual to the servant.

"Yes'm. The massah likes to rise early. He done ate his breakfast and rode out to the fields."

"Oh," she murmured and daintily placed the linen napkin on her knee. She then assumed a quiet manner

270

while the servant offered her a selection of delicacies that had been warming on the sideboard. "Did he mention when he would return?" She casually sipped her coffee.

"No, Miz Meghan."

"Thank you, Nicholas." She dismissed the servant and sighed. Well, *Mrs. Chandler,* she said to herself, it would appear that you are on your own for the day. Meghan shrugged her shoulders disconsolately. Certainly she would be able to find something within this rambling mansion with which to occupy herself.

She concluded her meal and was rising from the table when Sophie entered the room. Dogging her tracks was a very young girl, perhaps not yet sixteen, Meghan judged, and with skin as brown as chocolate and hair that lay in tight little curls all over her head. She was pretty, Meghan decided.

"Good morning, Miz Meghan," the housekeeper said cheerfully.

Meghan returned the greeting and stepped closer to better examine the girl. "Who is this?" she asked.

"This be Abbey, and Massah Derek says that she is to be your maid. That is, if'n you likes her," Sophie explained.

"Abbey, did you say?"

"Yes'm."

"Well, Abbey. I can hardly decide if you are suitable for my needs when you cower behind Sophie, can I?" Meghan said pleasantly in a soft, soothing voice. "Come here, child. There is no need to be frightened."

Very slowly, the young girl stepped from behind the housekeeper's skirts and awkwardly dropped into a curtsy before Meghan.

"There now. See. I am not such a beast." Meghan smiled.

"Oh, no, ma'am." Abbey hurriedly stood up. "Why, you're . . . you're beautiful. It's just that I ain't never worked in the big house afore."

"You will do just fine," Meghan assured her. "Now, run along and help Sophie for the time being. I shall summon you when I need your assistance."

"Yes, ma'am. Thank you, ma'am." She bobbed up and down as she backed toward the door.

Meghan wandered out of the dining room and up the wide, mahogany staircase. Never in her wildest dreams had she imagined the extent of Derek's wealth, nor had she expected Chandalara to be so extravagantly furnished. It was obvious that Derek's taste had been greatly influenced by his world travels. From the Persian carpet in the drawing room to the Waterford chandelier in the dining room, one could see that great care had been given to the furnishing of each room.

Meghan walked past the bedchamber she shared with Derek and paused momentarily before the door of the adjoining room. Slowly, she entered the sitting room that connected the huge master bedchamber and the smaller one that Derek had allocated for her own use. The furnishings in her room were quite similar to those in the master bedchamber, except where Derek had selected somber shades of brown for his chamber, her room had been accented in soft shades of blue.

She admired a delicate porcelain figurine that adorned the dressing table and solemnly sat down before the mirror to study her reflection. She had avoided mirrors as of late, afraid that the truth of her station in this household could be easily read on her anxious face. Meghan lifted trembling fingers to her lips. How old she looked. She was only eighteen and yet the events of the past weeks and the added burden of guarding Derek's secret had added years to her appearance.

"At this rate," she sighed wearily and gazed down at her lap, "he will cast me aside by the end of the month."

"Nonsense," came an unexpected reply.

Meghan's head snapped back and in the mirror, her eyes locked with Derek's as he leaned against the doorjamb.

"What sort of rubbish has your mirror been telling you?" He strode across the floor to stand behind her.

"I look so old," she blurted out mournfully. "How can you possibly bear to look at me?"

"It's not such an awesome task," he teased, then noting the seriousness of her downcast face, he added, "Meghan, you are as young and beautiful as you were on the day I beheld you in your father's library. The adventures you have experienced these past weeks have merely served to enrich your beauty. You have matured, my sweet, an aging process which wrinkles one's soul, not one's flesh."

"Mirrors do not lie," she mumbled desolately.

"No, but ofttimes we view ourselves with a more critical eye than is warranted. Believe me, love, I do not yet find the sight of you an unpleasant chore for my bleary eyes." He placed an affectionate kiss against the nape of her neck. "What are you doing here?"

"Surely, it's not uncommon for the mistress of the manor to lounge in her chamber," she snapped irritably. "Or am I not permitted to wander about *your* home?"

"It's your home as well," he said softly, stung by her sharp retort. "Please, Meghan, cannot one day go by in which you do not remind me of your resentment for me. Can we not at least try to be amicable with one another?" He suddenly looked very weary.

"I apologize." She glanced up in time to see him mask the wounded expression that darkened his handsome features for a moment. "Do not be angry with me,

Derek." She softened under the disturbing frown he turned on her. "It seems that my tongue has grown more spiteful of late." She shook her head, unable to account for her irritable moods.

"I suppose I should be accustomed to it by now." He grinned ruefully. "In any case, it was not my intent to imply that you should not be here. I gave this room to you freely to use at your discretion whenever you so choose, just as long as you remember in whose bed you lie at night." He leaned down to press a kiss against her tempting mouth.

"I am not likely to forget," she murmured against his warm lips. Meghan shivered slightly as the pressure of his mouth against hers left her giddy and as she parted her lips in eager anticipation of his hard, thrusting tongue, she lifted her arms to encircle his neck.

"Why, Meghan, did I not know better, I might suspect that you are trying to seduce me." His eyes twinkled merrily at the rose-colored flush that spread over her cheeks. "And at such an indecent hour of the morning," he said and clucked his tongue. Derek chuckled lightly and pulled Meghan to her feet, thereby breaking the spell of the timeless moment. "Does the room suit your tastes, or shall I have to spend a small fortune to redecorate?" he asked, abruptly changing the subject.

"Oh, no, no," she assured him. "It is quite elegant. But . . . but there is one thing."

"Yes?"

"I . . . I feel so inactive. Is there nothing for me to do?"

"Well, you could always help Sophie with the housework, or instruct Lettie in the preparation of some of your aristocratic dishes," he jokingly offered.

"Sophie manages the house quite well, and you

should pray that you never have the misfortune of dining on any concoction prepared by these humble hands," she honestly warned him. "I fear that I am sorely lacking when it comes to the artistry of fine cuisines."

"No matter." He pulled her to him and wrapped her in a snug embrace. "I did not bring you here to cook for me. I have servants who provide excellent domestic service. I brought you here to—"

"I know why I am here." She pulled away from him abruptly, but Derek caught her arm to prevent her escape.

"You do not think highly of yourself, do you? I assure you, Meghan, had your only redeeming attribute been the fact that you serve me well in bed, I would have left you in New Orleans. I brought you to Chandalara because you are pleasant company and have proven to be an interesting and intelligent companion." He drew her to him again, and staring meaningfully into her surprised eyes, he lowered his head and kissed her. "Of course, your *deeper* charms did play an intricate part in my decision to bring you to Chandalara." He slapped her playfully on her backside as he released her and walked toward the sitting room.

"By the way, you are mistaken about the management of this house. Sophie does an excellent job, mind you, and there is much you can learn from her. But, I fear, the household ledgers are in a terrible state. I thought it might interest you to see if you could restore them to some semblance of order." He vanished into the adjoining room, only to pop his head back through the door seconds later. "Does this project interest you?" he inquired.

Meghan quickly nodded.

"Good." He disappeared into the master bedchamber.

Thinking that he meant to leave again, Meghan quickly scampered into the room, but she stopped short when she discovered him slumped in one of the chairs in front of the fireplace. "Are you home for the day?"

"No, I still have many things to see to. I came back to ask if you would like to ride along with me. It would be an excellent opportunity for you to view the grounds. Besides, I passed Champion's stall this morning. Do you realize, my sweet, that you have not so much as inquired about the beast since we arrived here?" he asked accusingly.

Meghan bowed her head sheepishly. "I had not forgotten him, really. It's just that my mind has been elsewhere."

"I would offer to exercise him for you, but the last time I tried to mount the beast, he damn near killed me." Beneath his breath, he added, "He puts me in mind of his mistress in that respect."

"You *are* incorrigible," Meghan scolded. "But when did you attempt to ride Champion?" A frown wrinkled her brow, for she could not recall the incident.

"The day I delivered him from the ship to Yvette's dress shop. He refused me access to his stately back, and I was forced to *escort* him through the streets of New Orleans. A most humbling experience for a man of my stature, I assure you." He clucked his tongue in feigned annoyance.

"Champion *is* particular about those he allows upon his back." She smothered a titter, wishing that she had been present to witness the scene he had just described.

"So I discovered." Derek observed the amused grin that twitched at the corner of her mouth with mild disdain. "Would you like to ride with me?"

"Oh, yes! Just permit me a few minutes to change." She scuttled to the armoire to select a riding habit.

"Did Sophie not present Abbey to you?" he asked sternly.

"Yes."

"And did you not find her acceptable?"

"Oh, yes, Derek. I am certain that she will serve me well. It's just that I have done without the services of a personal maid for so long that I have grown used to dressing myself," she hastily explained. "Please, don't think for a moment that your thoughtfulness is not appreciated."

"That never occurred to me. I merely feared that your stubborn nature might be surfacing, and that you might reject the girl simply because I recommended her," he said. "I am pleased you have accepted her for appearance's sake. It would not do for the servants to suspect that we harbor animosity toward one another." He retreated to the door. "I shall see that Abbey comes to assist you while I ready the horses. I'll meet you downstairs in fifteen minutes." He closed the door firmly, but if he noticed Meghan's affronted expression, he gave no indication.

"Why, of all the . . ." She flung an ashtray at the neutral barrier and plopped down on the chair before the dressing table, completely oblivious to the thundering crash as the ashtray shattered against the door. As she drew the pearl-handled brush furiously through her hair, her anger increased. "So, his only concern is that I conduct myself with the deportment expected of his *wife*. Does the fool actually think that I want the world to learn of the despicable situation in which I am forced to live?" She slammed her delicate fist against the sturdy table, setting the bottles thereon rattling. "He is positively the most irritating man!"

The fervent strokes of the brush gradually subsided into a soft, rhythmic tempo and as her eyes beheld her image in the mirror, her fingers softly touched the lips that his had only moments before caressed. "Ah, but he is a *splendidly* irritating man," she sighed.

Chapter Twelve

As the days passed, Meghan developed an agreeable rapport with the serving staff and adopted a comfortable manner in her management of Derek's home. Lettie consulted her daily concerning the menus and food preparation, but Meghan suggested few alterations, conceding that there was little she could do to improve an already excellent kitchen. And as Derek promised, he presented her with the household ledgers.

It was with determination that Meghan tackled the enormous task of creating order from the chaotic state in which the ledgers lay. She began her work shortly after the noon meal and requested that her supper be served to her in Derek's office, so she would not have to interrupt her work. Midnight was upon her when Meghan leaned back in her chair, yawned sleepily, and stretched her arms wearily above her head. It was then that she noticed Derek standing in the doorway, his eyes regarding her with an almost sinister glare.

Meghan swiftly stifled her yawn, and retrieving a pen, she hurriedly dunked it into the inkwell and scratched some figures onto a blank piece of paper. But when she again glanced in his direction, she discovered that his expression was unchanged.

"Derek?" she blurted out nervously. "What have I done to provoke such an agitated scowl?"

A slight grin pinned back the corners of his mouth and he chuckled sourly, "I fear that it is not with you that I find displeasure." He eased his large frame into the office and closed the door behind him. "In complete honesty, I was silently damning myself for being the brainless dolt who suggested that you undertake this project." He stepped with measured stride across the floor and circled the desk to position himself behind her chair where he began to massage the tenseness from her tired shoulders.

"Mmmm," she sighed languidly. "But I don't understand. I thought that you wanted me to assume the duties of running your household."

"I do, love," he murmured huskily against her neck as he craftily slipped one hand beneath her robe to fondle her breast. "But it was not my intent that you should neglect your other obligations." He skillfully turned her head so that his mouth could capture the sweet nectar of her lips. "I missed you at supper. The table was not half as radiant as when you are in attendance." He flicked his tongue playfully along the corner of her mouth, retreating purposely to deny her contact.

Meghan moaned disappointedly at his teasing and slipped her arm around his neck to pull his head down to hers, but still he taunted her until Meghan, thinking she would go mad with this endless torment, sought to push him away from her in complete frustration. It was then that the pressure of Derek's lips against hers increased, and he thrust his tongue inside her mouth to sample the sweetness therein.

Meghan rose halfway from her chair to meet and return his demanding kiss, the blood thundering at her temples and her heart pounding so in her chest that Derek's sensitive fingertips could detect each pulsating beat.

When Derek finally released her, she collapsed breathlessly into the chair, one wayward arm knocking against the papers that lay on the desk, sending many of them fluttering to the floor. Immediately, Meghan was on her knees to retrieve the errant documents, but Derek's hand on her arm made her pause and look up at him.

His eyes were warm and his voice thick with desire when he spoke. "Can that not wait till the morrow?"

"From the looks of things it has waited too long as it is." She gathered all the papers and returned to the chair, the magic of the passionate interlude completely forgotten. "Faith, if you mismanage your other interests as badly as you do this plantation you may well find yourself a pauper one of these days," she said and clucked her tongue disparagingly.

"It cannot possibly be as ominous as you suggest." He peered over her shoulder to scan the papers that were piled high on the desk. "What is all of that anyway?"

"Mayhem is what it is!" she exclaimed. "Did you accomplish this all by yourself, or did someone assist you?"

"Wade handles the books for all my interests," he reminded her.

"Do you ever bother to review them, or are you totally satisfied to accept another's word as to the state of your affairs?"

"Wade is my friend, Meghan. He has never given me cause to suspect that he might be swindling me with fraudulent mismanagement of my records. And I *do* examine the books from time to time," he informed her haughtily.

"Oh, and just when was the last time you troubled yourself to balance these?" she demanded.

Derek stared thoughtfully at the floor and then shrugged his shoulders.

"I thought as much," she scolded. "Derek, there are several instances where funds have been allocated to purchase goods, and the items are not to be found. For example," she said, beckoning him to lean closer as she pointed out a particular illustration, "this voucher specifies the purchase of a pair of matching candelabra."

"A handsome price," Derek whistled.

"And yet Sophie says she has never seen them. There are similar instances throughout the ledger." Meghan lowered the pen and gazed up at him.

"Hmmm?" Derek stroked his chin, engrossed in deep concentration. "I shall speak with Wade. I'm certain he can explain this."

"Good." She returned her attention to the desk as if she intended to continue her labors. But Derek obviously had other designs, for he reached across the desk and extinguished the light as he pulled her from the chair.

"Meghan, I am truly flattered that you have taken such an avid interest in managing my home. But I must insist that you limit your efforts to the daylight hours, for when the sun sets your duty lies elsewhere."

"Yes, Derek," she sighed and wrapped her arm in his as he led her from the office, across the yard and up the porch to the spacious mansion.

The next morning Meghan returned to the task of balancing the jumbled figures, and she was still ensconced behind the ornate desk when Sophie came bustling into the office shortly before the noon meal.

"Lawd o' mercy, Miz Meghan! Is you still at them books?"

"Afraid so, Sophie." Meghan leaned back in the chair and cast a warm smile at the servant. "Would you be a dear and open the window? It's awfully warm in here."

"I can do better'n that, Miz Meghan. You come on up to the porch and I'll brings you a nice, cool drink."

"Thank you, Sophie, but I really should stay with this until I can make some sort of headway."

"Miz Meghan, this house been runnin' just fine this long with them books in the state they is. A few more hours ain't gonna hurt it none." The servant crossed to the desk where Meghan sat. "Now you git on outside and draw yourself a breath of fresh air."

"And just what would your master say if he heard you speaking to me in this manner?" Meghan tried to sound stern, but the sparkle in her eyes belied the severe intonation of her voice.

"Like as not, he'd side with me," the servant responded with a self-satisfied grin.

Obediently, Meghan followed the servant out of the uncomfortably warm office to the refreshing shade of the verandah. Sophie remained long enough to ensure that her mistress was comfortably situated, and then she scurried off to collect the promised beverage.

Meghan relaxed in her chair, thankful that Sophie had coaxed her from the stuffy office to the more amiable atmosphere outside. She was sipping on the drink that Sophie brought her when a young man that Meghan had never seen before rode into the yard. He dismounted and was ascending the front steps when Meghan stepped from the side verandah.

"May I help you?" Meghan asked.

"I got a letter here for Captain Chandler." The boy waved the missive eagerly before her. "Just came in

282

today. My pa said it looked mighty important; so he said I should deliver it to the captain personally." The boy beamed brightly as if he considered the assignment a personal achievement.

"I am Mrs. Chandler," Meghan informed the boy. "My husband is not presently at home, but you may give me the letter. I shall deliver it to my husband."

"I don't know." The boy hesitated. "Pa said the captain would be rightly pleased, seeing that I took such good care of his mail and all."

"Billy Joe Wilkes!" boomed Sophie's voice from the doorway. "You stop tryin' to weasel a reward for doin' yer job and hand over that there letter to Miz Chandler."

"I wasn't trying to weasel nothin'," he protested and lamely handed the missive to Meghan.

"Now, you jest climb on that there animal of yourn and skedaddle on outta here afore I take the broad end of this broom to yer backside." Sophie shuffled her large frame onto the porch and grasped the broom she had been using to sweep the main hallway with such menace that the boy nearly fell from the porch in his haste to return to his mount.

Meghan watched with subdued amusement as the boy scrambled on his horse and galloped out of the yard before turning to Sophie. "Really, Sophie, I could have spared a little something for the boy. Was all that necessary?"

"Beggin' yer pardon, ma'am. Massah Derek pays Mr. Wilkes extra to see that his mail is delivered to the house. Course, if'n you *wants* to offer young Billy somethin' for doin' his job, that's yer affair, but that don't give him no right to go askin' for no handout," Sophie said doggedly.

"I suppose not," Meghan agreed. "I did not mean to

283

scold you, Sophie. I guess I still have a great deal to learn."

"Shucks, I'm too old and ornery to take offense at a little scoldin'." Sophie smiled widely. "And as far as I can tell, you is doin' jest fine runnin' this here house."

"Thank you," Meghan whispered appreciatively.

"If'n that letter's from who I thinks it is, you better skedaddle on down to the barn with it. Massah Derek rode in awhile back." She ignored Meghan's curious gaze and started to sweep an already spotless porch. "Most likely he's tendin' to his horse. Massah likes to do that." She continued as if talking to herself. "Else he'd been here to wallop that young, upstart Wilkes."

Sophie disappeared inside the house, leaving Meghan standing on the porch, staring at the letter she still held in her hand. Derek's name had been scrawled across the envelope in a bold script, and she wondered pensively about its contents as she stepped from the porch and slowly sauntered toward the barn.

The barn door was standing ajar when Meghan approached, and as she drew near the huge door, she became aware of the deep sound of Derek's voice. She decided that she should not interrupt his conversation, but Meghan became suddenly puzzled when she realized that Derek was evidently delivering a rather lengthy dissertation to his horse.

"It's lucky you are that you do not have to deal with that female, Trojan, my lad." Derek applied a stiff brush to the horse's flanks and received a soft whinny of appreciation. "You had the right idea the moment you met her by letting her know who was in command. I, on the other hand, have not displayed the same wisdom. But Hank has presented me with some rather disturbing news." He slapped the horse heartily on the rump. "He said that Meghan was down here this morning with a

284

sugar cube for you and that behemoth of hers. Fact is, Hank said she had you eating out of her hand." He chuckled deeply as the horse turned to look at his master and snorted as if to deny the accusation.

"Nothing to be ashamed of, fella." Derek again slapped Trojan's rump and retreated to the railing where he had placed a bucket of oats. He gathered a handful of the grain and offered it to the animal. "She has the uncanny ability to set me blubbering like a lovesick swain. Why, if the fact that she is Thomas Bainbridge's daughter did not set so sorely with me, I am certain that I might be persuaded to relinquish my gay and independent bachelorhood for the more restrictive pleasures of wedded bliss." Derek was a little startled that he had actually voiced such a declaration, but he was even more surprised to hear Meghan calling his name just beyond the barn door.

"Derek?" She poked her head through the opening.

"In here, Meghan." He left Trojan's stall and watched Meghan closely as she approached him from the doorway. Had she overheard him?

"A young man delivered this a short while ago." Meghan handed him the letter.

"Young Wilkes?" Derek accepted the letter and examined the handwriting on the envelope.

She nodded.

"Was he up to his usual shenanigans?"

"He attempted to finagle a gratuity for doing his job," she admitted. "But Sophie put an end to his antics."

"I would like to have witnessed that scene," he said with a chuckle.

Meghan waited for Derek to open the envelope, but he gave no indication that the letter provided him with even a mild interest. Instead, his serious eyes studied her conscientiously, and Meghan grew increasingly uncomfortable.

"I thought that you would like to see the letter as soon as possible. It might be important," she added nervously as she stepped to Trojan's stall and cooed a soft greeting. The horse instantly responded by dropping his nose to nuzzle her cheek. "I shall teach you to push me down," she chided gently and scratched him affectionately behind the ear.

"Had I not witnessed this with my own eyes, I would have never believed it," Derek exclaimed. "Trojan is seldom that docile even for me. Who would have thought that a mere slip of a girl could tame the heart of this stalwart beast?"

"He has proven to be an easy conquest compared to some," she replied softly. "Man ofttimes proves to be more stubborn and unwilling to succumb to his feelings and yet it is the horse that is referred to as the dumb animal."

"Meghan," Derek spoke her name softly as he stepped nearer, his hand outstretched to touch her.

"Are you not going to read your letter?" Meghan blurted abruptly. "Sophie seemed to think it was of paramount importance."

"It can wait." He pulled her to him and forced her to look at him. "I have elucidated my position regarding our relationship on numerous occasions. Need we belabor the subject again?" he sighed wearily.

"No, there is no need, especially since your ears are deafened to my pleas," she said accusingly.

"I made you no promises," he reminded her. "Pray, do not allow your ponderings to lead you to expect that you can extract a formal commitment from me," he cautioned. "For if that is what you anticipate, I fear that you shall have a lengthy wait and be sorely disappointed."

"I *expect* nothing from you," she said, her eyes sparkling bitterly. "And I only await the day which will render my deliverance from you!" She jerked her arm from his grasp and whirled to present him her back. "Pray, do not waste your thoughts on me. Attend to your letter."

Derek solemnly considered her proud back, and he gave a disgusted sigh before ripping the envelope open. As his dark eyes quickly perused the bold script, the unsightly scowl that darkened his handsome features slowly blossomed into a wide grin. With a loud whoop, he grabbed Meghan about the waist and swung her around to face him. Without warning, he brought his mouth down upon hers in a tempestuous kiss that left her breathless. Her senses reeled when he finally pulled his blistering hot lips from hers.

"I assume that the news you received was of a pleasing nature." Meghan raised a shaky hand to assess the damage inflicted upon her coiffure.

"Indeed!" he cried, smiling happily.

"Oh," Meghan muttered. She was beside herself with curiosity as to the contents of the missive, but she vowed silently that she would swallow her tongue before she would grant him the satisfaction of jesting at her questions. "It's nearly time for Sophie to sound the dinner bell." She retreated toward the barn door. "I think I shall go up to the house."

"What! Are you not going to bombard me with a multitude of questions?" he teased her.

"No," she murmured quietly and slipped through the doorway to emerge into the bright June sunshine.

"But I have grown accustomed to your pesky inquisitions." Derek was at her elbow. "Indeed, I shall be sorely disappointed if you ask me nothing." He halted her with his hand on her forearm. "Go on. Ask me. I know your head is positively alive with all manner of suppositions." His eyes twinkled merrily with mischievous intent.

"Derek, I know not of what you speak," she mumbled tiredly. "If you wish to enlighten me as to the substance of your letter, so be it. If not, then it is my sincere entreaty that you play your little pranks elsewhere, for I am weary of *all* of your silly games."

"You may feel differently when I leave in a few days," he informed her curtly and resumed his progress toward the house.

"What? What do you mean? Where are you going?" she blurted out unthinkingly and hurried after him. It was then that she noticed the victorious gleam on his face, and she realized, too late, that she had fallen for his trap. "Forget I asked. You may leave and, I pray, never return," she said tartly as she stormed past him to clamor up the steps.

"Oh, no." Derek was again beside her, his eyes shining gaily with mirth. "It is your nature to be inquisitive, my sweet, and I would have you no other way." He opened the door so that she might enter the house. "To be frank, I rather like to imagine that your incessant questioning denotes an interest in my concerns." He gently nudged her chin upward till their eyes met. "Will you forgive me my childish taunting?"

Meghan looked into his warm eyes and shamelessly admitted to herself that she would forgive him anything if he but asked. But to Derek, she merely nodded her head.

"Good." He proffered his arm. "Shall we dine?"

Meghan linked her arm with his and stepped with him to the dining-room table. Derek held the chair for her while she sat down; then he claimed his own chair at the head of the table. Meghan sat quietly while Nicholas served them from the sideboard, her eyes ever glued to the slip of paper in Derek's hand.

She watched as Derek absently stuffed the letter into his pocket and addressed Nicholas, "Will you please inform Lettie that Mrs. Chandler and I will be dining out this evening?"

"Yes, Massah." the servant replied obediently.

"And tell Hank that I would like the buggy brought to the house by six-thirty," he continued. "Oh, and Nicholas, explain to Robert that we will not require his services this evening. I shall drive the buggy myself."

"Yes, Massah, I'll see to it right away." Nicholas exited the room to deliver the messages as instructed.

"Was that the content of the letter? An invitation to dinner?" Meghan could not fathom why Derek would be this secretive over a mere dinner invitation.

"No. I rode over to the Tyler's this morning following my routine inspection of the fields. I had not seen Jason and Miranda since I returned from England." He sampled a slice of the thick roast beef that had been piled upon his plate.

"And how were they?" Meghan politely inquired.

"Fine. They had just returned from Baton Rouge and had not yet learned of my *marriage*. So naturally, Miranda insisted that we join them for supper this evening. Fact is, they cannot wait to get a look at you." He put his fork down and gazed at her thoughtfully. "I realize it is short notice, and if you would rather postpone the meeting until a more convenient time, I could dispatch a messenger to the Tyler's with an appropriate apology," he offered.

"That will not be necessary. They are your friends, and I am quite able to suffer a little inconvenience from time to time," she conceded.

"Thank you." He grasped her hand and briefly

289

brushed it against his lips. "Not only is Jason a dear friend, he is perhaps the most influential member of this community. Some even feel that he will be our next governor. Why, the fact that Tylerville is named for him is just one tribute to his honor."

"Is this the couple I was supposedly going to serve as governess?"

"Yes."

"I shall not be able to look them in the eye," she sighed morosely. "To think how quickly I clutched at your suggestion. Had I but considered your plan more carefully, I would have realized that you likely had some devious scheme in mind."

"And if you had," he leaned closer to whisper his statement in her ear, "I would be tossing and turning my nights away in a cold and lonely bed."

"I sincerely doubt that *your* bed would have remained cold very long, Derek," she said sarcastically.

"Well." He shrugged his shoulders and raised one hand in a noncommittal gesture. "I would not worry overmuch about meeting the Tylers, were I you," he said, returning to the original topic of their conversation. "Jason and I will likely adjourn to the library for a political discussion while you relate to Miranda the intense joy you experience daily by being my wife."

"Oh, you!" Meghan scoffed, but she was not to be permitted the courtesy of a rebuttal.

Having concluded his meal, Derek excused himself and withdrew from the room, taking the mysterious letter with him. But later, when Meghan climbed the stairs to their chamber to select a suitable gown for the evening's dinner engagement, she found Derek soaking in a tub of hot water, flamboyantly puffing on a cigar.

Meghan eased quietly into the room, carefully closing the door behind her, but she suddenly gripped her stomach as the strong scent of the tobacco rendered her momentarily weak with nausea.

"Meghan?" Derek rose halfway from the tub, fearful that she was going to faint.

"I . . . I am all right," she stammered weakly.

"Does the smoke bother you?"

"I'm afraid so. I can return after you conclude your bath." She turned toward the door.

"Nonsense." He immediately extinguished the annoying cigar.

"Thank you." Meghan stepped to the open window and gratefully inhaled the summer-sweet fresh air.

"I am pleased you came. I was just about to send for you." He observed her curiously with a concerned expression. Derek extended his hand toward the bedside commode and the envelope that lay thereon. "I would like you to read that."

The color had returned to Meghan's cheeks by the time she plucked the letter from the commode and sat down upon the bed. She examined it for a long moment before she raised her eyes uncertainly to Derek.

"Go ahead," he urged.

Meghan carefully unfolded the paper and quickly scanned the words that were written on the page. "Andrew Jackson," she murmured. "I believe I have heard that name before. Yes, I am positive that Papa spoke of him, none too kindly, as I recall." She returned the letter to its envelope and replaced it on the commode. "Is he a friend of yours?" She stood up.

"Yes, I suppose you could call him that. And your father likely mentioned Andrew's name in association with the Battle of New Orleans in the war with England."

"Yes, that was it," she agreed. "Papa was furious that a mere Yankee should fare so well against British forces." She stepped to the armoire and began to rummage through her dresses.

"Can Abbey not do that for you?" he asked tersely.

"Yes, she could," Meghan said slowly then turned eyes widened with feigned innocence to him. "Would you like me to summon her *now*?" She glanced pointedly at his bath.

"No." His voice held an air of distinct agitation. "But you may wait until I have finished and *then* summon her. There is no need for you to do that when I have provided a maid to serve you."

"Yes, Derek," she sighed, glancing around hopelessly for some task to occupy her hands. Shyly, she approached the bathtub. "Would you like me to wash your back?" she offered timidly.

"Please." He leaned forward and Meghan dropped to her knees beside the tub and vigorously lathered his back.

"In the letter, Mr. Jackson invited you to the Hermitage for a visit," she quoted the missive. "Where is that?"

"The Hermitage is the name of Andrew's plantation," he explained. "It is located near Nashville, Tennessee, and that, my lovely"—he traced the line of her jaw with a dripping wet finger and watched as the water trickled a path down her slender neck to disappear between the crevice of her mounded bosom—"is a very long journey from here."

"Are you going?" she asked.

"Yes."

"Will you be gone long?" she continued reluctantly, afraid that she might anger him if she belabored the subject.

"Well, now, that will depend on how much money I gamble away." He witnessed the disapproving frown on her lips and chuckled deeply. "It is not what you think," he assured her. "Andrew has a stable of fine horses and an incurable weakness for racing them," he explained. "And the infuriating aspect is that he usually wins."

"Which only serves to make you more determined to be victorious." She nodded knowingly.

"Ah, little one." He looked at her with sincere admiration. "You know me well, considering that we have been together for only a few short weeks. I have not visited the Jacksons in some time; so that leads me to believe that Andrew suspects that I have acquired some formidable stock since my last visit. I did not own Trojan at that time," he added.

"Do you intend to race him?" Meghan rinsed the soap from his back and dried her hands on the towel before handing it to Derek.

"I have considered it." He stood up and fastened the towel around his trim waist. "But I've had my eye on another horse that has impressed me greatly." He glanced at her mischievously from the corner of his eye.

"Oh, and have I seen him?" she asked, genuinely interested in the topic.

"Yes," he chuckled slyly. "Meghan, I have taunted you enough this day. The horse I speak of is your own. I have admired Champion since that day in London when you rode him so magnificently."

"You wish to take Champion with you, so that you may race him against Mr. Jackson's horses?" Meghan asked softly.

"Only if you agree, my pet." He brushed his lips against hers as he walked past her to the chair upon which had been laid a fresh suit of clothes. "I would not race him if you did not grant me leave to do so."

Meghan thoughtfully considered all that had been said, and turning to him she said, "He has never been raced formally, you realize. I am sure that there is a great deal of training involved to sufficiently prepare a horse for a race."

"Yes, indeed. We shall have to search diligently to find a capable jockey."

"Here?"

"No, we would stand a better chance in Nashville," he admitted. "But fear not, my pretty, you shall have final approval of the man we select to commandeer your behemoth."

Meghan stared at him blankly for a full minute before she completely digested the implication of his statement. Derek had just concluded dressing and had turned from viewing his appearance in the mirror when Meghan flung her arms around his neck and covered his face with a covey of appreciative, butterfly kisses.

"Whoa!" he laughed good-naturedly. "To what do I owe this pleasant display?"

"Do you mean it?" She paused breathlessly. "Am I to go with you?"

"Of course." He snuggled her close to him. "True, the trip will be tedious, but I shall likely be away from Chandalara for several weeks, and I care not to take the risk of returning to an empty house."

"Where would I go?" she asked softly, lowering her gaze.

"I don't know, nor do I care to find out," he retorted.

Meghan smiled at him sweetly and rested her cheek against the broad expanse of his chest. The scent of the freshly laundered shirt mingled with his clean, masculine essence, and she sighed contentedly in his embrace.

"Meghan, you are positively beastly to entice me this way when you know well and good that I do not presently have the time to wile away in your arms. I have a number of matters to tend to before we can

294

depart for Tennessee," he scolded her lightly and set her firmly from his grasp. "But fear not," he granted her a devilish grin, "I shall remedy this afternoon's oversight when we return from this evening's engagement."

He sauntered casually toward the door as he delivered his next statement: "I shall send Abbey to assist you with your preparation for this evening, and perhaps you can begin selecting those articles you will take with you on Monday."

"*Monday*!" Meghan whirled, thunderstruck. "I cannot possibly be ready by the day after tomorrow!" she shrieked. But the door had already closed behind him and Meghan slumped to the bed in a daze, knowing that when Monday arrived, she would be prepared to embark on their journey.

Chapter Thirteen

As Derek instructed, Hank brought the buggy to the mansion at precisely six-thirty. Meghan was sitting before the mirror in the master bedroom, applying the faintest hint of rouge to her colorless cheeks. Morosely, she considered her reflection and concluded that she needed to spend more time outside to rejuvenate her waning complexion. She had risen from the chair and begun to smooth the delicate silk skirt of her mauve gown when her attention was drawn to the window by a curious clicking sound.

Somewhat perplexed, Meghan strode to the window and pulled back the curtain and narrowly escaped being pummeled by an airborne pebble. She poked her head through the opening and her eyes fastened upon Derek who was positioned by the buggy, his head turned upward toward the chamber window. He held his pocket watch in one hand and methodically bounced a handful of pebbles in his other open palm. But when Meghan appeared at the window, he dropped the rocks to the ground, positioned his hands on his hips and planted his feet firmly as he gazed up at her.

"Your chariot awaits, madam." He bowed formally, extending one arm toward the buggy in a gallant gesture.

"Really, Derek!" she chided. "Is this anyway to summon a lady to your carriage?" She aspired to sound disapproving, but she was actually quite amused.

"Perhaps not," he said with a shrug. "But it is *my* way and it usually works. For you see, my pet," he glanced purposely at his watch, "if I do not find you standing before me in precisely thirty seconds, I shall be forced to depart without you."

"You would not dare!" she challenged him, knowing full well that he would dare to do whatever might please him.

In response to her declaration, Derek calmly clasped his hands behind his back and began to rock gently back and forth on his heels. "Twenty-five seconds," he coolly informed her.

"Oh, you . . . !" she seethed hotly as she drew her head from the window and glanced about the room wildly for her shawl. She finally located it, draped across the back of a chair, and hurriedly grabbed it as she dashed frantically from the room. She raced down the steps, across the main hall and emerged breathlessly onto the porch with seconds to spare.

"Record timing, my sweet. Tell me, was your speedy arrival due to the fact that you did not wish to spend an evening apart from your endearing *husband*?" Derek chuckled merrily as she struggled to regain her breath. "Perhaps Andrew will have a footrace in which I can enter you," he continued to tease her.

"Pray not, m'lord," she retorted sourly. "For once given the opportunity to flee, you may well believe that I shall grasp it eagerly." She reluctantly accepted the hand he extended to steady her as she climbed into the buggy.

Derek guffawed loudly at her retort as he walked to the other side of the buggy and climbed in beside her.

Meghan ignored his laughter and shifted in her seat till she discovered a comfortable position, while Derek devoted his attention to maneuvering the team away from the plantation house. He handled the pair of matched bays with an expertise that Meghan now took for granted. Somehow she could not imagine Derek ever being confronted with an obstacle that he could not master.

The drive to the Tyler plantation was pleasant and they conversed easily as Derek maneuvered the team along the picturesque, country road. Never in Meghan's wildest speculations about America had she envisioned such a beautiful, breathtaking landscape. And her reluctance at meeting the Tylers seemed to vanish when Derek turned the buggy down the lane which led them to the Willow Wood plantation house. It was an impressive mansion, very similar in architectural design to Chandalara, although Willow Wood seemed larger.

"What do you think of it?" Derek inquired.

"It is lovely," Meghan murmured. "But I prefer Chandalara."

"I am flattered, pet, but please refrain from voicing such an opinion to Miranda." He pulled the team to a halt before the august mansion. "She takes great pride in showing off Willow Wood to her guests."

"Really, Derek," Meghan replied saucily. "I am well acquainted with the deportment one displays while a guest in another's home," she haughtily informed him.

"Just a friendly reminder." He kissed her hand as he assisted her from the buggy and led her to the house.

They were received by the butler who promptly escorted them to the plush drawing room where their hosts awaited them.

"So, this is the young lady who finally managed to strap a bridle on our bucking stallion," boasted the gentleman whom Meghan assumed to be her host. "Permit me to be the first to extend my sincerest felicitations." He bowed formally before her.

"Thank you," Meghan murmured sweetly.

Meghan estimated the man to be in his mid-fifties. And though he was well preserved for his age, there was a telltale hint of gray in his distinguished black mane. He was as tall as Derek and while the years had obviously added weary lines to his rugged face, Meghan decided that he was still a truly handsome man. He possessed a winning smile and he spoke with the same smooth tone of self-confidence as did Derek. He seemed to be an amiable person, but why did Meghan suddenly grow uncomfortable when Jason Tyler approached her?

To rid herself of this eerie feeling, Meghan gave her attention to Mrs. Tyler. She was near her husband in age, very small in stature, and quite slender. The uneasy feeling Meghan experienced earlier vanished completely when she met the warm, friendly smile of her hostess. Miranda Tyler was a genuinely kind person, Meghan decided, and she immediately felt at ease with the older woman.

"Tell me—it is Meghan, is it not?" Jason continued in a friendly voice.

She nodded.

"Miranda and I have been wondering the livelong day as to what you would look like. You know, exactly what kind of girl it took to finally get Derek to settle down. Lord knows he has had ample opportunity to do so before this, what with the entourage of females he usually attracts." He leaned closer to Meghan. "You will tell us your secret, won't you?"

"Jason!" Miranda gently scolded her husband. "You are embarrassing the child."

"Nonsense! Why, it's no secret that every eligible maid in Tylerville has tried to latch on to Derek."

"Your husband is absolutely right, Mrs. Tyler. Derek has made it a point to enlighten me as to his rather, how shall I phrase it, *infamous* past." She winked mischievously at her hostess and offered Derek a coyly submissive grin.

"Just my way of keeping her in check, Miranda." Derek defended his actions. "This way, Meghan knows that if she does not behave, I have a choice selection from which I may choose a replacement." He placed a secure arm around Meghan's waist and drew her to his side.

"You would be ten kinds of a fool if you ever allowed anything as ridiculous as that to happen." Jason stepped forward and took Meghan's hand in his. "You have won yourself a lovely bride, Derek, and one of whom you can be justly proud." He lifted Meghan's hand in a friendly gesture and gently brushed it against his lips. But only Meghan observed his startled expression when his eyes beheld the wedding ring that adorned her finger.

Whatever the reason for his reaction to the gem,

299

Jason quickly masked his wonderment and skillfully maneuvered Meghan away from Derek's side, carefully entwining her arm with his own. "Do you not think it is time we adjourn to the dining room, Miranda?" he addressed his wife.

"I certainly do." Miranda graciously accepted the arm that Derek proffered to her. "Why, Cora has been cooking and baking ever since your visit this morning, Derek."

The dining room was as elegantly furnished as the drawing room had been and the food on which they dined had obviously been skillfully prepared. The beef was thick and juicy and the wild turkey was tender and mildly flavored. The potatoes had been cooked in a smooth, creamy sauce and were served with an array of marvelously prepared vegetable dishes, and the bread was piping hot and fresh from the oven.

To Meghan's consternation, the conversation focused principally on them. The Tylers were sincerely interested in how Meghan and Derek had met and married and Meghan was intensely relieved when Derek took it upon himself to handle the response to their questions.

"Just imagine, Jason. A whirlwind courtship and marriage and then to be whisked away on an ocean voyage for a honeymoon trip. And to think, all those weeks in a ship's cabin," she sighed wistfully. "How utterly romantic!"

Derek noticed Meghan squirm uncomfortably in her chair, and his watchful eyes observed the faint blush that darkened her pale cheeks. Without thinking, he reached across the table and captured her trembling hands and gave them an encouraging squeeze.

"Romantic, indeed," he whispered hoarsely and though Jason and Miranda were aware of the words he spoke, when Meghan looked into his intense eyes, it was

300

as though they were completely alone. "We must make a note to repeat the voyage, say, on our tenth anniversary," he said warmly and Meghan smiled at him shyly in return and could but nod her head in agreement.

Dessert was served, and shortly thereafter Miranda suggested that she and Meghan retire to the drawing room with their coffee to exchange some friendly gossip. "I simply must fill you in on all the local families," she explained. "Besides, I am quite certain that Jason and Derek have some political issues to discuss. Mind now, Jason. Meghan and I shall grant you men but a reasonable length of time to hash over your infernal political schemes and smoke your smelly cigars, then we demand an equal share of your attention. Agreed?"

"Agreed, Miranda," Derek answered for the two men. And he gave Meghan an encouraging nod as she followed Miranda from the room.

"I do declare, Meghan. You have simply been the greatest help. Why, I should have sent this tablecloth off to my niece in Charleston weeks ago and if you had not helped me finish it, Lord only knows when I would have gotten around to it." Miranda stood to fold the piece, stopping momentarily to examine Meghan's work. "My dear, you do the most exquisite work, such tiny, even stitches. I simply haven't the patience, I suppose. Tell me, wherever did you learn to embroider so beautifully?"

"At school," Meghan replied. "But my stepmother taught me the finer points and encouraged me to take my time and do a neat job. But, Mrs. Tyler—"

"Tut, tut. Did we not agree to dispense with formalities, Meghan?"

301

"Yes, Miranda." Meghan corrected. "I was about to say that I would be happy to show you how to make the more intricate stitches, if you would like."

"Why, yes, dear. That would be lovely." She folded the tablecloth and placed it neatly on a side table. "Goodness me," she exclaimed suddenly. "Just look at the time." She pointed to the clock on the mantel. "I shall have to scold those two properly for keeping us waiting. Excuse me, dear."

When Miranda had gone Meghan suddenly felt very alone in the large room. During the time spent working on the tablecloth, her hostess had kept a vivid conversation going with Meghan offering but a few comments. But now Meghan felt stifled by the silence. She stood up, thinking that if she moved about the uneasy feeling would disappear, and began to examine the elaborate furnishings in the room.

Her eyes fell instantly upon an oriental, porcelain figure and she fingered it lovingly, wondering if Derek had brought it to the Tylers from one of his trips abroad. As if in a dream, a voice floated across the room to answer her unspoken question.

"That particular piece was a gift from your husband," Jason said, and he casually stepped toward her. "If memory serves me, I think he brought it with him on a return trip from the Orient two years ago."

"It is lovely," she whispered, looking beyond him to the door, hoping that Derek might be standing there, but to her extreme dismay, Derek was nowhere to be seen.

Jason noticed the direction of her gaze and hastened to account for Derek's absence. "They walked down to the stables for a moment. You see, Derek gave one of his young colts to Miranda just before he left for England and Miranda wanted to show him how the animal

302

was faring."

"I see." She smiled softly. But for some unfathomable reason, Meghan's uneasiness was growing more intense the longer she remained alone with Jason.

"I told them I would show you to the garden and that they should join us there." He extended his arm and Meghan knew of no way she could decline the invitation without appearing rude.

"I imagine the garden will be lovely this time of year." Meghan smiled at him warmly and accepted his arm, praying that her nervous anxiety was appropriately camouflaged.

If Jason was aware of her anxiousness, he gave no indication. "Miranda takes great pride in her garden, as she does the entire estate. You know, Meghan, we have been married for nearly twenty-five years. Miranda is the light of my life," he said fondly and Meghan knew that the words he spoke were genuine. Jason Tyler worshiped his wife. "I only hope that you and Derek experience the same happiness that Miranda and I have shared over the years."

"Thank you, Mr. Tyler." She looked away from him to view the garden and shield her face from his ever-searching eyes. "Miranda has every right to be proud. The garden is exquisite."

"She will be pleased to know that you approve."

They lapsed into a silence that only served to magnify the growing tenseness that Meghan had experienced ever since she found herself alone with Jason. But was she imagining things, or did he seem to be ill-at-ease with her as well? Meghan turned slightly to better study the man's profile and was startled to discover his gaze intently upon her.

"You're uncomfortable, Meghan. Perhaps the night air is too chilly for you," he suggested.

"No," she replied. "I don't mean to appear squeamish. It is just that I . . ." she faltered uncertainly. "May I be candid?"

"Please do."

"Earlier this evening when you noticed my wedding ring . . ." She nervously twisted the gem around her finger as she spoke.

"Yes?" He raised an eyebrow questioningly.

"Well," she stammered on, unsure of her next statement, "for a fleeting moment you appeared stunned, as if . . . as if you recognized the ring. You must admit that it has a rather unusual setting. There cannot be many like it in existence."

"How right you are. And, I might add, you are a very observant, young lady." He led her to a bench along the garden path and motioned for her to sit with him. "If you would permit me to reminisce for a few moments."

"Of course."

"You see, I was not born in America. Like Derek, I was uprooted from my home and sent to this land almost thirty years ago. While in England, I became infatuated with a very lovely girl and hoped to make her my wife." He paused for a moment to draw a cigar from his pocket. "Will it offend you if I smoke?" he politely inquired.

"Please, do whatever will make you feel at ease."

Thankfully, he lit the cigar and continued with his narrative: "A friend of mine in London was a goldsmith and he told me that he could fashion a wedding ring for me so beautiful and unique in design that no one else in the world would possess one exactly like it." He turned to gaze at Meghan. "When I first beheld your ring, I thought that time had played a cruel trick on me."

"Is this the ring you had made for your beloved?" Meghan's eyes grew wide with astonishment.

"The resemblance *is* remarkable, but the odds that the ring you are wearing and the one I commissioned are one and the same are slim indeed," he assured her. "Perhaps you would care to tell me how you came upon your ring." He seemed curious. "Did it belong to your mother?"

"Oh, no, Mr. Tyler. Mother died when I was quite young and whatever jewels she possessed were locked away by my father. He loved her so dearly that he could not bear to see me wear them," she explained. "The ring belonged to Derek's mother and when we were married, Derek insisted that I have it."

"Derek's mother?" Jason's eyebrows shot up in surprise. "I didn't know that he kept in touch with her after he left England."

"Well, it *is* a rather awkward story, Mr. Tyler."

"And one that need not be bantered about, my sweet," added a deep voice from the shadows behind them.

Meghan whirled to see Derek and Miranda emerge from the darkness onto the lighted garden path. The look on his serious face was brooding, although Meghan could not readily surmise if he was angry with her.

"We were simply discussing Meghan's exquisite, wedding ring, Derek. It was not my intent to pry into your private affairs," Jason genuinely apologized.

"I have never attempted to keep the fact of my illegitimate birth a secret, and while I admit that I am not overly proud of my origin, neither am I ashamed of it." His eyes locked with Meghan's as he spoke and they never wavered from their target throughout his delivery. "My mother is a particularly sacred topic and I prefer that she not be discussed as though she were some juicy bit of gossip."

"I . . . I would not do that!" Hot tears burned at

the corners of Meghan's eyes, and she knew that if she had to endure Derek's harsh stare much longer, she would not be able to prevent them from flooding her cheeks. Without warning, Meghan gathered her skirts in her hands and flew past Derek to the door that readmitted her to the house, granting her temporary respite from his scorn.

"Perhaps I should go to her," Miranda offered.

"That will not be necessary, Miranda." Derek placed a restraining hand on her arm to prevent her from leaving. "I instructed your man to bring our buggy to the front of the house. I shall likely find Meghan waiting for me there." He started to leave. "On behalf of Meghan and myself, I would like to thank you for your hospitality and apologize for Meghan's abrupt behavior."

"You *were* a bit harsh with her, Derek," Jason reminded him.

"Perhaps," he stated indifferently. "But I am a rigid taskmaster and Meghan well knows that. There are certain infractions I simply cannot abide."

"Humph!" Miranda snorted. "You sound as if Meghan were your pupil instead of your wife. A caution, Derek. Wield your whip carefully, lest you drive that sweet young thing from your arms." She lifted her skirts and followed Meghan's route of retreat.

"It would seem that I am outnumbered," Derek grumbled.

"Anytime a woman sides against you, you're outnumbered," Jason laughed good-naturedly and slapped him on the back. "I'm just grateful they don't have the vote."

"Perish the thought," Derek bellowed.

"Well, you best go and make up with her. Need I remind you how cold the nights can get on the trail?"

Jason walked with him to the front porch. "Have a safe journey," he called as Derek walked down the path to the buggy.

As Derek suspected, Meghan was already positioned on the front seat. Without a word, Derek took the reins from the stableboy and climbed into the buggy. The drive home started out to be as chilling as was the night air. But Derek could endure no more than ten minutes of the frigid silence before he directed the team off the road, beneath a clump of trees.

"Why are we stopping?" Meghan demanded.

"So, you have not lost your tongue after all." He tried to sound jovial. "For a moment I was concerned."

The venomous look she cast in his direction was enough to cause him to forgo any further attempts to humor her. Instead, he placed his hands firmly on her shoulders and forcibly turned her till she faced him.

"Meghan, I did not mean to attack you so mercilessly, but you are well aware that my mother is a touchy subject with me."

"And you are constantly overlooking one important factor whenever you mention her to me," she interrupted harshly. "Derek," her tone grew suddenly soft and she placed a slightly quivering hand on his to steady her jittery nerves. "Elizabeth was your mother and my father committed a vile and cruel act when he sent you away from her. But please try to remember that Elizabeth was my stepmother for a very long time. I would never defile her precious memory by spreading malicious gossip about her.

"Mr. Tyler had merely expressed an interest in my wedding band and I told him it had belonged to your mother. That is all." She folded her hands primly in her lap and focused her gaze away from Derek and onto the fleeting shadows the breeze created in the gently swaying tree branches.

"I see," he responded softly. "Forgive me my earlier outburst. It was totally unwarranted and I behaved like a brainless dolt." He reached over to claim her hand and was surprised that she did not jerk it from his grasp. "You must have loved her quite dearly," he whispered gently.

"I did." She sniffled at the tears which again appeared in her eyes. "She replaced the mother I lost as a child, and, in many instances, filled in for the father who did not want me around. I am quite certain she ofttimes found it difficult to care for the child of the man who so mistreated her," she said sobbing uncontrollably as she struggled to draw her shawl more tightly about her.

"Cold?" Derek asked.

Meghan nodded stiffly.

"Here." He extended his arm and drew her closer, placing an arm about her shoulder and pulling her securely against him so she could share his warmth. "Better?" He tipped her chin up and gazed into her flawless face.

"Yes, thank you," she murmured quietly.

They sat thus entwined for several moments before Derek stirred and, reaching for the reins, he asked, "Are you now ready to continue homeward, my pet?"

"Yes."

"As my lady wishes." He started to drive away, but halted abruptly. "How silly of me. I almost forgot," he murmured slyly and Meghan could see that his eyes twinkled mischievously in the dim moonlight.

"What?" she asked warily.

"It's an old Louisiana custom," he spoke smoothly, all the while pulling her toward him, encircling her with his powerful arms. "Whenever one pauses beneath a magnolia tree with one's favorite girl, he cannot continue his journey until he has coaxed a kiss from the damsel. Bad luck is certain to befall the unlucky lad who has an unrelenting sweetheart."

He tilted her head back and as he spoke, his lips started downward to claim their pleasant reward. Meghan moaned contentedly as he gently brushed her lips aside and inserted his tongue into her mouth to feast on its sweetness. His kiss was not harsh or demanding, but rather soft and searching, and his movements were slow and deliberate and, she suddenly realized, *tender*.

Always before, Derek had kissed her the way a man would kiss a harlot. His kisses had been fierce and demanding, as if he intended to reaffirm that he had purchased the goods and could handle them to his liking. Meghan could almost understand the harshness in his dealings with her and in her confused state, she rather welcomed them. But this tender, yes, affectionate display was a side of Derek she had never witnessed. And truthfully, Meghan was not certain that she could cope with it.

"Well, madam." Derek's voice was thick with desire when he finally tore his mouth from hers. "That will have to sustain you until I can get you home." He gave a whistle and the team jerked forward.

Meghan remained silent for the remainder of the trip, occasionally glancing upward to gaze into the handsome face that was silhouetted by the moonlight, but it was to no avail. She could extract no more from the expression on his face than she could from the kiss he had just bestowed upon her.

Automatically, Meghan's fingers lifted to stroke the flesh that had recently known the passionate caress of his lips. No, it was not possible that Derek might be developing some sort of romantic feeling for her, she decided. She must not permit her mind to harbor such a ludicrous thought. Had he not told her that very day that she should not expect anything from him in the form of a permanent relationship? That one day, without warning, he might cast his sights on another beauty and send her on her way.

Oh, Derek, she sighed inwardly. I did not mean for it to happen, but I have fallen helplessly in love with you and the thought that you could put me aside for another leaves me feeling empty inside. She hastily lowered her gaze, fearing that if he saw her expression, he might easily guess the contents of her troubled thoughts. And that was one thing she must never allow.

Derek must never learn of my feelings for him, she thought dismally. I think that I would truly die when he turned his mocking eyes on me and laughed at my folly. Have I not repeatedly told him that I hate him and await only the day of deliverance from him? Would it not be a grand victory for him to learn that he has won my stubborn heart? But it shall be *my* victory instead, for I shall never give him the opportunity to ridicule me by denouncing my love.

"It shall be my secret," she whispered beneath her breath and her words were carried off by the gentle, summer breeze. "You shall never know of my love for you, Derek Chandler."

Meghan awoke before Derek the next morning and quickly scrambled from the bed to begin preparations for their journey. After partaking of a light breakfast, she instructed Nicholas to see that the luggage was aired out before bringing it to the master chamber. She then returned to the upstairs chamber, entering the room quietly so as not to disturb Derek.

He lay on his back, arms folded neatly across his chest with the sternest of expressions adorning his handsome face, almost as if he contemplated some critical dilemma in his sleep. The sheet had been kicked aside in defiance of the early morning heat and while Meghan was not displeased with the view, she did not relish the thought of one of the servants coming in to be greeted by the same sight.

Meghan eased the door shut and tiptoed to the bed, reaching across him to pull the sheet above his waist. Once this had been accomplished, she made her way to the armoire to select those items she would take with her to Tennessee. As she examined each article for stylishness and durability, she softly hummed a popular tune, completely lost in her work.

Consequently, she did not notice that the figure on the bed no longer slept, but had lithely moved to stand just behind her. Nor was she to receive an advance warning as two powerful arms swept around her to capture her in their embrace. In one sweeping motion he lifted and turned her, enabling him to gaze into her bewildered face.

"Ah," he sighed wistfully as he leaned forward to place a kiss against the hollow of her throat. "Can it be that Venus, the goddess of love and beauty, has slipped into my chamber?" he whispered hoarsely against her throat as his lips traced a line of feathery soft kisses to her mouth, where he paused to grin at her devilishly.

"Derek!" she scolded sternly. "You simply must stop sneaking up on me like that. You startled me."

"Sorry, love." His hands expertly parted the material of her robe and slipped beneath the folds to caress the warm flesh along her waist.

"Derek," she whimpered pleadingly. "I have a mountain of things to do if you expect me to go with

311

you tomorrow. I have not the time to cuddle now."

"Cuddle?" Derek sounded amused at her choice of words. "Why do you protest, my sweet, when I am but warming my hands?" Even as he spoke his hands traveled to her breasts then down to her hips in a rhythmic motion that set her flesh afire with desire for him.

At last he ceased the maddening torment and removed his hands from her waist, taking care to retie the sash before he dropped his hands to his side. With an amused chuckle he strode to the bedside table upon which he had placed his personal effects upon retiring the night before. He selected his watch from the array of articles on the table and nonchalantly looked at the time.

"Meghan!" he addressed her menacingly. "What have you done, letting me oversleep this way? Do you know what time it is?"

"No." She shrugged her shoulders indifferently and returned to her work.

"It's nearly eight o'clock." He began to pull on his clothes. "You will have to hurry and dress, else we will be late for church."

"Church? Derek, how can you possibly expect me to get things organized when you keep dragging me away from my responsibilities?"

"Sophie and Abbey can help you when we return."

"But, Derek," she protested.

"Save your entreaties. Perhaps I am not the most religious man in the world, Meghan, but I realize that the Lord has given me a great deal for which I am truly thankful. Is it asking too much for me to grant Him one morning a week to express my gratitude?"

"No," she whispered humbly.

"Then you will accompany me?" It was more of a

command than a question.

"Yes, Derek," she sighed softly and turned to select a Sunday dress from the armoire.

"I shall instruct Hank to bring the carriage around and inform Robert that he will be driving us." He stepped to her and pressed an affectionate kiss to her cheek. "I'll meet you downstairs as soon as you are dressed."

"I shan't keep you waiting."

Derek nodded as he shrugged his broad shoulders into an elegantly tailored coat and hurriedly left the room.

On a day when she had hoped to secure a little rest before beginning the long, tedious trip to Tennessee, Meghan was to quickly learn that although the Sabbath was a day of rest for many, this particular Sunday was to hold no peace for her. After church services had been completed, Wade Hampton accompanied them home for Sunday dinner as was his usual routine. And it was late afternoon before she could extricate herself from Derek and his guest and climb the steps to the master bedroom to begin packing.

Nicholas had followed her instructions and brought the luggage to the room, and when Meghan opened the door, she discovered that Sophie and Abbey had already undertaken a major portion of the task. Upon seeing their mistress, they immediately suggested that she return to her guest and allow them to finish packing. But Meghan firmly stood her ground, insisting that she needed to discuss certain household matters with them before leaving.

It was nearly time for supper when Meghan next emerged from the chamber, her packing at last completed. She was at the top of the landing when she became aware of angry voices in the main hallway directly below her. One of the voices was new to her, but she immediately recognized Derek's embittered voice and she quickened her step, anxious for his safety. As she neared the bottom of the staircase, she was presented with the awesome sight of Derek involved in a heated confrontation with a man she had never seen before.

"You best pack your belongings and move the hell out of my house!" the man shouted at Derek and with a sagging heart, Meghan realized the identity of the stranger.

"I'll not discuss the issue further, Iverson," Derek replied stonily and motioned for Nicholas to open the door. "I paid you well for Chandalara and I shall not permit you to badger me about its ownership. If you have any questions concerning the legalities of owner-ship, I suggest you contact my lawyer." Derek grabbed the man roughly by the shirt, dragged him to the door, and shoved him ruthlessly out. Then he turned in disgust to reenter the drawing room.

At that moment Meghan's alert eyes observed the man pull a knife from his pocket, and with horror, she saw the man take three angry steps toward Derek and violently thrust the knife at Derek's unprotected back. The following sequence of events happened so rapidly that later Meghan could scarcely recall their content. But when her frightened eyes beheld Derek's perilous situation, common sense prevailed and she screamed a throaty warning to him.

In an instant, Derek turned and knocked the weapon from the attacker's hand. And this time when Derek escorted the man to the doorstep, he was none too gentle with his dismissal.

"I'll be back!" Iverson promised as he stumbled to his feet, gingerly testing the side of his face that Derek's angry fist had just moments before caressed.

"Iverson," Derek said threateningly, "many a man would kill you for attempting such a foolhardy stunt. And while I am indeed tempted to do just that, I shall squelch the overwhelming desire to see you squirm at my feet like the lowly worm that you are—this time. But you may rest assured that if you venture near my home again, the Lord God Almighty could not save you from my wrath!" Derek slammed the door and briskly turned toward the drawing room, only to have his progress halted by Meghan, who hurled herself into his arms to ensure for herself that he had not been injured.

"Oh, Derek!" she stammered helplessly. "Are you . . . are you all right? That awful man! He did not hurt you, did he?" she asked breathlessly, clinging to him so tightly that he could barely move.

"No." He gently fingered the silkiness of her fine cheek. "But had it not been for your timely warning, I could now be at the mercy of your skillful, healing hands." He gently tipped her head back and was genuinely surprised to discover that her wide eyes were bright with tears of concern for him. "Why, Meghan?" He caught a tear between thumb and forefinger. "Tears? For me? Can this perhaps mean that you *do* care—just a little?" His gaze grew more intent as he scanned her face for some explanation for her anxious behavior.

"Of course, she cares," Wade answered from the drawing room door. "My God, man, she *is* your wife and she was but doing her wifely duty by so heroically saving your life. Ah, my dear Meghan, you bungled an excellent opportunity to rid ourselves of the rogue," he added suggestively and was somewhat puzzled by the cold stares he received from the couple.

"My, but you've both grown so utterly somber. I was merely joshing, Derek, old boy." He quickly downed the remaining contents of the glass he held in his hand and retreated within the room to refresh his drink. As he

315

moved, he was overheard mumbling something about people not understanding his wit.

"I had forgotten about Wade," he whispered apologetically as he took her arm to lead her to the drawing room.

"No matter. You said nothing that should give him cause to be suspicious."

Derek placed a protective arm about her shoulder and held her close. "Perhaps we can persuade Wade to execute an early departure." He smiled at her wickedly and cast a glance toward the stairway that led to their chamber.

"As you wish, m'lord," she sighed wearily and offering him a coy grin, she added, "I prefer *almost* anything to Wade's boastful banter."

"I'm not certain I know how to interpret that remark." Derek eyed her closely.

"Good," she replied as they entered the drawing room to join Wade.

Later, when the three of them sat down to partake of the supper that Lettie had skillfully prepared, the topic that continually floated from Wade's incessantly wagging tongue centered around Sam Iverson's attack on Derek's life. Even after the meal had been concluded, and they returned to the drawing room to enjoy a quiet afterdinner drink, Wade still seemed to be obsessed with the gruesome story.

"Please, Wade," Meghan begged. "Derek was nearly killed by that madman. It is an incident that I truly wish to forget. Must we rehash the ghastly scene for the duration of your visit?" She glanced at Derek to see if he was angered with her forward manner and was surprised to note that his expression seemed to match hers.

"Derek," Wade chided, "it appears that you have neglected to properly train your wife as to her station. Are you going to sit idly by while your wife insults your dearest and closest friend?" The look on Wade's face plainly expressed that he was teasing, but had Wade taken the time to carefully examine Meghan's unhappy face, he would have surmised that she was amused by neither his monotonous chatter, nor his chastisement of her behavior.

"Were I not in total agreement with Meghan's apt appraisal, I might be persuaded to prescribe some slight reprimand," Derek replied slowly, more to intimidate Meghan than to accommodate Wade. "But the fact is, I am bored with the subject as well."

"Oh, how I yearn for the good old days when a woman knew her place and was content to hold her tongue while the menfolk discussed the more important issues of the day." Wade gazed wistfully off into space, ignoring Derek's comment.

By this time Meghan had heard all that she could endure and rising from the sofa in a huff, she walked defiantly to the door. "Important issues—humph!" she said as she pulled the door open. "I'll wager your important discussions consist of such squalid content as drinking, gambling and wenching and other such vile filth. If you will excuse me, I shall retire to my chamber and leave you *gentlemen* to your discussion." She presented them her back, and Derek was allowed the provocative view of the sway of her hips as she saucily stepped across the hall to ascend the staircase.

"She's magnificent, Derek! Why, an actress of the stage could not have delivered her lines more superbly," Wade cheered.

Even as Meghan ascended the staircase she could hear Wade's loud retort, and she had to forcibly quell the raging desire to run back to the drawing room and slap the leering smile from his hawkish face. How could Derek possibly stand to have that insufferable man around? How could he permit such a prankster to manage his businesses and invite him into his home as a friend? She paced back and forth till her temper mellowed considerably. She then washed and having changed into a comfortable dressing gown, selected a book, and climbed into bed. She was still sitting up in bed when Derek entered the room later that evening.

"Wade has departed," he informed her. "It's safe to leave your hiding place and rejoin me in the drawing room; that is, if you want to."·

"I was hiding from no one," Meghan retorted hotly. "I left simply because I could endure no more of Wade's insipid chatter. But if you have no objection, I think that I should like to retire for the night. I have suffered a tiring day and fear that tomorrow will be no better."

"As you wish." He came to stand beside the bed. "You are absolutely correct in assuming that tomorrow will be a taxing day. It shall likely set the pace for the remainder of the journey." The gaze that swept over her was warm and fondly appraising. "I shall join you later," he whispered meaningfully, leaning forward to place a kiss against her tempting mouth.

"Derek?" The sudden seriousness of her voice stayed his movement, causing him to pay special attention to her words. "Why do you tolerate him? Does he hold such an important position in your business that a replacement cannot be obtained? Are you bound to him in some way I have not been made aware?"

"Meghan . . ." The tone of his voice was ominous, and the look he turned on her warned that she was prying into an area that was not her concern.

"Did he save your life at some point in your past?" she continued, paying no heed to the threatening glint in his somber eyes.

"No."

"I thought not, for he did precious little to assist you

318

when Iverson attacked you this afternoon." She closed her book and placed it on the bedside commode. She then peered at him closely as she folded her arms across her bosom. "Perhaps the answer to my question is of a more personal nature," she said icily. "Tell me, Derek, is it because you have made love to his sister that you are obliged to retain her intolerable brother?"

"I am obligated to no one! And you would do well to remember that." He grabbed her savagely by one arm and dragged her forward; for one anxious moment, Meghan feared that he might strike her. But when she raised her free arm to shield her face, he abruptly regained control of his senses and lessened the pressure on her arm.

"I never made love to Deirdre," he said softly.

"But you said—"

"Oh, she satisfied my animal cravings for a time, I won't deny that. But there was never any love or tenderness shared between the two of us," he admitted honestly.

It is the same with you and me. The words formed in her throat, but when she opened her mouth, Derek covered her lips with his fingertips, as if he knew the words she was about to speak and would will her not to utter them.

"Do not say it, little one," he whispered gently as his finger traced a pattern along the delicate line of her cheek. "You do not know Deirdre; therefore, you cannot possibly imagine how things were between us. Now, as far as Wade is concerned, what can I say? Wade has been a good friend to me. He helped me purchase Chandalara and has assisted me on occasion when I suffered setbacks with my other enterprises. Aside from this, he looks after things here when I am away on business and Nathan is not around to care for Chandalara," he patiently explained to her.

319

"I realize that he sometimes oversteps the bounds of propriety in his speech, but that is only because the dear fellow feels that he is terribly witty. But if you cannot abide his company perhaps it would be wiser if you avoided Wade when he visits in the future," he suggested.

"Were I really your wife, you would not tolerate his behavior toward me," she said begrudgingly.

"Wade's tongue wags on, and I have long since learned to ignore it for the most part. His suggestions toward you thus far have been just that, but if he were ever foolhardy enough to attempt any advances, he would have my wrath to endure. He knows that." Derek carefully eased her back against the pillows and sat down beside her. "Don't let Wade's attitude upset you. He means well." He tried to coax a smile from her, but Meghan could not be drawn out of her somber mood. Derek emitted a long sigh and stood up. "If you will excuse me, I have arranged to meet with Nathan to discuss his responsibilities while we are away." He leaned over and pressed a kiss to her forehead. "Sleep well, for I fear that the accommodations we'll encounter on our journey shall not be as elegant as this." He extinguished the lantern and quietly withdrew from the chamber.

Chapter Fourteen

Meghan awoke early the next morning, her stomach fluttering with anxious butterflies in anticipation of the impending trip. Yawning sleepily, she rolled to her side and stretched out her arms to embrace her now familiar bedmate, only to discover that she was alone in the bed.

"Derek?" she whispered drowsily looking about the room. She was a little surprised when she did not receive a reply.

Puzzled by his absence, she ran her hand searchingly along the sheets where he usually lay and by their coolness, she determined that he had apparently spent the night elsewhere. Meghan hurriedly climbed from the bed and walked to the basin to wash the sleep from her eyes. She then donned a riding habit of brown muslin and brushing her hair till it shone, she pulled it tightly back and anchored it at the nape of her neck with brown, silk ribbons. After approving her appearance in the mirror, she descended the stairs to look for Derek.

She located him in the dining room. Derek stood at the sideboard, helping himself to a cup of coffee and, at first glance, Meghan did not recognize him. He had discarded the sleek, tailored trousers and coat she was accustomed to seeing him wear around the plantation for the more serviceable, tight-fitting buckskins he had worn on *The Lady Elizabeth*. And although Meghan was impressed with the striking picture of masculinity he presented in the garments, she was a little apprehensive. Would he revert to the cold, insensitive Derek he had been aboard the ship once they were away from his friends and he no longer had to act the part of the devoted husband for appearance's sake?

"Good morning, Meghan," he called cheerfully and sauntered over to her, pecking her lightly on the cheek. "Sleep well?" he asked as he escorted her to the table and held the chair for her till she was comfortably seated.

"It would appear that I fared better than you." She unthinkingly reached up to smooth away the dark lines that shrouded his sensitive eyes.

321

"Yes," he chuckled. "Nathan and I had a good deal to discuss." He caught her hand as she was about to withdraw it and brushed it against his lips before advancing to his own chair.

Nicholas came then to serve them and while Derek ate heartily, he noticed that Meghan picked lamely at her plate. "Is the food not to your liking?" Derek asked considerately.

"Oh, no!" she assured him. "Lettie is a marvelous cook. I simply do not have much of an appetite this morning."

"I fear that the cuisine aboard my riverboat will be sadly lacking in comparison with this feast. You should eat a hearty breakfast." He motioned for Nicholas to refill his cup. "This will be a strenuous trip and I should not like to see you grow fatigued from lack of nourishment."

Under Derek's watchful eye, Meghan dutifully cut another bite from the pile of pancakes that Nicholas had stacked upon her plate and washed it down with a drink of cold milk. "Riverboat?" She daintily wiped the corner of her mouth with a napkin. "I thought we were taking the horses."

"We are," he explained patiently. "But we shall travel aboard my boat to Natchez then overland to Nashville. I must apologize for being unable to furnish you with a proper maid servant on our journey, but I fear that Abbey would only impede our progress."

"I shall manage," Meghan murmured quietly.

"Good." He stood up. "Nathan has already departed with the wagon that is carrying our belongings, but we should be able to catch up with him before he reaches the river. I shall go and see if our mounts are ready."

Meghan joined him outside a few moments later and after tearful good-byes were exchanged with Sophie and

Abbey, Derek lifted her to her seat upon Champion. Meghan could scarcely believe how in such a short time she had grown to love Chandalara and its people, and she realized sorrowfully that she was going to miss it awfully. Her sentimental thoughts were hastily interrupted by Sophie's booming voice as she exchanged words with her master.

"Why you gotta drag that chile clean 'cross the wilderness is beyond me. Why, she barely had a chance to unpack her grip and here you is goin' traipsin' round the country agin." She wiggled her nose in abject disapproval. "Just cos *you* ain't got a lick o' sense don't mean Miz Meghan has to suffer none."

"Now, Sophie." Derek's eyes twinkled mischievously as he gave the old woman an affectionate hug. "Rachel and Andrew have been after me to take a wife even longer than you have and were I to appear at their home without my bride, I truly fear the chilling reception I would receive." He strode to his mount and lithely sprinted into the saddle. "I suggest that we strike a bargain, Sophie. You manage my house well while I am away and I shall return your mistress to you safe and sound."

"Bargain . . . humph!" Sophie placed her plump hands on her hips. "Ain't I always looked after your house whiles you rambled round the world like a stray pup with no home?"

"Yes, Sophie," Derek chuckled.

"You should start thinkin' 'bout settlin' down some now that you has finally gone and got yourself married, instead of takin' that sweet chile to that sinful city." She clucked her tongue and turned to waddle back to the house, still mumbling, "And that trail to Nashville. All that thievin' and murderin' what goes on by the no 'count trash that travels it. Decent folks ain't got no

323

chance. Ain't fittin', it just ain't fittin'!" She turned to shake one last warning finger at Derek. "You take care of that chile, you hear."

"I hear, Sophie, I hear," Derek called over his shoulder as he nudged Trojan down the long drive. "It would appear that you have captured the old girl's heart," he said admiringly to Meghan.

"What do you mean?" She glanced at him, puzzled by his statement.

"Well, I am certain if it were Deirdre I intended to *drag clean 'cross the wilderness*," he mimicked Sophie perfectly, "Sophie would have voiced no objection."

As Derek had predicted they caught up with Nathan and the wagons before they reached the river. And as they drew near Derek's riverboat, he pulled up beside her. "Is she not a beauty?" He gazed fondly at the vessel. "She's on her way upstream to St. Louis with a load of cargo we brought over on *The Lady Elizabeth* and while there, the men will load her with goods to bring back to New Orleans. It is perhaps the most profitable and rewarding of my investments," he said proudly. Derek paused and looked at Meghan, whose emerald-green eyes were glued to his face in complete fascination. "I have probably succeeded in boring you silly with all this."

"No, you haven't," she insisted softly.

"Well, shall we go on board?" He jumped down from his mount to assist Meghan from Champion's back and led her up the gangplank to the boat.

"Where will you stable the horses?" Meghan cast a concerned eye over her shoulder at Champion, who nervously pawed the ground as he watched his mistress abandon him.

"She may not, at first glance, appear to be spacious, but *The Cajun* quarters a fulltime crew of eight, has substantial cargo space, a stall for livestock, plus my own personal cabin as well as guest cabins for those I invite on board." He escorted her past a row of doors to one marked "Private" and, pushing it open, he stepped aside so that she might enter before him.

"It's lovely, Derek," she whispered.

A mere glance was all Meghan needed to recognize the rugged décor and dark color scheme as having been of his design. The room positively reeked of Derek's influence and Meghan knew instinctively that were she to open the box on the desk, she would find several of his favorite cigars, and a bottle of his special brandy would be encased in the small cabinet by the window. Yes, this was obviously Derek's cabin: immaculate, rugged and masculine . . . just like him.

"Make yourself comfortable." He gestured toward the room. "I shall rejoin you as soon as I have determined that our things are safely on board and the animals are secured in their stalls."

"But . . . Champion," Meghan started to protest.

"I do not intend to *ride* him aboard, Meghan." He kissed her abruptly. "Do you not think that you can permit me to handle him, just this once?" He was gone before she could offer any further protests.

When Derek returned, he found her sitting near the window, gazing wistfully toward shore and he went to sit on the arm of her chair.

"We are moving." Meghan observed the boat pull away from the dock, but then her eyes spied Nathan on the wagon and she turned to Derek thoughtfully. "Why did you not invite Nathan to accompany us? Does he not know Mr. Jackson?"

"Yes, he does. And I had intended for him to join us until that unfortunate incident yesterday with Iverson." He stood up and crossed to the small liquor cabinet and withdrew a bottle of brandy. "After Iverson's attack, I thought it would be wiser to leave Nathan behind to handle any unseemly situation should the bastard be foolish enough to return.

"Would you care to join me?" He lifted the glass of brandy toward her.

"No, thank you." She stood up and began to walk about the room, pausing now and then to examine a particular object that caught her attention. "It is much too early for me," she informed him politely.

"Yes, but you forget that I did not make it to bed last night; therefore, I am finding it exceedingly difficult to distinguish the hour." He lifted the potent brew to his lips and tasted it.

"I did not forget," Meghan murmured softly.

"What?" Derek sounded surprised as he drained the contents of the glass and returned the bottle to the liquor cabinet. "After our little discussion about Wade, I rather thought you might welcome a night of respite from me." He rubbed his eyes wearily and sat down tiredly upon the bed.

"No, when I awoke this morning and realized that you had not come to bed last night, I became concerned about you," she whispered the words so lowly that Derek had to strain his ears to hear her admission.

"Concerned? About me?" he asked in feigned disbelief. "Careful, dear heart. I fear that you are beginning to sound remarkably like a *wife*." He had intended his statement as a joke, but when he beheld the expression that darkened Meghan's pretty face, he quickly regretted his choice of words. "Ooohhh!" He stretched wearily, hoping to avert the conversation from the disastrous course it had just taken. "I never should have allowed Nathan to keep me up so late."

"You must be exhausted." Meghan observed his

haggard face and considerately stepped to the bed to sit down beside him and offer what comfort she could. "Will the trip to Natchez take long?"

"We should arrive late tonight." He yawned sleepily.

"Then why do you not get some rest?"

"That is not a bad suggestion," Derek agreed as he promptly stood and stripped down to his buckskin trousers before stretching out on the roomy bed. "Ahhh," he sighed pleasurably and reached out to grasp Meghan's hand. "Do you not wish to join me?"

"Need I remind you that I was not the foolish one who shunned the comfort of a bed last evening? I am not weary, nor do I wish to wrinkle my dress." She wrinkled her nose at him disdainfully.

Meghan started to move away from the bed, but Derek caught her by surprise and dragged her onto the bunk with him, pinioning her beside his muscular frame to prevent her from escaping him. "Oh, Meghan," he sighed dreamily. "I speak of sharing the ultimate rapture, and you can but fret over a mere wrinkled gown." His nimble fingers worked the buttons of her jacket while his lips fastened upon hers to explore their sweetness. "There is a simple solution to your plight, pet." His hand gently stroked her breasts, and he could feel the nipples stiffen through the soft material of her blouse. "Were you to remove the offensive garment, it would not get wrinkled." He playfully nibbled at her ear.

"And you would get no *rest*," she sternly reminded him. Meghan pushed away from him sharply and was able to escape his grasp before he recovered from the surprise of her movement.

Above all, Meghan feared that were he cunning enough to trick her into his arms again, she would not be strong enough to resist his amorous advances. Derek

327

had ruthlessly awakened her young body to the pleasure that the intimacies between a man and woman could bring. It was almost as if he alone held the key that could unlock her hidden passions and spark them to an all-consuming flame. And it disturbed her not a little that this rogue, who had caused her nothing but heartache and promised her but more of the same, could manipulate her body and drive her to such frenzied heights of sexual rapture that she could forget her breeding and respond so shamelessly at the slightest touch of his hand.

"Why so pensive?" Derek's voice shattered her troubled thoughts. "Does it disturb you to learn that you rather enjoy the way you feel when I make love to you? It shouldn't, you know, for you were born to be loved." His voice was rich with desire as he spoke and Meghan shivered involuntarily when she observed his piercing eyes intently fixed upon her.

"And to think that you wasted all those years learning to behave like a proper, young lady and for what? So you could marry a buffoon such as Charles Beauchamp, who would have left you in a cold and lonely bed while he dallied from mistress to mistress." He rolled to his back and folded his arms behind his head. "You realize, of course, that you should thank me for rescuing you from such a chaste, indeed, frustrating existence."

"I shall *thank you* to keep your offensive remarks to yourself." Meghan shot him a scathing look. "Why, the mere idea that I should enjoy your . . . your . . ."

"Lovemaking," he offered.

". . . is ghastly. Why, *decent* women do not enjoy such things, let alone speak of them!"

"Why, you little hypocrite." The wide grin that adorned Derek's handsome face plainly revealed that he was deriving great pleasure from their banter. "Next

328

time I make love to you, I shall endeavor to minimize your enjoyment so you may maintain your claim to decency." He laughed uproariously as Meghan whirled bitterly and marched to the door.

"For your information, *Mr.* Chandler, there is not going to be a next time. You have abused my flesh for the last time," she spoke grandly and would have executed a perfect flight had she not stumbled on the hem of her gown in her haste to vacate the cabin.

"Bravo!" Derek cheered her words. "You are a masterful opponent, Meghan. But just where do you think you are going, young lady?" He raised a suspicious eyebrow as he observed that she was apparently determined to withdraw from the cabin.

"Ooohhh! You lascivious leper, you . . . you spineless son of a slimy snake! I am going to throw myself in the river and rid myself of your foul stench once and for all!" She slammed the door furiously before he could voice an objection.

Derek stared at the door for a long moment. Then the room reverberated with his hearty laughter in response to the temper tantrum he had just witnessed and he could be heard to chuckle just before he drifted off to sleep, "That's my girl."

After Meghan left Derek's cabin, she stood on the deck of *The Cajun* for a long while, watching the various boats drifting down the river and permitting the cool breeze to calm her flaming temper. Meghan wandered about the boat for the better part of the day, exploring the different cabins and talking with Derek's men. And in the early evening, her empty stomach urged her to follow the trail of the delicious aroma that led her to the boat's kitchen where the cook was more than happy to provide his employer's wife with a bowl of hearty stew. And following her meal, Meghan made her way to the stall that temporarily housed Trojan and Champion. She was still there, sitting in a lonely corner of the stall, her head resting against the wooden railing, eyes closed in slumber, when Derek discovered her several hours later.

"So, here you are," he whispered gently and lifted her into his arms. "I see that you wisely decided against taking a swim."

Meghan's eyes fluttered open and the peaceful dream that had been floating through her head was obliterated by the mocking sound of his voice. But although his tone was sarcastic, in the darkness Meghan could not detect the look of relief that registered on his rugged face that he had found her safe from harm.

"What time is it?" she murmured sleepily.

"The middle of the night," he answered quietly as he carried her to their cabin. "You little vixen! I damn near had them turn *The Cajun* around to go back and search for you. You ever pull a stunt like this again and I shall tan your lovely backside," he scolded her severely and laid her gently on the bed.

"Careful, Derek," Meghan mumbled faintly. "I fear that *you* are beginning to sound remarkably like a *husband*."

"Not likely!" he bellowed, but his words went unheard, for Meghan had rolled to her side and was instantly asleep.

She awakened near dawn and, rubbing the sleep from her drowsy eyes, she sat up in the middle of the bed. The room was still dark and several moments passed before she was able to focus her eyes on Derek in the dimly lighted room. He stood by the washbasin, busily splashing water on his face and neck.

"Derek?" she called quietly.

"I did not mean to wake you, pet." He briskly dried his face with a towel and, retrieving his shirt from the chair, he walked over to the bed. "Go back to sleep."

"But where are you going?"

"I have some business in town, but I should return before nightfall. We shall leave for Nashville in the morning." He slipped the shirt over his shoulders and leaned over to press a kiss to her lips. "You stay here and we shall have an elegant supper when I return." He slipped into his coat, collected his hat and had stepped through the door before he realized that Meghan was behind him on the deck.

"But . . . but I do not want to be locked away in this stuffy old cabin all day." She stamped her foot impatiently. "I wish to accompany you."

"Oh, you do, do you?" Derek placed his hands on his hips and retraced his steps till he stood directly in front of her, their bodies almost touching.

"Yes," she replied defiantly, purposely imitating the stance that he had assumed.

"Unfortunately my dealings will not take me to the more progressive sections of the city, or to the refined plantations nearby. Take a good look, Meghan." He swung his arm toward the direction of his speech. "It is known as Natchez, Hell Under the Hill, and aptly named, I might add. Every form of lowlife, river rat, and mangy scum end up here at one time or another to visit the brothels and fill their bellies full of cheap whiskey. And if a man should be resourceful enough to avoid getting shot at or knifed in the back by some money hungry drunk, he has to be wary of the *ladies* who will attempt to lure him up to their chambers with sweet talk and empty promises and then proceed to club him over the head and rob him of his valuables." He stepped to

331

her side and made a grand motion as he extended his arm to her. "Come along then if you insist. But do not be surprised if I am accosted by some river scum who, after rendering me helpless, will likely drag you into the shadows to rape you and share you with his friends." He paused for effect. "Well?" Derek demanded impatiently, taking her hand roughly and placing it on his arm. "Are you not going with me?"

"No," she whispered hoarsely and tearing her hand from his arm, she ran back to the cabin and slammed the door loudly.

Derek stepped angrily to the door and as he stood facing the neutral barrier, he muttered, "Women! Bah! They fill their heads with senseless notions, but when presented the folly of their ways they invariably succumb to tears to make the man feel like an insensitive fool." He jammed his hat upon his head in disgust and strode quickly to the gangplank.

The boat was brightly illuminated with lanterns, and torches lit the path along the plank when Derek returned in the evening after concluding his business. The heavily laden packhorses that he had borrowed from an old acquaintance were handed over to one of the boatmen before he trudged along the deserted deck to his cabin.

The cabin was encased in total darkness, and thinking that Meghan might have chosen to retire early to nurse her injured pride, he gently closed the door so his entry would not disturb her. Then after a few moments of silent deliberation, he uncertainly crossed to the bed to gaze down at her sleeping form only to discover an empty berth.

"Meghan?" he asked anxiously, struggling again into the coat he had discarded upon entering the room and silently cursing himself for not posting a guard at the door to safeguard against her attempting an escape. Had she not warned him that she awaited only the opportunity to be free from him? And because of his stupid oversight, *he* had presented her the very opportunity she sought. Blinded with self-recrimination at his foolish blunder, Derek stalked to the door and jerked it open with the intention of summoning his men to instigate an organized search of the town.

"Derek?" Meghan called softly from the chair near the window. "Where are you going?"

"What?" He stopped suddenly and turned toward the direction of the sound. The tart inflection of his voice belied the expression of extreme relief that adorned his handsome face, but it was adequately shielded by the darkness. "What is it, little one?" His tone softened somewhat as he strolled over to her chair. "Still angry with me?"

"No," she muttered reluctantly.

"Then why so glum? And why are you sitting in the dark?" He instinctively reached down to finger a feathery wisp of her hair.

"I . . . I wish to apolo- . . . apologize for my behavior this morning." Even though they were enclosed in total darkness, she turned her head aside; so he could not see her face.

"Meghan." He slowly shook his head in amazement. "My sweet, innocent Meghan," he chuckled softly to himself as he drew her from the chair to encircle her with his strong embrace. "You are a constant delight to me." He kissed her affectionately on the lips and smoothed the hair from her downcast face. "Oh, I will admit that your moods sometime baffle me, especially when I am unaware of their basis, but you owe me no apology for this morning. I did my part in arousing your flaming temper. Besides, it was only natural that you should want to accompany me on an excursion into town." He tried to console her.

"I . . . I did not know that Natchez was such an . . . an unsavory place, or I would not have demanded to go with you," she explained.

"Of course you didn't, my sweet." He sat down in the chair and pulled her onto his lap. "In all fairness I should tell you that not all of Natchez has such a scandalous reputation and had we the time, I would rent a carriage and take you driving so you could see for yourself what a lovely city it is."

"That will not be necessary. I know that you are anxious to get to Nashville and visit your friend." She rested her head against his shoulder.

"Then shall we put this morning's unfortunate incident from our minds?" He pulled her tighter against him.

Meghan nodded.

"And in the future you must learn to trust me and exhibit more faith in my judgment, dear heart. I am concerned for your safety; therefore, you must strive to remember that although you may not agree with my decisions, I make them with your welfare foremost in mind." He repositioned her on his lap, taking her head between his masterful hands and stroking the silkiness of her cheeks with his fingertips. He kissed her gently and when he pulled away, he asked, "Are you hungry?"

"Starving," she admitted.

"Then why do you not change into one of those pretty gowns I purchased for you, and I shall take you to dine at one of the most reputable establishments in Natchez. The wine is mellow, the food is superb, the atmosphere is not to be surpassed and the company . . ." He paused and leisurely ran his hand up and down her arm.

"Well, the company, I daresay, shall be exquisite."

Cold chills washed over Meghan as she stared into his sensitive eyes, and she pushed off his lap to stand upon shaky legs. "I shan't be but a moment." She stepped to her portmanteau to select a fresh change of clothing.

They returned late with Meghan yawning sleepily as they walked up the gangplank arm in arm. Derek insisted that she retire immediately, and he considerately saw that she was comfortably tucked in before he ventured onto the deck to enjoy a cigar.

Derek stood on the deck, gazing toward the bright lights that illuminated the bawdy taverns and brothels which brazenly called out to travel weary boatmen, inviting them to step across their thresholds and ease their boredom. But the boisterous din of the music and laughter, coupled with an occasional blast from a trigger-happy gunman, did not so much as penetrate his beleaguered mind, for it was in much the same confused state as was the city at which he gazed.

"What is happening to me?" he grunted softly. "Can it be that after all the years of carefully evading the snares of countless other women that I have inadvertently fallen victim to the innocence of one so young?

"I have no one to blame save myself," he severely lectured himself. "Have I not repeatedly boasted that no mere woman would ever conquer my heart? Well, it would appear that the good Lord has presented me a fitting challenge, a challenge which I may no longer ignore." He became silent once more as he consciously struggled with the decision he knew to be forthcoming.

"Ah, Meghan," he whispered her name to the wind, "the sweet flower that has been incessantly crushed by my stubborn will and, yet, continues to blossom like the

335

daisies in a sun-drenched, spring meadow. I care for you, but I do not love you." He was genuinely surprised at how painful and forlorn those lonely words sounded on his lips. "I cannot—*will not* love Thomas Bainbridge's daughter!" He slammed his fist into the deck railing and the wood splintered at the ferocity of the blow.

He moaned despairingly and turned to walk in slow, determined steps to his cabin, mentally battling with the decision he had just made. The lantern still burned and the light from its glow irradiated Meghan's slender figure on the spacious bed. Closing the door behind him, Derek moved silently to the bed and stood for several minutes in quiet meditation as he stared listlessly at her.

"Meghan, my sweet," he breathed heavily, reaching down to fondle a fragrant wisp of hair that was spread upon her pillow. "What will your reaction be when I inform you of my decision to dispatch you to Charleston when we return from our travels? It was indeed a difficult decision to make, but one that will undoubtedly be for the best." He walked to the table to extinguish the light.

"Should I tell you of my intentions before we leave tomorrow?" he questioned aloud as he perched on the edge of the bed. "No." He determinedly shook his head. "You would likely request permission to depart for Charleston immediately, and I do want you to have this trip." He stood to remove his trousers and gripped the corner of the sheet and drew it back. "What is this?" he chuckled softly with mild surprise as he permitted his eyes to wander over her freely.

When Meghan had retired earlier, she had merely stepped out of her clothes and slipped between the sheets. But now she was clad from head to toe in one of her nightdresses, the pink, silk ribbons pulling the delicate lace collar snugly about her neck.

336

"It would appear that you have donned your armor in an attempt to thwart the dreaded attack." He climbed into the bed beside her and leaned over to gaze at her beautiful, sleeping face. "So, you would carry out your threat of yesterday. Meghan, my captivating, rebellious nymph, have you not yet realized that you have grown to anticipate these moments as much as have I?" He lay back on the pillows and drew her into his arms.

"However, I shall allow you this one insignificant victory," he conceded. "But while I will not force you to suffer the indignities of my lovemaking tonight, you could surely have no objection to my holding you in my arms for a time." He placed a kiss against her forehead and gently rocked her back and forth.

And as his strong hands gently stroked the softness of her honey-brown hair, Derek closed his eyes in contented slumber, completely oblivious to the tormenting tears of anguish that trickled down Meghan's cheeks and fell unnoticed onto his broad chest.

Part Three

The Confrontation

Chapter Fifteen

The sun glistened brightly on the Hermitage on the blistering July afternoon. And there was virtually no activity as the sweltering heat of the day drove those who might be easily tempted to shirk their responsibilities to seek respite from the weather with a cool drink from the spring, or a short nap beneath a tall shade tree.

It was a servant who first noticed the travelers who were slowly advancing toward the house. She had opened an upstairs bedroom window and leaned outside to allow a precious breath of air to whip across her bronzed face when she spied the small entourage. As she studied the troup slowly winding its way toward the mansion, a wide grin parted the lips of the girl when she recognized the man who sat astride the lead horse. With a jubilant yelp she rushed from the room and scampered down the circular staircase to search for her mistress and relate to her the news of the approaching visitors.

"Miz Rachel, Miz Rachel!" The girl bolted into the dining room where Rachel Jackson and a servant were busily polishing the family silver.

"What is it, child?" The older woman rose from her chair to confront the servant, long since accustomed to the young girl's excitable temperament. Accordingly, Rachel Jackson had determined that it was best to question the girl thoroughly before allowing herself to become unduly overanxious.

"They's comin', they's comin'!" The girl jumped up and down excitedly.

"*Who* is coming?" Rachel inquired patiently.

"Massah Derek, and he's bringin' someone with him," she responded happily, pleased that she should be the one to impart such favorable news to her mistress. "I seen them when I was upstairs, airin' out the guest room like you ask me to."

"Oh, Lizzie," Rachel sighed in relief. "Everytime you come screeching into the room like that my heart leaps with fear that something dreadful has happened to Andrew. I declare that you have frightened nearly ten years from my life this week alone with your antics." She smoothed the skirt of her modestly styled gown and checked her hair in the mirror before striding gracefully from the dining room to greet her guests.

She emerged from the house just as Derek was dismounting from Trojan, and when he turned to see her, he rushed forward to embrace her warmly. "Rachel, you are as beautiful as ever." He held her at arm's length and gazed at her fondly.

"And you remain the unfaltering flatterer, for which I am eternally grateful." She laughed. "It does wonders for my aging soul to have you about." She looked beyond him for the first time to see Meghan. "Well, when Lizzie came bounding down the stairs squawking, 'they's comin',' I half expected that you might be the visitor, knowing that Andrew had invited you. But I must admit that *this* is a total surprise, Derek." She extended her arm toward Meghan. "I suspected that your companion might be Nathan, but that is quite obviously not the case." She raised a questioning eyebrow toward Derek, who had moved to assist Meghan from Champion's back.

"Now, Rachel," Derek raised a hand to quell her rising suspicions, "I recognize that condescending scowl. You must strive to remember that I am no longer the irresponsible lad of sixteen that Andrew dragged from the Cumberland and delivered to you to nurse back to health."

"*I* did not say you were," Rachel stated with a calculating air.

"But your expression clearly dictates that you have jumped to an irrational conclusion concerning the relationship between the young lady and myself, and I simply will not have you thinking badly of me *or* my wife." He grinned at her broadly as he observed the dubious frown melt away into an elated smile.

"Wife?" she exclaimed. "When? Where?"

"I shall explain everything in due course," he assured her. "Where is Andrew? I would like him to meet Meghan."

"Meghan," Rachel repeated, stepping forward to grasp her hand. "That is a truly lovely name."

"Thank you, Mrs. Jackson," Meghan replied demurely.

"Tut, tut," scolded the older woman. "We are not so formal around here that you may not call me by my given name. In fact, I shall insist that you address me as Rachel." She squeezed her hand warmly and turned to Derek.

"Andrew had some errands to see to in town, but he will return shortly," she explained. "But we needn't stand here chattering in the sweltering sun." She turned to lead them into the house. "I shall send someone to tend to your things and see that the horses are properly stabled." She escorted her guests to the parlor and excused herself momentarily while she administered instructions to the servants.

"What do you think of her?" Derek asked of Meghan when their hostess had vacated the room.

"She seems to be a very grand and dignified lady, and should Mr. Jackson prove to be the same, I shall derive no pleasure in deceiving them with this disgusting sham of a marriage," she informed him curtly.

"Meghan." Derek's voice held a distinctly threatening tone, but he was prevented the opportunity of further reprisal, for Rachel rejoined them at that moment.

"I must admit that the two of you have duly aroused my curiosity." She claimed a seat opposite the young couple. "Derek has staunchly rebuked all of my worthwhile attempts to see him properly wed, Meghan. You must divulge to me the secret of your success." Her smile was friendly and directed toward Meghan, but she was ill-prepared for the response.

"Yes, I am well acquainted with Derek's steadfast confirmation to bachelorhood. *Everyone* has seen fit to make me aware of his heralded past," she said tartly, barely conscious of the cautioning hand that Derek placed on her shoulder as he stood behind her chair. "As for myself, I assure you that I used no demon's wiles, nor cast no witch's spell upon Derek to lure him to my side."

"Meghan!" Derek interrupted sharply. "Where are your manners?"

"It's all right, Derek." Rachel waved the incident aside. "Meghan has obviously been badgered with this before and it was not my intent to belabor a well-worn subject. As a woman, I can well appreciate the bitterness and frustration one experiences when constantly reminded that she is not the first to enjoy the thrill of her husband's warm embrace. But, my dear," she addressed Meghan cordially, "you may assuredly derive extreme satisfaction in knowing that you shall be the last to

344

do so."

"Forgive my outburst," Meghan murmured quietly, completely humbled by the older woman's gracious manner and wise words. "I am not usually so discourteous, and I can offer no excuse for my ill temper save the fact that it has been an extremely grueling journey and I am truly exhausted. Might it be possible for me to freshen up a bit, so that I do not present a totally disastrous first impression?"

"Of course, dear." Rachel was on her feet again and to the door to issue additional instructions to the servants. "I have traveled the Trace myself and it was thoughtless of me to have forgotten the tedium of the trail. Your bath will be ready shortly."

"Thank you," Meghan replied politely.

"I could rather stand to wash away some of this trail dust myself," Derek proclaimed as he took Meghan's hand to assist her from the sofa. "Come, my love, we go to transform you into the charming princess I am more accustomed to viewing." He winked at her as if to say that he was not angered by her behavior and she need not fear retribution.

Meghan sighed contentedly in the depths of the huge bathtub that the servants had carried into the room and filled with warm water. The door had barely closed behind the last departing servant before Meghan had stripped and plunged into the enticing bath. Now she closed her eyes and permitted her thoughts to drift aimlessly as the warm liquid soothed her aching flesh. And when she opened her eyes to discover Derek standing at the foot of the tub, her lips parted instantly in a lazy grin.

"Feeling better?" he asked softly.

"Mmmm," she moaned deliciously. "Heavenly. Oh,

Derek, I think that I shall never be clean again after all that time of dirt and mud and dust and *more* dirt." She vigorously lathered a sponge with perfumed soap and began to scrub her leg for the third time.

"Please, Meghan," he reached forward and snatched the sponge from her hands, "I rather enjoy the sight of your sultry legs with skin intact and I fear that if I permit you to continue this unwarranted abuse, there will be nothing left. Besides, you have already bathed longer than any five normal people and, I daresay, that if any particle of dust has managed to survive your merciless attack it will have been for naught, for your beauty doth outshine all that dares to venture near you."

"Derek." Meghan laughed gaily at his rhetoric, but she winced slightly as her sudden movement alerted a multitude of painfully overworked muscles. "Do not make me laugh so. I positively ache all over."

"Perhaps I can be of some assistance then." He gallantly strode to the head of the tub and began to gently massage the tired muscles of her shoulders and back.

"That feels wonderful," Meghan sighed dreamily as she allowed her muslces to relax under his adept touch. "But I fear that I have other parts that pain me more severely." She made reference to her travel weary backside.

"The prescribed treatment is the same and if you are willing," he reached around her with both arms to grasp and fondle her breasts with his large, capable hands, "I shall certainly try my best to accommodate you."

"That will not be necessary." Meghan playfully slapped his hands away. "I shall have to endure the discomfort for a few days, for I am not one of your horses that would have you groom it following a strenuous workout."

"My horses have never complained," he chuckled airily and expertly sidestepped the bar of soap that Meghan flung at his head. "You *are* a spiteful wench." He laughed and picking up a fluffy towel from the bed he offered it to her, but Meghan was reluctant to accept it.

"Can I not relax for a few moments longer?" The pleading eyes she turned to him were so innocently appealing that he could not refuse her.

"As you wish," he relented. "But only a few minutes more, or I shall be forced to present a very wrinkled wife to Andrew." He strode to the washstand; Meghan observed him while he washed away the dirt and grime of the trail, then prepared his shaving equipment to strip the growth of beard from his rugged face.

It was with a little sadness that she watched this last maneuver. Derek had shunned the use of a razor on their journey up the Trace, explaining to her that the last time he had tried to scrape his whiskers by the light of a fire he had very nearly cut his throat. As the weeks progressed the stubble on his face blossomed into a full beard and Meghan discovered that she genuinely approved of his bewhiskered appearance, for the addition of the facial hairs served to make him even more forcefully appealing. And as she watched him raise the razor to his chin, she found herself biting her lip to keep from suggesting that he permit the beard to remain intact.

This was the first time that Meghan had ever been allowed the luxury of watching him shave. Even when they had been aboard *The Lady Elizabeth*, Derek had accomplished this particular chore before she awakened in the mornings. So it was in complete fascination that her eyes were glued to him as he performed, what was to Derek a rather perfunctory task. Meghan was amazed at how in just a few quick strokes of the razor the thick growth of whiskers had been completely removed and Derek was once again transformed into the clean-shaven rogue to whom she was heretofore accustomed.

"Meghan?" He crossed to the bed to retrieve the fresh suit of clothes the servants had laid out. "Why do you stare?"

"I was merely watching you shave." She stood up and wrapped the towel around her as she stepped from the tub.

"Ah, yes, I wager that you are as relieved as I to be rid of the bristly stubble." He came up soundlessly behind her and smoothed his chin along her naked shoulder. "See, there is no more of the bothersome stuff to irritate your tender flesh." He placed a blazing trail of hot kisses from her shoulder to the nape of her neck.

"I did not find it bothersome," she said quietly.

"You should have voiced your opinion before this, Meghan, for there is little I can do to alter matters at the present." He returned to tend to the task of attiring himself.

Meghan had just wiggled into her undergarments when she noticed that Derek was having considerable difficulty arranging his stock. Uncertainly, she moved to him to offer her assistance, half expecting to be brusquely informed that he was quite capable of dressing himself. But to her surprise, he smiled broadly at her and gratefully submitted to her ministrations.

"Papa could never tie his stock, either, but he was too stubborn to permit anyone to help him," she jabbered unthinkingly as she went about her chore and once completed, she stepped back to critically analyze her handiwork. "Very handsome, indeed," she concluded proudly.

"To which do you refer, Meghan, the neckpiece, or

him whose neck it surrounds?" Derek asked curiously, his eyes alive with mirth.

"Why, Derek, what with every fair maid in the country simply pining for even the slightest of your favors, you cannot possibly imply that you are remotely concerned with *my* niggling opinion? Do I dare permit myself to hope for as much?" She placed the back of her hand to her forehead as though she were dizzy with faint. "Pray, m'lord, do not toy so unmercifully with the affections of one so young and meek." She lowered her lashes coquettishly and collapsed upon the bed with an uncontrollable fit of giggles when Derek stomped from the room, muttering that he had been a fool to expect a civil reply from such a troublesome wench.

Meghan had still not quite regained her composure when Lizzie knocked quietly on the door a few minutes later to announce that she had been dispatched to assist with Meghan's toilette.

Meghan sat patiently before the mirror as the servant skillfully arranged her hair in a becoming style. First, Lizzie brushed the long, luxurious strands until they glistened, then she piled them atop Meghan's head and wove a blue silk ribbon with intricate precision through the silky tresses. And as a final touch, Lizzie pulled several strands free from the ribbon and arranged them in attractive, feathery curls about her slender face.

"Lizzie," Meghan lifted a hand to her hair, "you have done a splendid job," she praised the young girl. Meghan stood up to smooth her gown and was quite pleased with the way her coiffure complemented her dress.

"Thank you, Miz Chandler." The girl edged bashfully toward the door. "I'll tell Massah Derek that you is ready."

"Thank you, Lizzie." Meghan again averted her gaze

to the mirror. She had been wise in her selection of gowns. Blue was definitely her most becoming color and the style of the gown was elegant, yet appropriate for the quaint, country setting.

The dress was made of India silk and boasted short, puffy sleeves and a bodice that fit snugly to her waist to accentuate her slender figure. It then flared in an inverted V-shape to fall in billowy swirls about her delicate ankles. In order to obtain the proper effect, several petticoats had to be worn beneath the full skirt, and although she had to endure the sweltering heat, Meghan had decided that she would suffer the mild discomfort in order to make a suitable impression upon Derek's friends. Finally she lifted her eyes to the décolletage of the gown. Admittedly, it was more modest than many of her dresses, but enough flesh was exposed to entice the masculine eye, causing Meghan to lament the fact that she had no jewelry to accent her dress.

One hand rested lightly against her throat as her brow tilted noticeably into a thoughtful frown, while the other hand fingered the rows of delicate, pearl buttons that adorned the bodice of her gown. Besides these, the wedding band was the only other gem she possessed.

"Perhaps I can alleviate your dilemma." Derek had entered the room unbeknownst to her and had been thoughtfully observing her studious confrontation with the mirror. He strode to the saddlebags that were draped across a chair and drew out a small, leather case which he proceeded to hand to her.

Meghan stared at the case and cast a puzzled frown in his direction before giving in to her curiosity and opening the box. Inside the case, against a red velvet background, lay a few pieces of jewelry that she recognized as a portion of the Chandler collection.

"I hope you can find something suitable to coordinate with your ensemble." He peered over her shoulder as her eyes wandered in amazement over the lavish assortment of jewels. "Of course, I could not handily carry the entire collection, so I took the liberty of selecting a few pieces that I thought would be flattering to your complexion."

"Must you always be so proficient in determining my needs? You will likely spoil me, thus making it more difficult for me to adjust to conducting my own affairs when the time comes," she said quietly, her eyes searching the case for the tiny heartshaped diamond necklace that Elizabeth had given her.

"I have not yet had the opportunity to have the clasp repaired." He correctly guessed the contents of her thoughts. "Perhaps you will allow me to choose for you?" And without waiting for her to reply, he selected a single strand of perfectly matched pearls that shined with a subdued, milky luster and placed them about her slender neck. "Do you concur with my selection?"

"Yes," she murmured lowly. "They are lovely."

"Yes, but in a subtle way. They do not bedazzle the eye so that the intrinsic value is overshadowed, nor are they gaudy in appearance." He turned her from the mirror and rested his hands lightly on her shoulders. "They radiate a beauty that is as irrevocably pure and untainted as your own." He looked at her proudly and for once his chocolate-brown eyes did not tease her. "And in the event I have neglected to tell you, permit me to say that you look exceptionally lovely this evening." He tucked her arm in his to escort her belowstairs. "I sincerely hope that this evening's fare is light, for I fear that I am already satiated after feasting upon your loveliness." He led her to the circular staircase and would have proceeded to descend the steps had Meghan not suddenly clenched his arm with an awesome strength that stayed his movement.

"What is it?" He observed that her other hand clung tightly to the banister.

"I fear that I have grown positively giddy with your lavish flattery." She wanted to draw as little attention as possible to the wave of dizziness that had just gripped her.

"You are probably fatigued from the journey. I shall make certain that you retire early this evening so you may receive a proper night's rest." He took one step downward, but Meghan still remained glued to the spot and when he turned to question her, he found himself gazing into her sparkling, green eyes and the sensitive awareness of their beauty unsettled him a bit.

Slowly, as if she would will the moment to remain suspended in time so that they might forever savor its gentleness, Meghan lifted her hand to his cheek. "My handsome cavalier," she murmured softly. "Unceasingly solicitous where I am concerned." She leaned forward until their lips embraced in a brief, but pleasant encounter.

"So, the truth be out at last!" he bellowed. "The lady does not find me unattractive to gaze upon." He took both her hands in his and squeezed them warmly.

"To deny it would be folly," she admitted, offering her lips to him again.

"Damn it, Meghan, do you realize how difficult you are making it for me to continue down these steps to dine at a table with friends and make polite conversation while my loins burn with desire for you? How am I to endure such an excruciating evening when my thoughts will be laden with visions of you in my arms?" He ran his fingers lithely up and down her arms, instantly setting her flesh afire with a multitude of stimulating tingles.

"We shall *both* have to endure the evening, Derek, but perhaps the acute anticipation will serve to make the adventure all the more satisfying," she suggested coyly and Derek's mouth spread wide into a provocative grin.

"If that be true, I shall look forward to the event with great zeal." He again offered her his arm and she accepted it without hesitation.

"And now," she fell in step with him, "I am finally to meet your legendary General Jackson."

Rachel was sitting in the parlor and when the couple entered, she came forward to greet them. "Meghan," she offered the girl a radiant smile, "you look positively stunning."

"Lizzie was a great help to me. I would like to thank you for your thoughtfulness in sending her to me," Meghan said graciously.

"It was unforgivable of Derek to drag you from Chandalara without the services of a personal maid." Rachel threw Derek a stern look.

"That was merely because I am acquainted with the excellent hospitality you provide, and if I have overlooked any of my lady's comforts, it is because I took for granted that you would graciously rectify any of my ineptitudes." He cast the woman a mischievous smile as he stepped to a table that held an exquisitely cut crystal wine decanter and matching goblets. "Since our host has not yet returned, perhaps you ladies will permit me to offer you a glass of claret."

"I wonder what is detaining Andrew." Rachel glanced at the clock upon the mantel.

"He's probably lollygagging about in one of Nashville's shoddy taverns," Derek offered in playful speculation.

353

"As I recall, young man," boomed a hearty voice from the doorway, "that was one of *your* favorite pastimes, but never mine."

All eyes focused on the tall, gangly figure of Andrew Jackson as he stood in the doorway, silently appraising the scene he had just emerged upon.

Meghan could scarcely believe her eyes. Could this almost frail looking man be the individual that Derek so admired and respected? Why, from all the glorified tales of heroic adventure that Derek had told her, Meghan had conjured in her mind a more formidable-looking man instead of the rickety bundle of battered injuries that now stood in the doorway. His narrow shoulders were hunched forward slightly, his forehead bore an ugly, disfiguring scar, and when he strode across the room to greet his wife with an affectionate kiss, Meghan could not help but notice the cane he gripped in one hand.

"Well, now that I have returned," he said as he stepped to Derek and relieved him of the wine decanter, "I can accordingly assume my duties as host." He filled each of the four glasses as he talked. "Yes, I can certainly appreciate your annoyance at my absence when you arrived, Derek, but had you displayed the common courtesy of responding to my letter, I would have accordingly postponed my engagement in town."

Derek shuffled his feet uncomfortably and coughed to clear his throat. It was the first time Meghan had ever seen Derek flinch before anyone, and the sight did not prove to be as self-satisfying as she had one time thought it might. Her eyes returned to examine Andrew Jackson more closely. Perhaps she had been a bit impulsive in her hasty judgment of the man's physical prowess.

"And what have we here?" He stood before her, the

glass in his worn, outstretched hand was steady as he offered it to her. "It appears that everyone has forgotten their manners this evening," he said gruffly, turning to Derek. "I presume she came with you."

"Yes, Andrew." Derek crossed the space that separated him from Meghan in two quick strides and placing a supportive arm about her slender waist, he addressed Andrew, "This is Meghan, my wife." He gazed at her fondly and Meghan looked at him from the cover of her lashes in complete bewilderment at the genuine pride he had displayed when he introduced her.

"Wife, is it?" Andrew's penetrating gaze returned to examine her with renewed interest. "It's about time you did something worthwhile with that miserable life of yours besides roaming the infernal seas, doing the Lord only knows what and with whom." He lifted a disapproving eyebrow to Derek.

"As I recollect, you sowed a few wild oats in your younger days as well," Derek challenged him.

"Ahem, yes, well, we can dispense with this tedious chitchat. We are no doubt boring these beautiful ladies." He carefully maneuvered the conversation back to the young couple by speaking to Meghan. "Tell us, Mrs. Chandler, how do you endure marriage to this devilish scoundrel?"

"Thus far it has not been so terribly difficult to bear," Meghan replied demurely, but she was thunderstruck to see the agreeable expression vanish from his face as the brilliant cast from his eyes grew ominously grim. She observed the man in total confusion as he wheeled from her and retreated to the wine decanter to refill his glass, returning it to the table with such force that Meghan feared the delicate crystal would shatter.

"*British!*" Andrew thundered furiously, and Meghan was certain that she had never before heard such

355

bitterness and resentment so thoroughly expressed in the articulation of a single word. "That's what becomes of permitting young people to make their own matches. You couldn't be satisfied with one of the young chits Rachel paraded before you. Oh, no, you had to go off half-cocked—"

"Andrew," Rachel's pleasing voice calmly interrupted. "Now that you have properly chastised Derek and nearly frightened this poor child to tears, do you think it might be possible for us to sit down to supper?" She captured her husband's arm and shrewdly directed him toward the dining room. "You may continue your tirade later." She offered him a winning smile and motioned for Derek to follow them.

"I have suddenly lost my appetite," Meghan said glumly, rejecting the arm Derek extended to her. She would have fled had he not placed a gentle, restraining hand upon her wrist.

"Pay no attention to Andrew," he said softly. "Believe me, Meghan, his bark is much worse than his bite." He gently nudged her toward the dining room. "Perhaps it would ease your anxiety to know that Andrew cared as little for me the first time we met." They had arrived in the dining room and their hosts quickly took up the story.

"I damn near tossed him back in the river," Andrew crowed. Then beneath his breath, he added, "A lamentable misjudgment on my part that I have ofttime had just cause to regret."

"You see, Meghan, my husband does not limit his objection to merely you and Derek. Oh, no, my Andrew would never do anything on such a small scale." She threw him a devoted glance, though her voice was light with her teasing.

"That's quite right." Derek again took up the tale.

356

"Andrew's animosity is directed toward all the British."

"But why?" Meghan asked flatly. She was unaccustomed to prying into the private affairs of total strangers, but she felt that an explanation was due her for his rude display.

"Well, she's a spunky little redcoat, I'll give her that." Andrew surveyed her with an amused, calculated stare. "I suppose you are entitled to an explanation of some sort for my hasty manner. You see, when I was a lad of thirteen, I joined the Colonial effort in our struggle for independence. But as luck would have it, I was captured by the British before I got to see any real action. The officer in command ordered me to clean his mud-spattered boots and when I *politely* refused to accommodate the bastard," Andrew's eyes grew bitter as he recalled the incident, "he gave me this endearing little remembrance." He gestured toward his scarred forehead.

"I see," Meghan murmured softly. "And did you clean his boots?" she inquired unwaveringly, completely oblivious to Rachel's sharp intake of breath and Derek's firm hand about her wrist. Instead she met, and held, her host's steadfast gaze as if to announce that this was her personal battle and she would not back down.

"*What?*" Andrew thundered, obviously affronted by her question.

"It seems to me that a truly *worthy* officer of the Crown would have seen you carry out his command regardless of your injuries," she stated simply.

A nerve-racking tenseness enveloped the room and an eternity seemed to tick away before a single sound was heard in the elegant dining room. Then slowly, Andrew's lips parted in a playful smile and he threw his head back in genuine laughter.

"Yes, by golly, she's spunky all right, Derek." Andrew

slapped him soundly on the back and gallantly offered Meghan his arm. "Come, let us get better acquainted over a leisurely supper." He spirited her away from Derek and seated her at the table.

Rachel and Derek exchanged huge sighs of relief, and Derek strode to Rachel and extended his arm to escort her to the dinner table. They dined on a flavorful soup, roast duck, a variety of fresh vegetables, and hot biscuits, topping off the meal with a delicious plum pudding. During the meal, Derek obligingly answered the questions that Rachel asked concerning their marriage.

And as usual, whenever this particular topic was being discussed, Meghan would endeavor to detach her thoughts from the unpleasant conversation. She was constantly amazed at Derek, for each time he told the story he grew more confident in his tale and the words rolled off his tongue so fluently that Meghan *almost* found herself believing that she was indeed his wife.

Meghan looked up suddenly to find Andrew's gaze fixed intently upon her, and she quickly averted her concentration to Derek, silently praying that her host did not prove to be as adept at reading her thoughts as Derek had. She took a sip of wine and cast Derek what she hoped would be considered by all a genuine look of loving affection. The story he related bore no actual lies, she admitted reluctantly to herself, but the fact that he omitted several pertinent facts concerning their relationship did not alter the circumstances; she was still his whore.

"Meghan?" The sound of Derek's rich voice awakened her from her musings. "Are you not feeling well? Rachel has been trying to attract your attention for several moments." He considered her thoughtfully.

"Forgive me," Meghan quickly apologized to her

hostess. "I am afraid that I was quite lost in my thoughts and did not hear you."

"It's of little consequence." Rachel dismissed the incident. "I was about to suggest that you and I retire to the parlor so the menfolk can enjoy an afterdinner smoke and talk over old times."

"If memory serves me, Rachel," Derek said, leisurely fingering the stem of his wine goblet and offering her a coy smile, "you used to join us *menfolk* in our afterdinner vendettas. Why, I even brought you a pouch of your favorite tobacco from New Orleans," he added deliberately for Meghan's benefit so that he could observe her reaction.

She did not disappoint him. Her mouth plopped open and her eyes widened in surprise at Derek's revelation. She had read of some women who privately enjoyed the taste of tobacco, but she had never been personally acquainted with a woman who actually admitted to using the stuff.

"Your thoughtfulness is appreciated, Derek, and I will surely see that your gift is properly utilized. But in deference to Meghan, I think that I will manage if I dispense with my pipe for one evening."

"I will not hear of it," Meghan interrupted suddenly. "I am not so frail that I cannot endure a little smoke and did you not say, Rachel, that friends do not have to behave so formally with one another?"

"Yes, I believe those were my exact words," replied the older woman pleasantly.

"Then it is settled." Meghan rose from her chair and went to stand beside Derek. "Besides, I rather enjoy watching Derek puff away on his cigar as he flamboyantly recounts one of his tall tales."

"Tall tales, is it?" Derek pretended to be insulted. "I assure you, Meghan, that you may acknowledge any

359

utterances from these lips as having divine inspiration and consisting entirely of factual events." He captured her hand and pressed it lightly to his lips. "How can you not believe such an honest face?" Ignoring Andrew's loud guffaw, he took her arm and directed her toward the parlor.

"Suppose you tell us one of Derek's stories, the way he told it to you, and we'll substantiate its authenticity," Andrew suggested as he and Rachel followed them into the room.

"Oh, I could never tell a story the way Derek does," Meghan insisted.

"Good," Andrew snickered. "We could do without his melodramatics," he said candidly and offered Derek one of his cigars.

"Well," she began uncertainly. "The most recent story he told me has to do with the Natchez Trace." She noticed that Derek's eyes had grown bright with amusement at her selection of anecdotes.

"You do not mean that he told you of those horrible tales of murder and robbery while you were on the trail?" Rachel shrieked in disbelief and shot a sternly disapproving look at Derek, who seemed to be thoroughly enjoying the exchange.

"Yes, he mentioned a man named Sam Mason and a . . . Little Harpe; yes, those were the men. He said that they were wont to attack unsuspecting travelers whom they suspected of carrying large sums of money. I am not ashamed to admit that the thoughts of those men possibly sneaking up on us in the middle of the night simply terrified me. Why, what with the sounds of the animals in the night and my ruminations on these ghastly men, I can assure you that I slept very little." She glanced at Rachel and was quite perplexed by her angered expression. "Did I say something amiss?"

Meghan asked hesitantly.

"Oh, no," Rachel assured her, "but I think that your prankish husband owes you an explanation and an apology as well." She clutched the bowl of her pipe in one hand and lifted the stem to her lips, while she offered Derek a pointedly agitated look.

"What do you mean?" Meghan was more than a little confused as she glanced helplessly from Andrew to Rachel, finally turning to Derek. "Surely you did not invent those horrible tales to purposely frighten me?" She could not believe that he would be so ruthlessly cruel to her.

"No, Meghan," Andrew was speaking to her. "Derek did not invent the stories he told you about the Trace. But I do fear that you have been deceived, my dear, for while Sam Mason and Little Harpe accomplished some of the most horrendous crimes of our time, their unfortunate reign of terror along the Trace ended several years ago." He smiled softly at the flabbergasted expression that lit up her face. "It would appear, Mrs. Chandler, that you have been hoodwinked." He unsuccessfully tried to suppress a chuckle.

"But for what possible reason?" Rachel demanded. "Derek, how can you justify deliberately frightening this child in such an abominable manner?" She lowered her pipe and leaned back in her chair as she awaited Derek's explanation.

Derek rose from his seat and went to share the sofa with Meghan, placing an arm around her as he took his place beside her. "As you stated this afternoon, Rachel, you and Andrew have had occasion to travel the Trace, and you are well acquainted with the stress and tedium that the journey places on one." He tenderly ran his thumb along Meghan's cheekbone, coaxing her to turn her head so he could gaze upon her innocent beauty. "Well, my Meghan has been quite irritable with me as of late and while I could accustom myself to her standoffishness during our traveling hours, I could not risk her duplicating the same behavior when we bedded down for the night." He grinned sinfully at the blush that reddened her cheeks, but he would not allow her to turn her face from him. "So you see, I was forced to formulate a foolproof plan that would ensure that my arms were never empty during those black, lonely hours of the night." He clasped Meghan's hand and raised it to his lips, offering her a waspish grin.

"I trust that your scheme proved to be successful." Andrew raised his glass in obvious approval as he laughed softly and, as a merry disposition often proves to be contagious, the entire room soon rang with the mirthful laughter of both couples.

"Well, Derek," Andrew began after the laughter subsided. "What sort of stock did you bring with you this time? I haven't had any decent competition around here in a good while, so I certainly hope you won't disappoint me this year."

"Now, Andrew," Rachel broke in. "You men can discuss your horses tomorrow. Don't you think we ought to be planning some sort of reception for this young couple?"

Meghan's mind was a whirlwind of confusion and she was only vaguely aware of the conversation that was taking place around her. Indeed, the one thing that held her complete attention was Derek's arm that surrounded her possessively and caressed her closely against him. She sipped the wine that Derek had poured for her and tried desperately to concentrate on the things that were being said, but her mind was groggy from the wine she had consumed throughout the evening. Derek, she thought dreamily, unaware that her head had dropped to rest on his shoulder, could be so nice when he was not busily plotting ways to torture her.

"It appears that we have bored your bride to sleep." Andrew observed Meghan's peacefully sleeping face as she reclined against Derek. "For all that she is British, Derek, I will admit that you have chosen well."

"Thank you, Andrew. Coming from you, I shall consider that a supreme compliment." Derek retrieved the wine goblet from Meghan's limp hand and placed it on the table. "You will forgive her, won't you? I know that she will be beside herself with embarrassment in the morning when she realizes that she fell asleep while you were planning a party for us."

"Nonsense," Rachel chided. "The poor dear is obviously worn out." She glanced at Meghan fondly. "Would you like me to summon Lizzie to assist you when you take her upstairs?"

"No," Derek said slowly, gathering her up in his arms. "I think that I quite know where everything is," he added wickedly and sauntered toward the door with his agreeable burden. And with his back to them, he did not see the look of genuine approval that passed between Rachel and Andrew as he left the room with Meghan.

Chapter Sixteen

Meghan sat in dismal contemplation before the dressing table mirror while the sounds of the music and laughter of the party drifted upward through the open window. But the gay atmosphere of the festivities below was not reflected on Meghan's pretty face. In fact, anyone seeing the distressing frown would never suspect that she was the guest of honor for whom the party was being given. Party, she thought bleakly. How could anyone expect her to be festive after the startling discovery she had made earlier in the day?

When she awoke that morning Meghan was not surprised to find that Derek had already risen and ridden off with Andrew. Derek never confided in her as to the purpose for their morning jaunts, but she suspected it had to do with the horse race she knew them to be organizing. Quickly, Meghan donned her clothes and descended the stairs to search for Rachel, finally locating her in the garden.

"Good morning, Meghan," Rachel called cheerfully. "Did you have breakfast?"

"I am not very hungry this morning," Meghan explained.

"As I recollect you haven't had breakfast a single morning this week." Rachel returned to her knees to inspect the progress of a particular plant. "Most folks are quite partial to my cooking."

"You are an excellent cook," Meghan hastened to assure her. "It's just that lately I have been suffering from a queasy stomach and it has affected my appetite." She kneeled beside Rachel. "May I help you with this? Perhaps it will help stimulate my faulty appetite."

They worked diligently in the garden until the sound of approaching horses and the lofty noon sun made them realize that they would soon be summoned to the dinner table.

"That must be the men returning." Rachel stood up slowly, placing a comforting hand to the small of her back. "Andrew keeps telling me that I am getting too old for this sort of thing, but I love it so. Well, we best get back to the house so we can freshen up before dinner."

Meghan stood up suddenly, but quickly regretted her abrupt movement, for she was momentarily crippled by a sharp pain in her abdomen that left her breathless and gasping for air, causing her to sink to the ground on her knees.

"Meghan!" Rachel was instantly by her side. "What is it?"

"I . . . I'm not sure. I suddenly felt so weak," she stammered and continued to clutch her hands to her stomach.

"Here, let me help you out of this hot sun." Rachel grasped Meghan firmly by the arm and assisted her to the shade of a large tree. "I'll summon Derek to carry you to the house." She turned to go, but Meghan's hand shot out and fastened tightly around her wrist despite her weakened condition.

"Please, do not leave me. I shall be all right in a few moments, and you will have disturbed Derek for nothing." She released Rachel's arm and the older woman returned to her side. "It was foolish of me to venture out into the sun without my bonnet and Derek will likely tease me unmercifully for my silly blunder."

"I believe that the sun is not entirely to blame for your present condition," Rachel murmured thoughtfully.

"What do you mean?" Meghan was puzzled by the soft smile that adorned Rachel's face.

"I was just considering the symptoms."

"Symptoms?" Meghan's eyebrows arched upward in a perplexed frown, but then her eyes widened and the color returned to her cheeks as she realized the hidden implication behind Rachel's statement. She lurched forward to grasp Rachel's hand. "Do you mean that you think I am . . ." She could not finish her question, but her eyes dropped instinctively to her stomach.

"I believe there is a strong possibility that you are carrying Derek's child." She patted Meghan's hand gently. "That would account for your tiredness and loss of appetite. And although the sun could have played a hand in this episode, my every feminine instinct tells me that you are with child." She stood up and carefully assisted Meghan to her feet and hugging her fondly, she said, "I am so happy for you, my dear. As you know, Andrew and I were never blessed with children of our own and, consequently, we adopted a son and assumed the responsibility of rearing two of my nephews. And while we love the children dearly, I am convinced that there could be no greater experience than presenting a baby, the result of your combined love, to your husband. You are indeed fortunate to be able to give this most precious gift to Derek." Her eyes misted over while she talked and she brushed the tears away before she again turned to Meghan. "When are you going to tell Derek the happy news?"

"I . . . I don't know," Meghan replied weakly, still thunderstruck by the revelation that she was pregnant with Derek's child. She had attributed her occasional bouts of dizziness and nausea to the recent events that had disrupted her life and she had dismissed the skipping of her last two monthly cycles to this supposition as well. Never had she dreamed that she was *pregnant*.

What am I to do, she thought desperately, and what will Derek's reaction be? She turned her head slightly; so that Rachel could not witness the worried expression that shrouded her face. Suddenly her mind was filled with reflections of the last night she and Derek had spent together on his riverboat and she recalled how, thinking her to be asleep, Derek had divulged his plan to send her away when they returned to Chandalara. If she were to tell him of her condition, he might decide to revise his plans and keep her at Chandalara out of some sense of obligation for the baby. And while Meghan would give anything to have Derek ask her to stay with him, she would not do so merely because he felt responsible for the child. She would readily accept his love, but not his pity and for this reason alone she realized that she would *not* tell Derek of her condition.

"Meghan?" Rachel asked hesitantly. "Are you all right? You seem to be distressed about something. Surely, it is not the news about the child that has upset you."

"Oh, no, it's just that I am a little surprised. Derek and I have only been married a few months and we have never discussed the possibility of children," she quickly explained. "Please, do not mention this to Derek. I need a little time to accustom myself to this discovery and I am sure he would make much a to-do."

"My dear, I wouldn't dream of spoiling your surprise." Rachel was obviously affronted that Meghan would suggest she might do such a thing. "But I do hope that you tell him before you return to Chandalara. Andrew and I are quite fond of Derek and would derive great pleasure in sharing this joyous news with him." She bent to collect the bouquet of flowers she had cut to decorate the dining room table. "Come along. The men are probably wondering where we are." She started down the path toward the gate that led from the garden. Meghan sighed deeply before she hurried after her.

Meghan was awakened from her silent deliberations by the sounds of two giggling girls who had entered the room to check their appearance. Offering them a warm smile she rose from the chair and smoothed the skirt of her gown, the same gown she had worn their first night at the Hermitage, and left the room to search for Derek.

Rachel had kept her promise about not telling Derek of the baby, but Meghan had been unable to prevent her from disclosing the fact that she had been overcome by heat exhaustion in the garden, so that Derek would not overtax her on the dance floor, she had explained. But Meghan loved the exhilaration of a lively dance, and she had finally coaxed a promise from Derek that they might have one dance together, and Meghan was determined that he should honor his agreement.

After dinner, the double doors between the parlor and dining room were opened and the furniture was pushed back so as not to hamper the dancers. The musicians had taken their station and the dancing had already begun when Meghan again descended the staircase. Several of the couples were involved in a vigorous country dance and Meghan stood wistfully aside, one dainty foot absently keeping time with the music, while her alert eyes carefully scanned the dance floor for Derek.

"He's out there," Rachel said, and Meghan glanced up in time to see her nodding toward the front door. "He and Andrew and some of the other men are discussing the race," she laughed.

"It is beyond me how men can place such importance on a trivial matter like a horse race and then claim that women are frivolous creatures." Meghan tapped her foot impatiently. "Well, I do not know how you feel, Rachel, but Derek promised me a dance and I am going to remind him of his bargain." She stalked toward the door with a determined gait, but paused uncertainly as she became aware of the men's voices just beyond the enclosure.

"Tell me, Chandler, rumor has it that you brought some fine, competitive stock with you this time. Is there any truth in that?" asked one of the men.

"Indeed he did," interrupted another voice that Meghan immediately recognized as Kevin Burwell. The man had sat beside her at the supper table and had proceeded to bore her enormously with his pomposity and egotism. Carefully, Meghan inched closer to the door so she might better hear the exchange.

"I brought my own horse, Trojan. I believe he is capable of showing your fine Tennessee thoroughbreds a thing or two." He drew on his cigar and glanced casually toward the house, catching a glimpse of the skirt of a blue gown before it was quickly jerked from his view. Derek smothered a crafty smile and again addressed his captive audience. "But my wife's horse, now there is a superb animal."

"We have all seen the animal, Derek," Burwell was talking again, "and we agree that it is perhaps the most impressive horse we have ever laid eyes on." He stopped for a moment to consider Derek. "But I'm curious. Why is it that you haven't entered him in the race? Perhaps there is some truth to the gossip that has been circulating," he laughed speculatively.

"Oh," Derek droned indifferently. "To what gossip do you make reference?"

"Only that you cannot enter your wife's horse because *she* won't allow you to ride it," he guffawed loudly. "Of course, I think that you are more of a man than that. A real man would not permit a mere woman to make his decisions for him," he scoffed.

"Whatever my reason," Derek's face grew somber, "it is *my* affair and you should not concern yourself with the matter," Derek pointedly informed him.

"All right, men." Andrew, thinking that the situation had gone far enough, decided to interrupt before the matter got out of hand. "We have tarried long enough. I imagine the ladies are wondering what has become of us."

With this declaration, Meghan gathered up her skirts and raced back to the parlor door so Derek would not suspect her of eavesdropping. But Derek was not among the men who returned to the house and again she marched determinedly to the door, intending to call to him, but she could not make out his figure in the darkness.

Where could he have disappeared to, she thought stubbornly, and stepped out into the night to continue her search. It was then that her sensitive nose caught the faintest hint of his aromatic cigar and the scent led her to the garden. He was leaning against a tree, his arms folded thoughtfully across his chest and he stared off in the darkness, his brooding eyes focusing on some distant star. He was completely oblivious to her silent surveillance, or so she thought, and occasionally she observed him lift his cigar to his lips then deliberately exhale the smoke in precise circles, the contemplative expression on his face never wavering.

"Are you going to stand there all night, Meghan? If you took the trouble to follow me out here you evidently have something on your mind." His voice sounded troubled, but his eyes were tender when he finally turned to gaze at her.

"How did you know it was me?" she asked quietly, approaching him.

"My dear, if I were to be blindfolded and placed in a room with a thousand wenches, I verily say that I could handily pick you from them." He crushed the cigar beneath his boot and captured her hands in his. "You have the most delightful fragrance about you." His lips parted in a smile and all the bitterness was gone from his face.

"I found you the same way," she said proudly.

"What?"

"Your cigar," she explained.

"Oh, a disgusting habit. I really should give it up. Now tell me, my sweet, why did you pursue me to the garden?" He released her hands and leaned his rugged shoulder against the tree, his warm gaze ever caressing her.

"A dance," she said gaily and clasping her hands behind her back, she gently swayed with the music that filtered from the house and mingled with the fresh, summer breeze. "You *did* promise me one," she reminded him.

"Yes, I seem to recall making some sort of commitment." His manner was light, but the troublesome frown had returned to blemish his attractive face. "Shall we rejoin the festivities?" He gallantly offered her his arm.

"It means a lot to you, doesn't it?" Meghan's voice was soft and she lifted her hand to smooth the worried lines from the corners of his eyes.

"The dance?" He wrinkled his brow in a puzzled grimace, feigning ignorance as to the purpose behind her query.

"Do not tease me," she pleaded. "I would like to help you if I could."

"Yes," he sighed heavily, "the race means a great deal to me, but you should not let it trouble you. And though I am grateful for your offer, there is really nothing that you can do." He grasped the hand that still caressed his face and pressed the palm to his lips. "Don't ask," he suddenly whispered and pulled her

371

gently into his arms.

"What?" she questioned softly and rested her cheek against his chest, feeling considerably reassured by the steady, even rhythm of his heart.

"You were about to ask me why the race is so important, and I am not certain that I can adequately explain my motives."

"You could try," she whispered faintly. "I'll listen."

He glanced down into her radiant, green eyes that sparkled like diamonds in the moonlight and he tightened his arms around her. "Perhaps it stems from my impetuous childhood," he began. "It would seem that whenever the circumstances of my birth were discovered there was always someone present to ridicule me, or offer a lewd comment. In fact, I started defending my honor at quite an early age—seven to be exact." He almost appeared prideful in his boast, but Meghan detected the lines of pain that creased his weary eyes.

"What happened?" she murmured quietly.

"One of the young locals made a base comment about Mother thereby forcing me to uphold her honor and prove to the lackey that I was not one to be toyed with." His eyes grew increasingly dark and Meghan shivered slightly at their intensity.

"And?"

"I whipped him until he was broken and bloody and crawled away from me on his belly like the snake that he was," he said coldly, but his wide shoulders sagged gloomily as he recalled the misfortunes his illegitimate birth had forced upon him. "I have had to prove myself to every righteous snob that ever questioned my ability as a man, and I shall continue to do so until I have proven to all the Thomas Bainbridges and Kevin Burwells of the world that it is not *who* a man is, but *what* he makes of his life that is the deciding factor when a man's ultimate worth is estimated."

He offered Meghan a wan smile. "You see, it was not so easy to explain."

"But I do understand," Meghan offered earnestly. "And you are wrong when you think that I cannot help you. Champion can win your race for you. I know he can," she hurried on excitedly.

"Meghan," Derek began patiently, "I have scoured the entire countryside for a man to ride Champion, but I fear you have spoiled him, my sweet, for he snubs all save you."

"Oh, pooh," Meghan chided. "The men you interviewed simply must not know how to handle horses." She fell silent, seriously considering their alternatives. Suddenly her lips parted in a wide smile. "Derek, *you* could ride Champion."

"Lest you've forgotten, your friend has displayed a similar discontent when I am on his back," Derek reminded her. "Besides, my weight would impede his speed."

"Perhaps," Meghan agreed. "But it cannot hurt to try. Come with me to the stable," she said abruptly as she hooked her arm in his and started down the path, leaving him no other alternative except to accompany her.

They strolled arm in arm to the stable. Meghan waited beside the door while Derek found a lantern that illuminated the entire length of the stable when he ushered her inside.

"Meghan, I admit that my curiosity is piqued." His eyes flickered merrily like the wick in the lantern. "Were it not that I know you so well, I might be inclined to speculate that you lured me here so that we might take advantage of that tempting mound of hay."

"I did not *lure* you," she replied indignantly. "But if you are not interested—" she threw up her hands in defeat "—we might as well return to the house. I am certain Andrew will grant me the pleasure of a dance." She tossed her curls haughtily and made a grand gesture as if she would leave.

"A moment, my fine lady." He grabbed her arm. "I did not journey this distance for nothing. Either you make known to me your little secret, or . . ." The implied threat hung in the hot, night air.

"Get your saddle," she instructed.

"*What*? Do you mean to go for a ride in the middle of the party that Andrew and Rachel have graciously arranged for us?"

Meghan's response to his insipid question was to cast her eyes to a sturdy beam that supported the roof and set her foot impatiently tapping upon the hard, earthen floor.

Derek studied her for a long moment and, recognizing the stubborn set of her determined mouth, he decided that the sooner he indulged her in her unusual request, the sooner he would be allowed to return to the party and his friends. With this thought in mind, Derek retreated into the tack room to gather his gear; when he returned, he discovered that Meghan had released Champion from his stall.

Meghan stood beside him, softly crooning to him in a gentle voice and turning to Derek, she offered him her sunniest smile. "It's all right," she said brightly. "You may saddle him."

"All the same to you, Meghan, I'd rather not tangle with your monster tonight." Derek eyed the animal warily.

"But you do not understand, Derek." Meghan persisted as she grasped his arm and urged him closer.

374

"Champion is perfectly willing to let you ride him."

"And just how did you arrive at such a divine revelation?"

Champion, having grown somewhat indifferent with the proceedings, lowered his head and began to nibble at the straw that had absently fallen to the stable floor.

"Oh, one just has to know how to talk to him. Trust me," she pleaded as she took the bridle and went to slip it over Champion's head. "He will offer you no resistance."

The expression that darkened Derek's rugged face was one of total skepticism as he cautiously strode forward. "I still don't understand why you think he will accept me today when but a few weeks ago he tossed me on my duff." He regarded Meghan cynically, but when his eyes met her resolute face, he shrugged away his doubts and promptly saddled Champion. And Meghan stood by the horse's head, cooing loving phrases in his ear, while Derek eased himself onto Champion's back.

Derek fully expected the animal to bolt with the unfamiliar pressure of his weight, but he could not discern that Champion even noticed the difference. He directed the animal through the wide barn and trotted him around the stable yard for a few minutes. Once thoroughly satisfied that Champion had accepted him, Derek returned to the barn and slid from the saddle to quickly enfold Meghan in his sturdy embrace.

"I am unconvinced as to your methods," Derek swung her around in a wide circle, "but you were right." His eyes caressed her fondly and when Meghan opened her mouth to speak, he quickly covered it with his forefinger. "Blast it, woman," he bellowed. "Can you not for once permit me to finish a single sentence before you interrupt me? I was about to ask your permission to ride your beloved Champion in the race

375

next Saturday." His lips parted in the familiar impish grin that Meghan knew she could not resist. "Well?" he asked anxiously.

"I would not have brought you to the stable had that not been my intention," she said softly.

Derek let out a wild whoop that Meghan felt sure could have been heard in the town had the noise of the party not cloaked it, and he again picked her up and swirled her around in a full circle. "Meghan, did I not promise you a dance?" He placed a tender kiss upon her upturned lips.

"Faith, and I was beginning to suspect that you were a man who did not keep his word." She placed her hands on her hips and stood away from him, fearful that if he spun her around again she might be overcome by dizziness.

"My word is binding, so you can well believe that we shall dance, just as you may also believe that I promise you a *ride* you will not soon forget." He bestowed upon her another long, lingering kiss then hurried to un-saddle Champion, leaving her to contemplate the dual implication of his last statement.

The race track was already a flurry of activity by the time Derek and Meghan and the Jacksons arrived. It appeared as if the entire county had turned out to witness the highly publicized affair. Children were running about willy-nilly, oblivious to the shouts of their parents, who sat idly by on blankets, recuperating from a recently devoured picnic lunches. In the distance Meghan could hear the nervous whinnying of horses that were being readied for the day's events, and it was in this direction that Derek turned his attention as he lifted Meghan from the Jackson's carriage.

"Nervous?" she whispered against his ear before he

deposited her on the ground.

"You would not believe me were I to tell you otherwise." He strolled with her through the grass until he selected a vantage from which she could ideally view the races. "You should be able to see quite well from here, though it is good that you remembered your bonnet." He glanced toward the sun and squinted against the glare. "I fear that it is going to be a real scorcher today." His eyes darted past her to discover Rachel and Andrew slowly making their way toward them. "Promise me that you will return to the carriage if you should feel unwell."

"You need not worry, Derek. I will see that no mishap befalls your lovely wife," Rachel promised as she and Andrew joined them.

"Thank you, Rachel. I knew I could depend on you. Well, Andrew, what do you say that you and I get this race started?"

"You appear mighty eager to get yourself whipped." Andrew slapped him on the back as the two men started off in the direction of the horses.

"Well," Rachel sighed, "I figure that we have a good half hour before the first race begins."

Meghan shook the daydreams from her head and turned to smile at Rachel. "Yes, that would be Champion and Mr. Burwell's horse, Stardust. I can hardly wait."

"Why don't you sit down here and rest for a while?" Rachel suggested, and she extended her hand toward the chairs that Andrew had carried to the site for them.

"Thank you, but I am far too excited to sit," Meghan responded eagerly.

"Perhaps you would care for a glass of cold lemonade," Rachel offered. "We have a scrumptious picnic lunch as well, but since Andrew and Derek seldom eat before a race, I thought we would wait till afterwards and have a victory lunch."

"Fine," Meghan agreed. "And I would love some lemonade." Meghan accepted the glass and proceeded to pace back and forth, absently sipping the refreshing liquid. Her wandering eyes irrevocably fastened upon Derek as he conversed with his friends.

But a sudden commotion a few yards away caused Meghan to avert her gaze momentarily. Kevin Burwell had just climbed atop his mount, but apparently the animal had not responded favorably to his master's command, for Meghan watched him jerk the poor animal's head viciously to one side. And the string of oaths he hurled at the beast could be heard easily by anyone in the vicinity.

Meghan frowned sourly that the man would stoop to such cruel treatment of a defenseless animal and forced herself to concentrate on Derek. He had worked diligently the entire week with Champion, practicing with him and getting him accustomed to responding to his unfamiliar weight. There had been many times when Champion had ignored Derek's command, but never had Derek reacted the way Burwell just did.

"Meghan, the race is about to begin!" Rachel called excitedly.

Meghan directed her gaze to the two riders who anxiously awaited the discharge of the gun that would signal the beginning of the race. Derek sat majestically upon Champion; his shoulders were squarely set, and a look of grim determination lined his sensuous mouth, which blossomed into a wide grin as he became aware of her close scrutiny. Meghan returned the smile and when Derek lifted his fingers to his lips to blow her a friendly kiss, she contentedly retraced her steps to her chair and sat down beside Rachel.

Meghan did not remain seated for long, however, for when the starting gun sounded, she jumped to her feet to urge Champion on and did not reclaim her chair for the remainder of the race. The horses were scheduled to circle the track twice and by the time Derek urged Champion across the finish line a full length ahead of Burwell's entry, Meghan's throat was hoarse and dry from shouting words of encouragement.

Meghan hurried toward the stable to congratulate Derek, but soon discovered a throng of people already surrounding him, making her progress discouragingly difficult. But her attention was suddenly averted by the painful whinny of an animal in distress and she whirled in time to see Kevin Burwell strike his horse savagely with a riding crop. Meghan uttered an indignant grumble and picked up her skirts as she started to run toward the man. Her path was blocked, however, as Derek maneuvered Champion in front of her and, reaching down with one powerful arm, he swept her onto the saddle before him.

"Have you no kiss for the victor?" He waited not for her answer, but covered her mouth with his and leisurely plundered its vulnerable softness while the crowd below whistled and cheered them on. Finally, Derek released her from his fiery kiss, but his lips continued to caress the loveliness of her fine skin and they traveled lightly from the corner of her mouth to her ear to whisper quietly, "I know you are upset, but there is nothing we can do about it."

"But—" She shifted on the saddle so she could better observe him and was surprised to see that the look that darkened his face was murderous. So, at last they agreed on something. He could not abide such cruel, inhumane treatment either.

"Shhh," he cautioned. "Burwell is coming this way."

"Well, Derek, may I be the first to offer my congratulations on a splendid race? You handled the beast magnificently." He paused in front of Champion and admiringly stroked the horse's head. "Tell me, would you consider selling him? I assure you that I can make it worth your while."

"No," Meghan informed him curtly. "Champion is not for sale."

Burwell regarded Meghan briefly with mild disdain before returning his attention to Derek. "As I stated, Derek, I am quite prepared to make you a handsome offer for the animal."

"You must forgive my wife's zealous outburst, Mr. Burwell," Derek apologized and threw Meghan a remonstrative glance as he slid to the ground to better converse with the man.

"Then, am I to assume that you might consider selling the animal?" Burwell looked hopeful.

"*No!*" Meghan shrieked. "Champion is mine! I have seen the way you handle your animals, Mr. Burwell and were I to consider selling my horse it would not be to the likes of you!" She threw her leg over the saddle so she sat astride his huge back, and dug her heels into Champion's flanks.

Champion bolted forward with such fury that Derek was momentarily stunned by the chunks of earth that his mammoth hooves flung in the air. They rode for a distance along the main road until Meghan's alert eyes caught the imprint of another trail and she directed Champion into the woods. The branches from low-lying trees snatched at her face and hair as she flew along the narrow path and bitter tears filled her eyes as she considered how Derek had very nearly betrayed her. How could he do such a thing to her? And worse still, how could she love such a man who would think so little of her feelings that he would barter off her only cherished possession?

She had no idea how far they had traveled. Her central concern was to get Champion safely away from Derek. He was all that she had left and she could not bear to part with him. If she could but find an inn where she could spend the night, perhaps she would be able to collect her thoughts and formulate a plan for the immediate future.

But I have no money, she thought disparagingly.

And then she remembered her wedding ring. That should bring a tidy sum that would sustain her until she could arrange for some type of gainful employment. But it was then that she became aware of the thundering hooves rapidly approaching her from behind and she realized that it would be but a matter of minutes before she was overtaken. In desperation Meghan spurred Champion faster along the trail. Although she was an excellent horsewoman, Meghan was unfamiliar with the path; her uncertainty was transmitted to Champion and he slowed noticeably.

Meghan heard the hoofbeats drawing closer and realized that the rider was almost beside her. And even before she saw the powerful hand reach out to jerk the reins from her grasp, she knew who her pursuer was.

In a flash Derek brought the horses to a halt and jumped to the ground. He hauled Meghan, none too gently, from Champion's back and stood her roughly on the ground before him.

"You little fool!" His shout reverberated in the dense forest, sending a frightened bird into flight from a nearby tree. "Are you trying to get yourself killed?" He shook her fiercely.

Meghan kicked at his legs and pummeled his chest with her fists; in one final desperate attempt to escape his cruel grasp, she raked his bare cheek with her nails.

With a bitter oath Derek shoved her to the ground and straddled her with his long legs. Her nails had opened a deep furrow which now bled freely, and Meghan instantly regretted her impulsive behavior that would likely leave him with an unsightly scar.

"Of all the stupid, scatterbrained, irresponsible tricks!" His face was beet red as he paced back and forth, pounding his fist in the palm of his hand. Suddenly he turned to her. "Just where in blue blazes did you think you were going?"

Meghan shook her head numbly unable to respond as she choked back tears. "I thought you were going to sell Champion to that awful man," she sobbed. "I could not bear to have him taken from me."

Derek dropped to one knee beside her, his mood more subdued than before. "You are always so quick to assume that I am going to hurt you in some way. Have I not taken care of you since we departed from England?"

"Yes," she mumbled lowly.

"The horse belongs to you, Meghan. Next time give me due credit to respond accordingly when approached in matters such as this. It was only natural for Burwell to question *me* about purchasing the animal," he sighed wearily.

"I will try not to react so harshly," she solemnly promised.

"Not only did you nearly scare me to death, bolting off like that," he scolded, "but I had to scratch Trojan from the next race and forfeit to Andrew. *That* did little for my ego, I assure you. In fact, I think that perhaps I should mete out some form of disciplinary action to discourage any similar displays from you in the future." He grinned at her mischievously.

"Derek?" Meghan tried to scamper from his reach.

"Oh no." He grabbed her securely about the waist. "You'll not escape me this time." He scooped her up in his arms and stalked to a fallen tree.

"What . . . what are you going to do?" she shrieked, frantically trying to squirm from his steely embrace.

"Why, my dear, I am going to beat you," he informed her flatly. "A practice that every husband should observe routinely to keep headstrong wives in line." He sat down on the log and, though Meghan continued her futile struggles, he finally managed to turn her over his knee.

"No! Please!" she cried.

"Give me one good reason why I should not administer the thrashing you have so richly earned," he said with placid detachment. Even as he listened for her reply he raised his hand to deliver the first blow.

"The baby!" she cried in utter despair. "You might hurt the baby." She fell into a fit of pitiful sobs.

There. Now he knew.

Derek slowly lowered his hand and lifted Meghan to a sitting position on his lap. The expression of shock and surprise was still on his face when Meghan finally succeeded in checking her sobs. With trembling fingers she brushed the last of the tears from her eyes and pushed herself from Derek's lap to stand on rather wobbly legs.

"Baby?" Derek questioned blankly.

Meghan nodded weakly.

"Are you certain?"

"Yes."

"When did you make this discovery?"

"A few days ago. I was too stupid to recognize the symptoms for what they were. Rachel was the one who guessed the truth." She turned her back on him and gazed off into the distance.

383

"When . . . when will the child be born?" Derek was still visibly shaken with Meghan's revelation, and he did not yet trust his legs to support him.

"Early in the new year," she replied quietly. "February . . . I think."

"Well," he sighed deeply and rose to his feet. "That would mean that you became pregnant on the ship."

"Yes," she muttered dismally. "It would appear that you may add fertility to my rapidly expanding list of faults."

"Meghan?" He reached for her hand and turned her so he could better observe her face. "Are you unhappy about the child?"

Meghan lowered her eyes, unable to muster a response and Derek gathered her to him. "I see. You feared that *I* would be displeased to learn that I am to be a father." The word in relation to himself sounded strange on his lips.

"Are you not?"

"I *am* a little surprised," he admitted. "Though I suppose it was bound to happen sooner or later." He smiled at her thoughtfully. "But the more I think on it, I rather like the idea."

"Really?" She lifted her eyes to search his face for some indication that he might merely be accommodating her for the time being.

"Yes. What man would not be proud of the fact that he has created an heir?" He still held her hand as he led her toward the horses.

"There are those who might not be so proud."

"I suppose," he conceded. "But you forget that I was the product of a situation that did not permit me the companionship of a father. I am not likely to allow the same misfortune to befall my own son."

"Oh, so it is to be a son, is it?" She tried to sound indignant.

"Of course," he boasted. "You would not dare present me with anything less." He observed her crestfallen look, and as he recalled the sour relationship between Meghan and her own father, he silently cursed himself for his thoughtless words. Gently, he tilted her head to enable him to gaze into her eyes and his heart melted when he saw the sadness that dulled their brilliance. "Unless," he continued softly, "you could manage to bestow upon me a daughter who is as beautiful as her mother." He ran the back of his hand along her cheek.

Meghan reached up to grasp his hand. "It really makes no difference to you?" she asked hopefully.

"No. Just make the child strong and healthy, and I will be proud to have it bear my name." He started to assist her onto Champion, but Meghan suddenly threw her arms around his neck and kissed him.

"And I shall be proud to be its mother," she declared happily and allowed him to lift her onto the saddle.

Later that evening, Meghan said good-bye to Derek at the front door of the Hermitage. "Will you be gone long?" She absently straightened the slant of his stock and smoothed the material of his shirt across his muscular chest.

"No. Andrew has an errand to run and I thought I would accompany him. I do not anticipate a late return, but should you grow tired you need not wait up for me. You are not to overexert yourself." He shot a warm glance toward her stomach.

"I won't," she assured him and tilted her head to accept his kiss.

He turned and went down the steps and Meghan watched him mount Trojan. He waved good-bye, and as he and Andrew started down the driveway, Meghan closed the door and walked to the parlor where Rachel sat reading and peacefully puffing on her pipe. Meghan smiled at Rachel as she sat down on the sofa to apply the finishing touches on an infant nightgown that Rachel had insisted she make after learning of the baby.

"So, you finally told him." Rachel lifted her eyes from her book.

"Yes."

"He did not appear to be overly distraught with the news." Rachel lowered her pipe and looked pointedly at Meghan.

"No, he was quite pleased." Meghan held up the tiny gown to inspect her handiwork and as she lowered the sewing again, she met Rachel's steadfast gaze. "I suppose you think me foolish to keep such news from him."

"Not foolish. You merely reacted as would any young bride who is still a bit insecure in her marriage," she stated flatly. "Granted, some women might find their husbands unmoved with the prospect of fatherhood, but I knew what Derek's reaction would be. You see, Meghan, Derek has been a favorite of ours for several years. We know him perhaps better than any of his friends, even you, my dear," she said candidly. "We were, of course, surprised to learn that he had married, for Derek had always declared himself to be a confirmed bachelor.

"But after meeting you and observing the two of you together, Andrew and I both agree that marrying you was probably the wisest move that Derek ever made. You possess the tender nature and gentle understanding that is the ideal foil for his somewhat rash tendencies." She went to sit beside Meghan on the sofa, and taking her hand in her own, Rachel patted it gently. "Therefore, when I realized that Derek was totally committed to you and your marriage, I knew that he would be

386

delighted with your gift of a child."

"I guess I should have exhibited more faith in Derek," Meghan murmured weakly.

"Well, men are funny creatures sometimes, but I have yet to find a comparable substitute for my Andrew." Rachel laughed softly as she stood up. "The excitement of the race has left me quite exhausted and if you have no further need of me, I believe I shall retire for the night."

"Go right ahead," Meghan urged. "I think I shall stay up a little longer."

"Can I summon anything for you before I retire?" Rachel inquired considerately.

"A bath would be heavenly, if it would not be an imposition."

"No imposition. I shall instruct Lizzie to draw you a bath. Oh, and Meghan." Rachel paused near the parlor door.

"Yes?"

"Just in case you are wondering, Andrew and I heartily approve of you. Derek has had a rather difficult life and we were both immensely pleased and relieved that he should display such excellent taste in selecting a wife." Her words were warm and sincerely delivered.

"Thank you."

"One does not expect gratitude for expressing the truth. I trust that you will have a restful night, and I shall see you in the morning."

"Good night." Meghan observed the closing of the parlor door before refocusing her attention on the tiny piece of clothing that lay in her lap.

Meghan tried to keep her thoughts from wandering to the one circumstance that she felt would drive her mad: the fact that the child she carried was not the result of a happy marriage, but of a relationship that was held together simply by Derek's lust and her own reluctance to aggravate his temper by attempting to run away from him. She had tried that only hours earlier and had quickly learned the folly of such behavior. Besides, if she were to be truthful she did not want to leave Derek.

"If he would but consider making me his real wife," she sighed forlornly.

The fact that her child in reality would be a bastard disturbed her considerably, but only slightly more than the deceitful life she was currently living. She abhorred the lie she lived with daily, and she especially detested the fact that Derek had presented her to the Jacksons with such clever aplomb that they, too, had been deceived. They were such a wonderful couple, so completely devoted to each other. What would their reaction be if they learned that she and Derek were entangled in a relationship that, in short, made a mockery of their own perfect marriage?

Meghan sighed desolately as she slowly climbed the stairs to her room. As she had requested there was a tub of warm water awaiting her. Lizzie had remained in the chamber to assist Meghan, but she dismissed the girl, assuring her that she could see to her own needs.

Meghan disrobed and gradually lowered her aching body into the tub and sighed languidly as the stimulating heat of the water relaxed her tired muscles and dissolved her apprehensions. Meghan vigorously lathered her legs and arms and was attempting to do the same to her back when Derek's mellow voice broke into the stillness.

"May I offer my assistance, madam?" He softly kicked the door closed and strode into the room.

"I can manage," she murmured lowly.

Derek placed the tray he carried on the bedside table then dragged a chair alongside the tub and sat down. "I am quite knowledgeable as to your proficiencies, but won't you grant me this one little request by allowing me to serve you?" He leaned forward to kiss her, but Meghan detected liquor on his breath and unthinkingly, she braced a wet hand against his chest to stay his movement.

"You, sir, are drunk!" she accused.

"Only a little," he said defensively.

"And exactly what became of your important errand?" she demanded, dubious that an urgent errand ever existed.

"We saw to it." He pushed her hand away and kissed her doubtful lips before continuing. "We had a little celebration is all."

"*Little!*" she exclaimed.

"Uh-huh." He took the cloth and soap from her hands and lathered the wash cloth as he spoke, "I am saving the *big* celebration for later." He winked at her. "That is why I drank sparingly." He leaned close to whisper in her ear, "I wanted to be sure that I was capable of conducting a proper celebration with you."

"You are positively shameful," Meghan chided. "Rachel shall surely thrash you for leading Andrew down such a wicked path, and I will not blame her."

"It was his idea." Derek scrubbed her back while he talked. "He suggested we visit the tavern in Nashville so we might suitably toast my accomplishment."

"*Your* accomplishment!" Meghan emerged from the bath amidst a flurry of wildly scattered water pellets. "Why, you boasting blowhard!" She jerked the soap-filled cloth from his hand and shoved it into his surprised face before he could react to her attack. Wrapping a towel about her, she began to pace back and forth furiously. "You brag of your deed as if I were a broodmare while you strut about town like a proud

389

peacock, assuming credit for doing little more than planting your seed within me. You could have done as much with any woman, but, no, you had to prove your dominance over me."

She abruptly halted her attack as Derek grabbed her and hurled her to the bed. Before she could move, he was beside her, pinning her to the mattress. His eyes were red from the burning soap, but they danced with smug amusement as they beheld her startled face.

"Yes," he murmured, "I suppose I did." He plucked a wisp of her hair from the pillow and used it to trace abstract designs along her shoulder. "Perhaps you provided a more provocative challenge than did all those other women."

"I was not aware that you found your other lady friends to be so uninteresting," she said. "It was lucky for you that a refined lady of quality, such as myself, happened along."

"You will do for the time being," he said jokingly, but when Meghan opened her mouth to utter a sharp retort, he quickly covered it with his hand. "Tut, tut, my sweet, I will not permit you to spoil the evening by allowing you to lash me with that vicious tongue of yours," he scolded her. "Faith, if the child you bear is as chatty as its mother, I fear that I shall never encounter another moment of peace," he sighed in exaggerated despair, shaking his head. "Now, sweet Meghan, I am going to remove my hand, but if I hear one discouraging word from you, I will be sorely tempted to remove your stubborn hide to the stable where you can sleep with the other mulish creatures," he said sternly as he cautiously lowered his hand.

"I will be good," she promised. "Do not be angry."

Derek pulled away from her and considered her for a moment before his mouth parted in a wide grin. "I am not angry," he managed softly. "How can I be angry with the captivating wench for whom I have planned a gala evening?"

"You have been promising me an exciting evening ever since you returned." She smoothed the material along the lapel of his jacket. "Just where is all of this going to take place?"

"Why, in the arms of your lover, of course," Derek chuckled and reached for the glasses and bottle that rested on the tray he had brought into the room.

"Champagne?" she asked.

"You sound surprised. Did you not think that I would supply the best for the mother of my child?" He sounded a trifle affronted, but Meghan knew that he teased her.

"Silly, it's just that I have not had champagne since the night of my betro—since we left London." She altered her statement and giggled nervously, hoping that she had not spoiled the magical moment by inadvertently mentioning the past. But if Derek had caught her slip, he gave no indication.

"One customarily giggles *after* the consumption of the beverage. I understand that it has something to do with the bubbles." He handed her the glasses while he opened the bottle.

Meghan adjusted the pillows behind her and leaned against the headboard, taking care to drape the towel around her naked torso. She held out the glasses while Derek filled them then she settled back to sip the beverage.

"A moment." Derek held up his hand to stay her movement. "I should like to propose a toast." He extended his glass to her. "To our son . . . or daughter. May it inherit its mother's beauty and its father's charm, wit, personality . . ."

"Oh, you," Meghan giggled helplessly at his antics.

"See what I mean. It's the bubbles." His statement only succeeded in making her giggle all the more.

Derek quickly drained his glass and held Meghan's to her lips till she had emptied hers as well. He then started to refill the goblet, but Meghan placed a hand over the glass.

"Sir," she said sternly, "is it your intention to render me under the influence?"

"To be truthful, I was contemplating that notion," he admitted seriously.

"Why?"

Derek again emptied the contents of his glass before responding to her question. "I thought that you might not find my lovemaking so repulsive were you a bit tipsy."

"Oh, Derek." She grasped his hand and slipped it beneath the towel to rest on her stomach. "If I found your advances to be unbearable, we could not have created the child that grows within me." She stared at him warmly and could have sworn that she observed his eyes mist over with tears. Then her eyes beheld the ugly scratch she had inflicted upon him earlier in the day, and she instinctively reached out to touch it, causing him to wince with pain. "It would appear that my impulsive action has left you with an unsightly remembrance."

"It's nothing." He drew her hand from his cheek to his lips and tenderly kissed it. "It will likely cause me some slight discomfort for a few days. Nothing more." He shrugged the incident aside.

"I fear that it may leave a nasty scar." She silently condemned herself for her behavior. "I'm sorry," she murmured softly.

"Don't be. I'm not." To her surprise he sounded

almost proud. "A scar adds a rather distinguished air to one's features, don't you think? Everyone will want to know how I acquired the ghastly thing, and I will be quite the center of attention, I think. I shall have to conjure up some daring tale to relate to my friends," he stated grandly.

"Shameful." Meghan shook her head.

"Pretty girls will likely be sympathetic and express a desire to console me." He glanced at her mischievously then quickly averted his gaze.

"You attempt any stunts like that and you may rest assured that you will find your other cheek similarly adorned," she warned him.

"I have experienced both the force of your wrath and the sweetness of your more womanly charms and, if I may be permitted to expostulate, I admit that I have a preference for the latter." He slowly removed her towel and let it fall to the floor.

His gaze wandered from her eyes to her abdomen, back to her eyes, and he smiled at her affectionately. "You are not very far along and yet, you already possess a certain glow and I think that I can detect the slightest beginning of a rounding belly." He stroked her stomach gently.

"Oh, Derek, that is the most distressing aspect of having a baby. It's I who will repulse you when I have grown fat and ugly with child," she pouted forlornly.

"Not likely." He laughed good-naturedly. "I shall hold you as dear as always." He leaned forward to kiss her fears away and his hand instinctively climbed to caress her breast. "Do you think the babe would mind a slight intrusion?" Derek asked huskily, his lips placing a constant trail of fiery kisses from her lips to her breasts and back to her lips.

"Humph! You were never so considerate of his

mother's wishes," she reminded him with feigned indignation.

"*His?*" Derek raised a puzzled eyebrow.

"I would like it to be a boy," she explained simply.

"Well, in reply to his mother's criticism." Derek stood to remove his clothing before joining her in the bed. Pulling the sheet over them, he draped his arm about her shoulder and said, "I never bothered to consult her, because I knew that deep within her heart she wanted me to make love to her." He caught the fist in his hand before it landed a blow, and, forcing her down in the bed, he covered her mouth with his to smother her fiery oaths.

Chapter Seventeen

Derek awakened in the night to discover that Meghan had disappeared from their chamber. Wiping the sleep from his eyes, he quickly donned his trousers and boots and abandoned the room in search of her, finally locating her outside. She was standing beneath a huge, oak tree, gazing up at the full moon. And he knew her thoughts were miles away when he came up behind her and encircled her waist with his arms and she did not so much as flinch at the sudden seizure.

"Was it my unbearable snoring that drove you from my bed?" He asked, gently nipping the nape of her neck with his lips.

Meghan shook her head. "You do not snore," she whispered.

394

"*Something* must have disturbed you to have driven you out into the night." He pulled her tightly against his chest and snuggled her close to him. "Is it the child that worries you?"

Meghan nodded reluctantly and her shoulders sagged wearily. "Yes, a little."

"But I don't understand. I thought you were pleased with the notion of motherhood."

"I am. It's just . . ." She whirled suddenly and flung herself into his arms. "Oh, Derek. I am frightened!"

"I suppose it is only natural for one who has never borne a child to have reservations." Derek gently soothed her. He smoothed the hair from her face and in the bright moonlight, he could detect that slight glimmer of tears in her eyes and the wet paths that trickled down her cheeks. "Tell me why you are frightened."

"You will think me foolish." She turned her head, so he could not see her face.

But Derek caught her just under the chin and compelled her to look at him. "No, I won't. Tell me," he insisted gently.

"I'm afraid that something may go wrong, that perhaps the child or myself will . . . will . . . die." She labored over the final word as if she feared that once it was voiced openly the chances of some misfortune would be drastically increased.

Derek could think of no comforting response so he compensated by pulling her more closely within the shelter of his embrace to reassure her. "Why should you harbor such unsettling thoughts?"

"Because, my own mother never regained her strength after I was born, and there was one time when I assisted Elizabeth as she attended one of Papa's tenants who was about to give birth. Oh, Derek," she gripped his arm fiercely, "it was horrible! The girl was in excruciating pain and she screamed and cried for hours. But her cries were not as jolting as was the hollow silence that filled the room when her screams abruptly halted."

"She died?" Derek questioned softly.

"Yes, as did the child. I shall never forget the terrible sight of her bruised and mutilated body." Meghan rested her cheek against Derek's broad chest, taking great comfort in his nearness.

"You *must* forget it, Meghan. Not all pregnancies end so savagely." He nestled her to him. "You have every reason to be a little apprehensive, I suppose," he conceded. "After all, you have been uprooted from your home and dragged to a strange land bereft of family and friends. You have been the object of scandal and you have been mercilessly beaten and threatened with measures to which no lady of quality should ever be subjected.

"Add to that my staunch refusal to release you even though we are not married and it is little wonder that you are frightened. Faith, a lesser woman could not have endured the hardships that you have suffered," he said flatly. "And while I will admit that I am chiefly responsible for your present situation, I must remind you that we can do little to alter what has passed between us. It does not dictate, however, that my attitude and feelings cannot change. I shall henceforth strive to be more understanding of your needs and perhaps you will become less tense as you approach your time." He kissed her suddenly and released her from his embrace. "There now, little one. Feel better?"

"Yes, except . . ." she began uncertainly, unsure if she could voice the request that was on her tongue.

"What?"

396

"Will you stay with me? I mean, when it is time for the baby . . . just for a little while. I think that I could be strong if you were there to . . . to . . . reassure me. I know that I should not ask such a thing, but I have no friends here except . . . except you." She turned her back to him shyly. "I would not expect you to remain throughout the entire ordeal, of course."

"Meghan," he gently scolded. "I shall stay as long as you have need of me. Now," he stepped in front of her, "is there something that I can do to obliterate the unbecoming frown that presently adorns your lovely face?"

"Yes," she murmured faintly.

"Anything."

"Take me home." She looked at him pleadingly and was surprised to observe his eyes darken bitterly at her request.

"That I cannot do," he replied curtly. "I have tried to be an honorable man, Meghan, but your request far exceeds reason. I shall *never* return you to England." He started to stalk past her, but was restrained by a gentle, but firm, pressure of her hand on his arm.

"I do not wish to return to England," she whispered quietly and lifted her hand to caress his cheek. "I want to go home to Chandalara."

"You're positive that we cannot persuade you and Derek to extend your visit with us?" Rachel asked hopefully.

Meghan daintily wiped at the corner of her mouth with the linen napkin before addressing the older woman. "You have been most kind to us and we deeply appreciate your gracious hospitality, but we were at Chandalara for such a short time and I long to see it again."

"I, too, am anxious to get home." Derek took up the exchange. "I left a great deal of unfinished business at Chandalara, and then, of course, there is my shipping firm as well."

"Does that mean that you intend to continue with your vagabond ways?" Andrew asked crossly, and Derek turned to survey him closely.

"Good heavens, Andrew." Rachel turned to him, surprise obviously shadowing her brow. "Derek has been involved with the sea ever since we've known him. Why this sudden objection?"

"He did not have a *wife* then." Andrew looked pointedly at Derek.

Meghan's heart froze at the scornful inflection of Andrew's voice. Had Andrew somehow discovered their carefully guarded secret? As she was faced with this horrifying possibility, the glass of wine she had been about to lift to her lips suddenly fell from her numb fingers.

"How clumsy of me." Meghan frantically rubbed at the unsightly stain that blossomed on her stylish gown. "I fear I have ruined my dress."

"Perhaps not," Rachel offered gently. "Come with me, dear." She stood up and took the soiled napkin from Meghan's nervous fingers. "I might have something that will remove the stain." She cast a quizzical look at her husband before escorting Meghan from the room.

Derek had sprung instantly to his feet when the women rose, and now that they had withdrawn, he was hesitant to regain his seat. Instead, he plucked a cigar from his pocket and pensively examined the slender rod before turning to face Andrew. "So." He casually leaned forward to light the cigar from the elegant candelabrum that adorned the table. "It would appear that you have found us out."

398

"Indeed."

"May I inquire as to how you learned the truth? I thought that we played the ideally married couple rather convincingly." He ambled across the floor to the window, carefully turning his gaze outdoors.

"I *was* convinced that you and the girl were married. Damn it, that's what I don't understand. Had I not overheard your conversation last night, the two of you would have left tomorrow and I would have been none the wiser."

"When?" Derek mentally struggled to recall the conversation that Andrew had overheard.

Andrew pushed away from the table and rose to his feet. "You and Meghan were not the only ones who suffered a sleepless night," he began to explain. "Thinking that a breath of fresh air would clear my head and help me sleep, I stepped outside. That is when I discovered the two of you. It was not my intention to eavesdrop, you understand, but neither am I sorry that I learned the truth about your relationship with the girl."

"I can understand your bitterness," Derek began, but Andrew interrupted impatiently.

"*Why*, Derek?" he demanded harshly.

"I rather don't care for the tone of your voice." The glare Derek turned on Andrew was coldly detatched. "My motives are personal and, therefore, none of your concern," Derek stonily informed him.

"*What?*" Andrew's head snapped back, and he literally shook with anger as he glared at Derek. "After all that you've done, that is the only justification you can offer. It is personal!" He shook his head in disbelief. "Have you nothing else to say?"

"Does Rachel know?" Derek asked quietly.

Somehow he could find it easier to endure Andrew's

hostility if he knew that Rachel had not yet been informed. For he could not bear to witness her disappointment were she to learn that he had fallen short of her expectations.

"If she were, do you honestly think that you and your *whore* would still be residing as guests in my home?" His eyes danced shrewdly as he awaited Derek's response.

"Andrew." Derek's voice was forcibly controlled as he slowly turned from the window, his brown eyes now black with intensity as he calmly surveyed the older man's face. "I have considered you to be my friend for many years; indeed, I owe my life to you. But if you ever slander Meghan's name in such a manner again, I promise you that you shall not live to do so a third time." He delivered the warning with such impassive confidence that Andrew fully believed he would carry out his threat. "Really, Andrew, I always thought you to be more of a gentleman," Derek curtly reprimanded his friend.

"As I did you," Andrew countered. Refilling his wine glass, he purposely strode to the fireplace and leaned his aging frame against the mantel. All the while his steadfast gaze never wavered from Derek's face.

"Since you have seen fit to flagrantly abuse our hospitality, do you not think you can humor me by answering a few questions? I realize, of course, that you believe my interrogation to be unwarranted, but you must understand that my curiosity has been duly aroused and you may as well know that I damn well intend to find out the basis for your behavior." He brought his cane down sharply on the wooden floor. "Now are *you* going to supply the appropriate answers, or shall I question the girl?"

Derek knew Andrew well enough to realize that he

was determined to have his way. If he did not provide Andrew an account of the situation, Andrew would summon Meghan to the room. And that must not happen. She had already suffered greatly because of him and he would not allow her to be humiliated before Andrew.

"Go ahead. Ask your questions." Derek shrugged his shoulders and ambled over to the table to retrieve his glass of wine.

"If the girl is not your wife and not your whore," Andrew said, completely ignoring Derek's sinister scowl, "then what the devil *is* she?"

"Thomas Bainbridge's daughter," Derek replied, as if this revelation should pacify Andrew. It did not.

"You have told me about him and I can fully understand your animosity toward the man, but what does his daughter have to do with this tale?"

"It's a long story, Andrew. And one I have not the desire to recount in full at the moment. However, I will tell you this much. It is because of my actions while I was in London to claim my inheritance that the girl is in her present predicament." With this admission, Derek sighed wearily as he sat down and leaned forward to extinguish his cigar in his plate of half-eaten food.

"It had been my intention to gain my revenge against Bainbridge for the years of suffering my mother endured at his hands, but the bastard did not retaliate against me. Instead, he brutally attacked Meghan and cast her from his home. I felt responsible for her and accordingly made arrangements to bring her with me." Derek hastily gulped down the remaining contents of his glass. "I trust that your curiosity has been satisfied."

"Hardly." Came Andrew's dry reply. "You have merely explained how you came to bring her to

401

America, not why you have neglected to make suitable arrangements for the girl. Instead, it would appear that you are content to flaunt her as your wife when you have never bothered to sanctify the relationship. Can you explain that?" Andrew demanded.

"She is Bainbridge's daughter!" Derek reiterated stubbornly, again assuming that this particular fact should serve as adequate justification for his actions.

"A biological injustice of nature over which the girl had no control," Andrew reminded him. "Do you love her?" he asked sternly.

Derek's head snapped back abruptly at the unexpected question. But he quickly masked his surprise and stood up, pushing the bothersome chair away from him in disgust as he carefully avoided Andrew's persistent scrutiny. Without offering to respond, Derek stalked across the floor toward the door and would have successfully executed his departure had Andrew not stepped in front of him and blocked his path.

"*Do* you love her?" This time the question was voiced more gently. Derek's shoulders sagged heavily as he realized that Andrew would not be satisfied until he received an answer.

"I care for her," Derek admitted painfully.

"And the child she bears; it *is* yours?"

Derek nodded.

Andrew slowly shook his head and walked back to the mantel where he picked up his wine glass; he absently twirled the goblet between his fingers as his eyes thoughtfully studied the tart liquid. Several tense minutes passed while Andrew deliberated his next words. At last, when Derek would have left him to his troubled meditation, Andrew slowly turned to address him. "Wait. If you would but indulge me a few moments longer."

Derek removed his hand from the doorknob and he turned to face Andrew; thereby, consenting to listen to the words that he had obviously given serious consideration.

"Derek, you have been like a son to me. I know that we've had our differences in the past, but I can honestly say that you have never done anything that has given me cause to be disappointed in you . . . until this moment," he added sadly. "Now, I know you believe that you have reached the age of maturity where you no longer need to heed the advice given you by your elders, but unfortunately I am not yet resigned to deny myself the opportunity of airing an opinion when the situation so warrants, as does this one." He drank the wine and placed the glass on the table. "It is due to this that I ask you to hear me out.

"What will you do when others learn of your secret?" he asked frankly.

"I shall deal with that problem when it arises," Derek replied coolly.

"And when others make lewd comments about Meghan; will you threaten to kill them as you just threatened me?"

"No doubt."

"Then prepare yourself for a difficult life and you should learn to harden yourself against the tears of your woman when she pleads with you to ignore the crude insults that slander her honor. For you will quickly discover that many a woman cares precious little about her *honor* when the life of her man is in jeopardy. But then you are remarkably like me, Derek, and each time some callous bastard so much as glances at Meghan disrespectfully, you'll likely as not end up in a skirmish. Believe me, I know what I'm talking about!" His narrow shoulders slumped noticeably and Derek realized that the conversation was not an easy one for Andrew.

"You are referring to the scandal that Rachel's first husband caused," Derek offered.

Andrew nodded.

"But you were not to blame for that misunderstanding."

"No, Rachel and I truly believed that Robards obtained a divorce. But by the time we discovered the error it was too late, for Rachel and I were already married," he explained.

"But you remarried."

"Yes. I balked at first because I married Rachel in good faith, and my love for her did not diminish because of Robard's ineptness and lewd accusations. But I finally relented, thinking I might be able to still the tongues of those that would wag when the news came out. But our remarriage did not satisfy the gossipmongers who would still strive to tarnish Rachel's name. For no matter where the true blame rested, she was always the one they chose to ridicule. Rachel is a fine woman, Derek, and those who would defile her name are not fit for her to walk on.

"I know you have heard much of this before, but I want you to realize that you can expect a similar reaction when your plight is made public. Every sanctimonious son of a bitch within a hundred miles will think it his God appointed duty to comment on your living arrangement and Meghan will be the target of much of their discourse.

"Are you ready for that? Are you prepared to watch Meghan grow old before her time? Can you bear to have her cry herself to sleep in your arms each night? And what of the child? You, of all people, should be aware of the reception it will receive. But above all, Derek, are you willing to risk your life in defense of their honor? It is not an easy decision to make, for I have had occasion to do so, and I still carry the scars from those confrontations." He sighed deeply and rubbed the strain from his eyes as he walked over to Derek and clasped him firmly by the shoulders.

"Think it over carefully before you reach a decision. If you want, I can arrange for the two of you to be wed before you leave for Chandalara, or you may leave Meghan here. Rachel would like nothing better than to play mother hen and perhaps we can find someone locally who would—" he started to offer.

"No!" Derek was adamant. "She is carrying my son, Andrew, and regardless of what you think, *that* is important to me . . . Meghan is important to me. I do care for her, but you must remember that for fifteen long years I have harbored a lethal hatred for Thomas Bainbridge. I simply cannot forgive what he did; therefore, you cannot expect me to fall helplessly in love with his daughter when the memory of his evil ways still burns heavy here." He thumped his fist against his chest to indicate his heart.

"I had not intended for it to be this way." His voice suddenly adapted a serious tone. "In fact, I had decided to send Meghan to stay with friends in Charleston when we returned to Chandalara, but that was before I learned about the child. I cannot abandon her in her present condition."

"You could marry her."

"Not yet, Andrew. Perhaps in time my animosity toward her father will dissipate and my conscience will permit me to make her my wife. But I need more time, for after years of disciplining myself to hate the Bainbridge family, I find it exceedingly difficult to accept the possibility that I *might* be capable of loving one of them."

"I see." Andrew heaved a sorrowful sigh. "I understand your emotional dilemma, Derek, and I will not harass you further." He removed his hands from Derek's shoulders and solemnly walked to the door. "The decision you will ultimately be forced to make will indeed be an arduous one; consequently, it is also one that you alone must make. I sincerely hope for your peace of mind that is one with which you can live."

Derek observed the closing of the door as Andrew withdrew from the room before he dared to voice his own nagging concern. "So do I, Andrew. So do I."

Meghan tiptoed quietly down the staircase, taking care to avoid disturbing the remainder of the household. She and Rachel had been sewing in the parlor following supper, and she had thoughtlessly forgotten the tiny gown she was making for the baby when she retired for the night. Derek's plans were to leave the Hermitage early in the morning, and fearing that she would leave the tiny apparel in the confusion, she decided to retrieve it while the notion was fresh in her mind.

Her bare feet padded soundlessly across the hallway. Meghan slipped soundlessly through the parlor door, taking care to close it before she made her way to the sofa. But as her hands closed upon the soft material the room was suddenly drenched with light from the lamp on the table. Meghan straightened immediately as the abrupt brightness startled her, and she clutched the sewing so tightly that she pricked her finger with the needle that was still attached to the garment. Squealing with pain, she instantly dropped the gown to the floor, and placing the injured appendage to her lips, she whirled to face the unknown intruder.

"I didn't mean to frighten you," Andrew apologized. "But I am unaccustomed to finding attractive young ladies prowling about my home in the middle of the night." He offered her a friendly smile, but Meghan could not help but notice the strained lines of worry that shrouded his eyes.

"I was not actually prowling . . ."

"A poor choice of words on my part." He crossed to her side and extricated her finger from her mouth to examine the puncture. "It isn't serious." He released her hand and it fell limply to her side. "Would you care for a glass of wine?" he asked as he walked to the table to collect the glass from which he had been drinking.

"No, thank you," she murmured quietly. "I came down to get the sewing I forgot earlier. I had not anticipated the chance that I would meet someone." She suddenly felt very self-conscious about standing before this man, clad, as she was, in only her nightgown. "Could you not sleep?" she asked considerately.

"What? Oh, no, not yet," he admitted. "My mind is a whirligig of motion at present, and I doubt that I would be able to rest properly were I inclined to retire to my chamber."

"I see." Meghan knelt to pluck the sewing articles from the floor. "Derek mentioned that you and he had words about us. Are you still disturbed?"

"To be frank, yes."

Meghan lowered her gaze in acute embarrassment. "I . . . I know what you must think of me, but do not think badly of Derek." She stepped forward to plead with Andrew. "The blame does not rest entirely with him."

"Blame is not the issue," Andrew informed her. "Derek is supposedly a mature, responsible adult, but in this particular instance, he is behaving like a dim-witted, schoolboy by allowing his baser passions to influence his conduct. And as for you," he continued, "you seem to be a sensible, young lady. You are obviously well-bred; therefore, I cannot fathom why you are content to live with him in this fashion."

Meghan turned slowly to walk to the door. She knew of no words that she could speak that would ease his troubled thoughts, for she was only too aware that her relationship with Derek could not be easily justified. But as her trembling fingers encircled the doorknob, her chin dropped sadly to her chest, and she offered him one last comment.

"I love him," she whispered forlornly. "I realize that does not make our situation any more respectable in your eyes, and I know that Derek does not return my feelings." She raised her head and turned a little thereby, allowing Andrew to detect the bright glimmer of tears that sparkled in her eyes. "But if I thought that there was an inkling of hope that Derek would one day return my love, I would cling to that hope and remain with him, no matter how long it took for him to declare his love for me." She hastily jerked the door open and disappeared into the dark corridor.

Andrew Jackson stared after the fleeing figure for a moment and chuckled hoarsely as he extinguished the light and plunged the room into total darkness. "Well, I'll be damned," he mused aloud as he lumbered down the hallway toward the chamber he shared with Rachel. Pausing briefly by the foot of the staircase, he glanced upward toward the second floor. "No, Meghan, you will not have to wait long before the lad comes to his senses, unless of course, I miss my guess, and he turns out to be a bigger jackass than I suspect."

Meghan shifted tiredly on Champion's back and placed a considerate hand to her travel-weary back. They had exchanged farewells with the Jacksons several days earlier and had embarked on their journey home. She had at first been saddened to leave her new friend, for she had found Rachel Jackson to be a pleasant companion, but as each day slipped by, drawing them nearer Chandalara, Meghan's mood brightened. She also noticed that the black lines of thought that had previously creased Derek's brow had lightened as well.

Meghan sighed happily and breathed deeply of the fresh, summer air. She was genuinely enjoying the picturesque landscape that had escaped her notice on their initial excursion up the Trace. Derek had so thoroughly frightened her with his horrible tales that her mind had been preoccupied entirely with thoughts of thieves and murderers; every shadow or rustle in the underbrush had sent her imagination into a frenzy of anticipation. But now she was relaxed and able to concentrate on the beauty of the foliage and wildlife that inhabited the Trace.

The path before them suddenly widened, enabling two horses to travel side by side and Derek slowed Trojan's pace until Meghan was beside him. As the sun filtered through the overhang of thickly gathered leaves, it cast a shimmery glow about her, but Derek's favorable perusal soured somewhat as he recalled his heated argument with Andrew on that final evening at the Hermitage.

Andrew had been correct in many of his allegations, Derek reluctantly agreed, and Derek was resourceful enough to realize that a solution must eventually be formulated. But was he prepared to accept Meghan as his wife? Was he ready to put the memory of Thomas Bainbridge behind him? These were pertinent questions that he must thoroughly consider before he could act decisively.

"Why do you frown so?" Meghan asked, interrupting his thoughts. "It's such a lovely day that I should think a more appealing expression would lighten your brow. Does something trouble you?"

"No. I was merely pondering the notion of stopping for the night," he lied. "The afternoon grows late, and you are weary. We shall be stopping soon."

"I can continue a little further," she informed him. "I am not as frail as you seem to think."

"I am well-acquainted with your stamina; it's the child I consider." He smiled at her, and they again fell silent as they continued to make their way along the deserted trail.

They paused to make camp just before sundown, and while Derek tended to the horses, Meghan set up the campsite. She carried the blankets and cooking utensils from the packhorses and scurried off to gather firewood while Derek entered the forest in search of their supper. That task finally completed, Meghan had but one more chore to accomplish before she could relax. It was with this thought dancing through her head that she plucked up the bucket and started through the dense undergrowth of brush and fallen trees to the rippling brook to which Derek had directed her. When she came upon the spring, she fell immediately to her knees and thoroughly splashed her face and arms with the cool, refreshing liquid. Unthinkingly, she undid the top laces of her bodice and similarly scooped up handfuls of water and doused the sultry flesh as well.

It was then that her alert ears heard the gunshot in the distance, making her realize that Derek had probably found their supper, and she needed to complete her task and hurry back to the campsite with the water. But as Meghan leaned forward to dunk the bucket into the glistening brook, she heard a twig snap and was suddenly overcome with an intense sensation,

410

as if the eyes of some sinister being were boring into her vulnerable back. Meghan quickly filled the bucket and stood up, valiantly trying to remain calm as she turned to make her way back to the camp.

Once safely at the campsite, she placed the bucket of water by the cooking utensils and sat down on a rock to settle her nervous stomach. She folded her arms across her abdomen and her head drooped as she rocked back and forth, trying to relax her jangled nerves. Consequently, she did not hear the footfalls behind her, nor did she notice the intruder to her peaceful solitude till she felt the hand on her shoulder. The color instantly drained from Meghan's face as she whirled at the contact, her hand falling instinctively to a tree branch that she would utilize to defend herself against the unknown assailant.

"Meghan?" Derek regarded her carefully. "You are as pale as a ghost. What's that for?" he referred to the stick she clutched in distraught fingers.

The limb crashed to the ground as her fingers grew limp with relief, and she rushed forward to throw herself into Derek's arms.

"Honey?" His comforting arms instantly surrounded her. "I did not mean to startle you. I called to you when I entered the clearing. Did you not hear me?"

Meghan shook her head. The initial shock had subsided, but she was reluctant to leave the security of his reassuring embrace. "When . . . when I was by the stream, I . . . I thought that someone was watching me," she explained.

"Are you certain? I saw no one while I was in the woods." He thoughtfully pondered her statement. "Did you see someone?"

"No, it was just an intense feeling." She shuddered.

"Perhaps it was your imagination," he offered, trying

411

to ease her anxiety. "The forest can ofttimes play tricks with an imaginative mind. Besides, had there been a stranger passing by, I could hardly blame him for pausing to gape at you," he whispered huskily, and Meghan lifted her eyes to his questioningly. "I imagine you presented quite an alluring distraction, kneeling by the pool with your breasts bared." He removed his hands from her waist and they instinctively reached to secure the laces of her open bodice that she had forgotten in her zeal to return to the camp.

When he had finished, Meghan awkwardly moved away from him on the pretense of arranging their blankets in a comfortable pallet upon which they would sleep. "I did not mean to be such a silly bother."

"No bother, and I never regret the opportunity to hold you in my arms," he added. "Faith, I can safely say that you have never before this day hurled yourself at me with such vigor. I shall treasure the moment for some time to come, I can assure you." He chuckled as Meghan openly winced at his rhetoric.

Derek ignored the insolent glare she bestowed upon him and instead devoted his efforts to preparing the rabbit he had shot for their evening meal. Once he had the fire going, he skewered the meat and placed it on the spit above the blaze. The sun had drifted behind the western hills and darkness had enveloped them before Derek and Meghan settled behind their steaming plates of food. They ate hungrily, neither one speaking, but both content to satisfy their mutual need for the nourishing food.

"Is it not remarkable how tasty a rather bland plate of hot beans and wild game can be to one's palate? Especially when one is accustomed to a more genteel cuisine." He drank thirstily of the strong coffee and leaned forward to refill his cup. "More?" He extended

412

the coffee pot to Meghan.

"No, thank you. I fear I can barely force down one cup of the bitter stuff." She glanced down at her empty plate and put it aside, grimly determined that she would ignore the hunger pangs that still gripped her stomach.

"Still hungry?" Derek noticed her hesitation and immediately guessed the reason. He retrieved her discarded plate and generously filled it with a second portion. "You are eating for two now." He handed her the plate. "And if the child has inherited my ravenous appetite, I fear the meager portion you just consumed will not be nearly enough to satisfy him. Go ahead. Faith, you have eaten very little these past weeks and I am elated to see that you have finally recovered your appetite." He stretched lazily, crossing his arms behind his head, and settled back against the trunk of a tree to observe her fondly as she continued her meal.

It was then that he heard the noise. It was not the familiar sound of the forest, but the nervous rustling of a nearby bush and the crackling of a twig that alerted him to the threat of danger. Derek casually leaned forward and unobtrusively pulled a sharply honed knife from his boot; encircling Meghan's waist with his arms, he gently dropped a kiss to the back of her neck, then maneuvered his lips to nibble at her ear.

"We are being watched," he whispered.

And when the plate of half-eaten food would have tumbled anxiously to the ground, Derek caught it and nonchalantly tossed it aside. He turned her in his arms, and when she opened her mouth to question him, he covered it with his own to silence her. Quite naturally, he lifted her in his arms and carried her to the blankets that she had earlier spread for them. As he lowered her to the ground, their lips parted, but Derek placed a warning finger to her lips to caution her against making

413

a sound.

"Shhh," he whispered and pressed the knife into her trembling hand. "I'm going to look around. The light from the fire does not extend this far and you can easily spy anyone who might emerge into the clearing before they detect you. If that should happen," Meghan could not see his face in the darkness, but she could ascertain by the serious inflection of his voice that he was gravely concerned, "slip as quietly as you can into the forest and hide. I will find you." He reached beneath the blanket to claim his gun and started to leave.

"Derek?" Meghan murmured his name so lowly that he did not hear it, but her desperate hand against his arm brought him momentarily back to her side. "You are not putting on this lavish display to frighten me, are you?" she asked hopefully. "For if you are, you must know that you have surely succeeded."

"No, my sweet," he voiced the words she feared most. "Perhaps it's just a wild animal in search of food, but there is something or *someone* out there, and I'll not sleep this night till I have learned what it is." And with that, he disappeared into the dense forest.

Meghan's heart fell as she witnessed him vanish in the darkness, and time stood still for her as the endless seconds grew into endless minutes. She sat motionless upon the hard ground, her body curled into a tight knot as she nervously awaited Derek's emergence from the forest. Meghan tried desperately to calm the accelerated pounding of her heart. Derek had left the knife with her, but did he actually think she could maintain the presence of mind to use it if she had to? Her mind was awhirl with these thoughts when the air abruptly reverberated with the deafening blast of a gun.

Her heart stopped pounding—indeed, it very nearly stopped beating entirely—as the breath caught in her

414

throat, and she turned anxious eyes to the clearing, diligently praying that Derek would appear by the firelight to eliminate her fears. But the ominous figure that emerged from the forest to be illuminated by the firelight was not Derek, but Garth McTavish.

Meghan's breath came in a rush, and her desperate attempt to smother the startled scream that rose in her throat, came too late.

"Come on out here, gal."

The sound of his repulsive voice made her blood run cold, and she wrapped the blanket about her tightly as if she were in the midst of a horrible nightmare and Derek would miraculously appear at any moment to awaken her and hold her in his arms and kiss away the frightening visions. But the nightmare was *real*, and the next words McTavish uttered left her feeling totally helpless and at the mercy of the vile man.

"Don't go thinkin' yer man's gonna come bustin' in here to save ya cos I jest put a bullet through his uppity head," he boasted proudly. "He's daid, lady, and no good to ya now. So jest mosey on out here and let ole Garth show ya a real good time."

Meghan's brain was numb. Derek could not be dead, but . . . but she had heard the gunshot, and then McTavish had appeared. "Oh, Derek," she murmured quietly. "It will do me no good to hide in the forest, not if what he says is true, for you cannot come to me now, or . . . or ever." Mournful tears began to trickle down her cheeks.

"I'm waitin', gal," Garth's voice shattered her moment of grief, abruptly reminding her of the terrifying situation with which she was presently confronted.

Meghan deliberately wiped the tears from her face and slowly climbed to her feet, clutching the knife fiercely in one hand behind her back. She knew what she must do. For now that Derek was dead, her fate at the hands of the revolting man was certain, and she resolved that she would rather die by her own hand than submit her body to the loathsome swine. But first, she realized, her fingers tightening around the handle of the sharp blade, Derek's death must be avenged.

"It's 'bout time. I was jest fixin' to come lookin' fer ya."

His lips parted in a wry, self-satisfied grin to display an evil mouth full of repulsive, yellow teeth. His black eyes raked her wantonly, and Meghan could surmise by the pulsating bulge in his dirty buckskins that she had little time to organize an effective course of action.

"I'm the kind of man what don't like to be kept waitin', even by no quality lady. So, you drag yer prissy ass on over here so we can commence to sportin'." His grubby hands suggestively stroked the material along the front of his dirty buckskin britches that housed his throbbing organ.

Meghan's tense eyes could not avoid the deliberate movement of his hands, and she glanced nervously to her right, as if calculating her chances should she dart into the forest to escape the inevitable.

"Now don't ya go thinkin' I'll let you git away from me. I've been hard pressed to have ya ever since I seen ya by the stream, what with yer tits glistenin' in the sun and all." He openly leered at her. "I'll not likely let you git away from me." He smacked his lips together as if he were savoring a dish of food, and Meghan could almost feel his sinister eyes burning through her gown to sear her delicate flesh.

Meghan's heart began to pound with an increasing fierceness, and the blood coursed through her veins as McTavish started across the clearing toward her.

"Yep. The way I see it, you and me got some unfinished business to tend to."

He was in front of her now. His breath smelled grotesquely of whiskey; the stench of soured sweat and horseflesh clung to his foul body. Meghan tried desperately to control the nausea that rose involuntarily in her throat as the vile man ran his thumb along her quivering chin and finally hooked it in the bodice of her gown.

"I've waited a long time fer this. I'd a had my pleasure with ya this afternoon 'cept I had to take care of Chandler first." He laughed evilly, obviously satisfied with himself for having killed Derek.

"But enough of this parley." He pulled her roughly against him and his eager hands squeezed the flesh of her buttocks through her dress. "We're wastin' time."

Meghan threw her head back, and bright tears of anguish trickled from beneath tightly closed eyelids as her assailant covered her mouth with wet, repulsive kisses.

"No need fightin' it." He felt her stiffen in his arms. "Cos ya know what's gonna happen." His hands returned to slip into the bodice of her gown, and he rubbed his hard knuckles against her breasts. "There jest ain't no way to avoid it," he jeered at her.

Meghan forced her mind to disregard the obscene man and she balanced the knife reassuringly in her hand. She did not even flinch when he ripped open the front of her gown to better his accessibility to her voluptuous flesh. It was then that he became overcome with his inflamed passions, and in his frantic haste to wrestle her to the ground, he did not notice the weapon that rose purposefully above his head and stroked swiftly downward through the air.

McTavish roared painfully as the point of the blade

417

tore savagely into his shoulder, and he instantly released her and stumbled backward, anxiously groping the injured arm.

Realizing that the wound she had inflicted upon her attacker was far from fatal and fearing the repercussions of her act, Meghan took advantage of the man's momentary paralysis and sprinted toward the protective cover of the forest. But she had traveled only a few feet into the forest when she was tackled from behind and sent sprawling to the grassy, woodland floor, knocking the knife from her hand.

In an instant, Garth flipped her to her back and pinned her to the ground beneath his unbearable weight.

"Bitch!" he spewed, slapping her viciously. "You'll pay fer that!" His cruel hands yanked ruthlessly at the tattered threads of her shredded bodice in an attempt to render her completely naked beneath him.

Meghan was temporarily stunned by the blow, but the sound of tearing material helped her recover her senses, and she began to struggle frantically.

"I'm warnin' ya, if'n ya keep this up, little lady, I'll like as not break yer pretty neck." He took the sensitive nipple of her breast between thumb and forefinger and squeezed it brutally.

Meghan's excruciating scream filled the air, but Garth continued to increase the pressure until she gradually lay still beneath him.

"That's better." His slobbery, wet lips traced a path from her mouth to the breast he had just mercilessly mistreated. "I like a fiery wench as well as the next man, but yer makin' it damn hard for me to concentrate on my pleasure." His knee was between her thighs, persistently forcing her legs apart while he fumbled with the opening of his buckskins to release the hardened

418

flesh that he would use to defile her young body.

The palms of Meghan's hands pressed the hard earth and she turned her head to one side to avoid his slovenly kisses. She could not bear to have his vile lips caress hers the way Derek's had. . . . Derek . . . The tears began to slide down her distressed cheeks and she whispered his name forlornly. "Oh, Derek, I loved you so." She felt the urgent prodding of her assailant's swollen manhood against the softness of her thighs, and an intense fear gripped her stomach.

Oh please, dear Lord, she prayed silently, let me die. I cannot bear to live at the mercy of this monstrous man . . . or without Derek. I do not wish to live without him. She began to sob uncontrollably.

"Go ahead and cry, lady. But don't go thinkin' them tears is gonna sto—augh!" His breath came swooshing forth and escaped his body in a violent rush as he suddenly lurched forward, his dead weight crushing her helplessly to the ground.

Meghan screamed hysterically and pushed frantically at the dazed man who, in a semi-unconscious state, was attempting to climb to his feet to confront his assailant. In her muddled condition, Meghan could not fathom what had happened to thwart Garth's attempt to rape her, but she did possess the presence of mind to try to escape while his attention was devoted elsewhere. Gathering her tattered dress about her, she stumbled to her feet and started to run deeper into the forest. But even as she ran, she could hear the shouts of the two men and the skirmish that was taking place behind her, and she forced her trembling legs to carry her onward.

She did not know the identity of her liberator, nor was she particularly anxious to find it out. In all likelihood he was some thief or murderer who had witnessed her struggle with Garth and quite probably had rescued her so that he might have her for himself. With this thought foremost in mind, she diligently plodded on through the dense foliage.

But suddenly the forest reverberated with the unmistakable, agonized, bloodcurdling scream of one who had obviously been mortally wounded. The sound made her blood run cold. And her heart thundered in her chest as she came to an abrupt halt, her feet frozen to the ground. But the sudden sound of someone crashing through the forest behind her forced her into action, and she was running again, furtively trying to put distance between her and her pursuer. But the persistent pounding behind her soon made her realize that her stalker was gaining ground. In her frantic zeal to escape him, her foot caught on a tree root, sending her sprawling to the hard earthen floor. Meghan tried to scramble to her feet, but in an instant her pursuer was on her, his arms reaching out to capture her.

"*No!*" she screamed. "Don't touch me!" She kicked and scratched at him, her arms flailing wildly at his head.

"Meghan!" The familiar voice called out to her. "Meghan, honey, it's Derek." He shook her roughly.

"Derek?" She abruptly halted her wild assault and permitted her eyes to focus on him. "Derek," she repeated his name vaguely.

Even when the familiar arms lifted her in their strong embrace, she was not certain she could believe that it was really true, that Derek had not been killed by that horrible madman.

Derek carried her back to the camp and placed her near the warm, glowing blaze of the fire, for even though the summer night was hot, she shivered uncontrollably in his arms. And when his eyes observed the nasty bruise that had already darkened her left cheek, Derek became enraged.

"The bastard!" he swore hotly and his work-hardened fingers softly caressed the blemished area. "I should have castrated the son of a bitch." He noticed the blank, almost bewildered cast to Meghan's ravaged face, and it was with great concern for her welfare that he was prompted to inquire urgently, "Honey, are you all right?" His gentle fingers pressed her shoulder lightly.

It was then that the tears that had been frozen in fear behind her lashes began to slip down her cheeks. As her body shook with convulsive sobs, she leaned forward and weakly extended her arms and wrapped them tightly about his neck. "He said . . . he said . . . you were . . . dead." She buried her head against his broad chest.

"I very nearly was," he said softly, holding her to him.

He ripped a piece of material from her ruined petticoat, and dipping it in the bucket of water, he applied the cool compress to her discolored cheek in an effort to diminish the swelling that had already begun.

Meghan winced at the contact, but she relaxed considerably as he nestled her in the crook of his arm, her eyes ever glued to his serious face. She could still not believe that he had escaped death and was sitting safely beside her.

"How did you escape that awful man? He was quite sure that he had killed you." She trembled despite the arm that was possessively draped about her and snuggled closer to him, reveling in his nearness.

"No doubt he did." He pointed to an area of his scalp directly above his left ear that was drenched with sticky, red blood and caked with dirt. Blood still oozed from the open wound, and Meghan was instantly concerned.

"Derek! Why did you not tell me of this sooner? I

must see to the wound at once." She tried vainly to extricate herself from his arms, but Derek steadfastly reaffirmed his grip about her waist and held her to him.

"It's nothing," he said placidly. "First, I would have you calm yourself. You have been through quite an emotional trauma," he crooned softly, but Meghan was persistent.

"I'm fine, really," she insisted and pushing away from his embrace, she went to collect a bar of soap from her bags. And as she carefully cleansed the ugly wound, Derek described his encounter with McTavish.

"I found his camp about a hundred yards away from ours, deeper in the forest. And while I was rummaging through his belongings, he crept up from behind and shot at me. Luckily, his aim was faulty, and he only grazed me. I was stunned momentarily, and by the time I recovered, I realized that Garth had probably headed straight for you." He placed his hand on her arm and Meghan paused to look down at him, their eyes locking in a timeless embrace. "Had Garth not been so preoccupied with his lusty cravings for you, I fear that he might have taken a more precise aim, and I probably would have been killed," he said solemnly. And for the first time since her youthful body had been awakened to the sexual pleasures it could provide a man, Meghan was genuinely grateful that she had served as a temptation. "In effect, you saved my life," he continued.

Meghan's eyes misted over again, recalling the desperate moments during McTavish's savage attack. "But you saved me, too." The tears began to fall freely, and she clung desperately to his neck, her tormented sobs being cushioned by his durable shoulder. "Had you not stopped him, he was going to . . . to . . ." Her last words were choked off by an anguished sob that was literally torn from her throat.

"I know . . . I know," Derek whispered faintly, nestling her against him, rocking her gently as he soothed her frayed nerves. "It's over, honey," he assured her. "You're safe now. I'll keep you safe," he promised.

Chapter Eighteen

Meghan was on her knees in the middle of the flower garden at Chandalara. She had been impressed with Rachel's garden at the Hermitage and had concluded that as long as she continued to reside at Chandalara she might as well put her talents to good effect. Consequently, she had determinedly set to work in the sadly neglected garden. But as she labored over the flowers, her thoughts were not focused entirely on her work. Instead, she reflected on Derek.

He had grown moody, almost distant, ever since that terrible night on the Trace when Garth McTavish had assaulted them. Her fingers thoughtfully hesitated over a delicate, orchid-colored gladiola as she recalled the ensuing events immediately following that fateful night.

Derek had staunchly decided against delivering McTavish's body to the sheriff in Natchez. Instead, he buried it in a shallow grave, carefully marking the gravesite in the event the authorities were not satisfied with his tale and determined that further investigation was required. Fortunately, that had not been the case. The sheriff was well-acquainted with McTavish's shady character and seemed totally willing to accept Derek's account of the attack. Subsequently, he had been cleared of any charges, thereby, making Meghan even more concerned with his dismal mood. It would seem that some great burden weighed heavy on his mind, and he was reluctant to confide in her the nature of its source.

She had thought it strange that Derek had not mentioned the skirmish with McTavish to anyone, and thinking that he preferred to forget the disgusting episode, she similarly did not speak about it. But she continued to worry about him, for each day the lines of anxiety seemed to be more pronounced on his handsome face, making him look a good deal older than his twenty-nine years.

Meghan carefully gathered up the flowers she had cut and strode to the table on the verandah. Sitting down, she thoughtfully arranged the bouquet in the crystal vase that adorned the table. All the while a distinct frown tugged at the corner of her mouth, for in her heart she believed she knew the reason for Derek's somber mood and his hesitancy to approach her.

Had he not said he would send her away when they returned from the Jacksons? Perhaps that was the decision with which he currently struggled. Had she been mistaken to believe that once he learned of the baby he would want to assume the responsibility of father and . . . and husband? Was she now to be cast adrift to fend for herself and her child?

"Lawdy, Miz Meghan, a body'd think a cloud of gloom had settled on this here house by the looks of yore unhappy face."

Sophie had ventured outside to make certain that her mistress was not overtaxing herself. Ever since the housekeeper had learned of Meghan's condition, she had fluttered about her like a mother hen, seeing that

424

she ate properly and received sufficient rest.

"No, Sophie, not a cloud of gloom, rather a cloud of uncertainty I should think," Meghan murmured quietly and tried to force a smile so that Sophie would not feel a need to question her further. "What brings you out into the heat of the day?"

"I come to remind you that it's time fer yore nap. You might be feelin' fit as a fiddle, but that chile you is carryin' needs his mama to lie down fer a spell so he can get some rest." She waddled over to the only shady spot on the sun-drenched verandah and waited for Meghan to conjure up some sort of excuse to avoid taking the prescribed nap.

"I am not tired, Sophie, and the baby will be fine, I promise you." She caught a sudden movement from the corner of her eye, and the sound of hoof beats cautioned her that someone was approaching the house. "Besides, you would not confine me to my bed when I have guests presently arriving." She placed her hand to her brow to shield her eyes from the glaring sun as she averted her gaze in the direction of the carriage that was progressing toward the house.

"Shucks, Miz Meghan. That ain't no *guest*. That's only Massah Wade's uppity sister, Miz Deirdre," Sophie stated matter-of-factly.

"Sophie!" Meghan scolded. "Is that any way to speak of your master's friends?"

"Humph!" Sophie barked. "She ain't no friend of Massah Derek's."

"Be that as it may, we must try to make her as comfortable as possible while she is a guest in Derek's home. Now, run and ask Lettie to prepare us a pitcher of cold lemonade and a plate of her tastiest pastries," she instructed the housekeeper, her eyes never wavering from the expensive carriage. When she moved from the

425

table to go to the front stoop to welcome Wade's sister, however, she noticed that Sophie had not left to follow her instructions.

"Shoo!" she commanded and Sophie dutifully shuffled off in the direction of the kitchen.

Meghan stood aside to silently scrutinize the young woman who stepped confidently from the carriage and strode forward, graciously extending her hand to Meghan. She was as tall as her brother and quite slender, but Meghan's eyes were fastened on the girl's hair which was as black as the dark of night and was arranged attractively in delicate curls all over her regal head. The sharp contrast of the dark curls against her pale skin was indeed startling, and Meghan imagined that the girl derived immense pleasure in the initial shock her appearance provided.

She was pretty, Meghan conceded, and she could easily understand how Derek would have been enticed by her beauty. She courteously accepted the woman's hand and offered her a friendly smile, but the smile that parted Deirdre Hampton's lips was conspicuously overshadowed by a scornful glare that deepened her bright, blue eyes as she shrewdly examined Meghan.

"Well, well, you must be Meghan. I've heard so much about you." She clasped Meghan's hand for a brief moment then released it instantly, sweeping past her grandly as if she intended to enter the house uninvited. "Has Derek returned? I simply must have a word with him."

"No, Derek had business in town." Meghan tried vainly to disguise the anger that strained her voice, for she had taken an instant dislike to Deirdre's blatant display of arrogance. "Perhaps I can be of service to you, Miss Hampton," Meghan offered.

"Perhaps," Deirdre agreed slyly and reached for the

426

handle to the huge door, but Meghan's voice staid her movement. "When I saw your carriage approaching, I instructed Sophie to collect us some refreshments. She will serve us on the side terrace." Meghan strode past her, chin held regally high, and led the way to the table. Both had claimed a seat before Meghan continued. "I trust you will be comfortable here."

"Oh, yes." A cunning smile parted Deirdre's lips. "Derek and I used to breakfast here. I am quite at home, thank you."

Meghan bristled immediately at the crass statement and realized that whatever the underlying reason for Deirdre's visit, she was apparently going to flaunt her past relationship with Derek. Consequently, Meghan resolved that she would not allow this domineering woman to spoil the beautiful day, and she similarly vowed that she would take lightly any of Deirdre's implications concerning her past involvement with Derek. Had he not told her that his relationship with Deirdre held no fond memories for him?

Meghan folded her hands primly in her lap and turned a sunny smile to her guest. "How can I be of service to you?"

"I am planning a small get-together this Friday evening in honor of Derek's marriage. Nothing elaborate, you understand, just a few old and dear friends who are interested in getting better acquainted with the girl who finally latched onto our darling. But Derek said something that I fear will simply spoil my plans." She regarded Meghan speculatively, contentedly awaiting the question she knew the naïve girl would be unable to withhold.

"You have spoken with Derek?" Meghan struggled to air the question casually, for she did not want Deirdre to think that she objected to Derek conversing with her, even though Meghan found it difficult to discourage the jealous stirrings that tugged at her dubious heart.

"Why, yes, dear. As a matter of fact, he invited me to dine with him at the coffeehouse in Tylerville little more than an hour ago." She giggled sweetly as if hiding a delicious secret. "During lunch, he casually mentioned that you would be leaving soon to visit friends." Deirdre paused deliberately and leaned forward nonchalantly to rearrange the flowers that Meghan had meticulously placed in the vase.

Meghan was indeed perplexed by Deirdre's statement, but she refrained from making an immediate reply when she saw Sophie approaching with the requested refreshments. Instead, she satisfactorily camouflaged her surprise and devoted her attention to filling the glasses with the cold lemonade.

Deirdre accepted the glass, but politely refused to sample any of the delectable pastries that attractively garnished the silver tray.

"They look positively scrumptious, but I am watching my figure. How fortunate for you that you do not have to be as frugal." She offered Meghan a condescending smile.

"I beg your pardon." Meghan's fingers hesitated over a particularly sinful-looking cherry tart.

"Derek mentioned that you are with child. And now that you have successfully bound him to you by providing him with an heir, I suppose you need not concern yourself by keeping up your appearance. You can grow as plump as you please and everyone will think it is due to the child." An insincere smile was staunchly plastered upon her stony lips.

"Humph!" muttered Sophie. "You ain't never been concerned about what you ate afore this as I recollect." Sophie's apparent dislike of Deirdre darkened her eyes, and she folded her arms across her bosom and stared accusingly at the woman.

"Really, Meghan, do you encourage such behavior from your *servants*? I am certain that *Derek* would not approve." She undauntedly locked glares with the housekeeper.

"You may leave us, Sophie." Meghan reluctantly informed the faithful servant.

"But—"

"I am sure Deirdre meant no harm by her words," Meghan cautioned Sophie.

"That's right, Sophie, dear. I wouldn't dream of doing anything to upset Derek's *wife*."

Sophie smothered a guttural reply and slowly moved away from the table. She was none too keen with the idea of leaving her mistress alone with the crafty woman and she muttered her inaudible disapproval as she disappeared inside the huge house.

"You must forgive Sophie, but she has grown quite protective of me since she learned of the baby."

"Oh, and will she be accompanying you on your little excursion?" Deirdre asked shrewdly.

"That is the second time you have referred to some sort of holiday. I assure you, Derek and I have not discussed an upcoming journey," Meghan calmly informed her.

"You misunderstand, dear. Derek said only that *you* would be leaving, but he failed to tell me when. You can, of course, appreciate my dilemma. I can hardly hope to plan a reception for you and Derek if you are going to be leaving." She could not successfully conceal the smug look of amusement that highlighted her face.

Meghan was thunderstruck! So, Derek had finally grown weary with her and would revert to cavorting with his old lady friends. But had she not seen it coming? Derek had not once attempted to make love to her since that horrible night when McTavish had very nearly raped her. It would seem that Derek had grown tired of the game they played and now desired to terminate their relationship. After all, had he not ofttimes told her that there were no lasting ties that bound them? But how could Derek be so cruel as to allow this woman to confront her with his decision to send her away?

Meghan tried vainly to ignore the triumphant smile that Deirdre bestowed upon her, and she successfully checked the hurtful tears that sprang to her eyes. Meghan was still in a confused daze when she rose to her feet to accompany Deirdre to her waiting carriage, but Deirdre turned to her abruptly on the front stoop.

"You need not accompany me all the way to the carriage. I wouldn't want you to overexert yourself in your *delicate condition*."

Meghan could not fathom why Deirdre's voice held such an embittered tone. Granted, Meghan felt no great fondness for the woman, but she had endeavored to be hospitable even though Deirdre had proven to be a vast trial to her congenial nature.

"By the by, when will the blessed event take place?" Deirdre asked coyly.

"Shortly after the new year. February, if our calculations are accurate." Meghan smiled happily and placed her hands lovingly across her stomach. She was not about to let this lady demoralize her.

Deirdre's precisely plucked eyebrows lifted in mock surprise, and she cast a scoffish glance at Meghan's abdomen. "It would seem that the New Orleans ceremony was a wee bit *after* the fact."

"Oh, no, Deirdre, you are misinformed. Derek and I were wed in London *before* we set sail for America."

430

Meghan made certain that she recounted the tale as had Derek.

"Oh, I see. Now that I think of it, Wade told me the same story. It must have slipped my memory." Deirdre stepped toward the awaiting coach. "You will remind Derek of the party, won't you, dear? I'm certain you will agree that there is no need for him to sit alone by the hearth while you are away."

"I shall remind him," Meghan said shortly.

She watched as the driver handed Deirdre into the carriage and without a backward glance, she quickly ran inside and up the stairs to fling herself across the bed and unleash the flood of tears she could no longer restrain.

And as the carriage swayed gently down the long drive, the occupant therein was heard to mumble sourly, "Married in London, indeed."

Derek entered the master chamber to find Meghan seated solemnly before the mirror. Her eyes were still noticeably swollen from the deluge of tears that had scourged her delicate cheeks, and she mechanically pulled a pearl handled brush through her glossy curls. Derek immediately spotted her tear ravaged face and he mentally damned the one he knew to be the cause of Meghan's distress.

He strode to the bedside table and placed a tray of food thereon before he moved behind her chair. Purposely, he put his hand on top of hers to stay the desolate movement of the brush and the serious look in his eyes caused Meghan to shiver nervously when she met his appraising gaze in the mirror.

"I brought your dinner," he stated simply after studying her stricken face for a lengthy moment.

"Had I been hungry, I would have joined you in the

431

dining room when Sophie announced supper. I fear that you have wasted your time and energy by carrying that tray up here," she replied, her voice distinctly laced with a saddened air.

"Nevertheless, you are going to eat." His big arms swooped downward to surround her, and he determinedly carried her to the chair beside the table on which the food lay. "I am not about to allow your stubborn nature to jeopardize the welfare of our child. Now, eat!" he commanded.

Meghan regarded his powerful, rigid back as he stood near the window, absently staring out into the black night. His thoughts seemed to be as far adrift as the stars that dotted the darkened horizon, and his square shoulders sagged slightly as if a great burden weighed heavy upon them.

Disconsolately, Meghan averted her gaze to the plate of food before her, and she obediently lifted a forkful of fresh peas to her lips. Derek was right, of course. She must not allow her disappointment to cause her to neglect the baby, for she would love and cherish Derek's child regardless if he permitted her to remain at Chandalara, or cast her off to some unfamiliar city.

"Sophie tells me that you had a visitor this afternoon."

Derek's voice was soft, but he did not turn his gaze from the window.

"Deirdre was concerned that I might not be able to attend a party she has planned in our honor Friday night," Meghan offered quietly, forcing her voice to sound calm and indifferent.

"Yes, she mentioned the affair to me at the coffeehouse in Tylerville today." Derek ran his rugged hand along the back of his neck to ease the tension he felt building there.

"Then you *did* invite her to dine with you!" she exclaimed accusingly.

"Hardly!" Derek bellowed. "Nathan and I were seated at a table when Deirdre plopped down, *uninvited*, and proceeded to bombard us with her usual boorish chatter."

"But she said . . ." Meghan began, then hesitated, totally befuddled by the contradiction in the two tales.

"That I invited her to dine with me?" He turned to observe Meghan slowly nod. "Deirdre believes what she chooses and ofttimes misconstrues the truth to suit her fancy."

"Did she also misconstrue your conversation about sending me away?" Meghan's question was barely audible above the sudden rush of wind that parted the draperies in a wild dance.

"So, *that* was what she said to unsettle you." Derek nodded knowingly.

"*Unsettle?*" Meghan was affronted that Derek would regard the matter with such passive insensitivity and she turned on him bitterly. "Why, no, Derek. I am deliriously happy with the news that you have decided to cast me off to Charleston, wherever that is, so that you may revert to your philandering ways. She is very pretty, Derek, although a bit spiteful for my taste, but she should serve you well."

"Charleston?" Derek swiftly moved to her side and placed a consoling hand on her shoulder. "Deirdre said I was sending you to Charleston?"

"No, *you did*!" She lifted her eyes to his accusingly.

Meghan sensed that he was mentally searching his thoughts to recall having made such a declaration, and she quietly reminded him of his soliloquy aboard *The Cajun.*

"I thought you to be sleeping that night." He

unconsciously smoothed her cheek with his hand. "I was merely speaking my thoughts aloud, and I have since altered my plans." He drew up a chair before her and leaned forward to clasp her hands in his.

"It *is* my intention to send you away for awhile, but not for the reasons you think and certainly not to Charleston." He placed a finger to her lips when she started to question him. "Please, grant me the courtesy of explaining my position before you attack me," he said fondly.

Meghan relaxed slightly, but her anxious eyes never wavered from Derek's.

"I have reason to suspect that Iverson hired McTavish to attack us on the Trace. I explained my suspicions to Nathan, and he agrees with me. Therefore, if I am correct, I am certain Iverson will try to dispose of me again." He suddenly pulled her from the chair onto his lap.

"I want you to return to Dulcie's Image for a short time, just until I've settled the score with Iverson. McTavish is no longer a threat to you and Dulcie will watch over you. You may take Sophie if you like." He cocked his head, so he could better determine her reaction. "I cannot take the chance that you will inadvertently be hurt should Iverson attempt anything else." He cradled her to him.

Meghan stared at him in disbelief. She had been mildly surprised when he suggested she return to Dulcie's Image, but his open concern for her safety completely astounded her. Meghan's eyes warmed suddenly, and she draped her arms about his neck as she gazed at him quizzically.

"You mean you aren't suggesting I leave because you have grown weary of my company?" she asked hesitantly.

"Lord, no!" he exclaimed. "Whatever gave you such

a notion?"

Meghan was far too embarrassed to formulate a verbal reply, but her bright, green eyes glanced uncertainly toward the huge, fourposter bed.

"Ah, so you have pined for my amorous advances after all." He teased lightly as he eased her head down onto his shoulder. "I merely wanted to be certain that you had sufficiently recovered from Garth's attempt to rape you before I—"

"Derek," she interrupted. "Garth was a horrible, horrible man, and the experience I suffered at his hands is one I chose to quickly forget. I would never associate his vicious assault with the way you treat me," she said honestly and snuggled closer to him to bask in the security of his nearness.

"Well," Derek smiled ruefully, "some women would not have survived such an experience. And the idea that you might fight me out of fear bothered me severely." The arms surrounding her tightened instinctively. "For you see, my sweet, I am well-acquainted with your stubborn moods when you would deny me the pleasure of your bed, and I can cope with them easily enough. But were you to resist me out of genuine fear, well, I'm not certain I could adequately handle such a situation," he admitted.

"Indeed, sir?" Meghan whispered softly. "I cannot imagine you being presented with any situation that you could not easily master. But in any event," she ran her fingers lightly through his hair, "I'm not likely to offer you any resistance."

"Well, before I attempt to make . . . er . . . retribution for my *inattentiveness*," he grinned at her mischievously, "we must settle this issue about returning you to New Orleans."

"I don't want to go," she murmured gently.

435

"But what if Iverson—"

"Derek." Meghan leaned forward and stared intently into his chocolate-brown eyes. "If Iverson thinks that he can hurt you by harming me, then what is to keep him from following me to New Orleans? Surely, Dulcie cannot guard me every minute of the day." She deftly ran her hand along the neatly trimmed growth of beard that had sprouted on their journey down the Trace, and that Derek had never bothered to shave. "Do you not think I would be safer were I to remain at Chandalara under your protection?" She slipped her hand beneath his shirt and gently ran her hand along his chest as she offered her lips to him.

"Meghan?" Derek pulled away and looked at her suspiciously. "It's unlike *you* to try to seduce *me* especially when you know that I shall do whatever I deem is best."

"Have you not regularly berated me because I do not come to you willingly?" she pouted.

"Yes, but . . ." He groaned pleasurably as Meghan's roving hand boldly passed over the hardened bulge between his thighs. "You must be a witch." He caught her against him and quickly carried her the short distance to the bed. "There can be no other explanation for your constantly changing moods," he whispered breathlessly as his fingers fumbled nervously with the bodice of her gown. Derek swore. "Look at me. I'm behaving like a lovesick swain about to experience a woman for the first time."

Meghan giggled airily at the preposterous comparison and waited patiently while Derek hastily removed his restrictive garments. She then pushed him gently back against the sheets.

Derek observed her curiously as she discarded her own clothing and climbed into the bed beside him. And

436

he was puzzled further still when she avoided his grasp and began to place a trail of sensuous kisses from his mouth to the sensitive nipples of his chest, along his flat stomach, creeping lower still till he suddenly shuddered violently as Meghan's moistened lips uncertainly encompassed his stiffened manhood. The breath caught in Derek's throat, and his entire body quivered with the agonizing pleasure her timid application ignited within him.

Derek's nimble fingers tangled in the luxurious curls of her flowing hair, and, quite reluctantly, he lifted her head from the throbbing shaft and carefully positioned her astride him. Meghan's eyes grew round with anticipation as Derek rocked gently from side to side, his virile manhood filling her completely while his hard fingers masterfully fondled her breasts, then slid down her waist to her hips and buttocks, igniting a burning flame wherever they touched.

Instinctively, Meghan moved her fingers along his chest and stomach as she began to sway with him, gently at first, then faster and faster as they rode the crest of a turbulent wave that took her further and further out to sea. She struggled against the swell that threatened to swallow her in its raging whirlpool, but her struggles came to an abrupt culmination as the water came lapping around her flaming body, leaving her content to float on the cool, ocean wave, aimlessly, languidly.

"Oh . . . oh, Derek," she whimpered breathlessly, unable as of yet to voice a coherent sentence. "Please . . . stop." She tried unsuccessfully to push away from him.

But instead of releasing her, Derek rolled with her to her back and continued to plunge deeper and deeper into her with a rhythmic tenderness that caused her to moan with ecstatic rapture, and she crushed her breasts against his chest and lurched upward to receive his demanding thrusts and cry out with unbelievable pleasure. But, in time, the thundering of the ocean waves subsided for Derek as well, and he lay serenely atop her, totally satiated and breathless as he marveled in wonder at the abandon she had displayed and, more, at the initial foreplay she had instigated.

Immediately, his lips captured her mouth in a blazing kiss that left her blissfully dizzy and content to lay beneath him to luxuriate in the feel of his nakedness against her own soft skin. Meghan permitted her fingers to move along the contour of the relaxed muscles of his back, and she smiled happily as she realized that she had given of herself completely to the man she loved. And even though they were not joined together by the clergy, she reveled in knowing that she belonged to him.

"Where did you learn to do *that*?" Derek's thick voice permeated the night air that gently whipped across their entwined bodies.

"You . . . you do it to me," she shyly reminded him. Meghan awkwardly met his sensuous gaze, suddenly realizing that in their zeal to be in each other's embrace they had neglected to extinguish the candles. "Did you not like it?" she asked demurely.

"Like it!" he crowed. "I *loved* it!" He started to roll away from her, fearful that his superior weight might cause her some discomfort, but Meghan clung to him fiercely, refusing to let him leave her.

"Are you still going to send me away?" She lightly ran her fingers through the mass of curly hairs that decorated his broad chest.

"You little vixen," he chided. "Have you no shame? Taunting me this way. You do not play fair, madam." He kissed her nose. "How can I possibly say I will pack you off to New Orleans when you tempt me this way?"

He lowered his lips to flick at her nipple, and he moaned as the peak grew taut with his touch. "God in heaven!" he sighed heavily, running a hand through his unruly hair.

"Does that mean I may stay?" Meghan giggled shamelessly.

"*Yes!*" he bellowed. Derek left her a brief moment as he extinguished the candles, then he quickly returned to her side. "I only hope it is a decision I do not live to regret." He cradled her against him, gently rocking her back and forth until she drifted off to sleep. And staring down at her brilliant face which was outlined by the pale light of the moon, he suddenly realized that he would be stung quite deeply were any misfortune to befall the lovely creature that slept trustingly in his embrace.

"No, Abbey." Meghan wrinkled her nose in mild disdain. "I wore that dress to afternoon tea with Mrs. Tyler only yesterday. I should like to wear a more festive gown to Miss Hampton's soirée." Meghan sat in undecided confusion before the pile of haphazardly strewn dresses. Surely, there was one suitable gown among the dozens that Derek had purchased for her that she could wear to Deirdre's party.

Moments later, Derek entered the room and leaned his handsome frame against the doorjamb while he studied her serious face. Surely, this meek creature could not be the same who had shamelessly shared his bed the past few nights. He chuckled wistfully as he closed the chamber door.

"Is madam presented with a problem of some sort?" Derek asked, a sly smile parting his full lips.

Meghan glanced at him, her pretty face shadowed by a perplexing frown. "I simply cannot decide upon a gown to wear tonight."

"I see." He stroked his bearded chin considerately and stepped to the chair in which Meghan sat, legs crossed and arms folded tightly as she thoughtfully examined each dress as Abbey held it up for her inspection. "That one." He pointed to a rather plain, muslin gown, indicating that Abbey should hold it up for his perusal. Knowing what the impending reaction would be, Derek casually suggested that she consider wearing the selected dress to the party.

"Really, Derek." Meghan recognized the playful glint in his eyes and calmly suggested that his opinion might be better appreciated elsewhere. "Men are totally incapable of understanding the importance of selecting the proper wearing apparel for these occasions," Meghan patiently explained to Abbey.

"Is that so?" Derek took her hand and pulled her from the chair to lead her to the connecting chamber.

Meghan regarded him curiously as he gently pushed her across the threshold into the sitting room, but the puzzled expression on her pretty face turned to one of elation when she beheld the gown that Sophie happily held in front of her. It was the exquisite gown that Meghan had admired in Yvette's shop in New Orleans.

Derek extended his hand to assist Meghan from the carriage and gently placed her on the ground before him. She was absolutely stunning. He had been wise to haggle with Yvette over the dress, for no other could complement the gown as did Meghan. He grasped both of her hands in his and stood her at arm's length while he caressed her admiringly with his eyes.

The gown was made of soft, green silk that whipped lightly about her delicate, kid slippers. It was high-waisted, and the material was pulled tightly so that it gathered in the back, allowing it to fall gracefully to the floor, creating an elegant train that glided regally behind her. The sleeves that capped her upper arms had been trimmed with a pale, green ribbon onto which tiny, perfect pearls had been sewn to complete the exquisite effect. The same ribbon and pearls ornamented the waistband that clung firmly beneath her breasts, lifting them provocatively above the daring cut of the décolletage. She wore the gown off her shoulders, and it was cut shockingly low in the back.

Derek hungrily eyed the creamy curves of her voluptous breasts and he had to forcibly suppress the jealous urge to remove his blue satin coat and place it about her shoulders in an effort to protect her from the leering stares he knew she would receive once they entered the house. Suddenly, Derek reached forward and gently tugged on the decorative lace of her chemisette in a futile attempt to conceal more of her alluring flesh.

"Derek!" Meghan slapped at his hand and she immediately adjusted the décolletage the way it had been prior to Derek's interference. "I thought you rather liked the way I look."

"*I do!*" he roared as he took her arm to escort her to the house. "But that does not mean I expect you to parade your charms before the whole bloody town." He paused for a moment and turned her face to his. "The flesh you so tantalizingly display is meant for *my* eyes alone, none other's," he sighed deeply and they continued toward the house. "I daresay the hungry wolves within will devour you in seconds. I shall no doubt be forced to spend my evening fighting off the young pups."

Meghan squeezed his arm gently. "You need not worry that my head will be turned, m'lord. I will remain by your side as would any obedient wife." She smiled at him gaily and Derek laughed heartily at her words.

"Obedient, indeed!" He chuckled deeply as he rapped sharply on the wide door.

The door was immediately opened by a servant and when he stepped aside to bid them enter, Deirdre strode forward to take Derek's hand possessively in hers. "Derek," she said joyfully. "How dashing you look this evening."

"Thank you, Deirdre." Derek gently but firmly pulled his hand away and drew Meghan to his side. "You're looking lovely." His eyes fell instinctively to the bold cut of Deirdre's décolletage that barely held her breasts in check, and Meghan wondered fleetingly why she had even bothered to don the gown.

Meghan noticed the prolonged direction of Derek's gaze and, unthinkingly, her fingers gathered a section of his coattail, giving it a sharp yank. Derek's head came up quickly and he glanced with amusement at the jealous scowl that darkened Meghan's pretty face. He was prevented the opportunity to comment on her behavior, however, for Deirdre chose that moment to address her.

"Why, Meghan, darling, don't you look . . . *sweet*?" Her eyes took in Meghan's appearance in one, brief glance, then she again turned to Derek. "Most of the guests have arrived and are waiting in the ballroom. Shall we join them? The dancing is about to begin." She started to take Derek's arm, but was chagrined to see Meghan place her arm snugly in his, leaving her no alternative but to lead them into the ballroom.

When they entered the ballroom, the festivities were about to get underway. Immediately, Derek claimed Meghan for the first dance, and he led her to three other couples who had taken up the stance for a quadrille. And as soon as that dance ended, Wade requested her to be his partner. In fact, Meghan was to dance every dance with a different partner. And even though

442

Meghan dearly loved the carefree feeling the dancing ignited within her, she was greatly relieved when Wade announced that the musicians would be taking a break while everyone helped themselves to the buffet. Eagerly, Meghan sought out Derek who had been whisked away to the study to discuss politics with Jason Tyler and his advocates, and claimed him as her dinner partner.

Derek took one look at her flushed face and instantly scolded her, "I should have known better than to leave you on your own. You no doubt danced every dance."

"Yes," she replied happily. "And it was absolutely marvelous. I haven't danced like that since I left London."

"And if I have my way, you won't again, at least not until after the babe is born."

Meghan looked up at him carefully as she slipped her arm in his. "The child is not nearly such a weakling as you seem to think. It could not be, not with such a strong and powerful father," she murmured admiringly.

Derek gazed down into her upturned face, and he could not resist the temptation to place a fleeting kiss upon her attractive mouth. "Flattery, my dear, will not move me to change my mind. You are not to overexert yourself, and I shall remain by your side for the remainder of the evening to ensure that you adhere to my wishes."

"Yes, Derek," she sighed forlornly. "If you will excuse me, I need to check my appearance. I fear my hair is out of place, what with all the dancing. I will join you in the dining room presently."

Without a backward glance, she spun away from him and made her way up the spectacular staircase to the room that had been set aside for the ladies. Meghan quickly repaired her coiffure, and was about to exit the room when Deirdre's haughty voice filled the air. "How

443

does it feel to be the center of attention, *darling*?"

Meghan recognized the intimidating sound of her voice, and she slowly turned from the mirror to meet Deirdre's cold gaze. "You planned the affair, Deirdre. I rather thought that Derek and I were to be the honored guests, thereby, making us the center of attention."

"Only Derek. You were to be in New Orleans by now, so that you could grow fat and ugly in some isolated room and not burden Derek with the brat you are going to force upon him."

"I don't have to listen to your ravings, Deirdre." Meghan started past her, but Deirdre blocked the exit.

"Even my brother finds you totally bewitching. He has spoken of little else since you arrived this evening, but I wager your saintly image will be tainted somewhat when he learns what you *really* are!" Her mouth was drawn into a thin, white line.

"What do you mean?" Meghan demanded.

"Never mind!" she replied sharply.

Meghan stared crossly at her adversary for a moment, then she adapted a cool and indifferent manner that surprised even her as she said, "Really, Deirdre. To behave in such a common manner. What do you hope to gain by this display?"

"Derek," Deirdre said flatly. "He's mine. He loves me. He always has. We were to be married!" She stepped closer to Meghan, who had become visibly shaken by Deirdre's declaration.

"But . . . but Derek told me that he ended his affair with you long ago," Meghan said weakly, a seed of doubt beginning to grow, tearing at her beleaguered heart.

"It's a lie!" The look Deirdre turned on Meghan was murderous. "Derek and I *were* to be married!" she insisted. "He promised me . . . just as soon as he concluded his business in London, and I returned from

444

my holiday in Europe. And then I returned to discover that you had ensnared him with your feminine wiles."

"No, it wasn't like that."

"Yes!" Deirdre cried. "But you may have been a little hasty in your zeal to present Derek with an heir, for he is still a young, virile man. Pray, what will he do when he has a need for love and discovers that he is encumbered with a wife who is so enormous with child that she cannot adequately satisfy him?" She masterfully twisted the knife that penetrated Meghan's already confused heart. "I will tell you what he will do. He will turn to another source to satisfy his need, and I will be waiting with arms open wide to welcome him back *where he belongs!*"

Meghan again tried to shove Deirdre aside, but the embittered girl grabbed her arm roughly, her sharp nails tearing at the delicate flesh. "Of course there are methods to rid yourself of the bothersome brat, but then you're likely too squeamish to consider *that*, even if it would mean that Derek would remain faithful . . ."

Her remaining words were to go unheeded, for Meghan at last jerked her arm free, shoved Deirdre ruthlessly out of her way, and raced down the staircase. She did not enter the dining room to search for Derek, but continued down the hallway, out the main entrance, and finally paused on the huge porch to rest her head against one of the massive pillars that supported the structure. All the while, Deirdre's spiteful words kept filling her head: there are methods to rid yourself, *there are methods* . . .

"Meghan?"

She whirled about to find Nathan's eyes curiously fixed upon her. Quickly, she tried to dissolve the look of despair that shadowed her brow, and she smoothed the skirt of her gown with nervous fingers as she addressed him. "Why, Nathan, are you just arriving? The buffet is just now being served if you hurry inside." She valiantly tried to control her voice, but it shook noticeably regardless of her efforts.

"I can wait." He gazed at her, his concern for her anxious appearance was quite obvious. "Are you all right? Is Derek the cause of your distress?"

"Oh, no, Nathan." She was quick to absolve Derek of any blame. "You are mistaken, there is nothing wrong."

"That, Meghan, is a bold-faced lie," he said bluntly. "You are obviously distraught, and if Derek is free of the blame, then I must assume that Deirdre has accosted you with her vile tongue." Meghan's downcast eyes told him that he had correctly guessed the identity of the one who had caused her emotional stress. "The bitch!" he whispered hoarsely. "Does Derek know about this?"

"No. Please, Nathan, I'm fine. There is no need to bother Derek with this trivial matter. It was foolish of me to allow Deirdre's thoughtless words to upset me."

"Do you wish to go inside?" he asked quietly.

"No, not yet. Could we perhaps walk in the garden for awhile? I would like to regain my composure before facing Derek's friends again."

Nathan graciously extended his arm and Meghan rested her hand lightly on his sleeve. "A stroll in the refreshing air could not harm my disposition either."

The couple started around the side of the house to enjoy the peaceful atmosphere of the secluded garden and were totally oblivious to the pair of chocolate-brown eyes that clouded over angrily as they observed the couple's departure.

Chapter Nineteen

Meghan watched Derek through shielded lashes as she absently speared the omelet that lay upon her breakfast plate. She had already attempted to make light conversation with him twice this morning and had received little more than a grunt and a noncommittal sigh for her efforts. In fact, he had been little more than civil to her since the previous evening when she had returned from her innocent walk in the garden with Nathan.

Meghan sighed desolately as she recalled the disastrous events of the past evening. When she had reentered the grand ballroom, she discovered Derek lavishly pouring his attention upon Deirdre. He danced with her, fetched champagne for her, and whispered gay anecdotes in her ear that made her giggle divinely. But it had been the outside of enough when the couple disappeared through the terrace doors to wander through the secluded garden, leaving Meghan to endure the piteous stares and calculating whispers of those near her. She had immediately requested that Nathan take her home, and he had reluctantly agreed after observing her distraught condition.

Once at Chandalara, Meghan had shunned the master chamber, choosing instead to retire to her own smaller one. She bolted the doors securely to avoid a confrontation with Derek, should he even bother to return, and climbed wearily into the unfamiliar bed. But her reprieve was to be a short one, for the door that separated the chambers splintered in the night to admit Derek, resembling the devil himself, to Meghan's room. She clutched helplessly at the thin sheet, realizing too late that the flimsy material would serve as little protection for her, and gazed uncertainly at the menacing shadow that took up an ominous stance at the foot of her bed, hands on hips, jaw set firmly, and sinister eyes that bore tiny holes through her. Meghan was suddenly terrified as the pungent odor of whiskey reached her nostrils, and she realized that he had been drinking quite heavily. Clamoring to the middle of the bed, she glanced around furtively for something she could use to protect herself should Derek attempt to harm her in his drunken state.

"Derek?" she managed guardedly.

"Silence, woman!" His voice was thick, and he had to grasp at the bedpost for support. "You would do well to fear me, after your vulgar display this evening. Humiliating me before my friends, abandoning me at the party and going off in the night with that . . . that . . ."

"Nathan is your friend, and you are not the only one who suffered this evening, *husband*. Or in your drunken state, can you not remember whisking *that woman* off to the garden? It was I who was left to endure the humiliation as your friends offered me sympathetic glances at being so quickly cast aside, and in such a public fashion." Her breasts heaved at her angry words. "Was it worth it, Derek? Was she as you remembered her?"

"Shut up!" He suddenly lunged at her, but Meghan moved quickly to evade his grasp.

Meghan soon realized the error of her ways as she witnessed the angry expression on his face darken to a black fury, and he leaped from the structure and in two long strides, caught her by her hair and dragged her back to him. She winced in pain, but he ignored her pleas as he jerked her head back so sharply that her neck actually popped, and he crushed his lips against hers in a ruthless manner that she assumed was intended to teach her a lesson of some sort. But what lesson did he have in mind? How one submits to the demands of an overbearing man? Had she not been subjected to that particular lesson often enough?

It simply was not fair. She was expected to sit idly by and bear him an heir while he resumed cavorting with his past mistress. "*No!*" she screeched and attacked him so fiercely that he momentarily lessened his hold on her. "You'll not have me tonight, not after you've just come from *her!*" She turned to run, but his fingers caught in the neck of her gown and in the following struggle, the delicate material gave way and sent her sprawling to the floor.

"Vixen! I did not *have* Deirdre. Oh, she wanted me right enough, but the tantalizing image of another is unfortunately branded upon my brain." He was on top of her before she could scramble away. "And then I return to my home to find that the little firebrand has spurned my bed and would bar me from her chamber." His fingers cruelly massaged her breasts and he thrust her legs apart with his knee. "Have you not yet learned that there is no obstacle great enough to keep me from getting what I want?"

"Yes, *master!*" she spat vehemently.

Derek swore and for a frantic moment, she thought he might strike her. But then she realized that she would have preferred a beating to what was about to happen, for he started to pull savagely at his clothing to remove them. And when Meghan tried to escape, he

449

shoved her harshly back upon the carpeted floor, his evil chuckle resounding in her reeling head. He was going to rape her, just as Charles had tried to do and . . . and Garth McTavish.

She was suddenly drained of the will to resist and, consequently, lay limp beneath him, her horror-filled eyes turned to him pleadingly. "No. Not like this . . . please, not like that. Not you, not *you*, too," she whimpered over and over, unaware that her hysterical mumblings had been heard.

But when Derek's arms encircled her and lifted her from the floor, she again cried out in anguish. "Shhh, my love," he cooed against her ear. "I am merely returning you to your proper place." He stepped through the sitting room and across the threshold and laid her gently upon the turned down sheets of the huge, baronial bed. "Rest now, Meghan. I've behaved abominably." He lay down beside her, but despite the harrowing moments just past, she immediately accepted his comforting arms about her.

Derek rubbed his bloodshot eyes and winced at the pain in his whirling head. What had he been thinking of the night before that had encouraged him to drink so profoundly and behave like a jealous fool? He leaned back in his chair while the half-empty plate of food was removed and a dish of fresh berries, floating in a rich, thick cream was set in its place. He had not meant to spend so much time with Deirdre, but after witnessing Meghan stroll into the garden with Nathan, he had lost all sense of reason. He scowled harshly as the quaint scene was recalled to him and he shoved the bowl of berries away in disgust. What was happening to him? Had Deirdre accompanied Nathan to the garden he would have voiced no objection. But it had not been Deirdre, it had been Meghan.

He observed her seriously as he stepped to the sideboard to refill his coffee cup. Damn! Why did she always have to assume such a look of martyrdom, as if she was constantly being wronged, yet valiantly shouldered each horrid experience as would any hallowed saint. Then his murky memory recalled the tattered nightgown he had seen strewn on the floor of her bed chamber that morning, and his expression softened as he gazed at her.

Why had he drunk so accursed heavily the night before? He could not remember the things he said or did, but they evidently had been vile, for Meghan seemed to shrink from him each time their eyes met. Thoughtfully, he drained the cup and turned to her. "I have some business in town this morning, but would you be interested in a ride when I return?" He regarded the eager smile that she quickly suppressed and knew that his invitation would not be declined.

"If it would please you," she replied softly.

"It would." He strode from the room without a backward glance.

Meghan watched his departure with saddened eyes before she stood up from the chair.

"Feelin' poorly this mornin', Miz Meghan?" Sophie's voice exploded beside her. "Mmmm mmmm! 'Pears the massah's not feelin' hisself either, cos he never eats such a piddlin' breakfast." She boldly stared at her mistress. "Seems to me, though tain't none of my business, that the chile you is carryin' is gonna be the one what suffers just cos you two is too stubborn and contrary to patch up yore diff'rences."

Meghan stared at the outspoken servant and had just opened her mouth to offer her a severe reprimand when Lettie burst into the room.

"Lumas!" she screeched. "Has you seen that boy,

451

Sophie?'' She noticed Meghan and greeted her properly before continuing her search for the errant lad.

''What has Lumas done this time?'' Meghan inquired wearily. Having heard various stories about the mischievous youngster, she felt it her duty to exhibit at least a passing interest in the boy, even though she felt far from dealing with wayward servants at this particular moment.

''I sent him down to the egg house to fetch me some fresh eggs for the massah's birthday cake, and that rascal done went and run off somewheres. I can't find him nowhere.''

''Derek's birthday? Is it today?'' Meghan asked excitedly, totally oblivious to the curious stares of the servants who thought it indeed odd that the mistress of the manor was ignorant of the fact that it was the master's birthday.

''Yes ma'am, but I can't make no cake without them eggs,'' Lettie insisted.

''Oh, pooh! Sophie, send one of the other boys to fetch the eggs. Lumas probably slipped off to the watering hole for a swim. Shoo, now.'' She scurried Sophie off with a wave of her hands, then turned back to Lettie. ''Come, Lettie, let me assist you with the master's cake.''

When Meghan emerged from the kitchen it was midmorning and the sun was already a bright, blazing inferno in the heavens as she gaily made her way along the path that led to Nathan's small cottage. The cake had been set aside to cool before the decorative trimmings could be added. In the meantime, Meghan decided to visit Nathan and invite him to sup with them that evening to share in the celebration of Derek's birthday. Meghan carefully climbed the wooden steps and crossed the porch to rap on the door, but when she received no reply to her knock, she turned the knob and quietly entered the modest domicile.

The cottage was quite small, but like Derek, Nathan had chosen to surround himself with treasures he had collected on his worldly travels. Meghan was intrigued with the various paintings on display, and it was not until she spied the easel near the window that she surmised that Nathan must have created the delightful paintings himself. Noting that a canvas still rested on the easel, Meghan curiously stepped forward to examine the painting.

It was of a ship riding the crest of a magnificent wave. The sky above was a brilliant contrast of blues, and seagulls dipped and soared with wings spread wide as they glided alongside the ship. The scene before her seemed to burst to life in her vivid memory as she recalled the weeks spent with Derek aboard *The Lady Elizabeth*, and as she moved a little closer to better scrutinize the canvas, she realized that the ship in the picture was indeed a replica of the one in which she had traveled to America.

"So, you have discovered my secret passion." Nathan's softly spoken words caused her to start and she turned from the canvas.

Meghan hurriedly began to explain her reason for standing in the midst of his home when she had never been issued an invitation, but Nathan lifted a hand to silence her. "You are always welcome here, Meghan, and I would be delighted to join you and Derek for supper. I intended to drop by later with his gift anyway." He nodded toward the painting she had been admiring.

Meghan again turned and gazed wistfully at the picture, but her shoulders sagged sorrowfully as she

453

muttered, "I have no gift for him. I did not even know it was his birthday until this morning."

"Derek will not expect a gift. In fact, he usually loathes being reminded of his birthday," Nathan said kindly.

"Nathan?" She suddenly turned to him, her eyes brilliant with color and he wondered if she had heard a word he had spoken. "Do you paint portraits?"

Nathan put the brushes that he had been cleaning on a table, and turned to her. "Yes, now and again. Why?" he asked, thoroughly intrigued by her question.

"I've just had the most clever thought, but first I need to know what became of my portmanteau that I carried with me from London. I must locate Nicholas and inquire about it immediately."

Nathan put a gentle restraining arm about her waist to prevent her from streaking past him. "There is no need for that. I can show you where it is."

She obediently followed him back along the path she had trod to his cottage, across the yard, and into the barn. She ascended the sturdy ladder that led to the loft, after assuring Nathan that she was quite capable of climbing a few paltry steps, and waited patiently while Nathan rummaged through the pile of crates and trunks, finally emerging with the portmanteau she had requested. It thumped loudly as he let it drop to the floor in front of her, and Meghan was instantly on her knees searching through the contents of the musty case.

"Might I inquire as to what you're looking for?" Nathan asked, his boyish face smiling down at her.

"Oh, I'm not even certain that Millie included it when she packed my belongings, but she knew how much it meant to me. . . . ah . . ." she squealed happily as her dainty fingers clamped upon the object of her vigorous search.

Nathan watched as she withdrew an ornate music box from the satchel and with loving care, opened the lid and removed a delicate, lace handkerchief that still carried the aromatic scent of a fragrant perfume. Meghan slid to the hay strewn floor and lovingly placed the folded handkerchief in her lap. Very carefully, she lifted each fold to reveal a heavy, golden locket which she dangled before Nathan as he stooped before her on his haunches. "Open it," she said softly.

Nathan accepted the locket and gingerly tripped the catch which permitted the oval enclosure to spring open. He hastily scanned the miniatures of the two women that appeared before him, then his pale, blue eyes darted at Meghan curiously.

"This is my mother," she pointed to the younger woman whose likeness she closely resembled, "and this is Elizabeth, Derek's mother." The light was dim in the loft, but the intense brown eyes of the deceased woman seemed to smile at her approvingly, and she lifted her hand and rested it upon Nathan's sleeve as she inquired, "Could you paint Elizabeth's portrait from this? I have no money, but I'll pay you somehow. It's just that Derek loved her so completely and yet he has no remembrance of her. And I have not the talent that you possess to make such a gift for him. Would you consider it, Nathan?" she asked hopefully.

Nathan studied the eager face that waited patiently for his reply and knew that he could not deny her request. "I will do it, but the only payment I shall even consider is that you consent to pose for me after this portrait is completed."

"Oh, yes!" She threw her arms about his neck and kissed him lightly on the cheek. "Derek will be so pleased, and I shall be forever in your debt for making this possible. But it must be our secret. Derek must not know of the portrait until it is completed."

"Now *that* might present a small problem, for he is wont to drop in now and again to chat and check on the progress of my paintings, particularly those in which he is interested. Had the devil of a time convincing him that I wouldn't part with the painting of *The Lady Elizabeth*. I couldn't very well expect him to purchase his own birthday present, could I?" He grinned at her fondly.

"No, but where . . ."

"There is a deserted cabin back in the woods a ways, just the ideal location for a part-time, vagabond artist to set up work." He pocketed the locket and extended his hands to assist her to her feet. "Perhaps you would care to see it?"

"Oh, yes, Nathan, I would like that very much, but I fear I must ask that I be permitted to reserve acceptance of your kind invitation another day." She hurriedly brushed at the pieces of straw that clung insistently to her skirt. "Derek has invited me to go riding with him this afternoon, but I shall visit the cabin one day very soon," she promised and looked at him wishfully as she eagerly posed her next question. "May I watch you paint sometime?"

"We shall see."

He led her to the ladder and steadied her as she began to descend the wooden steps. They said farewell at the door of the barn and Meghan again thanked him for agreeing to paint the portrait, then she scurried to the house to complete the preparations for the small dinner party.

Meghan had just put the finishing touches on Derek's birthday cake when he appeared at the kitchen door. "What's this?" His amused voice filled the spacious

456

kitchen. "Has Chandalara perhaps obtained a new scullery maid of which I have not been made aware?" His eyes twinkled mischievously as he added, "And quite a handsome piece it would seem."

Surprised by the interruption, Meghan whirled to find Derek's frame filling the doorway, a roguish grin highlighting his handsome face as he stepped closer to her. Not wanting him to discover her surprise, she stood firmly in front of the table where she had been working and attempted to draw him into casual conversation. But Derek was undaunted by this maneuver, and he picked her up and easily set her aside; thereby, revealing the gaily decorated birthday cake to him.

"Oh, Derek!" Meghan exclaimed. "You've spoiled my surprise!"

"Surprise?" He looked at her blankly.

"It's your birthday, silly. Do not tell me you've forgotten your own birthday," she gasped in total exasperation.

"It's not an occasion I look upon with great fondness," he aired blandly. "But since you have apparently gone to such trouble—you did prepare this offering, did you not?" His eyes enveloped her warmly.

"I helped." She nodded. "I had not the time to make you a proper gift. You see, I just discovered this morning that it was your birthday," she explained.

"No matter." He instantly waved the incident aside and pulled her against him and proceeded to place a rather ardent kiss upon her astonished lips.

Meghan was scandalized and her eyes darted around the kitchen to see who might have witnessed his impulsive action. But thankfully the servants had conveniently disappeared when they noted the master arrive to converse with their mistress.

"Pray, do not flush so, my proper miss. No wayward

eyes observed my husbandly kiss of thanks." He held her from him and scanned her pretty face. "Methinks, madam, that in your zeal to prepare this token for me, you have forgotten my invitation to go riding." He examined her wan complexion with obvious concern and added, "It would appear that you are not aptly suited for this type of labor, little one." He forced her to look at her reflection in a brightly polished silver platter that hung against one wall of the immaculate kitchen. "You have grown pale and quite fragile looking. Perhaps you should retire to your chamber and rest to restore a healthy glow to your cheeks. We shall ride another day." He started to escort her from the kitchen as if the discussion were at an end, and she had no recourse in the matter.

"Oh no, Derek!" She caught his arm. "I was so looking forward to this outing. I'm fine, *really*, and I daresay that the fresh air and sunshine will do more for my health than sitting in a stuffy, old bedroom."

"I well recognize the stubborn set of your brow, madam, and, thereby, yield to your pleas. Otherwise, you will doubtlessly strive to make the remainder of the day a misery by ignoring me, or pouting at me with those glorious, round eyes of yours." He sighed with mock acquiescence. "Run along," he swatted her playfully on the behind, "and change into more suitable clothes. I shall see to the mounts and have Lettie prepare us a picnic lunch to take with us."

He watched as she scampered off to do his bidding and shook his head in wonder as he muttered, "Were she not such a willful, headstrong chit our circumstances could be much more simple and uncomplicated."

But would I rather have her as a doting, submissive wench, who followed me blindly, never questioning me, he mused silently and was bewildered to discover that

458

he would have her no other way. "No. It makes for a much more *interesting* relationship to have the little firebrand balk at me now and again." He laughed lowly.

Meghan sat patiently on the front stoop with the picnic basket resting beside her when Derek led the horses up from the barn. Carefully, he lifted her into the saddle, claimed the basket of food, and jumped atop Trojan to lead the way across his properties. They paused by a shimmering lake that glistened brightly in the rays of sunlight that slipped through the leaves of the magnolia trees, and it was here they decided to partake of their lunch.

They both ate heartily and Derek complimented her cooking by hungrily devouring a huge slice of the birthday cake that Lettie had thoughtfully included. Afterwards, Derek leaned against the trunk of a tree and watched as Meghan went about gathering a bouquet of wildflowers, and he was reminded of an afternoon some months past when he had observed a similar routine.

How his life had changed since that early spring day when he entered the Bainbridge library intent upon receiving his inheritance and seeking revenge against Thomas Bainbridge. Had he known that in acting out such a scheme he would acquire this volatile, young thing in the bargain, would he have acted so rashly?

Derek sighed restlessly and rubbed his tired eyes. Yes, by God, had he the opportunity to reenact the episode, he would handle it in the exact same fashion, save for one thing perhaps. He glanced longingly at Meghan. Were he presented with the indentical circumstances, he would make her his wife, for he knew now what Andrew had tried to make him see . . . what he himself had, in truth, known for some time, but had been too stubborn to admit, blinded by hatred for her father as he was. He *loved* her, something he had never thought to realize with Meghan, or any other woman. But she was not just any other woman. She belonged to him. And she was bound to him by a force more absolute than had they been united by the sacred vows of a dozen clergy: She was to bear his son.

Surely, she did not still despise him as viciously as she had proclaimed on the morning her father and Charles had discovered them abed. Granted, he had said and done things to her which were, to say the least, unjustified, but certainly her scorn would have mellowed somewhat by now after all that they had shared together. He studied her as she cautiously approached him from across the meadow.

"But, how do I tell her?" he muttered beneath his breath.

For all of Derek's worldly experiences, he was in the awkward position of never having openly expressed his affections for a woman. Oh, he had lain with many and had whispered words of endearment at the appropriate moments, but fortunately he had been shrewd enough to recognize the symptoms of a marriage-minded female and had quickly culminated any dangerous relationship . . . until now. Certainly, one did not simply blurt out words of love. Of course not! He would have to wait until the right moment. He would court and woo her with tender words and gentle kindnesses. He would be solicitous of her every need and grant her slightest whims. With new determination, he watched as she neared him and never once was his mind overshadowed with the nagging doubt that she might not return his love.

"What a lovely bouquet." His lips parted in a friendly smile.

"Yes," she murmured, "the flowers are lovely this time of year."

Quite naturally, Derek took her hand and pulled her down beside him. She sat facing him, her arm wrapped around his bent leg while she rested her chin on his knee. Meghan stared into the darkly intense eyes that seriously studied her and secretly wondered at his thoughts. Unconsciously, she leaned forward to smooth the lines of concentration from his face, but when she would have removed her hand, Derek captured it in his and, turning it over, pressed his lips against her open palm.

Meghan sighed languidly.

"Tired?" he asked softly.

"A little," she admitted.

"I feared the outing might be too much for you, little one. You never listen to me, even though I am usually correct where you are concerned." He considered her for a moment, then said, "I think I should like Dr. Samuels to examine you."

"But I feel fine, only a little tired," she protested. "One should surely expect a certain amount of fatigue when she is carrying a child."

"Yes, I suppose, and you don't look as peaked as when I found you in the kitchen. In fact, I believe that a little color has returned to your cheeks." He nonchalantly cupped her chin in his hand and gazed at her longingly. "But I still insist that you be examined by a learned physician. I want no mishap to befall either you or the child."

"As you like, m'lord," she consented.

"Here," he pulled her head down against his hard chest, "rest for awhile before we return to the house."

Thankfully, Meghan did as he asked, but she quickly recoiled from him when her delicate cheek struck a hard object in the pocket of his coat. "Sir, have you taken to carrying bricks in your pocket?" She gingerly rubbed the offended cheek and playfully scolded him.

"See for yourself." He folded his hands behind his head and casually leaned back against the tree, his eyes dancing merrily.

Meghan regarded him curiously as her slender fingers slipped beneath the elegant material and plucked a rectangular box from the inner pocket of his summer coat. One hand still rested upon his chest, and she could feel the rapid pounding of his heart as she considered the box with obvious indecision.

"Open it," he urged.

Meghan slowly lifted the lid and the sun caught the shimmer of the contents that lay against the red velvet lining, creating a brilliant sparkle that dazzled her eyes. She immediately recognized it as the necklace he had requested the night of her betrothal party. She stared at the gem for a long moment, then cast a quizzical frown at Derek.

"You had the clasp repaired?"

"Uh-huh. This was the errand I had to attend to in town this morning." He extracted the necklace from the box and placed it around her shapely neck. He then critically scrutinized it as it lay against the mauve blouse of her riding habit, and he unthinkingly undid the topmost buttons, thereby allowing the gem to lie against her creamy skin. "There," he approved his alteration, "it now rests where it belongs."

Meghan's hand flew to her throat. "You mean, it is mine?"

He nodded.

"But it's *your* birthday, Derek, not mine. You shame me, for I have not such a lavish gift for you."

He lifted the sullen chin till their eyes were level, and he regarded her warmly as he said, "But you are vastly mistaken, m'lady." His hand crept over her slender figure till it came to rest upon the softly rounding curve of her stomach. "In a short time you will present me with the most precious gift that a woman can give a man."

"Oh, Derek!" Her eyes brimmed with tears. She threw her arms around his neck and as he held her close, the tears began to slide gently down her cheeks.

"It would seem I have acquired a somewhat emotional wife." He used the term naturally, with no hint of mockery lacing his voice. "Tears for every occasion—when she is angry, when she is sad or frustrated. I trust these are happy tears?"

She nodded and dabbed at her eyes with the handkerchief from his lapel, her other hand still clutching the diamond necklace.

He breathed in the fresh scent of her hair and sighed heavily. "Meghan," he began suddenly, and she detected a serious note in the inflection of his voice. "I wish to apologize for my behavior last night. In truth, I was so crazy-blind drunk that I don't remember what I said or did, but I am quite certain I was not very pleasant." He paused and encircled her hand with his. "Did I hurt you?"

Meghan carefully scanned his eyes. He did not remember. Then she must forget as well. But could she forget the sight of Deirdre in his arms, or the cruel words the embittered girl had hurled at her? She must try.

Bravely, she said, "No, you did not hurt me. I suppose that I behaved badly when I departed so abruptly, but you seemed to be . . . to be enamored of Deirdre . . ." She quickly glanced away, but Derek forced her to look at him again.

"Enamored? Hardly. Is it not proper for a guest to have one dance with his hostess, or retrieve her a

463

refreshment when she requests it? Granted, I *had* hoped for a more beguiling wench to accompany me to the garden, but my lady fair had forsaken me." He looked at her meaningfully. "On my honor, Meghan, it was not passion that drove me to Deirdre's arms."

"But she said . . ." Meghan began, but then stared at him in confusion. Would he believe the horrible things Deirdre had said to her?

"What?" he gently coaxed.

"Oh, dreadful things. She insisted that you and she were to be married, that you had promised as much. She said that you would return to her when . . . when my time grew near, and I could no longer attend to your needs." Meghan had been unable to look at Derek as she revealed to him the bluntness of Deirdre's scathing words, but her head dropped even lower as she continued chokingly, "She even suggested that I . . . do away with the baby. I'm not sure what she meant by that, but she seemed positive you loved her and would resume your relationship with her regardless of what I might do." She winced as he grabbed her shoulders, but his eyes were clouded with anxiety rather than anger as they scanned her anguished face.

He had heard of secretive operations taking place in the seedy establishments in the less desirable sections of New Orleans and Natchez and other large cities. They were usually conducted by unclean charlatans who had no regard for the safety of their patients once they had received payment for the immoral act. As often as not, the young women who sought out these unsavory characters for assistance suffered a grueling death. Derek shuddered. He could not bear the thought that Meghan might consider such an alternative to bearing his child. Moreover, he could not endure the vision of her being subjected to such cruelty.

"Meghan, you would not harm our child?" he asked anxiously.

"No, Derek," she assured him and he was instantly relieved. "Why should an innocent child suffer because of the hysterics of a cruel, heartless woman? You may rest assured that I will not endanger the baby's life."

Derek's hold on her relaxed. "So, that is why you spent your evening with Nathan," he mused aloud. "Deirdre upset you with her vile accusations, and yet you confided your despair to another man rather than trusting me." His tone was not harsh as Meghan might have expected, but it was distinctly accusing.

"Derek, I could not. She claimed that you loved her still and I was terribly confused." She looked at him pleadingly. "I did not wish to see anyone after Deirdre's contemptible display. Nathan happened upon me on the front portico quite by accident." She halted abruptly and her eyes grew round in disbelief. "You certainly did not think that Nathan and I . . . that we . . ."

"I suppose I did harbor a few unkind thoughts."

"But he is your friend, and I would not—"

"Yes," he gathered her in his arms, "we were both foolish." He kissed her lips, her neck, and then pressed his lips against the necklace as it lay against the pulse in her throat. "Mother was wise in her choice of gifts to you. Diamonds suit you, my sweet."

Meghan smiled at him as she touched the costly necklace that had played such a prominent role in bringing them together. She would cherish it always. "Elizabeth was wise in many ways." She gently ran her fingers through his beard.

"Meghan?" He looked at her strangely, and she thought that he suddenly seemed extremely vulnerable when he softly asked, "Would you tell me about her?"

"Yes, Derek," she said, and leaned her head against

465

his shoulder as she began to tell him of the mother he
never saw again after her father sent him from London.

Meghan carefully climbed the rickety steps of the
ancient cabin and quietly slipped through the open door
to discover Nathan staring pensively at the canvas
before him. Lost in thought as he was, he did not notice
her entrance until he heard the gentle click of the door
being closed.

"Leave it ajar, please." He offered her a dazzling
smile and went on to explain, "I fear the lighting in here
leaves much to be desired and every ray is richly
appreciated. Besides, we musn't risk jeopardizing your
reputation."

"Oh, pooh, Nathan." Meghan nevertheless reopened
the door, then went to sit on the stool by the window.
"How are you progressing?"

"About the same," he replied noncommittally.

"You have said that exact same thing for nearly three
weeks now. When will I be permitted to see the
portrait?"

"When it's finished."

"But when will that be?" she persisted.

"When it's finished," he repeated patiently.

"Nathan," she stamped her foot soundly on the hard,
earthen floor. "You really are being fretfully unreasonable about this whole matter."

"Now, Meghan," he scolded kindly. "Do you not
know that artists are notorious for their temperamental
tendencies, even part-time artists like myself?"

"But—"

"I am staunchly set in my ways, you may be sure."
He halted her protests. "You need run along before
Derek grows concerned about your absence from
Chandalara and comes in search of you." He con-

siderately observed the downcast look upon her face and went on good-naturedly, "I promise that you will be the first to behold the unveiling of the portrait."

"Promise?"

"Yes, now scoot. I'd like as not have Derek's wrath to contend with should he find us here."

Meghan, her spirits refurbished by Nathan's promise, bid him a good day and stepped out of the cabin and into the warm, afternoon sunshine. Her thoughts were cluttered with the portrait and how pleased Derek would be to receive the gift and, consequently, she did not hear the footsteps behind her until it was too late. Frightened, Meghan started to run, but her progress was impeded by a burly arm that encircled her waist and pulled her against a hard chest. She was hindered from calling to Nathan for assistance, for a hand suddenly covered her mouth, smothering her startled cries.

"Hold still, Meghan!" the voice ordered and although she immediately complied with her assailant's command, it was not fear that forced her submission, but rather the astonishment that seized her as she recognized the voice of her captor.

"I'm going to remove my hand, but I must caution you against trying to summon your friend in the cabin, for it would certainly be unhealthy for him," the voice advised. "Do you understand?"

Meghan nodded numbly. The mysterious hand fell from her mouth, but she was not to be freed completely, for the hand clamped onto her wrist and whirled her about.

"Charles!" she breathed heavily. "What are you doing here, and . . . and what do you want?" She desperately tried to appear unaffected by his sudden appearance, but her knees trembled despite her valiant efforts to control them.

"Why, Meghan, dear heart, I'm here because you are here."

"Oh?" Meghan sounded dubious. "And what do you want?" Meghan observed the meaningful gleam in Charles' eyes and frantically tried to free herself from his grasp.

"You're becoming repetitive, sweet, and frightfully hysterical, I believe. Do calm yourself." The pressure on her arm increased and Meghan forcibly suppressed the nervous flutterings of her heart. "I was about to explain when you rudely interrupted me." He twisted her arm cruelly. "Please refrain from doing so again," he warned. "Pray, why should you frown so, love? Are you not pleased that your father and I have come to rescue you?"

"Papa? He is here, too?"

"Certainly. You must realize what a scandal your flight with Chandler created. So, in order to preserve your good name, your father and I discreetly circulated the rumor that Chandler kidnapped you. Then we set off to save you from the cur, though it would appear that we have arrived a bit late for that." He offered a scoffing glance at her rounding stomach.

"You flatter me, Charles. But would it not sound more believeable to state that you and Papa perpetrated this tale in an effort to save your own worthless skins? I know for a fact that the genteel crowd with which you associate would cut you in an instant were they made aware of the contemptible truth about this whole sordid affair," she spat vehemently.

"Ah, well." He hastily cleared his throat and released her so suddenly that she stumbled a few feet from him. "As for that, it is my intention to see that my influential friends never learn of this matter."

"I'm quite sure," Meghan jeered.

"And you're going to help me," he confidently informed her.

Meghan was abashed. "What do you mean? Oh, what do you want with me, Charles?" she cried in total exasperation. "Why can't you leave me alone?"

He stepped near her and pulled her roughly against his chest, forcing her to suffer his embrace. "Because, dear heart, Chandler has you, and, despite all that has happened, I still want you . . . *and* the jewels, of course. He thwarted me in England, but I shall have the last laugh, yet." He brushed his lips against her throat and Meghan cringed at their moist touch. "You see, pet, you are going to take the jewels from Chandler and flee with your father and me to France."

"You're mad!" She pushed away from him in disgust.

"We shall eventually return to London, of course." His waspish eyes fell to her stomach. "But we need to pass some time in France if I am to successfully pass Chandler's bastard off as my own child."

"You're vile!" Meghan cried vindictively. "I would not go that far with you"—she snapped her fingers viciously—"therefore, it is ludicrous of you to presume that I would go to France with you."

"Nevertheless, you shall."

"But . . . but I am married to Derek. I cannot possibly leave with you," Meghan insisted desperately.

"Are you, indeed?" Charles tucked his thumbs in his vest pockets and rocked on the heels of his shoes as he surveyed Meghan's stricken face with open skepticism. "Really, Meghan, you did not seriously think that I would be gullible enough to believe the tale that you and Chandler have concocted. There was no wedding in New Orleans, for I checked out that possibility when Thomas and I arrived. And lest you forget, you were in no condition to be married the night you fled London, nor was there time. So, you see, pet, you have no recourse. Either consent to do my bidding, or . . ." he paused purposely.

"Or what?"

"I'll inform all of Chandler's fine, upstanding acquaintances of the whole bloody affair," he sneered.

"*All* of it, Charles? Shall you tell them of your own evil doings?" she challenged him.

"I daresay that won't signify once the local residents learn that the young lady Chandler has been parading before them as his wife is nothing more than a common whore!" He ignored Meghan's indignant gasp and continued. "These Americans are a damned haughty lot, and I can safely wager that they'll not take this lightly. He'll be ruined, blame you for his misfortune, and like as not, he'll kick you out, brat and all."

"No, Derek would not do such a thing." Meghan wanted to run, but she knew it would do her no good to attempt an escape, for Charles would not free her till he was ready.

"Wouldn't he? Do you trust him enough to test his loyalty? And even if he did not throw you out, could you withstand the snobbish gossip? Why, you could never hold your head up again in public."

"You have planned well, Charles," Meghan sighed wearily.

"Then you will do it?" He eagerly clasped her hand to his chest.

Meghan shook her head as if to clear it of the incredible events the afternoon had wrought. She knew that she would never betray Derek, but if she did not do as Charles instructed, Derek would be ruined. She was damned at every turn. She needed time to think.

"I . . . I need time," she muttered forlornly.

"I thought as much," he snickered. "How much time?"

"I don't know. Where can I reach you?"

"Clever ploy, Meghan, but I'd rather like to avoid a confrontation with your burly friend. Never fear, sweet Meghan, I'll contact you in due course." He started to walk away, but returned for a moment to brush his lips along her cheek. "I'm confident that you'll make the right decision." He turned quickly and disappeared into the dense undergrowth of the forest.

As Meghan observed his departure, she could not control the sinking, empty feeling that enveloped her, as if all meaning had been drained from her life. Turning slowly, she made her way through the mid-afternoon sunshine, back to the home and the man she had grown to adore, and to the difficult decision she must make.

Part Four

The Conquest

Chapter Twenty

Meghan gently pushed aside the huge barndoor and mechanically made her way to Champion's stall. The barn was in virtual darkness, but Champion instantly recognized his mistress by her scent and came to nudge her shoulder with his impressive nose.

"Oh, Champion," she sighed desolately. "What am I to do?" She leaned dejectedly against the railing and stroked the horse's forehead.

Two weeks had passed since her fateful meeting with Charles, and yet he had not returned to inquire about her decision. Her mind was an abyss of confusion as she struggled to find a solution to her dilemma. And thusly lost in thought, she failed to hear Derek's footsteps as he entered the barn, nor did she become aware of his presence till he spoke to her.

"Can it be that my boorish parlor discourse has driven you to seek solace with this beastly creature?" He hung a brightly lit lantern against a sturdy beam and turned to examine Meghan's distraught face. "Or can it be that you find his conversation," he jerked his head at Champion, "more engaging than mine?" he prodded.

Meghan could not suppress a smile despite her dismal contemplations. "Nonsense," she chided. "Your conversation was as lively as ever." Her smile quickly faded. "Deirdre was certainly hanging onto your every word."

"I thought we had settled the matter concerning Deirdre, but if her occasional visits are going to evoke this sort of response from you, I shall hereafter suggest that Deirdre remain at home when Wade comes to Chandalara."

"No, Derek. Deirdre's presence did not upset me. I simply wanted to be alone for a few moments, that's all."

"Do you wish to be alone now?" he asked softly.

"No," she said simply, stretching out her hand to him.

Derek accepted the hand and pulled her close. "Tell me what it is that disturbs you these days," he urged, gently nuzzling her cheek with his.

Meghan longed to cleanse her plagued mind of the fear that was currently making her life a living hell. But her most commanding fear, that of losing Derek, precluded any threat that Charles had imposed, and she dreaded Derek's reaction should he learn of Charles's deceitful plan. She needed more time!

"I'm not disturbed, Derek. What a silly notion." She hooked her arm in his and walked with him from the barn. "However, I *have* been preoccupied with decorating the baby's nursery, nothing more."

"I wasn't aware that selecting a particular color or fabric could serve as such a depressing distraction," Derek remarked sardonically.

Meghan hesitated for a moment and looked up into Derek's face, but the darkness prevented her from reading his expression. "I . . . I don't know what you mean."

"Don't you?" He took a few steps toward the house before he turned to face her. "You haven't slept in days, you don't eat properly, and you have developed a general nervous condition. An incompleted nursery

476

hardly seems adequate justification for the emergence of such extreme peculiarities in one." His broad shoulders slumped noticeably as he gave a long sigh. "Why can't you bring yourself to trust me, Meghan? God knows I haven't always dealt fairly with you in the past, but I thought we had finally settled our differences on that score." He looked at her hopefully, but when she made no effort to respond, he continued his progress toward the house. "I'm here if you decide to confide in me." These final words floated through the darkness to Meghan as she watched him enveloped by the gloomy night.

Meghan lay very still, but the comforting sleep that had eluded her in recent evenings would still not befriend her. She lay silently and savored the memory of Derek's passionate lovemaking. He had been slow and deliberate that night as he had tenderly lifted her to the heights and depths of his sensual netherworld. It was almost as if he had tried to transmit some new feeling for her through his lovemaking, a feeling that he was unable as yet to communicate to her openly.

She turned a little to one side to better view his handsome face, and the arms that surrounded her tightened automatically. If only she could summon the courage to confide in him. If only she could be sure that he would not unleash his wrath on her when she told him of her meeting with Charles. But even as she gazed at him in the darkness, she arrived at a hasty decision, for suddenly in the depths of her being there gently fluttered the evidence of the new life that she and Derek had created. It was just the vaguest of sensations at first, but as she lay quietly, she felt it again, the faintest of movements, as if a delicate butterfly gently flitted about inside her. Meghan's eyes warmed over with loving tears, and as she tenderly rested her cheek against Derek's furry chest, she realized what she *must* do. She must seek Derek's guidance in dealing with Charles. Perhaps through loyalty and trust she could melt the rough edges of his heart and earn his respect and love. At least she had to try. For the sake of their child and the chance of a happy life with Derek, *she had to try.*

Meghan's eyes fluttered open to reveal Derek leaning over her, a disturbing frown clouding his features. Her heart leaped with fear as she interpreted the scowl as discovery of her well-kept secret, and she hastily glanced toward the window to avoid his gaze.

"What time is it?" she inquired casually.

"Much too early for you to consider rising. I was merely going to place a kiss upon your brow and be on my way. It wasn't my intent to waken you," he assured her.

"But where are you going?"

"I've been summoned to the fields. An accident has befallen one of the men," he explained.

A vast relief flooded her veins as she realized that Derek was still ignorant of Charles's plan, but she was concerned about the worker. "Was he seriously injured?"

"Now, I cannot possibly know the answer to that till I've spoken to the doctor. Nathan has gone for him." He smiled at her and leaned forward to kiss her lips. "You go back to sleep."

"Derek." The softness of her voice momentarily checked his movement away from the bed.

"Yes?"

"The baby . . ." she faltered.

"Yes, is something wrong?" he asked anxiously.

"No, silly." She laughed and captured his face

478

between loving hands. "Last night . . . while you were asleep . . . the baby . . . well, it *moved* is all. I . . . I just wanted you to know." She studied the expression on his face and awaited his reaction.

Carefully, he pulled her to him and rested his chin on her head as he lowered one hand to caress her abdomen. "You should have wakened me."

Meghan sighed contentedly as she nestled her cheek against his comforting chest. "It was the slightest of flutters. I, myself, could barely feel it. Just wait till I'm great and round and he kicks you in the back while you try to sleep," she warned him happily. "You'll like as not heave us both from your bed."

"I anticipate the event with great zeal." He kissed the crown of her head and his gaze caught the sultry view of her rounded breasts where the sheet had slipped away. Wickedly, he lowered his head and playfully nibbled at each one till the nipples were rosy and firm when he finally withdrew. "You discredit me, madam," he whispered thickly. "I'd never heave such a fetching wench from *my* bed." He gently laid her back against the pillows and covered her with the sheet. He then stood to button his shirt, and he was tucking it inside his trousers when Meghan again spoke to him.

"Derek, I need to . . . *want* to talk to you." She looked at him hopefully.

Derek turned to gaze at her from his position at the foot of the huge fourposter. And as their eyes met, Meghan at last read comfort and understanding in the two shining orbs that contemplated her statement. "I have some matters to discuss with Wade after I see to the injured field hand, but I should return to the house around two. We'll talk then."

Meghan watched him stride confidently from the room, then rolled to her side and hugged his pillow to

479

her while she drifted into the first peaceful sleep she had encountered in weeks.

Later that afternoon Meghan sat by the window in their room, gazing out at the bright sky. She had long since lost all concentration on the needlepoint that lay dormant in her lap, as her thoughts largely centered around Derek and the conversation they were going to have. How much should she tell him, or rather, to how much would he listen before he erupted into a violent rage? Regardless of his reaction, Meghan had arrived at two decisions on that mid-September afternoon. Whatever Derek's decision concerning Charles, she would abide by it, and secondly, she would tell Derek of her love for him. At best, she could only guess at his reception of such a declaration, but she could no longer live in the same house with Derek, share his food and his bed, and give birth to his child, without sharing his love as well.

"Miz Meghan." Nicholas's voice interrupted her silent deliberations. "I knocked, but you didn't ansuh," he apologized for the interruption.

"That's all right, Nicholas. What is it?" She favored the old servant with a stunning smile.

"They's a man downstairs. Said he was a friend of the massah's, but I don't recollect ever seein' him afore. I told him the massah's not home, but he's set on talkin' to you fer some reason."

Meghan placed her needlepoint on the table and stood to press the wrinkles from her gown. "Did he give his name?"

"No, ma'am. Said he'd introduce hisself when you came down."

"Did he now?" Meghan was slightly taken aback by such a brash attitude. "Well, he certainly sounds like someone Derek would know. Did you show him to the drawing room?"

"Yes, ma'am. Pardon me, Miz Meghan, but do you intend to see him?"

"Certainly. As mistress of this hall, it's my duty to greet visitors, even impudent guests like the one belowstairs." She swept past the servant and went to the dressing table to check her appearance.

"Pardon me for sayin' so, Miz Meghan, but the massah won't take kindly to me leavin' you alone with no stranger," Nicholas wisely advised.

"Nonsense. If he's a friend, all will be fine, and if he's not, I'll quickly send him on his way." She noticed the servant's downhearted look. "I'll summon you if the need arises," she assured him. And with that, Meghan left the room and descended the stairs to the drawing room.

She gently pushed open the door and stepped across the threshold, but her first impression made her think that Nicholas's enigmatic visitor had changed his mind about speaking with her, for the room appeared empty. Meghan turned and was about to summon the servant when a slight movement out of the corner of her eye stayed her. But when Meghan turned to face her guest, the warm words of greeting she was about to offer froze on her lips when her bewildered eyes met those of the caller.

"Papa!" Try as she might, Meghan could not calm the sudden thrashing of her heart, nor could she efface the memory of her father angrily straddling her crumpled body, bloody whip in his clenched fist, mercilessly punishing her for foiling his evil scheme.

"Do stop staring at me, daughter. Surely, my appearance cannot have startled you that much." He returned the porcelain figurine he had been examining to its stand and began to move toward her. "Charles said he told you I was with him."

Nervously, Meghan avoided his approach and cautiously stepped to the sofa and sat down. "He did, but—"

"But you didn't anticipate *my* coming to confront you in your sordid little paradise," he concluded for her.

"My relationship with Derek is not sordid!" Meghan said defiantly.

"Well, whatever your relationship with the bastard *was*, it is now over," Thomas informed her. "We're wasting time. Gather your belongings, Meghan. Charles is waiting for us."

"Then go to him," Meghan suggested bitterly. "But I'll not accompany you."

"*What?*" Thomas stormed to the sofa and stood glaring at her, his dark eyes biting into her sensitive flesh.

But Meghan would not allow his forbiding appearance to intimidate her. "I'll not go with you, Papa, and there is nothing you can say or do to make me change my mind," she said unwaveringly.

"Yes, there is, my proud, stubborn daughter." Thomas grasped her wrists roughly and drew her cruelly to her feet. "You spoiled my plans once on this score, but it's not likely I'll stand for your disobedience a second time. I am your father and you will do as I bid. Now, get those cursed jewels and let's be gone."

"You are no longer my father," Meghan cried bitterly. "You relinquished your claim as my parent when you whipped me like a common stable creature. Then you *gave* me to a man you despised, not caring what he did with me. You undoubtedly expected that I would perish at the hands of the man who swore vengeance against you. But ironically I did not perish,

482

Papa. Indeed, I have done quite well for myself and, Derek, for all that he still hates you quite thoroughly, has proven to be very kind to me."

"Yes, I can see how his *kindness* has affected you," Thomas snickered at her rounding stomach. "I have listened to enough of this prattle. I shall tell you but one last time to collect your belongings."

"No!" she screeched as she tried desperately to pull away from his ruthless grasp. "I *love* Derek! You cannot force me to betray him!"

"Insolent brat!" Thomas raised his hand to strike her.

Meghan closed her eyes and turned her head aside to steady herself against the impending blow, but Derek's steely voice cut the air behind them like a knife. "You'll be dead before you land the first blow, Thomas."

If the ominous tone of Derek's voice did not convince Thomas that the threat was not an idle one, the pistol that was aimed at his chest did, for Thomas instantly released Meghan.

"You will understand my flagrant display of bad manners, Thomas, when I ask you to leave my home at once." He stepped away from the door to indicate that Thomas should use it as an exit. "I'll not trouble you for an explanation as to why you dared to venture to my home. I'm sure Meghan will fill me in quite nicely after you have departed."

Thomas blatantly ignored Derek and turned again to Meghan. "Come with me." His tone was less harsh, but it still sounded more like a command than a request.

Meghan could not look at him, nor could she bring herself to look at Derek, for she knew that his face would be alive with anger and pain at having found her father in his house. She also knew that she would likely suffer his outrage for the untimely incident. Therefore,

483

it was with slumping shoulders that she turned her back on both men and with a heavy sigh, she softly said, "No, Papa, I won't go with you."

With her back to him, Meghan did not witness the mask of black fury that instantly covered her father's face, but she did hear the bitter threat that he uttered before vacating the room. "You know what to expect, then, don't you, daughter?" And with this final rejoinder, he turned on his heels and stomped from the room.

Several minutes elapsed before Meghan turned from the bright glare of the window to face Derek. He had not moved from his stance beside the door, and she had been correct in predicting the harsh set of his jaw. But his mood seemed to mellow a little when he realized that the scene had been as distressing for her as it had been for him. Meghan was the first to break the haunting silence.

"I . . . I'm sorry that Papa came here, Derek," she began uncertainly.

"You knew that he was in the vicinity?" he asked.

Meghan nodded. "Charles, too," she admitted.

"That is what has been troubling you these past weeks," he offered for her.

Again she nodded.

"You have a tongue, Meghan. You have skillfully demonstrated its potency in the past. Pray, don't tell me that I'm finally delivered from its vindictive retorts." He angrily holstered the pistol and, replacing it in the table drawer, he strode toward her.

"I didn't know what to do!" She looked at him pleadingly, wringing her hands in sheer desperation.

"You could have come to me," he whispered softly and reached out to stay the frantic movement of her hands. "Did I not promise your father would not harm you again?" He seated her on the sofa and went to pour them a drink.

"Yes, and I desperately wanted to discuss the matter with you, but—"

"But you still don't trust me," he finished for her, waving aside her protestation to the contrary. "Drink this," he instructed as he extended the glass of Madeira to her. Derek then sat beside her on the sofa, leisurely sipping his brandy as he carefully studied her. "Tell me, Meghan, were you going to mention Charles and your father during our afternoon tête-à-tête?"

"Yes." The word stumbled from her trembling lips, and she nervously twisted the crystal goblet while awaiting Derek's next conjecture.

"Well, I suppose even such slight progress should be applauded," he mocked her. "Drink your wine, Meghan. It will steady your nerves, though I cannot fathom why you fear me."

"It's not you that I fear." She took a drink of the wine and hesitantly turned to face him. "Are you not even remotely curious as to Papa's purpose in coming here?"

Derek shrugged his rugged shoulders and crossed to the liquor cabinet to refill his glass. "Money, I suppose, or the jewels, and you, of course. I imagined his tune would change considerably after he sobered and realized the repercussions his unfortunate decision would have." He chuckled devilishly, then added, "How *does* one explain to polite society that he has relinquished his daughter, even a slightly tainted one, to a rogue of my notorious reputation? I'll wager Thomas was hard-pressed indeed to find you, little one." He returned to the sofa and draped a comforting arm about her shoulders. "Tell me," he said, lifting her drooping chin, "why did you not go with Thomas? Can it be my captivating wit and charm that makes you reluctant to flee with your father and would-be lover?''

"The situation is not at all amusing, Derek, and once you realize the full implication of Papa's reappearance, I think that perhaps you will share my sentiments." She glanced down at her lap before continuing. "My reasons for not going with Papa are personal and somewhat selfish. Papa never kept the fact that he despised having a daughter a well-guarded secret and, consequently, my life with him was not a pleasant one. I shall never again willingly place myself under his domineering guardianship, and Charles is no better." She finished her wine and rested the glass on the table.

"It's indeed enlightening to discover that you don't consider me to be domineering." He chuckled.

"You're worse than the lot of them!" She surprised him with her candor. "But in a different way," she added softly. "Derek." The sudden serious inflection of her voice caused him to raise an eyebrow. "I have something that I wish to say to you, but you must promise to hear me out before you interrupt." She looked at him tentatively.

"As you like." He sat back, a little puzzled by her sudden melancholy attitude.

Meghan took a deep breath before beginning. "I want you to know that I have given a great deal of thought to what I am about to say and, though I shall likely have to endure your wrath, I feel that I should make you aware of my plans." She glanced aside to witness his inquisitive gaze thoughtfully perusing her.

"Yes, I assure you that I'm thoroughly intrigued. Do continue." Derek started to select a cigar from his pocket, but Meghan's next statement checked his movement.

"I'm . . . I'm going away." The words that had

seemed stuck in her throat suddenly came in a rush as though they had been torn from her.

"*The hell you say*!" he thundered.

"You promised not to interrupt!" Meghan stood up quickly.

"To hell with that!" Derek cried. "I didn't know what an insane little speech you were going to make. What nonsense is this?"

"You don't know to what lengths Papa and Charles will go to destroy you!" She wrung her hands nervously as she turned to face him. "With my refusal to assist them, they are going to make it publicly known that I'm your—that we are not truly married." She checked her statement and dropped to her knees before him. "Don't you see? I can't bear to suffer the shame when all of your friends learn the truth about us, about the baby. And what will happen to your standing in the community? Surely, your business associates will not take this lightly."

"I think that you sorely overestimate the seriousness of your father's threat. My friends are not likely to take the words of two complete strangers to heart." He tried to minimize her fears.

"But what of those who do?" she persisted.

"I'll handle the situation *if* and *when* it develops. But whatever recourse I'm forced to take, it will not include sending you from Chandalara, I assure you," he informed her shortly.

"But—"

"No, Meghan! Consider the subject closed to discussion."

"Then . . . then you *must* marry me," she blurted out. She had not considered that he would denounce her plan after he learned of her father's intent to expose them.

"Meghan," Derek's voice held a warning note, and he tiredly rubbed his eyes. "We have settled the matter on this score as well, and you cannot possibly expect me to rationally discuss marriage to you after your father has only moments ago tarnished my home with his wretched presence," he said tartly.

"I'm not accountable for my father's actions," she moaned helplessly. "Please, Derek. It's not for myself that I ask this. I don't expect you to love me, only marry me in order to give our child a name," she pleaded.

"Don't badger me, Meghan!" He angrily pulled away the hand that she had clasped and directed his stern gaze toward the fireplace.

"I see." She slowly climbed to her feet and turned her back to him. "Then I shall be leaving in the morning."

"And I shall bring you back before noon," he countered wearily.

"And I shall leave again and again until you grow tired of chasing me and free me from an association that I cannot abide," she hurled at him hysterically.

"Damn it, Meghan!" Derek jumped to his feet. "For someone who only moments ago professed her undying love for me, you certainly have a strange way of exhibiting it."

Meghan whirled on him, completely dumbfounded with the realization that Derek had heard her decree, and she was infuriated that he would be glib about her admission. "You were obviously mistaken, sir!" she retorted loftily. "What you overheard was merely an attempt to trick my father into leaving me alone. I would have told him anything, *anything* to achieve that!" she screamed uncontrollably.

"Calm down," Derek cautioned. "In your present state, you're likely to harm yourself, or the child."

"I don't care!" Meghan wildly pushed aside the two arms that reached forward to restrain her. "*I hate you*! Hate you for the insensitive way you treat me and for the child you forced on me." She hung her head as the deluge of tears she had been fighting to control suddenly burst forth and streamed down her cheeks. "I'd rather it die than be forced to suffer a lifetime of hardships with a selfish and uncaring father such as you!"

Furiously, Derek stepped forward and grabbed her by the shoulders. "Stop it!" he commanded. "You don't know what you're saying! You don't mean that!"

"Yes, I do," she assured him. "Oh, what evil thing have I done that I am forced to bear the humiliation of having your—"

"Enough!" Derek released her abruptly, causing her to stumble backwards. "You're quite obviously over-wrought what with this afternoon's events. I can only hope that by this evening you will have regained your reason, and we can have a more rational discussion of this matter," he said formally and turned on his heel.

Meghan watched until he reached the door before she attempted to halt his departure, but the words she was prepared to speak were never to leave her lips. For as she stepped toward Derek, the window behind her shattered and a searing pain tore through her left side. The fierce impact of the bullet propelled her forward, causing her to strike her head on the edge of the table as she fell in a crumpled heap upon the floor.

Derek strode anxiously back and forth across the plush sitting room carpet. It had been hours since the doctor arrived to care for Meghan. He had not emerged from her room even once to brief him on the extent of her injuries.

"Here, Derek." A brandy snifter was coaxed into his hands as Nathan gently eased him into a comfortable chair.

"What time is it?" Derek mumbled.

"Midnight."

"What the devil is taking so long?" Derek asked impatiently.

But even as he voiced the question, he recalled the frantic moments in the drawing room when he had heard the gun blast and had turned to discover Meghan slumped on the floor. The events immediately following the attack happened so quickly that even now it was a struggle to recount them clearly. He remembered sending Nathan to summon Dr. Samuels, and he had similarly scattered the servants on a multitude of errands. Consequently, he alone had observed the deathly white pallor of her delicate skin as he carried her to the safety of her bedchamber. But the doctor had immediately ordered him from the room upon his arrival, so all Derek could now envision was the grim picture of Meghan lying motionless upon her bed, almost as if she were . . . No! Derek pounded his fist against the arm of the chair. *She must not die*! She might lose the child; there was that possibility. But there could be other children. He could never find another Meghan.

"Derek." Nathan's hand lightly pressed against his shoulder. "The doctor wants to speak with you."

Derek was instantly on his feet. "How is she?" he asked anxiously.

Dr. Samuels was a short, stocky, middle-aged man, who had served as Tylerville's only physician for the past twenty-five years; the years of hard work and responsibility were carved on his worn face. "She received a nasty blow to the head when she fell, Derek," the doctor began as he glanced wistfully at the drink in

490

Derek's hand. "Could I persuade you to share a glass of that?"

"What? Oh, yes. Pardon my lapse of manners. Nathan, would you?"

Nathan promptly obliged, and the doctor took a grateful swallow before continuing. "Luckily, the bullet passed completely through the fleshy area of her side. No major organs were struck and since she is young and strong, I anticipate a complete recovery," he reassured Derek.

"And the child?" Derek asked apprehensively.

"At the moment, Derek, I'm uncertain as to the welfare of the baby," the doctor replied honestly.

"But she hasn't lost it yet?" Derek inquired hopefully.

"No, but you must remember that she has sustained a severe shock, and has lost a great deal of blood. The chance of a miscarriage is present, but I believe that if she can make it through tonight and the next few days without suffering a setback, then the probability of Meghan losing the child will be greatly reduced. Right now, I'm more concerned with her state of mind. She seemed deeply troubled by something—I mean, other than this." He looked at Derek for an explanation, but when it became apparent that Derek was not going to offer one, he patted him on the shoulder and walked to the sofa and sat down. "I can remain the rest of the night if you want. She should be through the worst of it by morning."

"Yes, by all means. I'll have Sophie prepare a room for you." He rang for the servant. "Doctor, may I see her?"

"Yes, you may go to her, but see that she doesn't become upset," he warned.

Derek wasted little time in racing up the majestic

491

staircase to Meghan's room. He quietly pushed aside the heavy door, and, soundlessly slipping inside the room, he crossed to the foot of the bed. Abbey had been vigilantly sitting by her mistress's bedside, but she rose to her feet when she observed Derek enter the room. Derek smiled warmly at the young girl and whispered that he had come to relieve her of her duties for the duration of the night. He then devoted his entire concentration to the slight figure that seemed engulfed by the huge bed. She looked so small and helpless. How could he have been so cruel to her that afternoon when she had pleaded with him to marry her for the sake of their child?

Meghan was sleeping peacefully, so Derek drew the chair closer to the bed in order to be near her in case she should call out to him. His eyes momentarily fell on the nasty cut along her forehead, and he lightly brushed his lips against the wound before he sat down to begin the long vigil. The events of the day had occurred in such a whirlwind fashion that he had not yet had the time, or the presence of mind, to put them into perspective. But now that he knew Meghan was going to recover, he could devote the lonely hours of the night to solving the identity of his would-be assassin. For surely, the bullet that felled Meghan had been intended for him.

The most obvious of suspects was Thomas, of course, but Derek seriously doubted that he possessed the courage to pull off such a stunt. Charles, on the other hand, could have easily accomplished the cold-blooded deed; of that, Derek was certain. But he had a nagging doubt that prevented him from placing the blame entirely on Charles. After all, Sam Iverson had also threatened his life.

Derek stood up and stretched wearily in an attempt to clear his drowsy mind. He stepped to the window to continue his silent deliberations. The hot September night breeze wafted his tired body, and he leaned against the window ledge to observe the moon drenched lawn below. The sheriff and his makeshift posse had been of little help that afternoon. In fact, they had accomplished little more than the complete destruction of Meghan's flower garden and had destroyed any trace of a clue that the attacker might have left behind. But no matter, Derek mused. Whatever the identity of the culprit, he would doubtlessly return again. "Only next time, I'll be prepared for the bastard," Derek whispered hoarsely.

He returned to Meghan's bedside and tenderly applied a cool washcloth to her face and throat. "Meghan," he murmured softly. "You must be strong and give your strength to the baby. You cannot have meant those angry words earlier today. You have every right to be bitter with me," he lifted her limp hand to his tear-moistened cheek, "but don't turn that bitterness on our child. I *do* care, my angel, you must sense that somehow, and I'll prove to you how much as soon as you're well again." He lovingly kissed the hand he held, then returned to his chair where he soon drifted off to a peaceful slumber.

Meghan's slumber, however, was not to be so peaceful. She had remained blessedly unconscious throughout much of the ordeal, and the few moments of consciousness she had experienced had been clouded by the powerful sedative the doctor had administered. She stirred a little and her eyes fluttered open briefly; she imagined she saw Derek, sleeping quietly in a chair beside her bed.

You're just dreaming, a small voice in the corner of her mind assured her.

But if this was a dream, then so must she have dreamed his voice in the darkness, urging her to be strong for the baby. The voice that had told her he cared for her and would prove it to her when she was well again. Oh, how she longed that that particular dream might have been a reality rather than a drug-induced fantasy. Why did the doctor's medication make it so very difficult to distinguish reality from her muddled dreams?

Meghan sighed heavily and again Derek appeared before her. This time he was wearing the blue velvet dress coat he had worn the night of her betrothal party in London, and he was beckoning her to join him on the dance floor. Her immediate impulse was to decline, but then she relented. After all, what possible harm could there be in one innocent dance, and it had been so long since she had lost herself in the gay, carefree melody of a romantic waltz. She timidly accepted the outstretched hand and easily fell into step with her masterful partner. But when she lifted her head to offer him a radiant smile, she stiffened with horror, for the face into which she stared belonged to Garth McTavish, not Derek.

"*No!*" she screamed and tugged viciously to escape the dead man's grasp. "Let me go! *Let me go!*"

But it would seem that the apparition was not going to accommodate her. In fact, the harder she struggled the more intense his powerful grip became. But suddenly the awful man did release her, and she vaguely became aware of Derek's deep voice comforting her, his strong arms caressing her, holding her against him.

But no, she desperately tried to pull away from him. It was probably just another trick of her imagination. She would not give into this dream as she had the other one.

She felt the sensation of being pressed against the sheets and a cool cloth was placed on her brow. Oh, and the breeze. The breeze felt so luxurious as it floated across her hot flesh, and she was again transmitted to another time she had spent with Derek.

They were aboard *The Lady Elizabeth* and Derek had just made love to her. She could see his handsome face above her in the darkness, and she felt herself flush with embarrassment as he pulled her from the bed and wrapped one of his fresh-smelling linen shirts around her. He then led her from the cabin and onto the deck where the gentle ocean breeze served to cool her burning flesh. But the soft breeze abruptly turned into a violent gale that rocked the ship precariously, sending gigantic waves splashing over the ship's decks.

Meghan wanted to flee, but her feet were glued to the deck. She was hopelessly doomed to witness the ensuing storm. Meghan watched, horrified, as Derek was thrown off balance by the violent motion of the ship and fell into the deck railing which splintered upon impact, sending him sprawling into the abyss of the raging sea.

Meghan screamed and rushed forward, her arms outstretched to him. He seemed suspended before her, arms flailing wildly against the wind and the sea as he struggled to reach her. She glanced around for someone to help her, and there, calmly approaching her through the storm, was Nathan. Yes, Nathan would surely help her.

"Help me, Nathan!" she pleaded. "You're the only one who truly understands. *Help me!*"

But the storm abated as quickly as it had surfaced and Meghan was again at Chandalara. She was seated on the terrace overlooking her beautiful garden, sipping a cool glass of lemonade. Beside her was a cradle trimmed with a blue skirt, and when Meghan peeked inside, she was surprised to find a tiny baby, sleeping peacefully. "My

495

baby," she whispered lovingly as she continued to stare in awe at the tiny infant.

"No!" Deirdre's haunting voice shattered the precious moment. "Derek said you didn't want him, so he gave him to me." Her wicked laugh penetrated the air and to Meghan's horror, she lifted the baby from the cradle and started to walk away.

"*No!*" Meghan screamed hysterically and tried to free herself from the chair to stop Deirdre, but she was immobile. It was almost as if she were being physically restrained. She thrashed about wildly in the chair, but to no avail. Deirdre was nowhere to be seen by now, and yet, Meghan's head reeled with her cruel, inhuman laughter.

"My baby, my baby," she mumbled piteously as huge tears tumbled down her cheeks. Her clenched fists pummeled the chair with weak blows. She had to get to her baby! With one final surge of strength, Meghan tried to extricate herself from her captor, but the effort caused her to cry out as a tremendous pain ripped across her lower abdomen. She gasped for air and clutched at her stomach, and then there were no more terrifying nightmares, only blessed darkness.

Chapter Twenty-one

Meghan could hear the voices floating above her. She had heard them at different intervals since that final stabbing pain that had rendered her unconscious, but this time she could distinguish the voices more clearly than ever before. But even as she struggled to leave her somnolent world, a nagging emptiness clutched at her as if to caution her that all was not well in the conscious world.

"She seems better today, Massah Derek." Sophie had just concluded bathing her mistress and had tucked the clean sheet around her when Derek entered the room to inquire of Meghan's condition.

Meghan moaned softly and shifted in her sleep, tugging fretfully at the tight sheet.

"Oh, I done forgot," Sophie scolded herself. "Miz Meghan don't like her sheets tucked in so tight." She quickly corrected the oversight, then set about putting away the articles she had used in bathing Meghan. "Is you gonna sit with Miz Meghan fer a spell?"

"Yes," Derek responded distantly.

"I sure dreads the time when this chile wakes up and finds out she done lost her baby." Sophie shook her head sadly and turned from the dresser to wipe a tear from her cheek.

"What . . . what did you say, Sophie?" Meghan's voice sounded like a hoarse whisper.

Her unexpected inquiry startled the two occupants of the room, but Derek was quick to regain his equanimity. Instantly, he stepped forward and grasped Sophie by the arm, ushering her to the door. "Dr. Samuels insisted that he examine Meghan the moment she awakened. Instruct Nicholas to send one of the boys to summon him."

"Yes, Massah Derek." She glanced eagerly toward the bed. "Praise be, Miz Meghan done finally woke up. Now I can take proper care of her, and she'll be fit as a fiddle in no time. You just wait'n' see if'n she ain't," she promised a somewhat subdued Derek as she hurried out

497

the door to find Nicholas.

Derek walked slowly to Meghan's bedside and stared down at the wan face that regarded him somewhat pensively.

Meghan underwent his close scrutiny with mild discomfort. She had just survived a terrifying ordeal, the exact nature of which she was still uncertain, and she was not yet ready to go to battle with Derek.

"Derek, please don't look at me that way. I apologize if my illness has caused you some concern." She wasn't certain, but she thought his expression grew even more somber before he turned from the bed and faced the window. "Have I . . . was I unconscious long?"

"Ten days," he replied shortly.

"Ten days?" she repeated incredulously. "Was I wounded that seriously?" She could remember the thunderous impact of the bullet and Derek carrying her to her room, but her memory failed her beyond that point.

"There were other *complications* that impeded your recovery for a time," he said emotionlessly and moved away from the window to sit on the edge of the bed.

"What . . . what complications?" Meghan was growing increasingly uncomfortable with his cold attitude, and instinctively her hands ran across her stomach to caress the plump bulge where her baby grew. She somehow struggled to a sitting position when her fingers encountered the now flattened area of her abdomen. "Derek!" She clutched his arm and her eyes searched his for an explanation.

"You lost the baby," he said bluntly.

"*No!*" She shook her head adamantly. "Why are you always so mean?" She covered her face with her hands. And then she remembered the awful dream she had prior to the terrible pain that left her helpless for so

498

many days. Slowly, she lowered her hands and focusing a cold stare on Derek, she said, "*She* took my baby. You gave him to that heartless woman!" she accused him hysterically as her clenched fists pounded against his hard chest. "Give me back my baby! Make her give him back to me!"

Derek was temporarily stunned by Meghan's wild accusations, but her attack against him soon made him take charge of the situation. He captured her flailing hands in his and pinioned them by her side. "Listen to me!" he commanded and the raging sound of his voice shocked her to submission. "No one *took* our son. He is dead! *You* killed him. Do you understand?" He saw the bright tears well up in her eyes, and he released her hands, but their eyes remained fixed on each other. "Such a to-do for one to make over a child she had hoped never to bear. I rather thought that you would be pleased with the notion that you had been relieved of *that* particular burden." His words were purposely cruel, for he intended to hurt her the way she had hurt him.

Meghan felt her heart grow cold as she stared in complete horror at Derek. She had never before witnessed this calculatingly insensitive side of him, and she was not emotionally capable of dealing with his odd behavior. "Get out of here," she ordered hoarsely.

"As you wish, madam." He clicked his heels and performed a mocking bow over her bed.

"You're vile," she whispered harshly. "I hate you . . . hate you for what you have done to me." She turned on her side and wept freely into her pillow.

"Yes, I'm well aware of your sentiments, and you may be sure that I return them in full." He strode angrily toward the door, nearly upsetting Abbey as she was entering the room. "See to your mistress!" he said bitterly and stomped down the staircase to the drawing room for a badly needed snifter of brandy.

Meghan sat alone in the dimly lit nursery, her fingers clasped in a tight knot and folded primly in her lap. She stared fixedly at a blank space along the wall where the baby's dresser had stood. They had tried to remove all the furnishings and the clothes she had made from the nursery, but Meghan had caught them at their wicked task and had made them stop. Now all that remained of the furniture was the cradle that Derek had made for the baby and the rocking chair in which she sat. But they would not succeed in taking these things from her as well. No, she would have need of them when Derek made Deirdre return their son to her. She continued to rock and stare into the dim corners of the room, and, consequently, she did not hear the gentle click of the door being carefully closed.

On the far side of the door, Dr. Samuels shook his head slowly and turned to Derek. "How long has she been like this?"

"Three days ago I decided the nursery should be cleared, so as not to serve as a reminder to Meghan that she lost the baby. But my idea had an adverse affect, I fear, for she became like a madwoman, screeching at the servants and yelling that she needed the things for her baby." He directed the doctor into the sitting room that separated his and Meghan's chambers. "Then she took up vigil in that accursed rocking chair and no amount of persuasion can coax her from it. She permits no one entrance to the room, speaks to no one, and eats virtually nothing. I'm at my wits' end." Derek raked his fingers through his thick mass of black hair in total exasperation. "I suppose I could physically remove her, but—"

"No, Derek. I fear that's not the answer," the doctor

advised him. "I've seen similar cases and we have before us a very delicate situation. It must be carefully treated." He sat down in a comfortable chair and stretched his tired legs in front of him. "You see, Meghan hasn't yet accepted the death of the child," he explained, "and it will be difficult to reason with her till she does." He regarded Derek closely as he accepted a glass of brandy from his distraught host.

Dr. Samuels could not recollect ever having seen Derek in such a disheveled condition. His eyes were ringed with dark, ugly circles that spoke of sleepless nights and intense worry. And his clothes were in such a state of disarray that the doctor could only surmise that they had been worn constantly for several days.

"Derek." The doctor placed a comforting hand on the younger man's shoulder. "Get hold of yourself, man. Meghan needs you, and she needs you to be strong and healthy. Get yourself a good meal and a decent night's sleep. And stop swilling this stuff like it's lemonade." He took the brandy decanter from his hand and returned it to the table. "I've got a feeling there's a good deal more on your mind than what you've told me already, but I'm not going to pry. Not yet anyway. The important thing is that you get her out of that room and interested in living again."

"What do you suggest?" Derek asked dryly.

"I'm fresh out of suggestions at the moment," he confessed. "But then you should know better than I what would pique Meghan's interest enough to get her out of the doldrums." He picked up his medical bag and walked to the door. "But whatever you plan, do it soon. That's a lovely wife you've chosen for yourself, and I hate to see the spirit plucked from one so young."

Derek remained standing by the window for a long time after the doctor departed. The hot September sun burned like a torch high in the sky and Derek basked in the warm glow of its rays before turning his thoughts again to Meghan.

"So, the doctor fears for her sanity, too," Derek reasoned aloud. "Oh, he didn't say it in so many words, but he implied as much." His large, sun-browned hand impulsively reached for the brandy decanter, but the doctor's words were still fresh in his memory and he selected a cigar from his pocket instead. Aimlessly, he paced the length of the room while puffing thoughtfully on the cheroot.

Deep down he knew that Dr. Samuels was right. Meghan had to be coaxed out of her depression and encouraged to participate in life again. He had a plan he was certain would be successful, but he was not the man to initiate it. Meghan would not respond to him at all. Ever since the day she had awakened and he had ruthlessly told her of the baby's death, she had withdrawn from him daily.

There must be someone who could breach the barrier she had erected and persuade her to emerge from the shell into which she had retreated. There must be someone she trusted. He dropped wearily into the nearest chair and rested his head against the back of the chair. When he finally opened his eyes again, they fell upon the painting of *The Lady Elizabeth* that Nathan had given to him.

"*Help me, Nathan*," he mumbled aloud. "*You're the only one who truly understands*," Derek slowly repeated the painful words he had overheard Meghan cry out in her troubled sleep. And it was with considerable bitterness that he swallowed his pride and set out upon the worn path that led to Nathan's cottage.

The creak of the door signaled to Meghan that her quiet solitude was about to be interrupted, but she did not even honor the intruder with a nod. They came at regular intervals during the day. Sometimes they brought her food, sometimes they just stared at her, but she always ignored them. Eventually they went away when they discovered that she would not acknowledge them. Would they never grow tired of their silly games and leave her be?

"Meghan?" Nathan's voice softly called out to her.

Meghan could barely see him in the dark room, but his voice sounded warm and friendly. At last, here was someone she could trust. She extended her hand to him and his name fell freely from her lips with a relieved sigh.

Nathan clasped her hand between his and gave it a reassuring squeeze. "Do you feel up to a visit from an old friend?"

Meghan raised her head slowly till her eyes met Nathan's in the semidarkness, then she turned a suspicious gaze to the door. But Nathan gently smoothed the disheveled hair from her face and coaxed her gaze back to him. "There's no one else," he assured her quietly. "May I stay?"

Nathan watched her closely as she considered her reply and was half-expecting a rejection, when Meghan finally said, "Yes, I rather think I should like that."

"Good!" He straightened and put his hands on his hips. "But we can hardly converse in this dreary light." He stepped to the window before Meghan could offer any resistance and pushed the heavy drapes aside to flood the room with bright sunlight. But when he turned, he was ill-prepared for the ghastly condition into which Meghan had lapsed. She was clad in a dressing gown and robe that had obviously not been changed for several days; her eyes were red and swollen from crying; her hair was a mass of tangled, uncombed curls; and she was as weak as a newborn kitten. Nathan carefully masked his surprise at her appearance and walked to her, offering her his hand. "It's such a beautiful day, Meghan. Come share it with me."

Meghan withdrew from his outstretched hand and shook her head. "No, I mustn't leave the nursery," she whispered desperately.

"We don't have to. I promise I won't force you to do anything you don't feel ready to attempt," Nathan soothed her in a consoling voice. "Just come to the window and enjoy the fresh air and sunshine. Besides, there's something on the lawn I think you'd like to see." He again proffered his hand.

Meghan still appeared somewhat reluctant, but she found herself accepting his hand regardless of her apprehension. Her legs were unsteady due to her recent illness and subsequent inactivity, and Nathan obligingly slipped an arm about her waist and assisted her to the window. There she leaned against him for support and allowed the warm sunshine to wash over her for a few relaxing moments.

"Meghan," Nathan gently urged her, "open your eyes and have a look outside. A very special friend of yours is touring the grounds."

She glanced at him questioningly, then shielded her eyes against the glaring sun and looked out. There before her, Hank, the stablehand, leisurely led Champion along the wide, graveled drive. Meghan watched him longingly and felt a sudden twinge of sorrow as she observed her restless Champion tugging anxiously on the reins.

"He wants to run," she mumbled sadly.

"Yes," Nathan agreed. "I'm afraid he hasn't been properly exercised since your unfortunate accident. It seems that everyone is a bit reluctant to mount your

504

impressive friend."

"*He* isn't." Meghan could not bring herself to speak Derek's name aloud.

"No, but then Derek has many responsibilities around Chandalara. One can't expect him to think of everything," Nathan said casually to see what sort of response he would receive.

Meghan was embittered by his remark and decided that perhaps she had made a mistake in agreeing to let Nathan stay. "I have grown to *expect* nothing from Derek except heartache, and if you insist on discussing him, I shall be forced to ask you to leave." She started to make her way back to the rocking chair, but her trembling legs would not support her.

Nathan caught her before she struck the floor, and he swiftly collected her in his arms and carried her back to her chair. "I'm sorry if I upset you, and I promise not to mention Derek again until you're ready to talk about him."

"That won't likely happen for quite some time," she pertly informed him.

"Well, I'll not force the issue; however, there is another urgent matter I think we should discuss." He tilted her chin till their eyes met and offered her a friendly smile.

"Oh, and what might that be?" she inquired petulantly.

"You." He sank down on one knee before her and gently covered her hands with his. "You've grown so wan and frail. You should be out in the fresh air and you need to eat properly, so that you can regain your strength."

"But—" she began to protest.

"No, hear me out." He placed a finger to her lips to discourage an interruption. "We could begin by sitting

505

on the terrace a few hours each day. And when you're strong enough, we can stroll about the grounds and take buggy rides, and before you know it, you'll be ready to give Champion a real workout."

Meghan glanced sorrowfully about the nursery before her eyes returned to hold Nathan's. "Deirdre is never going to bring my son back, is she, Nathan? That's why you're here."

"Deirdre?" Nathan was genuinely perplexed by her statement.

"Yes. Oh, you needn't try to lie to me. I *saw* her take him," she insisted.

"Meghan, what you saw was a horrible nightmare, just an ugly dream that must have seemed very real to you. But you can believe me, Deirdre doesn't have your baby. I wouldn't lie to you about a thing like that," he told her kindly.

"Then what Derek said was true. I killed our son. It *was* all my fault." Her hands trembled uncontrollably beneath Nathan's.

"No," he said comfortingly. "If anyone is to blame, it's the man who shot you. And as soon as he's found, he'll be suitably punished, of that I assure you."

"Then why did Derek say those awful things to me?" She looked at him, her eyes full of hope that he would know the answer to her gnawing question. "Why does he hate me so, Nathan?"

Nathan slowly stood up and again took up his stance by the window. "Derek doesn't hate you, Meghan. He was deeply saddened by the baby's death and quite frantic with concern for your welfare. Why he said the things he did is known only to Derek, and you should discuss that with him. And so you shall as soon as you're well enough to see him again." He turned from the window to face her. "Now, if you'd like, I'll assist

506

you to your room and summon your maid to help you dress."

Meghan closed her eyes and tiredly rested her head against the back of her chair. Deep down she supposed she had always known that her baby had died, but it had been so much easier to blame Deirdre than to accept reality. But now that she had, there was yet another reality she must face. Now that the baby was gone, there was no longer anything that bound Derek to keep her at Chandalara. At the moment, he thought she despised him, and she was not so certain about his feelings toward her. Therefore, she would accept Nathan's friendship and then when she became strong enough, she would leave Derek and Chandalara before he could contrive to resume their former relationship. But in order for her plan to be effective, Meghan realized that she must shun all contact with Derek. For she knew only too well that if she again succumbed to his passionate embraces and caresses, she would be forever a prisoner of her love for him.

"Will I have to see Derek?" she asked quietly.

"Meghan, you share his home. I can't guarantee that your paths won't cross from time to time, but I can promise you that I won't arrange any secret rendezvous. You won't have to face Derek alone until you decide the time is right."

Meghan mulled this over thoroughly before she carefully replied, "Then, if that be the case, I should like very much to sit on the terrace with you." She offered him a weak smile and gratefully accepted his supporting arm.

Meghan's recuperation progressed rapidly in the following weeks. At Nathan's suggestion, they began their outings by sitting on the verandah, but Meghan grew stronger with each passing day, and she quickly

507

advanced to the more vigorous stages of her exercise program which included buggy rides and daily strolls through the garden and along the river.

Through it all, Meghan maintained her staunch policy of avoiding any contact with Derek. She ate her meals alone in her room, or on the terrace with Nathan. But on the rare occasions she had encountered Derek, she had pointedly averted her eyes and swept past him as though he had not existed. In truth, the only completely happy moments for her were those she spent with Nathan away from the tension-ridden house. With Nathan, she could assume a gay, frivolous spirit and temporarily forget about the trials that currently made her life so utterly miserable. But her mood would grow somber again the moment she returned to Chandalara.

Meghan had no time for dismal contemplations this morning, however, for Dr. Samuels had declared her fit enough to ride again, and Nathan had agreed to accompany her while she exercised Champion. She hurriedly ate her breakfast and could barely stand still while Abbey helped her don her prettiest riding habit.

She ran the entire distance from the house to the barn, but when she rounded the corner she came up short because Derek stood in front of the barn, conversing with Nathan and holding Champion's reins. Her first instinct was to dart around the corner again until he departed, but she was not quick enough, for Derek's next words halted her escape.

"Here she is now, Nathan." Derek's familiar voice penetrated the morning air.

Meghan remained glued to the ground where she stood. Her eyes darted helplessly toward Nathan for support, but he had wisely turned away on the pretense of attending his mount, daring not to interfere in the couple's private matters. Meghan swallowed hard and regarded Derek coldly when she realized that she alone must deal with him. She stiffened noticeably when Derek stepped to her and took her hand in his.

"Nathan tells me that you are going riding this morning." He tucked her arm in his and strolled with her toward Champion.

"Yes," she whispered, startled to find that the simple contact of her hand in his could stir her dormant passions.

"Pardon me?" Derek paused and leaned down to better hear her reply.

Meghan nearly swooned with the awesome effect of his nearness, and she forced her voice to remain calm when she said, "Yes, I am quite looking forward to it."

"Good." They had reached Champion and Derek effortlessly settled her atop the horse before proceeding to his own mount. "Nathan mentioned that you are riding over to the Tylers'. If you have no objection, I should like to accompany you as far as the crossroads to Tylerville. I have some business to attend to in town." He eased himself astride Trojan and turned to watch her face as she voiced her response.

Meghan shrugged her delicate shoulders indifferently and followed Nathan onto the graveled drive. "It hardly matters to me, I assure you. It's a public roadway, after all, and who am I to dictate who may or may not travel upon it?" She tapped Champion lightly and rode up beside Nathan to converse with him as they rode along the roadway. Therefore, with her back turned on Derek, she did not witness the smile fade from his handsome lips, nor did she view the bitterness in his eyes as he watched her familiar exchanges with Nathan.

As promised, Derek turned off at the crossroads, leaving Nathan and Meghan to continue toward the Tyler estate. But they had traveled only a short distance

509

before Nathan veered from the roadway and directed his mount into the trees.

"I thought we were going to visit Jason and Miranda," Meghan protested mildly.

"There's been a slight change in plans," Nathan informed her as he carefully guided his horse through the thick undergrowth. Curious, Meghan settled herself upon Champion and dutifully followed him.

They drew up a short time later before the abandoned cabin that Nathan used as a studio. He jumped to the ground and assisted Meghan from Champion's back, then started up the cabin steps.

"Why did we come here?" she asked.

"I suddenly remembered some unfinished business."

"The portrait of Elizabeth?"

Nathan nodded.

"I'm not so certain that I'd like you to finish it now," she said stiffly.

"Look, Meghan, you placed me in a very awkward position back there, favoring me with your company and completely ignoring Derek. Derek and I have been friends for a long time, and I don't think you sufficiently realize the strain your behavior is putting on that relationship." He descended the steps and walked back to her, resting his hands gently on her shoulders. "Don't be too severe with him, Meghan, for had Derek not taken the initiative, you'd likely still be cemented to your rocking chair, wallowing in self-pity."

"What do you mean?"

"It was Derek's idea that I visit you in the nursery those many weeks ago. He seemed to think that you wouldn't distrust me and that I might be able to coax you out of that dismal room. It was also Derek who arranged to have Champion strutting about the yard, knowing that if all else failed, he would serve as the

510

catalyst that would jar you from your isolated world." He noticed the offended look on her face and hastened to explain, "Now, don't take umbrage, Meghan. We only did what was necessary to help you. For regardless of what you think, we were all gravely concerned about you." Then, more softly, he added, "Hate is an ugly emotion and can ofttimes cause more anguish to the one who bears it than to the one at whom it's aimed."

"I . . . I don't hate Derek," Meghan muttered sorrowfully. "Indeed, I . . . I truly love him."

"Have you told Derek that?"

Meghan's proud shoulders slumped sadly as she shook her head. "No, he thinks me simple and foolish. Were I to tell him of my love for him, he would no doubt have a great laugh, and I cannot bear his mockery."

"I think that perhaps you sorely underestimate him," Nathan responded lowly.

"Do you? Well, it matters not, for he has told me on numerous occasions that he will never marry me, because of Papa. And I simply cannot continue to live in his house under our present arrangement. Therefore, since I am almost fully recovered, I think it would serve both our interests were I to leave Chandalara."

"You're certain?" Nathan raised her chin, so he could better scrutinize her face.

Meghan nodded.

Nathan leaned forward and placed a friendly kiss upon her forehead. "I understand." He slipped his hand in hers. "Then, do you not think that Elizabeth's portrait would serve as an appropriate parting gift for Derek?"

Meghan lowered her eyes, humbled by his words, and slowly nodded.

"Good." He escorted her to the cabin door and

pushed it aside for her to enter. "I think you'll be pleased when you see what I've completed thus far." He closed the door and neither one was aware of the pair of intense, blue eyes that shrewdly observed the scene from behind the heavy foliage.

Derek sighed as he angrily discarded the cigar butt and crushed it into the ground with the heel of one dust-covered boot. He then pushed away from the tree against which he had been leaning and strolled a few yards to the gently flowing creek that reflected the early morning rays. There he bent down to retrieve a handful of pebbles and stood to casually skip them across the peaceful water.

His thoughts, as usual these past weeks, were preoccupied with Meghan. There had been no business meeting in town. He had invented the appointment as an excuse to ride with her, hoping that he might be able to penetrate the cold wall she had erected between them. But she had remained unflappable, devoting her attention entirely to Nathan and ignoring his every attempt to melt the icy barricade.

Derek squatted down to better observe a school of minnows flitting in and out of the rocks in the shallow stream. "I've lost her forever," he mumbled softly on the wind. And he recalled the harsh words he had hurled at her when he accused her of deliberately losing their child. "I pushed her too far," he cursed himself. "Had I but weighed the impact of my words before voicing them."

But hindsight was of little value to him now. Meghan was almost fully recuperated and, knowing well the inclination of her stubborn temperament, he realized that she would soon announce her intention to leave Chandalara. But perhaps this was for the best. He could cope with the mildly irritating problems that had thus far beset their relationship, but her unwavering hostility was something with which he could not contend.

Derek's thoughts were suddenly interrupted by the sound of approaching hoofbeats. He surveyed the horizon and saw a figure on horseback rapidly crossing the meadow towards him. When he realized that the rider was feminine, his hopeful heart believed it to be Meghan. But as she drew nearer, Derek saw that although the lady held her seat well, she lacked the confidence and dignity that Meghan demonstrated atop Champion.

Derek's curiosity turned into dismay as he recognized Deirdre.

"Hello, Derek," Deirdre called cheerfully as she pulled up before him. "Are things going so well at Chandalara that you can permit yourself the luxury of a few carefree moments in the wilds? Or is there a more personal dilemma that drives you to seek solace elsewhere?" She giggled as if she knew a delightful secret.

Against his better judgment, Derek politely assisted her from her mount. "I'm in no mood for childish riddles, Deirdre. You've never been one to beat around the bush. What did you mean by your coy insinuation?"

"Oh, nothing," she replied coquettishly. "It's just that after what I've just witnessed, I suppose there must be *some* truth to the rumors I've been hearing."

Derek did not grasp the bait as Deirdre had expected, so she continued. "I mean, after all, they are sequestered together in that intimate little cabin, and you are here . . . all alone with nothing more than your thoughts to entertain you." She suddenly stepped forward and ran her hands suggestively along the front of Derek's shirt. "How lucky it is that I happened along

513

to console you."

Derek's large hands encircled Deirdre's as they methodically massaged his chest, and he removed them, forcing them to her side. "All right, Deirdre, if you insist, I shall play your little game. What rumors have you heard, and what makes you so infuriatingly certain that I need your consolation?" he asked tiredly, his indifference to the entire situation plainly visible upon his handsome face.

"Why, Meghan and Nathan, of course. They are simply on everyone's tongue these days." Deirdre beamed brightly, but had she been aware of the ugly scowl that blackened Derek's face, she might have unraveled her tale more cautiously. But, she was so overjoyed to be the one to deliver her news that she did not consider the rage it was likely to inspire. Therefore, she chattered on heedlessly, "Everyone is simply scandalized by the way she openly flaunts her lover all over the countryside."

"Lover?" Derek prompted. "You *are* referring to Nathan, I assume."

"Why, of course, silly. You cannot mean to stand there and pretend to tell me that you are ignorant of their shenanigans." She was visibly shocked. "Why, it's common knowledge that she and Nathan have been lovers for several weeks."

Derek's temper had subsided somewhat, but he was curious as to how Deirdre had arrived at such a conclusion. Moreover, he was determined to find out. He nonchalantly gathered another handful of pebbles and skimmed each one across the brook as he inquired, "And just what makes you so convinced that Meghan and Nathan are having an affair?"

"Derek," she chided. "I am not blind, but evidently you are. Are you not aware of the way they jaunt about

514

the countryside together?"

"Yes, Deirdre. As a matter of fact, they do so at *my* urging," he curtly informed her.

"Your—?"

"Yes." He smiled at her bewildered expression. "Meghan was quite weak after her recent illness and the doctor felt a few hours in the fresh air each day would hasten her recovery. My rigorous schedule does not permit me to spend much time with Meghan, so Nathan kindly agreed to serve as her escort in my absence."

"Yes, I suppose he would," Deirdre began dryly as her eyes settled on the pebbles that lay in Derek's hand. "And I can see that your schedule is *quite* full."

Derek threw the pebbles to the ground in disgust and stalked to his mount. "Believe what you will, Deirdre, but if I hear that you have been spreading this malicious gossip about, you'll have to answer to me."

He started to climb upon Trojan, but Deirdre rushed forward to stop him. "Wait, Derek. Perhaps that is how you meant it to be, but I sincerely doubt that you suggested they spend a number of intimate hours in the abandoned cabin on Jason Tyler's property, for that is where I saw them not more than an hour ago."

Derek was thunderstruck, and he whirled on her viciously. "You lie!"

"Do I?" Now she was the one wearing the triumphant smile. "I daresay they are still there. If you don't believe me, you can always check it out for yourself on your way back to Chandalara. It's not so very far out of your way," she said. She stepped to him and slipped her arms around his waist and pressed her cheek against his chest. "Do not trouble yourself with her, Derek. I love you. I want you. I always have. Forget about the little tart. Send her away, so that we can be together again. I can make you happy."

"You think that you can make me happy?" Derek muttered vaguely. "I sincerely doubt that, Deirdre, for I never knew happiness until I found Meghan." He firmly set her from him and settled himself atop Trojan.

"Where are you going?" she cried.

"Home," he sighed. "Where I belong."

"But . . . but what about the things I just told you?" she insisted. "Meghan can't possibly mean anything to you now."

"On the contrary," Derek rebutted. "Meghan means *everything* to me." He turned Trojan around to confront her. "But on the outside chance there is any truth to the rumors you have conveniently recounted to me, I'm quite confident that I can coax her back into my arms again. Good day, Deirdre." He tipped his hat and galloped off in the direction of Chandalara, leaving a very frustrated Deirdre staring after him.

Chapter Twenty-two

Meghan hummed an airy melody as she relaxed in her bath. Her thoughts centered lazily around the day just spent with Nathan, for at last the portrait of Elizabeth had been completed. Nathan had recreated Elizabeth's likeness admirably and Meghan could hardly wait to present it to Derek. She knew that he would be pleased with the gift and, similarly, she was sure of his reaction once she presented him with the news of her intention to return to London with Nathan on *The Lady*

Elizabeth's next voyage. But now her musings were interrupted as the chamber door opened and Sophie lumbered into the room.

"Abbey'll be up in a minute to help you dress, Miz Meghan," the housekeeper began.

"Thank you, Sophie." Meghan stepped from the tub and hurriedly wrapped a soft, fluffy towel about her. "But you did not have to come all the way up here to tell me that."

"No, ma'am they's more." She paused.

"Yes?" Meghan could not fathom the reason for Sophie's hesitancy.

"It's Massah Derek. He wants you should have supper with him downstairs." Sophie, and all the servants, had been aware of the friction that existed between the couple the past few weeks. She wanted to see them patch up their differences more than anything and now that her master had made the first gesture, she prayed desperately that her mistress would swallow her pride and accept it. "He sent me up here personal to ask you," she added hopefully.

Meghan seated herself before the dressing table mirror and began to brush the tangles from her hair. "Did he?" she inquired remotely. "You may inform your master that it is with my regrets that I must decline his generous invitation. I shall dine here as usual. Instruct Abbey to bring my supper tray when she comes to assist me."

"Yes, ma'am." Sophie hung her head sadly and went to do as she had been instructed.

Meghan stood with her back to the door, vainly struggling with the hooks on the back of her gown, when the door next opened. "At last," she sighed with relief. "Place the tray on the table, Abbey, and come help me, please."

517

But the fingers that quickly accomplished the task of securing the gown did not belong to Abbey. No, the hands that now rested menacingly about her throat belonged to Derek.

"Sophie tells me that you have declined my invitation to sup with me. Have you a worthwhile reason to snub me so?" he asked.

"I . . . I did not mean to snub . . ."

"Then you accept," he surmised.

"No! I . . . I prefer to dine alone." Fearing that she might succumb to his nearness, she attempted to put some distance between them, but she could not move, for his hands still encircled her neck.

"But I do not," he informed her. "Have you any notion as to how frustrating you have grown these past weeks, and how tempting it would be to strangle you, so that I may free myself of this conflict once and for all?" The pressure of his fingers slowly increased against the fragile skin and for one frightening moment, Meghan feared that he might actually harm her.

Meghan would not give Derek the satisfaction, however, of knowing that he had successfully frightened her. But she did place her hands over his fingers as if she challenged him to continue.

Derek took her hands in his and turned her to face him. "It's such a dainty neck." He lowered his mouth to kiss away the slight redness that the pressure of his hands against her neck had caused. "I daresay I could snap it with hardly any effort at all." His lips traveled further down into the valley of her breasts.

Meghan could feel her nipples grow hard as they strained beneath the material of her gown to experience Derek's sensual manipulation. It had been so long since these familiar passions had flamed within her and she longed to succumb to them, but her reason forced her to spurn him. Determinedly, she pulled away from him and set about repairing the damage he had inflicted upon her gown.

"You disgust me," she spat hoarsely.

"Do I?" Derek guffawed. "You certainly could have fooled me. But if m'lady insists, then it must assuredly be so. Tell me, have you grown accustomed to another's kisses, Meghan? Is that what prompts you to spurn mine?" He eyed her shrewdly.

"I don't know what you are talking about," she replied coldly.

"Do you not?" he sounded doubtful. "Then dine with me, and I shall endeavor to enlighten you." He extended his arm.

"I think not."

"And I think you shall." His eyes grew black with cold determination as he stalked to her side and resolutely gripped her arm. "Have you a desire for the servants to witness their mistress being forcibly dragged to the supper table, or shall you give up this annoying behavior at once and accompany me peacefully?"

"You're hurting me," Meghan protested at the cruel hold he had on her arm.

The pressure let up instantly, but he did not release her. Instead, Derek tucked her arm in his and led her from the room before she could offer him further resistance.

Recognizing the unyielding set of his jaw, Meghan decided that it would be more to her advantage to relent and have her meal with him. After all, the opportunity to inform him of her impending return to London might arise, and she just might have the last laugh yet.

They arrived in the dining room, and Meghan was mildly surprised to find Nathan seated at the table. "Good evening, Nathan. Derek neglected to tell me that you were going to share our repast with us." She glanced up suspiciously at Derek as he held her chair for her.

"A slight oversight." He shrugged his shoulders and claimed his seat at the head of the table. "But I did not think that Nathan's presence at our supper table would distress you, darling." He signaled for the maids to begin serving the meal.

"It doesn't," she murmured in reply and selected a slice of the fresh, wild turkey. She then lapsed into a subdued silence and solemnly listened to the casual exchanges between Nathan and Derek.

After the meal had been served, Derek dismissed the servants and lifting a forkful of the succulent meat to his mouth, he said, "Is the turkey not exceptionally tasty this evening?"

Nathan and Meghan nodded agreeably and Nathan ventured, "Did one of your men bring it in?"

"No, actually, I was out hunting this morning and I happened upon the rascal. You may be familiar with the area," he added purposely. "It was near that old, abandoned cabin on Jason Tyler's property."

His observant gaze took note of the apprehensive look that the couple exchanged, and he continued to torment them. "Oh, I gather that you are acquainted with the place. I rather thought you might be, for I saw your horses tethered before the cabin, then Meghan emerged an hour or so later, the most radiant smile adorning her face." His stony gaze settled on her. "You cannot imagine how I have missed that smile, but fortunately you have restored it, Nathan. Now, the only dilemma facing me is my indecision as to whether I should thank you, or kill you." He returned his wine glass to the table and purposely cast Nathan a challenging look.

But Meghan was the one who took up the gauntlet.

520

"How dare you!" Her fork clanked noisily against her plate and she rose unsteadily, shaking with fury. "I should have suspected that you had some ulterior motive in mind by having Nathan and myself here this evening. But I shall not remain in this room while you attack my character and your friend's by accusing us of having an illicit love affair." She started to run from the room, but Derek's next words halted her.

"And what did you expect me to believe, madam?" He moved to stand in front of her. "I observed on several occasions your return from outings with Nathan. You were always so gay and carefree, but as soon as you returned home, your melancholy mood draped you like a blanket, and no attempt to cheer you proved successful," he reminded her.

Meghan's shoulders slumped sadly and in a small voice, she whispered, "This house is a constant reminder of the baby I lost. It holds no happy memories for me."

"Hah!" His laughter was heartlessly cruel. "You expect me to believe that you still mourn the death of a child you never wanted! Were not your exact words that the child would be better off dead than to have an uncaring and selfish father such as myself?" Derek caught the wild fist that she flailed at him and pinned it behind her back. "Tell me, madam, would our son have benefited with a mother who wished him dead?"

"Derek!" Nathan sought to intervene.

"Sit down, *friend*!" he spat sharply. "I shall see to you presently."

"No, Meghan." Derek again devoted his attention to her. "I rather suspect that the separation from your *lover* might be a more accurate explanation for your saddened heart rather than maternal bereavement." His fingers bit cruelly into the softness of her delicate skin

521

and his eyes burned into hers as he awaited her response.

But Meghan withheld the ugly retorts that sprang to her tongue. Instead, she calmly removed his hand from her arm and stepped back to survey him with a cold, indifferent glare. "Then believe what you will, Derek, for I assure you that your speculations mean precious little to me." She presented him her back and defiantly strode from the room.

"Do you know what an insensitive son of a bitch you truly are?" Nathan confronted him. "In truth, I never really knew until this moment. Does it reaffirm your masculinity to run roughshod over one who cannot adequately defend herself against your superior strength?"

Derek turned slowly to face Nathan, and purposefully sauntered over to the table to claim his wine glass. He took a generous swallow, then returned the goblet to the table before deliberately choosing his next words. "That sounds remarkably like a challenge, Nathan. Was that your intent? Do you intend to provoke me into combat to defend Meghan's honor?"

"If it comes to that, yes. But hopefully an altercation can be avoided—not because I fear you, but because, were I to allow you to goad me into a confrontation, that, in effect, would be an admission of guilt." He regarded Derek with a composed manner. "But I assure you, my friend, Meghan and I have not betrayed you."

"Humph!" Derek snorted. "Then just how did you manage to wile away the hours in Jason's cabin?" he demanded.

A slight smile flitted across Nathan's handsome face as he pushed away from the table. "If you will follow me, I can perhaps better demonstrate my answer than relate it with words."

"*What?*"

But Nathan paid no heed to Derek's exclamation as he led the way to the drawing room. "Sit down." He pointed to a chair and walked straightway to an object that was curiously wrapped in a clean, white sheet. "This was to be Meghan's surprise, but since you have thoroughly spoiled that, I have no alternative." He ceremoniously drew the sheet back to reveal the completed portrait of Elizabeth Chandler.

"*Mother!*" Derek's face was alive with confused emotion. "But how . . . why . . ." he began uncertainly.

"Meghan can more aptly supply the answers to your questions, Derek, for it was her idea," Nathan informed him kindly. "So, you see, we were not using Jason's cabin as a lovenest. I worked on the portrait there because I feared you might discover it in my cottage. By the way, how did you discover our little hideaway?" He noticed Derek's shamefaced expression and he laughed loudly. "You mean to say that you followed us?"

Derek nodded slowly, a trifle piqued that his surveillance had been discovered. "I happened onto Deirdre a few days ago, and she could hardly wait to inform me that she had seen the two of you enter the cabin. At first, I placed no credence on her words, for we both know how she babbles, but then each day you and Meghan would disappear for hours on end. And finally, today, I had to seek satisfaction of my nagging curiosity; so I followed you," he explained. "You would have done the same, Nathan."

Nathan mulled this over before he replied, "Yes, Derek, if Meghan were mine and I feared I might be losing her to another, I no doubt would have reacted the same way," he agreed. Then as an afterthought, he added, "Though not as harshly."

Derek cleared his throat uneasily and reached inside

his pocket to retrieve a cigar. "I *was* rather hard on her, wasn't I?" He lit the slender cheroot and puffed on it thoughtfully as he studied his mother's portrait. "That is a remarkable likeness, Nathan." He pointed at the portrait with the butt of his cigar. "And you say it was Meghan's idea." He cast a contemplative glance out the open door and up the staircase to the room in which he thought her to be sulking.

"Yes, but this one was entirely my idea, Meghan knows nothing about it." He pulled another portrait from behind the sofa and held it up for Derek's appraisal.

The breath caught in Derek's throat as he turned to behold another portrait: Meghan's. She appeared so lifelike that at first glance, he imagined she was actually there before him.

"Yes, it rather affected me the same way," Nathan murmured quietly.

"But if Meghan knows nothing of this, how did you . . ."

"From sketches I made secretly when we were together, and as for the gown, who could ever forget the way she looked in it at Deirdre's soirée?" Nathan explained. "A blithering idiot could have painted *that* from memory."

"Yes," Derek sighed. "But this is no mere painting, my friend." He stood and walked nearer to obtain a better view of the canvas. "You have managed to capture her very essence . . . her womanly innocence, her alluring beauty . . . why, you even mastered that proud, little upturned nose. And the eyes . . ." Derek's voice trailed off aimlessly, and he turned away from the painting dismally. "Will you allow me to purchase it?"

"Derek, the portrait is yours. I want no recompense, but if you will permit me to say as much, this painting will be a small consolation indeed if you allow its inspiration to slip away from you," Nathan advised softly. Leaning the portrait against the end of the sofa, he went to place a reassuring hand on his friend's shoulder and offered one parting thought. "She cares for you, Derek, and if you'd but swallow that pigheaded, stubborn pride of yours, you would realize that you care for her as well. And the fact that she is Thomas Bainbridge's daughter be damned."

Derek remained in the room long after Nathan had gone and the house servants had retired for the night. All that remained of the candles that burned in the wall sconces were short stubs, and Derek routinely extinguished them before he slowly made his way up the steps. In his room, he removed his coat and stock and had started undoing the buttons of his shirt when his eyes fell upon the door of Meghan's chamber.

On impulse, Derek stepped through the sitting room that separated their chambers and tapped lightly on the door. "Meghan?" he began softly. "May we talk, please?" Half-expecting some object to be hurled viciously against the door, Derek was indeed surprised when she did not respond to his inquiry at all. "Meghan?" he repeated as he gently opened the door. "I know I behaved badly—" He came up short when he realized that she was not in her chamber.

Derek's heart raced with anxiety as he immediately grew concerned for her whereabouts. Surely, she had not fled in the darkness, and had she run to Nathan, he would have seen that she was returned safely to the house. Where could she have gone? His troubled concentration suddenly recalled the heated argument that occurred in the dining room.

"Of course," he mumbled and soundlessly made his

way to the nursery.

The room was in total darkness, but he saw her when he opened the door. She was kneeling on the floor beside the cradle that would have held their son. Her head rested on her crossed arms and, at first, Derek thought her to be sleeping. But as he moved to stand behind her, the moonlight caught the glimmer of a single tear as it trickled down her cheek and on reflex, she stirred and tiredly wiped it away.

"Meghan," he spoke her name softly and, placing his hands around her shoulders, assisted her to her feet. "I've been searching for you. You cannot imagine how anxious I became when I discovered that you were not in your room." He forced the solemn chin up and by the dim light of the moon, he could detect the sadness in her eyes. "Why did you come here, little one?" he asked quietly. "This room holds no pleasant memories for you."

"Oh, Derek!" Her voice trembled uncontrollably and she covered her face with her hands. "I did not mean those awful things. I only said them to hurt you because . . . because you had hurt me. I did not want our baby to die. I wanted him more than anything. You cannot believe me insensitive enough to wish death on an innocent babe." Her words came out in a rush, and they were full of anguish as a fresh flood of tears ran down her ravaged cheeks.

Derek pulled her hands away from her face and gently cradled her in his arms. "Shhh, shhh, honey," he comforted her. "I fear that I am the insensitive one, for I am to blame for much of your grief. We have both been on edge these past months, and, consequently, we have not always been kind. It was ruthless of me to blame you for the baby's death, for the fault did not lie with you, little one. Can you ever forgive me for my

526

heartless behavior? Say that you will, else I shall have to take to roaming the seas again, for I cannot pass another day in the same house with you, not being able to talk to you, or hold you, or touch you . . ." His fingers traveled along her shoulders and up her neck to caress her cheek.

Meghan raised her eyes reluctantly to search his, and as she lost herself in the abyss of his intense gaze, she realized what her reply *must* be. "I shall always forgive you." The words were barely from her lips before Derek's mouth covered hers hungrily.

It had been so long since she had surrendered to his demanding kisses and the passions they could ignite within her. With desire building rapidly, Meghan accepted his mouth eagerly and wrapped her arms around his neck as her lips parted to accept his gently probing tongue. Meghan moaned as his sweet-tasting tongue softly fluttered between her lips, rekindling emotions she had never thought to experience again with Derek. She languished in the urgency of his kiss and they were both breathless when he at last pulled away.

"God, how I've missed you . . ." he said thickly as he again kissed her lips, ". . . needed you," he kissed her closed eyes, ". . . wanted you." His lips fell to her neck and as his hand passed over her breasts, he could feel her taut nipples straining against the material of her dress. "May I have you, Meghan?" His breath was pleasantly warm against her skin and his lips rested a breath's pace from her own, his eyes caressing her. "Please, say that I may?"

"Yes, Derek, oh, yes!" Her reply was inaudible to her own ears, for she was aware only of the intense pounding of her racing heart. But she knew by the jubilant look on Derek's face that he had heard it, for he tenderly lifted her in his arms and carried her to his chamber. They swiftly removed their clothing, then Derek turned her toward the moonlight, so that his thirsty eyes could drink in her exquisite beauty. Meghan grew increasingly timid during his somewhat lengthy and sensual perusal of her nakedness, and she sought to shield her body with her hands.

"Don't!" Derek commanded huskily. "God, but you're magnificent. *Come here*," he added throatily, extending his hand to her.

Meghan stepped forward to accept it and allowed him to pull her into his embrace. She thrilled at the electric sensation of flesh against flesh as their naked bodies were at last reconciled. They walked hand in hand to the bed. Derek threw back the covers with an easy gesture and carefully lifted Meghan onto the structure. In an instant he was beside her.

They were on their knees, facing each other. Derek's sinewy arms encircled her waist and pulled her against him as his roaming hands traveled lower to caress her hips. And as his hands fondled her, his lips feasted on the succulent honey of her lips before falling to the temptation of her breasts.

Meghan trembled involuntarily as wave after wave of pleasurable tremors coursed through her body. She thrilled at Derek's skillful manipulation as his lips moved from her breast to her navel, then traveled leisurely back to her other breast. Here, his tongue expertly fondled the vulnerable flesh and flicking at the hardened tip, he created sensual rivulets of excitement that evoked contented sighs from Meghan.

"This pleases you?" he murmured softly against her throat.

"Yes," she sighed breathlessly.

"And this?" His eyes sparkled passionately as his

hands moved along the velvety softness of her back, around her trim waist and down to her hips. There, they altered their course to skim along her legs, traveling along the inside of her thighs until . . . Meghan suddenly convulsed and lurched forward as his nimble fingers came into contact with a highly sensitive area, causing Derek to chuckle lowly, "Yes, I can see that it does."

Meghan clasped her arms fiercely about Derek's shoulders and her head fell forward to rest against his chest until the consuming sensation that had momentarily stunned her subsided. Once it passed, though, Meghan began to nibble a trail of kisses along Derek's shoulder to his neck. Her teeth playfully nipped at his earlobe while she permitted the palm of her hand to roam freely over his chest to his stomach, then it slowly edged lower to purposely caress the flesh along his muscular thigh. Meghan heard his sharp intake of breath and pressed an ear to his chest to listen to the rapid rhythm of his pounding heart.

"And do I please you, m'lord?" She pressed a kiss against his chest, her tongue gently flicking at the hardened nipples.

"Can you not tell?" he coyly referred to the hardness that was currently pressed against her lower abdomen.

"Indeed." Her lips parted in a coquettish grin before Derek's fell upon them greedily. He crushed her against him so tightly that their entwined bodies seemed melded together.

They remained thusly entwined for a long time, the precious, intimate moment suspended for them. And all the while Derek held her against him, his hands roved all over her, refamiliarizing himself with the feel of her glorious, silky flesh.

Meghan soon became enraptured with the sensation

of his manhood positioned so near her own femininity and finally, she could no longer endure the nerve-racking suspense. "Now, please, *now*," she whimpered and started to roll onto her back against the firm mattress. But Derek's large hands caught on either side of her waist to stay her movement. Meghan regarded him curiously as he leaned forward to press his lips between the valley of her voluptuous breasts.

"But . . . but how . . ." she began, obviously puzzled.

"Be patient." He leaned back on his haunches and effortlessly lifted Meghan to position her astride him.

Meghan choked back a startled cry and her eyes grew steadily wider as his manhood nestled deep inside her, causing her to gulp breathlessly, "What . . . what do you want me to do?"

Derek's hands now rested on her hips. "Why, make love to me, of course," he whispered huskily. And as he spoke, he began to rhythmically rotate her hips from side to side. "For that is what I intend to do to you . . . quite thoroughly," he added thickly.

In response, Meghan ran her hands along his muscular chest and pressed her legs tightly against his sides. At first the position was awkward for her, but her inhibition rapidly dissipated as she discovered herself surrendering to the tumultuous emotions that flooded her very being. Her hands roamed down his arms and she clung to him as she lay her head back and lost herself in her passion. They swayed together in perfect harmony, almost as if they kept time to the gentle melody of a romantic waltz. But with a well-schooled expertise, Derek slowly increased the tempo and then, without warning, he thrust upward, taking Meghan quite by surprise.

She tensed instantly and her head snapped forward,

her eyes locking with Derek's in a tempestuous embrace. Her face was alive with emotion and when she would have looked away, Meghan found that she could not, for she was totally submerged in the depths of his sensual gaze.

His eyes sparkled wickedly as he continued to thrust deep inside her, simultaneously pivoting her hips against him as he leaned forward to flick at the tantalizing nipples of her quivering breasts. The contrasting movements caused Meghan to experience a diversity of complex sensations. And it seemed an eternity had passed when these tension-building senses at last came rushing together in one unmistakable, exquisite explosion, causing Meghan to cry out as she collapsed in a helpless bundle against his chest.

Derek gently lowered her to the mattress and lay down beside her, tenderly cradling her against him, stroking her lovingly and whispering sweet endearments in her ear until her breathing became more even. A contented smile parted his handsome lips as he basked in the afterglow of the pleasurable experience, knowing that Meghan had reveled in it as well. Perhaps now they could finally put their differences behind them and begin their relationship anew. He was certainly willing to give it a try, as was Meghan, or so he thought. But only moments later, he became quite startled by the muffled sobs that escaped her trembling lips.

Derek could not see her face, for her back was turned to him, but he placed a comforting hand upon her shoulder to quell its vibration and asked softly, "Meghan, why do you weep?"

Meghan could not bring herself to look at him, nor could she stifle her sobs long enough to formulate a reply. Instead, she shook her head firmly and buried her face deeper in the pillow to smother her broken sobs.

But Derek was not to be so easily dismissed. His hands gently clasped her shoulders and he easily turned her to face him. He smoothed away the errant strands of hair that clung to her tear-dampened face and with the moonlight as his candle, he observed her distraught expression.

Derek was shocked. "Meghan?" He leaned forward to better scrutinize her desolate face. "What is it, honey? What has happened to distress you so? Was it our lovemaking? Did I hurt you?"

"No . . . no," she reassured him. "Indeed, it was . . . it was exquisite," she added wistfully, wiping at her face with the corner of the sheet.

"Then what, darling?" He pulled her into his arms to comfort her. "Tell me. I cannot help ease your troubled mind unless you confide in me."

"It's . . . it's not that simple, Derek," she sighed heavily.

"Ah, then offhand I would speculate that I am the cause for your misery," he said seriously and when Meghan offered him no response to the contrary, he continued, "I see. Do you want to leave Chandalara? Is that it?"

"N-no," she replied slowly. "Would that I could, but my departure would resolve nothing, for I fear that there is no easy solution to my problem. Because, you see, I . . . I love you, Derek." Her eyes lowered, for she was not certain that she could bear to witness the satisfied, mocking look that he would bestow upon her. But had Meghan observed him, she would have been surprised to note his rather relieved expression. "There was a time I could have gladly left you, but to do so now would be folly, for I know I should only be miserable. But, in turn, if I remain . . ."

"Yes?"

"It shall be the same," she muttered sadly.

"Shall it?" He rested his shoulders against the headboard and pulled her across his lap. "Meghan," he began softly, "you humble me. In all my years of experience with women, I have never felt prevailed upon to express my feelings of love for any of them. Indeed, I am not certain I would recognize the emotion if I were beset by it. But of this I am convinced." He turned her head; so he could gaze into her bewildered eyes. "I care not to consider the thought of a single day of the rest of my life of which you are not included. Chandalara would lose its luster if you left and I . . . well, I should be totally devastated. If these are symptoms of love, then so be it. I readily succumb to them." He lowered his lips and gently caressed her mouth. And when he pulled away, he looked at her longingly, his dark eyes sparkling with bright, unshed tears, and at last he said, "For I do love you, my darling Meghan." His declaration came in a rush as he gathered her to him to kiss away the joyful tears that streamed down her radiant cheeks.

Two weeks had passed since that emotional night when they had at last proclaimed their love for one another. Their days were a bustle of activity as they began preparing Chandalara for the coming winter, and their nights were filled with love and passion. Meghan was happier than she could remember, her troubled mind was finally at peace.

They had received no more threats from her father and Charles and since there had been no reported sightings of the duo in the area, Derek told her that they must assume that they had abandoned their scheme and left the vicinity. The only problem that still vexed Derek was the identity of Meghan's assailant. Derek prodded the sheriff daily for any clues that might have been discovered, and each day found him further discouraged.

"I fear we may never find the bastard," he had confessed to her upon his return from Tylerville after another disappointing visit with the sheriff.

Meghan had considerately handed him a cool drink and sat down beside him on the drawing room sofa. "Perhaps you worry needlessly. The culprit has doubtlessly vanished forever and will not bother us again."

"I cannot take that chance. Meghan, you could have been killed," he had reminded her gently. "I'll not rest a day until the offender is found and the motive for the vicious attack is uncovered."

Meghan shook these reflections from her mind and stood up tiredly, placing a comforting hand to the small of her aching back. At first glance, anyone not knowing her position in the house might think her to be one of the servants, such was the condition of her state of dress. She was clad in one of the worn dresses she had brought with her from London, the sleeves of which had been pushed up to her elbows to allow more freedom of movement. She and Sophie were in the middle of cleaning and airing out one of the upstairs guestrooms, and the smudges from her cleaning endeavors were present upon her pretty face. She portrayed quite a contented picture in this domestic scene as she instructed servants to carry the heavy, rolled-up carpet outside and thump it until it contained not even a single particle of dust. She then turned her efforts to the draperies that hung at the window.

"Miz Meghan, why don't you let the menfolk do that?" Sophie chided as Meghan dragged a chair to the window and fingered the soiled draperies with obvious distaste.

"Pooh, Sophie. This won't take but a moment." She

534

started to climb atop the chair, but Nicholas appeared in the doorway to announce that Jason Tyler was in the drawing room, requesting to see her.

Meghan hurriedly checked her appearance in the mirror, brushing aside the strands of hair that had slipped from their confines and wiping hastily at her smudged face. Removing the apron that protected the skirt of her gown, she said, "Be a dear and help Sophie take the draperies down, won't you, Nicholas?" But before the reluctant servant could voice a reply, his mistress had already bounded from the room.

"You heard Miz Meghan, old man." Sophie turned on Nicholas. "Now, git on up on that chair. That ain't no job fer a lady, nohow."

"Cleanin' ain't no job fer a *man*, neither," Nicholas objected.

"I ain't askin' you to clean'em, fool. Now, take them curtains down afore Miz Meghan comes back'n' tries to do it herself."

Meghan could hear their bickering in the downstairs foyer and shaking her head in amusement, she stepped across the hall to the drawing room. The door was open and she slipped inside, prepared to sound a cheerful greeting, but she stopped short when she observed her visitor.

He stood facing the fireplace, his eyes glued to the portrait of Elizabeth that hung above the mantel. At first, Meghan was perplexed at the emotion-filled look upon his face, but then she read recognition in his troubled eyes and at last Meghan understood his bewilderment and this revelation left her momentarily stunned.

Meghan slowly made her way across the drawing room carpet and rested her hand on his arm. "Mr. Tyler? Are you all right?"

Jason turned to her, visibly upset, and nodded stiffly. His eyes fell to the hand that caressed his arm and beheld her wedding band. They darted back to the portrait. "Elizabeth . . ." he mumbled faintly. "But how can that be?" His serious eyes searched her face for an answer.

"You . . . you knew Elizabeth?" She was somehow able to stop her voice from shaking, but she could not control the tremor in her hand that still rested against his arm.

Jason's shoulders sagged heavily as he tore his eyes from the portrait and sank into a nearby chair. "Yes," he finally answered, "I knew Elizabeth Chandler." Jason nervously ran his fingers through his greying hair and glanced at her appealingly. "I seldom indulge in spirits before the noon hour, Meghan, but could I prevail upon you for a glass of brandy?"

"Certainly." Meghan filled a glass from the decanter, then sat down in a chair opposite him.

"Forgive me," he apologized, "I'm not usually this excitable, but the portrait did take me by surprise."

Meghan allowed him time to drink his brandy and compose himself before she prompted, "You said that you knew Elizabeth."

"Yes, a very long time ago in London . . ." His voice trailed off aimlessly.

"Were you friends of the Chandler family?"

"Friends? Hardly," he scoffed. "Elizabeth and I were in love and wanted to be married, but her father forbade it. He forced me to leave England and my home. But I arranged one final, secret meeting with her. That is when I gave her the ring which you now wear and she gave herself to—" He suddenly glanced up into Meghan's startled face. "I wanted her to run away with me, but she said that no good could come of that."

536

Meghan sat rigidly upright in her chair, anxiously twisting her lace handkerchief until it lay in a knot on her lap. Somehow she found her voice, "You're Jonathon Marley?"

Jason nodded weakly.

"Then, Derek is your—"

"My son," he finished for her, with a laborious sigh. Jason noticed that the color had drained from Meghan's face and he considerately asked if he should summon assistance.

"No, thank you. I do not easily succumb to the vapors, Mr. Tyler," she assured him. "It's just that I've suffered quite a shock."

"Yes, as have I." He stood and began to pace back and forth before the fireplace and the story he had kept inside him all these years came spilling out as he walked. "I went back, you know. I moved to France when I left London, but I returned twice in the following year to find Elizabeth, only to be turned away time and time again by her family. But I swear to you, Meghan, had I known there was a child, I would have moved heaven and earth to find them. Thinking my attempts futile, I gave up and came to America to start a fresh life with a new name."

"And when you met Derek, did you never think it odd that his surname was Chandler?" she asked quietly.

"It rekindled some memories, to be sure, but Chandler is a common enough name. I had no reason to suspect that he was my son."

"No," Meghan sighed wearily. "I suppose not." She glanced up seriously at Elizabeth's portrait before she continued, "Derek needs to know."

Jason nodded in agreement.

"Would . . . would you like me to tell him?" she offered.

"Your offer is most kind, Meghan, and I'm sorely tempted to accept, but I believe that Derek should hear this news from me. I'll need a few days, though. There are many things to be considered . . ." He picked up his hat and bowed over Meghan's hand. "You do understand?"

"Of course." She smiled kindly. "It must be quite shocking to suddenly discover that one has a thirty-year-old son. I shall not betray your confidence."

"Thank you." He gratefully kissed her hand. "But I almost forgot my original purpose in dropping by. I am just on my return from a business trip in New Orleans. And I am happy to inform you that you may tell Derek that he need not concern himself with Sam Iverson any longer. It seems that he got involved in a card game at Dulcie's Image some two months ago and became a lucky winner. But unfortunately for him, his opponent was not a happy loser. They found him the next morning in an alley with a knife through his . . . well, he was dead."

"I'm sorry he is dead, but as you said at least he will not be coming around, upsetting Derek anymore." She walked with him to the door. "Thank you for taking the trouble to stop by and deliver your message. I'll be sure to tell Derek the news about Iverson."

Meghan waited until the man had mounted his horse and ridden away before she returned to the drawing room and collapsed tiredly into a chair. She was emotionally drained with the morning's revelation and she sat in her chair, numbly trying to sort things out in her confused mind.

Jason had said that there were many things to be considered. Exactly, what had he meant by that? It would certainly be a shock to Miranda to learn after all these years that her husband had a natural son. But

538

then it was not uncommon for a man to sow a few wild oats before settling down.

What else?

Derek had mentioned that Jason was politically ambitious. Meghan knew virtually nothing about politics and cared about them even less. But one did not have to be a political genius to surmise that the sudden appearance of a bastard son might put a damper on a promising political career. One must consider the possibilities. This information, if used effectively by a political adversary, might sully Jason's honorable reputation.

She thought back to the night she had first met Jason Tyler. He had acted strangely when he beheld her wedding band and later, in the garden, their conversation had principally centered on the ring. Had he suspected the truth even then? Could he have believed his political career endangered enough to hire Garth McTavish to attack them and, that having failed, taken matters into his own hands? Was Jason Tyler her baby's murderer?

"From your earnest expression, I can only surmise that after days of beating rugs, polishing floors and stuffing mattresses, you have decided you made a vast error in judgment by not returning to London with Nathan aboard *The Lady Elizabeth*." Derek strolled into the room and sat down beside her on the sofa, stretching his long legs in front of him.

"Of course not, silly." She smiled at him warmly. "One of us had to remain here to keep you out of trouble." She offered him her lips and they kissed, tenderly, lovingly. "And what of you?" She pulled away, tucking her arm snugly in his. "Are you not a little homesick for your ship and the ocean breezes?"

"Not at all. The breezes at Chandalara suit me just

fine. Besides, it's high time I took over the management of this plantation permanently. I never bothered to hire an overseer after dismissing McTavish, for Wade always looked after things whenever I had to be away. But now, perhaps I can make Chandalara pay for itself as do my other enterprises." He gently squeezed her knee and gazed at her affectionately. "No, my love, I am not sorry to put an end to my roving days. I am content to make my home here with you." He kissed her hand, then stood and pulled her to her feet. "Was that Jason I saw riding away from the house when I returned a few moments ago?"

"Yes."

"You should have invited him to dine with us." He led her toward the dining room.

"Oh, Derek," she sighed, "if you but knew the exhausting morning I've experienced, you would perhaps understand the reason for my faltering manners."

"Don't tell me that Sophie and Nicholas have been haggling again." He laughed knowingly as he seated her at the table.

"Yes, but at least it's friendly haggling. Then I suppose it is only natural for two people who like each other to exchange a few discourteous words now and again, is it not?"

Derek settled in his chair and leaned forward to capture her hand. "If that be true, love, you and I must be prime examples of a totally enraptured couple." His eyes twinkled mischievously as he released her hand and leaned back in his chair as the servant began to serve the meal. "Did Jason have any newsworthy item to recount?"

"As a matter of fact, he did. He learned of something in New Orleans which he thought would interest you."

"Oh?"

"Yes. Sam Iverson won't return again to badger you about Chandalara. He was killed two months ago in New Orleans." Meghan placed her napkin on her knee and turned her attention to the delicious food before her.

"Two months, you say." He thoughtfully considered her statement.

"Yes."

"That would mean that Iverson was dead when you were attacked," he murmured slowly.

"Yes." Meghan looked at him, a little perplexed by his studious mood.

"Well, then, that *does* interest me. You see, Meghan, I've just come from the sheriff. It would seem that he has received a note from an anonymous source, claiming that Iverson was seen running away from Chandalara the day you were shot."

"But . . . but that is impossible."

"Yes, providing Jason's report is accurate. It can easily be verified."

"And if Jason's report proves to be true?" she questioned.

"Well," he sighed, his fingers seriously tracing the rim of his coffee cup. "That presents us with two possibilities. Either our Mr. Iverson has acquired Lazarus-like capabilities, or . . ."

"Or what?"

"Your assailant is still in the vicinity and having grown nervous with my insistence that the sheriff continue his investigation, he has sought to dangle a wild goose before my nose, hoping that I'll take up the chase." He stepped to the sideboard to refill his cup and reaching for the decanter, he laced it with a liberal portion of whiskey and lifting the cup to his determined lips, he said purposely, "Well, I suppose I mustn't disappoint the cur."

Chapter Twenty-three

Derek's plan was quite simple. He persuaded Jason to refrain from spreading the news of Iverson's death. Instead, he encouraged the sheriff to circulate the story about the anonymous letter he received. He even went so far as to offer a reward for information that might lead to Iverson's arrest. And he spent a good portion of each day combing the local woods and countryside, questioning anyone he saw about Iverson's whereabouts.

"Just what do you hope to achieve by all this?" Meghan asked him one evening as they were preparing to go to bed. She helped him out of his coat and then led him to a comfortable chair. "You're wearing yourself to a frazzle and for what purpose?" She sat on the floor in front of him, resting her cheek on his knee.

"I assure you, pet, there *is* a method to my madness. I had hoped to draw the culprit out into the open by pretending to believe the story about Iverson. That is why I've been galloping willy-nilly about the country-side these past few days." He lovingly caressed her cheek.

"You mean that you are using yourself as some sort of bait to attract this murderer's attention!" She instantly came to her knees, her eyes anxiously searching his. "What purpose will it serve if this maniac succeeds in killing you?" she asked desperately.

"He won't."

"How can you know that?" She stood before him and stamped her foot in exasperation, then she turned her back to him and went to stand before the window. The moderately warm November day had grown into a chilly evening, and Meghan shivered as the cool breeze washed over her. She could feel his presence behind her, but she was determined; he must not take such foolhardy chances by risking his life in this fashion.

"Cold?" he murmured against her ear.

Meghan shook her head stiffly.

"Stubborn." She heard him chuckle.

"No more than you," she accused him petulantly. Turning slowly, she let him take her in his arms and resting her cheek against his chest, she said, "Derek, if Papa and Charles are no longer a threat to us and Iverson is dead, what makes you so certain that there is still someone who wishes to do us harm?"

"Just call it a hunch, darling." He kissed the top of her head.

"How much longer do you intend to proceed with your plan?"

"If by the end of the week my plan to draw the scum out into the open has not succeeded, I promise that I will abandon it and return to my duties at Chandalara . . . and you." He pulled her chin up, so that their eyes met.

"Promise?" She made him vow.

Derek nodded.

"And you will be careful?"

"Yes," he cried.

"Derek," she whispered gently.

"What now, little one?" he sighed.

"I love you." She buried her face in his shirt and held him to her tightly.

"And I love you, my darling." He tenderly stroked

her hair and lifting her in his arms, he returned to his chair, settling her on his lap and holding her until her fears dissipated.

But the next day, Meghan's greatest fears were to be realized. She was relaxing with a book in the upstairs sitting room when she heard a rider approaching the house. Meghan was not certain if it was the anxious pounding of the horse's hooves that prompted the wild beating of her heart, or perhaps it had been the romantic sonnet on the page before her making her long for Derek's secure embrace. In either case, Meghan's concentration had been forced from the book and it now settled upon the approaching horseman.

Meghan crossed to the window to glimpse her visitor, but the road before the driveway was covered in a cloud of dust screening the rider's identity. Who would drive his horse so relentlessly—unless . . . unless he carried an urgent message.

"Oh, my God," she whispered faintly. "Derek!" Her heart leaped with possibilities. Had he been injured, or—or had her worst fears been realized and he now lay dead on some deserted country road?

Her book suddenly slipped from her fingers, falling with a resounding thud to the floor. This distraction served to dissolve her frozen stance before the window, and she turned and fled from the room. She arrived at the foot of the stairway just as the door flew open and Deirdre Hampton hurried into the foyer. In an instant, Meghan could detect from Deirdre's distressed appearance that something was terribly wrong.

"It's Derek, isn't it?" Meghan was surprised at how calmly she voiced the question.

"Yes," Deirdre replied anxiously. "He's been shot. Wade and I found him, but I fear that the wound is serious and we were afraid to move him far. Wade has gone for the doctor," she hastily explained. "I instructed your man to have your horse saddled. Come quickly, Meghan, he's asking for you."

The color drained from Meghan's cheeks and she unconsciously gripped the handrail for support. Oh, had she not warned him that something like this would happen?

"Meghan," Deirdre stepped forward. "Did you not hear me?"

Meghan shook her head to clear her anxious thoughts and she stared at Deirdre blankly. "What? Oh, yes, yes, I'm coming." She rushed forward and collecting her shawl from the chair, she wrapped it about her shoulders and started out the door, Deirdre dogging her tracks. "Wait. I must tell Sophie."

"There isn't time. We must hurry." Deirdre urged her forward.

Hank had saddled Champion and brought him into the yard. But as Meghan hurried forward for the servant to assist her atop him, a resounding clap of thunder echoed in the distance, causing Meghan to stop and gaze heavenward. Now was not the time to succumb to her silly, childhood fears. Derek needed her and she must go to him. In seconds, she and Deirdre were astride their mounts, racing down the driveway to the main road.

They rode swiftly, Meghan forcibly restraining Champion, for he could have easily overtaken Deirdre's sluggish mount had she allowed him free rein. But for her to take the lead would be useless, for she did not know Derek's whereabouts. "Where did you take him?" she shouted above the rising wind.

"Jason Tyler's old cabin," came the reply.

Silently, Meghan whispered a prayer of thanks, grateful that she and Nathan had utilized the cabin as a studio, for she knew a shortcut to the cabin. And if Derek's wound was as serious as Deirdre indicated, even a few wasted seconds might mean the difference between his life and death.

She pushed Champion harder than he had ever been ridden. And even though they rode like the wind, to Meghan an eternity passed before they emerged from the forest and into the clearing where the cabin stood. She reined Champion in before the cabin and jumped from his back. She started up the steps just as Deirdre entered the clearing behind her.

Without a moment's hesitation, Meghan threw aside the door and hurried across the threshold. "Derek, my darl—" The exclamation died on her lips and her heart turned cold.

Derek was not there. What was Deirdre's purpose in luring her to an empty cabin? The sudden scraping of a chair against the floor in the darkened corner alerted Meghan to another occupant of the room. Her heart pounded fiercely, and she pressed her hands to her breast as she slowly turned to face the intruder. The room had grown uncommonly dark with the approaching storm, but even in the obscure light, Meghan recognized the menacing figure that steadily moved toward her.

"No!" she screamed and whirled to bolt through the open doorway, only to discover that Deirdre blocked her only means of escape.

Feeling like a caged animal, Meghan glanced about her wildly for some sort of weapon she might utilize to defend herself. But even as she lunged for an old broom handle, her arm was gripped roughly and she was dragged across the floor and shoved into a chair.

"Sit down, Meghan," the man's voice commanded harshly. "Why, with your abrupt behavior, one might think that you are none too eager to sample our hospitality." His evil laugh filled the small cabin and as Deirdre's shrill laughter mingled with his, Meghan's heart sank as she realized the hopelessness of her situation.

Derek rode into the yard at Chandalara only moments after Meghan and Deirdre had made their hasty departure. He left Trojan at the stable with Hank and tiredly made his way up to the house. He walked leisurely to the drawing room, fully expecting to find Meghan waiting for him there. It had become customary for them to meet in the drawing room in the afternoon to share a glass of wine and discuss the day's activities. Therefore, he was mildly surprised to be greeted by an empty room. Thinking her to be upstairs, Derek strode to the foot of the stairs and called her name.

"Miz Meghan ain't here, Massah Derek," Sophie informed him as she emerged from one of the upstairs chambers and waddled to the top of the stairway. "Miz Hampton came bustin' in here awhile back and the next thing I knows, her and Miz Meghan went boltin' outta here on their horses."

"Did your mistress not inform you of her destination?"

"No, suh." Sophie started down the wide staircase. "But from the looks of things, they wuz in a powe'ful hurry."

Derek stroked his bearded chin thoughtfully as he walked to the door and threw it open to step out onto the porch. His concentration was focused on the ominous looking sky and the dark storm clouds that were rapidly rolling toward Chandalara. And as the distant thunder sounded in the heavens, he recalled Meghan's fear of storms and he was enveloped with an unmistakable uneasy feeling. Meghan would never leave the house with the threat of an impending storm unless something was amiss.

"Perhaps there is some trouble at Wade's plantation," Derek mused aloud. "I believe I should ride over there and find out what's afoot. Besides, Meghan will need someone to escort her home."

"I thinks yore right, Massah Derek." Sophie had joined her master on the porch. "I don't trust that Deirdre Hampton neither."

"Sophie!" Derek laughed and patted his housekeeper on the back. "So, you have grown fond of your mistress, have you?"

"Yes, suh." The woman nodded proudly. "And I don't wants to see her git hurt by that spiteful woman."

"Nor do I," Derek assured her. "You tell Lettie to prepare a special supper and I shall go fetch your mistress home."

Derek sprinted down the steps and loped across the yard to the barn where Trojan was stabled. "Sorry to roust you again so soon, my friend, but I need collect my wandering lady and bring her home before the storm outside erupts." He quickly saddled Trojan and in moments, he was astride the animal, racing along the road toward Wade's plantation.

Their journey was hampered slightly by the rising wind. And at one point, Derek was tempted to abandon the main road for the shortcut across Jason Tyler's property. But if Meghan were on her way home, he would miss her if he opted for the shorter route. Therefore, he decided to remain on the main road. And a quarter of an hour later, he arrived at the Hampton plantation.

Derek was admitted to Wade's study moments later, chagrined to find him the sole occupant of the room.

"Derek," Wade called good-naturedly, lowering the paper that he had been reading. "What brings you here?"

"My wife."

"Ah, abandoned you, has she? I always knew she would," he said airily, but noting Derek's serious expression, he changed his tone. "Is something amiss?"

"That's what I am trying to find out." Derek took a chair opposite Wade. "Have you seen her?"

"Nary a sign, I swear." Wade folded the paper and set it aside. "What makes you think that Meghan would come here?"

"Because, Deirdre came to Chandalara earlier today. Sophie said she was in quite a dither and when your sister departed, Meghan went with her," Derek explained. "I naturally assumed that something was wrong here . . ."

"No, nothing."

"Well, now I *am* baffled." Derek strolled over to the window just as the first raindrops began to pitter against the windowpane. "Where do you suppose they went?"

"I shouldn't worry, Derek," Wade offered. "The girls probably decided to ride into town together to buy some frilly trifle."

"I'd like to believe that Wade, but Meghan is positively terrified of storms. I cannot believe that she would leave the protection of Chandalara with a storm brewing unless it were for something important. Besides, Wade," he turned away from the window to face his friend, "you must admit that Deirdre has not been overly friendly with Meghan."

"To be fair, Derek, Meghan has done little to encourage a friendship," Wade reminded him.

"Well," Derek shrugged his shoulders, "I suppose I am to blame for that. One should not expect his wife

and former girlfriend to become fast friends overnight."
A loud clap of thunder drew his attention back to the
window. "I should be getting back to Chandalara."

"Oh, why not stay? The girls probably took shelter
from the rain, so there is no need for you to rush off."
Wade stood up and placed his arm about Derek's
shoulder. "They will no doubt show up here when this
storm abates, then the four of us can sup together."

"Thanks, Wade, but perhaps another time. Meghan is
likely home now, waiting to chastise me for chasing all
over the parish after her. She can be so frustratingly
independent," he sighed and shook his head.

"Yes," Wade nodded knowingly, "Deirdre is the
same." He walked to the door with Derek and watched
as he ran out into the rain. "If you see my wayward
sister, send her home," Wade shouted above the wind.

Derek acknowledged the request and removing his
rolled-up rain slicker from the saddle, he slipped it over
his head. He climbed atop Trojan and gently nudged the
horse's flanks to start him forward. This time, however,
he decided to take the shortcut that traversed the Tyler
properties.

Meghan sat stiffly in the straight-backed chair, her
eyes staring at the lantern that sat upon the crudely
shapened table. The tears that usually came so freely
were frozen behind her dazed eyelids. She sat in a
listless state for a long time, totally detached from the
conversation that was taking place at the opposite end of
the cabin, and from the raging storm outside.

Her thoughts centered around the hopelessness of
her situation. The fact that Derek probably knew that
she had left Chandalara with Deirdre was of little
consolation to her, for he had no inkling of their
location. He was probably lounging in the drawing room

at that very moment, reading his paper and relaxing with a glass of brandy while he awaited her return, so they could share a leisurely supper. But she was not going to return to him, at least, not if her captors had their way. And by the time he did grow concerned over her prolonged absence, he would be unable to follow her trail, for the heavy rains would have long since washed away any trace of their path.

Meghan sighed forlornly, but Deirdre's shrill laugh suddenly cut through her thoughts like a sharp knife. The effect on Meghan was like a slap in the face, for her lifeless eyes grew dark with bold determination. They will soon learn that I shan't be a docile prisoner, she mused silently. Lifting her head, her eyes settled on her captors, and she wondered for the thousandth time how Deirdre and Charles had ever become acquainted.

She was resolved that she would learn the entire story from them and she was further determined that, regardless of the consequences, she would not leave the cabin with Charles. For surely even death would be a welcome blessing compared to the type of life that he would force her to lead.

Meghan pulled herself straight in the chair and folding her arms across her breasts, she fastened a stony gaze on Charles and Deirdre. "I believe that I am entitled to some sort of explanation," she said coldly.

"Really?" Charles turned away from the narrow window where he had been watching the storm with some consternation. He had not worried that Chandler would discover Meghan's disappearance until they had long since vacated the premises, but the storm was causing him to delay their departure. And he realized that a mere thunderstorm would not keep Chandler from searching for Meghan if he thought her to be in danger. "And just what bit of information could I offer

551

that would appease your curiosity?"

"How did you become acquainted with Deirdre?"

"Yes, I rather supposed that might pique your interest," he replied casually. Sitting down in a chair opposite her, he regarded her with an arrogant eye. "And since we seem doomed to remain sequestered in this hole until this accursed storm ends, I see no harm in humoring you with the details of our scheme. Perhaps once you learn the extreme measures your father and I have taken to see that you return to London, you will think twice ere you dare cross us again," he added meaningfully. "But I seem to have tarried from your question. You inquired, I believe, as to my association with this lovely young lady."

Deirdre stood behind Charles, her hands resting on his shoulders. Her lips parted into a sneer, and she eyed Meghan coldly as Charles reached up to caress her hand familiarly.

"You see, Meghan, Deirdre and I met, quite by accident, in France last summer. She was quite distraught at the time because her lover had unexpectedly terminated their relationship—"

"Derek," Meghan blurted out, and she surmised by Deirdre's stony gaze that she had correctly guessed the identity of the *lover*.

"A slight misunderstanding that time could have healed had *you* not interfered," Deirdre spat hotly, taking a threatening step toward Meghan.

"Tut, tut." Charles put a restraining hand on Deirdre's arm. "I fear that we are getting ahead of our story."

Deirdre reluctantly returned to her stance behind the chair where she continued to eye Meghan with a hateful glare.

"So, you see, Meghan, I felt compelled to console

Deirdre and help her through her distressing time. Later, I learned that her lover had been Derek Chandler, the same Derek Chandler who stood to inherit the Chandler family jewels when Elizabeth passed on. It was then I realized the opportunity presented me. If Chandler did not bother to claim the inheritance, I would sell the gems to Deirdre for a handsome profit which I would, in turn, share with your father. For once I told him of my plan, he readily agreed to give me your hand in marriage, offering the jewels as your dowry."

"But Derek *did* elect to claim his inheritance," Meghan handily reminded him.

"Yes, your bastard lover has proven to be a thorn in my side from the very beginning," Charles conceded. "It was then I decided to steal the jewels back from Chandler. Deirdre had arranged to be in London with me at the time. She had the available funds and was ready to return to America when Chandler foiled my scheme a second time."

"I don't understand. What did you hope to achieve by purchasing Derek's inheritance?" Meghan demanded from Deirdre.

"Derek knew that I was on holiday in Europe. I intended to tell him that I bought the collection at an estate auction," she explained. "If Derek recognized the collection as his mother's, we could have reconciled our differences and become lovers again—perhaps even wed, such would have been his joy at having recovered his family inheritance."

"And had he not recognized the collection as his own?" Meghan countered.

"The end result would have been the same. No man could resist acquiring such a richly endowed wife," Deirdre informed her snidely.

"I fear that you sorely overestimate your charms,

Deirdre," Meghan informed her bluntly. "Had Derek known the jewels were his mother's, he may have attempted to purchase them from you, but I sincerely doubt that he would have married you for them."

"You are a fine one to talk, you hussy!" Deirdre hissed viciously. "Derek never saw fit to marry you, not even when you were carrying his brat!"

"Do control yourself, ladies," Charles said in a calm, soothing voice. "Can you not feel satisfied that you shall have the last laugh, Deirdre? Now, do behave yourself and allow me to continue." Charles was evidently quite proud of his accomplishments and was anxious to fill Meghan in on every detail.

"You followed us to America," Meghan accused.

"After your father's foolish stunt, I was left with little recourse," Charles sighed. "We arrived in New Orleans shortly after you and Chandler. I must admit that New Orleans is an enchanting little city with some rather *colorful* inhabitants. People like . . . Garth McTavish and . . . Sam Iverson." He spoke the names slowly, purposely.

Meghan's eyes grew wide at this revelation. "*You?*" she cried hoarsely.

"Yes." Charles smiled proudly as he buffed his manicure along the sleeve of his coat.

"But . . . but how . . . why?" she cried incredulously.

"Because"—he eyed her sternly—"Chandler humiliated me. I was determined to see him pay for my sufferings. I soon learned that if one waved a sufficient number of gold coins beneath Mr. McTavish's greedy nose, he would do just about anything. And to further advance my scheme, he fortunately harbored a particular animosity against Chandler. We also engaged the services of Sam Iverson by persuading him to believe

554

that Chandler swindled him out of his plantation. The man was a drunkard, so the plan worked easily enough."

"You sent him to Chandalara to assault Derek?" Meghan charged.

"No," Charles admitted. "Unfortunately, Mr. Iverson proved to be a trifle overzealous in his actions. That is precisely why we had to deal with him in New Orleans a few weeks ago. The man's appetite for gold could simply not be satisfied. At any rate, to draw suspicion away from us, we encouraged Iverson to employ McTavish to ambush you on the Trace."

"I see. You *loved* Derek so much that you paid someone to kill him." Meghan looked accusingly at Deirdre. "How could you betray him that way if you truly cared for him?"

"Derek wasn't to die." Deirdre quickly admonished herself of guilt. "You were supposed to think him dead, so you would never try to return to him. And as for my actions, Derek hurt me. And for that he had to pay before I could forgive him."

"Yes," Charles sneered slowly. "Just as you shall pay for embarrassing me before my friends in London. But that is another story." He waved his hand aside. "McTavish was to disable Chandler long enough to deliver you to me." He returned to his explanation.

"And did you give him permission to rape me?" Meghan tried desperately to control her trembling voice.

"I instructed him to do whatever was necessary to teach you a well-deserved lesson," he informed her bluntly.

"And when your evil scheme failed again?" Meghan inquired.

"We were hard pressed for a time, to be sure, what with McTavish dead and Iverson badgering us for more

555

money to keep quiet. That is when I finally decided to openly confront you, threatening to expose you and your lover. But then Thomas bungled everything. I told him to bring you with him, even if he had to drag you along, but your accursed lover intervened again."

"Did you shoot me, Charles? Did you murder my baby?" Meghan asked him point blank.

"No—" he began.

"I did." Deirdre interrupted Charles's explanation, a slightly self-satisfied smile parting her lips as if she were proud of her sinister accomplishment.

"*You!*" Meghan's head shot up instantly. She mentally recounted the horrible nightmare that had tormented her when she dreamed that Deirdre had taken the infant. Meghan had been correct in blaming her, for, in effect, Deirdre *had* taken her son from her. Her heart was suddenly encased with a bitter resentment and she focused a cold, heartless stare at Deirdre. "Why?" she demanded hoarsely.

"I warned Charles that if his attempts to get you to leave Derek failed again, I would take matters into my own hands. I was waiting outside on the verandah after Derek instructed Thomas to leave. I waited until I had a clear shot." She looked pointedly at Meghan. "I am an expert marksman, Meghan. Had you not moved at the last second, you would now be dead and Derek would be mine."

Meghan had never before experienced a hatred as intense as the one that enveloped her now. "*Murderess,*" she whispered thickly. "Derek will not have *you!* The murderess of an innocent babe: *his* child."

"Derek shall never know," Deirdre said loftily. "Thanks to Charles, Derek has been scurrying about the countryside searching for Sam Iverson."

"So, you sent the anonymous letter to the sheriff,"

Meghan correctly surmised.

"Guilty." Charles stood up and stepped across the floor to stand before her. "With Chandler conveniently indisposed during the day, it was quite simple to devise a scheme to lure you away from the protection of his plantation. And to culminate our effort, Deirdre shall go to him in a few hours and inform him that you elected to elope with me and return to England."

"Derek will never believe such a story!" Meghan exclaimed.

"Oh, and who will be present to dispute me?" Deirdre spat hoarsely. "The servants observed your eagerness to leave with me. No one forced you from your home," she callously reminded Meghan.

Meghan fell silent, totally drained of all emotion as she realized that Deirdre's scheme was plausible.

"Now, have all your questions been satisfactorily answered?" Charles asked.

"All save one."

"Oh?"

"You have no money, Charles, nor has Papa. Just how did you manage to finance this little vendetta?" she demanded.

"Deirdre," he replied simply.

"Deirdre?"

"Yes," the accused offered. "Wade provides me with an allowance."

"A generous one, evidently."

"True, but not liberal enough to meet my expenditures. Several months ago, I convinced Wade to assign to *me* the responsibility of managing Derek's household account. At that time, everyone believed that Derek and I would surely reconcile and be married, so it wasn't considered unusual when I signed the vouchers and banknotes," Deirdre explained. "And no one will be the wiser when Charles presents a signed note at the bank in New Orleans tomorrow."

"You see, Meghan," Charles stroked her cheek with his hand, "Deirdre and I were quite willing to go to any lengths to be reconciled with the ones we love."

"You don't love me," Meghan spat disgustedly as she shoved his hand away from her face. "Deirdre no doubt paid you well to remove me from Chandalara, so that she would be free to pounce on Derek."

"Perhaps I don't *love* you," Charles admitted. "But I have grown *obsessed* with the idea of possessing you. The money has simply made the sport a worthwhile venture. Come," he pulled her from the chair, "your father waits for us in New Orleans. We sail for London tomorrow." He read the stubborn set of her jaw and hastened to warn her: "A caution, Meghan, if you dare attempt to resist me in this, I promise that your punishment will be severe." He increased the pressure on her arm to accentuate his threat.

Meghan pulled her shawl tightly about her weary shoulders and stood up, but she refused to surrender to the helpless sobs that threatened to overcome her at any moment. She must keep her wits about her, for if Charles should weaken his defenses, even for an instant, she might be able to escape. The rain had stopped when Charles rudely pushed her through the doorway, but the sight that greeted Meghan was more welcome to her than would have been the most spectacular rainbow that could have painted the heavens. Derek stood about a hundred yards away from her, leaning against a tree, coldly staring at Charles.

"It's indeed good to see that you are well, darling," Derek said gently to Meghan, but his eyes never wavered from Charles. "I was just returning from Wade's when I spied Champion in front of the cabin, so

558

I decided to wait and escort you safely back to Chandalara. And now that you have concluded your visit, we are free to go. Come to me, darling." He extended one hand toward her and in the other, Meghan noticed, he held a gun. Derek recognized her apprehension and in a soothing voice, he comforted her, "Do not be afraid, honey."

Meghan's heart took flight at his encouraging words, but her feet remained immobile, for Charles clamped a steely arm about her waist, preventing her escape.

"Release her, Charles!" Derek demanded.

"I think not, Chandler. Meghan has expressed a desire to return to London and I have graciously consented to take her there. Now, I suggest that you climb upon your horse and ride for your home and leave me to my affairs," Charles said blandly.

"*No!*" Meghan screamed wildly as she struggled to be free of his cruel embrace. "He lies! Don't leave me with him!" she pleaded.

"I would never consider such a notion, love," Derek assured her. "Now, step aside, Beauchamp and face me like a man. A *man* does not hide behind a woman's skirts," Derek challenged.

"No, indeed not. Most men choose instead to assert their masculinity beneath that garment." Charles' hand slipped purposely lower across Meghan's stomach, and he suggestively raised the hem of her gown to permit Derek a view of her shapely legs.

Meghan was sickened and humiliated to be displayed in such a vulgar fashion, but Derek's reaction was quite the opposite. His face drained of all color as he erupted with an all-consuming rage. "Beauchamp, I shall take great pleasure in making you wallow in the mud like the lowlife swine that you are," he spat between tightly clenched teeth. Slowly, he began to stalk toward Charles.

"Stop!" Charles commanded.

"Stop?" Derek grunted. "Neither the angels in heaven, nor the devils in hell can stop me now," he whispered thickly.

"I'll not hesitate to shoot . . . *her*." Charles pulled a gun from beneath his coat and leveled it at Meghan, causing Derek to halt abruptly. "I'm quite capable of doing what I say, I assure you. She means nothing to me, just an amusing, little trinket. But I should not be crushed if she were to die. Can you say the same?" He observed the tormented play of emotions that crossed Derek's face. "Yes, I thought not. Now, throw your weapon aside." He motioned at the gun in Derek's hand.

Derek looked helplessly at the gun that was poised just inches away from Meghan's head and with an oath, he cast his gun aside.

Deirdre had been standing on the porch alongside Charles, but when Derek threw his weapon to the ground, she sprang forward to embrace him. "Let them go, darling," she pleaded. "She isn't worth the trouble. I can make you happy. I love you!" she cried.

Derek emotionlessly pulled Deirdre's hands from his neck and with one arm, he stiffly set her from him. "It is truly unfortunate that you feel that way, Deirdre, for I can never return your love. It has taken me a very long time to realize it, but I love Meghan. I shall always love her and none other." His dark eyes held Meghan's for an instant before they settled murderously upon Charles. "And I shall not allow this scum to defile her."

"From my vantage point, there is little you can do to prevent me from doing as I please," Charles informed him. And he watched the play of anger that twisted Derek's handsome face as he casually slipped his hand beneath the folds of Meghan's blouse to caress her

560

breasts. "Shall you not allow this?" He laughed. "Or this?" Charles turned Meghan's head and covered her lips with his. "Ah, you have doubtlessly taught her well, Chandler. For that, I owe you my gratitude, for she shall certainly serve me well on the cold nights to come."

"Where I shall presently send you, Beauchamp, you shall suffer few cold nights, I assure you." Derek held his arms stiffly at his side as he began to step toward Charles with a purposeful, measured gait.

"I'm warning you, Chandler," Charles threatened.

But Derek continued, heedlessly.

The relentless, determined expression on Derek's face served to unsettle Charles and without warning, he leveled his gun at Derek and fired.

Meghan screamed hysterically and expected to see Derek slump to the ground. Instead, he stumbled backwards slightly as the bullet penetrated his left shoulder, but he quickly recovered his equanimity and continued toward Charles, the blood that trickled down his coat sleeve being the only visible sign that Charles's aim had been accurate.

Meghan shoved violently at Charles, who was finding it increasingly difficult to reload his pistol and retain the struggling girl in his arms. With an oath, he pushed Meghan aside savagely. Successfully reloading the gun, he again aimed the weapon at Derek and fired.

Again Charles's aim found its mark as the bullet exploded into Derek's right thigh, successfully halting his forward momentum. And with a triumphant sneer parting Charles' lips, Meghan watched in horror as he began to patiently reload the gun a second time.

Meghan's head had struck the wooden floor of the porch when she fell, momentarily rendering her senseless. But as her dazed mind cleared, she struggled to her feet and hurried toward Derek. Charles, she realized,

561

was not going to cease this torment until he succeeded in killing Derek. With tears streaming down her face, Meghan raced toward her beloved.

Meanwhile, as Derek fought to pull himself to his feet, he too, observed Charles's sinister expression as he leveled the gun at Meghan's unprotected back. "No, Meghan," he frantically tried to warn her, but she was oblivious to everything except reaching Derek's side. Derek was seized with an awesome feeling of dread as the explosion thundered in his head and Meghan stumbled to the ground just inches from his grasp.

For an instant, time seemed to stand still for Derek as he tearfully dragged himself toward Meghan's fallen body. And as he lifted her limp head with one trembling hand, he raised the other in outrage toward the heavens and the forest reverberated with his cry of anguish. Then all became black as he slipped into unconsciousness.

Epilogue

Derek sat up in the huge fourposter, reclining his head against a mountain of fluffy pillows. His shoulder ached abominably and was accompanied by an even stronger, more persistent pain that throbbed relentlessly in his leg. But even knowing the seriousness of his injuries, Derek had been none too pleased to learn that the doctor still insisted that he remain abed.

"Why?" he had roared at Sophie that morning when

she served his breakfast. "There is too much to be done at Chandalara for me to be lying abed. I'm not a sick puppy, you know."

"No, suh," Sophie had readily agreed. "If'n you asks me, you is actin' more likes a stubborn mule," she had informed him pertly, then hurried from the room before he could offer a reprimand.

Derek's lips parted in a slight grin as he recalled the confrontation with his housekeeper. But then he suddenly became aware of another's presence in the room and as he slowly opened his eyes, his lips parted in a wide smile as he beheld his visitor.

"Good morning, darling," Meghan whispered softly from the foot of the bed.

"Good morning," he returned the greeting and then laughing loudly, he added hoarsely, "Come here, wench!"

Meghan did not wait to be summoned a second time. She moved quietly to the bed and seated herself beside him. Taking his hand in hers, she rubbed it against her cheek, then leaned forward and kissed him lovingly. And as she pulled away, Derek lifted his hand to caress her cheek.

"God, I thought I had lost you," he sighed deeply.

"And I, you." Meghan caught his hand as it slipped to her shoulder and squeezed it firmly. "You were so very sick at first. We were all frightfully worried for you. You had lost quite a lot of blood and you had to lay there on the wet ground while Deirdre summoned the doctor. Doctor Samuels said you contracted some type of infection on top of your other wounds," she explained. "You were burning with fever for days. Why, it sometimes took three of us to hold you in bed when you became delirious." She slipped into the bed beside him, taking care not to disturb his injured leg,

563

and happily accepted his arm about her. "It's so good to see you sitting up in bed again."

"And what of you? Sophie tells me that the doctor confined you to your bed for a few days." He regarded her speculatively. "Are you recovered?"

"Fully." Meghan nodded. "I had grown weak is all. After sitting by your side day and night for the past two weeks. I hope you remember my devotion," she teased him.

"I shall."

"I wanted to come to you when you wakened the day before yesterday, but Dr. Samuels forbade me." She lowered her head awkwardly. "I understand that Wade and the sheriff came to see you yesterday afternoon. Did they explain everything to you?"

"Yes, Wade read your statement to me—how Charles and your father and Deirdre had plotted against us all along. I never realized how twisted Deirdre's mind truly was."

"She loved you, darling," Meghan whispered. "A woman will do many things out of love."

"Yes, including running off unthinkingly with a deranged woman, placing her own life in jeopardy," he softly chastised her.

"Deirdre said you had been hurt," she quickly reminded him.

"And did you realize that there was a storm brewing when you rushed off to my assistance?" Derek gently lifted her chin up, so that he could gaze into her lovely eyes.

"Yes," she murmured in reply. "But you did not let the storm deter you in your search for me."

"I, little one," he kissed her upturned nose, "am not the one who is terrified of storms."

"I guess I put the storm from my mind."

564

"And where was your reason when you placed yourself in the line of Charles's gun?" he questioned sternly.

Meghan shook her head helplessly. "I could think of nothing except that he was going to kill you. I had to do something. I could not continue to live without you!" She buried her face in his chest.

"Nor I, you." Derek gently stroked her hair. They were quiet for a few moments and then Derek continued, "I suppose I do owe Deirdre a debt of gratitude."

"Yes," Meghan mumbled, "had she not reacted when she did, and used your gun to kill Charles, I am certain he would have killed us both."

"I thought he *had* killed you," Derek murmured gently.

"I know," she said quietly. "It was clumsy of me to stumble over that fallen tree limb."

"*Clumsy*!" he bellowed. "You damn near frightened me to death."

"I know. Can you ever find it in your heart to forgive me?"

In response, Derek lowered his head and covered her lips with his own and kissed her thoroughly. "I shall try." He chuckled.

"What will happen to Deirdre now?" Meghan asked.

"The sheriff has agreed that she should not be held for Charles's murder since she acted in our defense. And I promised Wade that I would not bring charges against her for her other activities if he agreed to take Deirdre away for a *long* rest."

"And did he agree?"

"Yes." He shook his head slowly. "I still don't fully understand why she had such a change of heart and became our defender."

"She believed, as I did, that Charles was going to kill you. She killed him to save you, my love. Believe me, darling, the fact that she saved my life as well was purely coincidental. It would seem that she unwittingly spoiled her chance to have you all to herself again." She reached behind him to plump up his pillows.

"I never wanted Deirdre, especially after I found you." He clasped her hand in his and pressed it to his lips.

"Well, that is behind us now," Meghan murmured softly. "But what . . . what have you decided to do about Papa?" she inquired reluctantly.

"As I understand it, he was apprehended in New Orleans as he attempted to board a ship to London. I sent my lawyer to him this morning to make him a similar offer. If he consents, my lawyer will present him with a rather large sum of money, and he is never to darken our door again," Derek explained.

"Derek!" Meghan pushed away from him in disbelief. "How could you possibly agree to give my father money after all that he has done, especially when you despise him so?"

"Because, dear heart, he happens to have an exceedingly lovely daughter whom I have grown to cherish, and I intend to devote the rest of my life to making her happy." He pulled her to him and his eyes fondled her warmly. "I am no longer amused with Thomas's little games, so if a few dollars will satisfy him, I shall readily pay the price." He stared down into her emerald eyes and was immersed in their beauty. "How long has it been since I told you I love you?" he asked softly.

Meghan gazed into his eyes and her heart swelled with love at the devotion she read there. "I . . . I can't recall," she whispered lowly.

"Well, if you cannot remember, then it has been far

too long, for you must know that I truly love you, my darling." His hand coyly slipped beneath the bodice of her gown to fondle her firm, round breasts.

"And I love you, Derek." Meghan determinedly gripped his hand in hers and resolutely removed it from her gown. "I shall always love you, but I fear that you shall have to wait a few days until you have recuperated somewhat before we attempt* what you are presently contemplating." She slipped out of his embrace and walked to the other side of the bed to check the dressing on his left shoulder.

"But—"

"No!" she reiterated.

"Well, I must have some diversion if I am to remain condemned to this accursed bed *alone*. Fetch me a brandy and a cigar, woman!" he shouted gruffly, but the twinkle in his eyes belied the sternness of the command.

"Faith, from the sound of things, you appear almost normal." She poured a glass of brandy from the decanter and retrieved a cigar from the box on the dresser and returned to the bed. "Here, m'lord, this will have to appease you until you recover your strength."

Derek begrudgingly accepted the brandy and cigar and then he shifted to a more comfortable position against the pillows. Meghan lit the cigar for him before she retired to a chair beside the bed to her embroidery. Derek observed the rather domestic scene with fondness, and as he silently contemplated their future together, he puffed thoughtfully on the cigar, filling the room with the aromatic scent of tobacco.

Meghan sat in her chair, her head bent over her work. But when the strong scent of tobacco enveloped her nostrils, the color drained from her cheeks and she stood up suddenly, sickened by the strong aroma. She dropped her needlework to the chair and ran to the window, throwing it open to breathe in the cool, December air.

"Meghan!" Derek sat up quickly. "What's wrong, honey?"

But Meghan did not respond to his question. Instead, she turned from the window and scurried into the adjoining room to avoid his curious stare.

"Meghan, by thunder!" he bellowed. "Come here at once!" But when she did not heed his command, Derek said determinedly, "Very well, then. I shall come to you."

With this declaration, Meghan abruptly reentered the room. "No, you musn't get up yet. You aren't well. The doctor said that any sudden movement might reopen your leg wound."

"The hell with that!" he exclaimed. "I want to know what is wrong with you. Come, sit by me." Meghan hurriedly closed the window, then she hesitantly walked to the bed and carefully sat down. "I can recall but one other occasion when my cigar smoke affected you in this manner, and a few weeks later I discovered that you were carrying my child. Meghan"—the gentle tone of his voice forced her head up and their eyes met—"are you pregnant?"

"Yes," she murmured faintly. "I became ill when Dr. Samuels was here to see you one day and he insisted on examining me. He confined me to bed because he feared that in my weakened condition, I might miscarry again. That is why I could not come to you until today. But I am feeling much stronger now."

Derek pulled her closer and cradled her to him with his uninjured arm. "I must take better care of you this time." He brushed his lips along her forehead. "Meghan?" He suddenly regarded her seriously. "You do *want* this baby, don't you?"

568

"More than anything," she quietly assured him.

"Good. Because as soon as I am able to travel, we shall depart for St. Louis aboard *The Cajun*."

"To St. Louis? Whatever for?" Meghan exclaimed.

"Oh, a honeymoon perhaps," he suggested coyly.

"Honeymoon! But . . . but we would have to be married for that." She regarded him in total confusion.

"Precisely," Derek agreed. "I have an old acquaintance there who would be more than happy to preside over the ceremony that would join us together as man and wife. That way, no one here need ever know that we were never married in London."

Meghan could scarcely believe her ears. "W-wife?" she repeated incredulously.

"Yes." He smiled at her amazement. "You *will* marry me, won't you?"

"But . . ."

"Now, please don't remind me of the lame excuses that I offered you in the past, for you must remember that I did not know then what I know now."

"What is that?"

"That I love you, completely, and I care not to live without you," he murmured gently. "Your answer, please, madam. I would propose on bended knee, but as you can see, I am incapacitated. Well?" he prompted.

"You're certain this is what you want?" she asked. "You are not doing this just because of the baby? For if you are—"

"Damn it, Meghan!" he swore. "I have loved no other and it is my sincerest intention to never love again. There is *you*, only you, my sweet. Is it not fitting that I wed the woman who has so completely captured my stubborn heart? Now, answer my question," he demanded.

"Well, when you phrase it that way, there can be but

569

one reply. *Yes!* Yes, my darling, I'll marry you." She threw her arms around his neck and surrendered her lips to his. When they at last parted, Meghan sighed and rested her head against his shoulder. "May we have a lot of children?"

"We shall fill this mansion," he promised.

Meghan ran her fingers across her stomach and glanced up at him lovingly. "Yes, I believe we shall."

The sound of a horse plodding up the drive suddenly drew Meghan's attention to the window.

"Who is it?" Derek asked.

"Jason. He stopped by several times while you were unconscious to ask about you. I shall greet him and send him up to you." Meghan walked to the door. "I believe he has something he would like to discuss with you in private."

"Do you not want to be here when I tell him the good news?"

"What news?"

"That he is going to be a *grandfather*." Derek waited patiently as Meghan turned slowly from the door and regarded him bewilderedly.

"*You know!*"

"Why, yes, of course." He laughed at her reaction. "Meghan, darling, a coincidence like this could only occur in some silly, romantic novel. A few years ago, I became obsessed with the notion of finding Jonathon Marley. After months of searching through the records of various London shipping firms, I discovered his name and was able to locate the man who captained the ship that brought him to America. The Captain remembered Mr. Marley right enough. He recollected him as a sad and troubled man who kept to himself. At first the captain thought him to be running from the law, but as he got to know the young man, he realized that his trouble stemmed from a different source altogether. In short, the Captain recalled that Mr. Marley changed his name to Jason Tyler, so that he could start his new life in America with a fresh identity. The ship put in port at New Orleans, so that is where I started my search," Derek explained.

"What did you plan to do?"

"I wasn't sure," he admitted. "I suppose, at first, I wanted some sort of revenge, but after I got to know Jason and Miranda, I realized that I could never purposely harm them."

"It must have been difficult for you, knowing that he was your father, yet unable to have a father's love," Meghan sympathized.

"I had his friendship. That proved to be comforting at times. Well," he sighed. "You may send him to me now."

"Yes, my love." Meghan opened the door, but Derek's softly spoken question halted her departure.

"Meghan? You will come back after Jason leaves? You won't go away?"

"Silly." She laughed happily. "Where would I go? I'm already where I belong." She blew him a kiss and hummed a cheerful melody as she closed the door on her old life with the promise of a fuller, happier life ahead of her, as Derek's wife. Her place was at his side for as long as she wanted. She was at peace with herself at last. All the nagging insecurities vanished as she descended the staircase, and she emerged at the foot of the stairs, a peacefully contented woman. She was home at last.

MORE ROMANTIC READING
by Cassie Edwards

PASSION'S WEB (1358, $3.50)

Natalie's flesh was a treasure chest of endless pleasure. Bryce took the gift of her innocence and made no promise of forever. But once he molded her body to his, he was lost in the depths of her and her soul. . . .

SAVAGE OBSESSION (1269, $3.50)

When she saw the broad-shouldered brave towering over her, Lorinda was overcome with fear. But a shameless instinct made her tremble with desire. And deep inside, she sensed he was so much more than a heartless captor—he was the only man for her; he was her SAVAGE OBSESSION!

SILKEN RAPTURE (1172, $3.50)

Young, sultry Glenda was innocent of love when she met handsome Read Baulieu. For two days they revelled in fiery desire only to part—and then learn they were hopelessly bound in a web of SILKEN RAPTURE.

FORBIDDEN EMBRACE (1105, $3.50)

Serena was a Yankee nurse and Wesley was a Confederate soldier. And Serena knew it was wrong—but Wesley was a master of temptation. Tomorrow he would be gone and she would be left with only memories of their FORBIDDEN EMBRACE.

PORTRAIT OF DESIRE (1003, $3.50)

As Nicholas's brush stroked the lines of Jennifer's full, sensuous mouth and the curves of her soft, feminine shape, he came to feel that he was touching every part of her that he painted. Soon, lips sought lips, heart sought heart, and they came together in a wild storm of passion. . . .

Available wherever paperbacks are sold, or order direct from the Publisher. Send cover price plus 50¢ per copy for mailing and handling to Zebra Books, 475 Park Avenue South, New York, N.Y. 10016. DO NOT SEND CASH.